APOCALYPSE

World

NOCT

aethonbooks.com

APOCALYPSE WORLD
©2024 NOCT

This book is protected under the copyright laws of the United States of America. No part of this publication may be reproduced, stored in a retrieval system, or transmitted, in any form or by any means, without the prior permission in writing of the publisher, nor be otherwise circulated in any form of binding or cover other than that in which it is published and without a similar condition including this condition being imposed on the subsequent purchaser. Any reproduction or unauthorized use of the material or artwork contained herein is prohibited without the express written permission of the authors.

Aethon Books supports the right to free expression and the value of copyright. The purpose of copyright is to encourage writers and artists to produce the creative works that enrich our culture.

The scanning, uploading, and distribution of this book without permission is a theft of the author's intellectual property. If you would like to use material from the book (other than for review purposes), please contact editor@aethonbooks.com. Thank you for your support of the author's rights.

Aethon Books
www.aethonbooks.com

Print and eBook interior formatting and design by Josh Hayes.

Published by Aethon Books LLC.

Aethon Books is not responsible for websites (or their content) that are not owned by the publisher.

This book is a work of fiction. Names, characters, places, and incidents are the product of the author's imagination or are used fictitiously. Any resemblance to actual events, locales, or persons, living or dead is coincidental.

All rights reserved.

ALSO BY NOCT

Apocalypse Me

Apocalypse City

Apocalypse World

Check out the entire series here! (Tap or scan)

1

RUN

Zeke stared up at the familiar armored form. Tendrils swayed on the wind. A mouth jam-packed full of vicious teeth grinned down at him, while another four mouths opened at its hands and feet. A white Oxford clad its chest, moving on a separate breeze from the rest of its body.

"You're...me?" Zeke breathed, staring at it.

"Hi, me. How's it going?" the other Zeke replied. "Conquer the world yet?"

Zeke stared, wordless.

"What am I saying? You're me! Of course, you did!" Stepping down from the rift, the other Zeke looked around. "Hey, is your Ryan still alive? Or—"

He jolted to a halt. His mouths gaped.

"What?" Zeke looked over his shoulder, following the other Zeke's gaze.

Mia blinked back at both of them. She shied back. "Er, can I help you?"

Zeke's eyes widened. *That's right. The other Zeke was so broken up over Mia's death that he destroyed the world, according to Ryan, anyway. If it's true, then this Zeke should be—*

He moved at the same time the other Zeke did, jumping in front of the other Zeke's path as he reached for Mia.

The other Zeke paused, then retracted his hand. He laughed lightly, though it sounded strained. "Of course. Yeah. I mean, I wouldn't let anyone near her either. After all, you must have worked hard to keep her alive. How did you do it?"

Zeke cleared his throat. "Er, Mia mostly did it herself. I rescued her from the Coffee Apocalypse, and I guess the Cartoon Apocalypse, but..."

"What? How? We always get stuck in the Museum Apocalypse for too long...even if we break free, it's—"

Again, Zeke cleared his throat. "Er, Ryan shoved me off the balcony. So...I started outside the museum. I had to fight through the Museum Apocalypse, but I didn't get swallowed up by it. Maybe that's the difference?"

"Ryan shoved..." The other Zeke put his hand to his forehead and laughed. He stumbled back, laughing so hard his whole body shook. "God *damn!* He's bloodthirsty, isn't he? No hesitation! Just straight up tries to murder his friend in cold blood!"

"Yeah, I thought it was pretty nuts, too," Zeke agreed.

The other Zeke shook his head. "You've had it rough, huh? My Ryan was still in his playing-nice phase. Tried to 'gently guide me' to do the right thing, or something." He chuckled. "Didn't do a great job of it, did he."

Zeke eyed him. He shook his head slowly. "No, doesn't seem to have."

Taking a step back, the other Zeke tried a disarming smile. It didn't work with his monstrous mouths. "Hey, so what's your deal, man? What happened? How'd things go, how'd you kill Ryan? What's going on in this world?"

Zeke rubbed the back of his neck. He glanced around. "Look, man, we just killed an Apocalypse. We're all tired, we just want to go home. Could we catch up later, maybe? Over coffee or something?"

"Sure, sure. I'll just. You know. Hang around," other-Zeke said. With a last wave, he darted off, speeding down the road faster than a car.

Domi stared after him, then looked at Zeke. "You have superspeed?"

"I don't. Other me does," Zeke grumbled.

Domi snorted. "I wonder what he ate."

Zeke startled. "Huh?"

She turned, giving him a look and planting her fists on her hips. "Seriously, Zeke? You're the Eating-Things Apocalypse, or whatever. Hunger? You eat shit. And then you get something from what you eat. Like those chicken wings on your back. It's obvious. We all know."

"You all...?" Zeke looked around him.

Mia nodded.

Isaac pursed his lips and shrugged, caught in the middle of walking away.

Olivia blinked, startled. "You eat— Is that why—"

"I had no idea, honest," Eric said.

"He doesn't know a lot of things, and she just joined the crew, so they don't count," Domi said dismissively.

"Hey," Eric muttered.

Zeke sighed. "All right, all right. Yeah. That's...about how it works."

Domi nodded. She gestured after the other Zeke. "What are we doing about him?"

"I don't know. I don't...I really don't know. Is he an enemy? Is he an ally?" Zeke pressed his lips together, then shrugged. "I guess we stall for now. See how he behaves, keep an eye on him."

"Seems like a mild reaction to your evil twin showing up. I mean, he probably destroyed the world," Domi commented.

"Right, but... Fuck, what am I supposed to do?" Zeke muttered, putting his head in his hands.

"Take a rest. Go home. Let's get a good night's rest, and a good meal, and we'll figure it all out in the morning. We've had a long day," Mia said.

"What if he follows us home?" Eric asked nervously.

Zeke hesitated, then rolled his eyes, as much at himself as anyone. "He knows where his base is. There's no point pretending like he doesn't. The best thing we can do right now is get home and hunker down."

"Right. After all, what if he gets there ahead of you and pretends to be you?" Mia pointed out.

Zeke snorted. "I'm not actually worried about that. So what? Ryan will suspect him of being everything wrong with the world and spend the whole time trying to kill him. Business as usual."

"What if he kills Ryan?" Mia asked.

"That... Huh. Yeah, okay. Let's get home. Quickly," Zeke decided. *As far as I know, the Dead Man's Switch is still active. If this Zeke kills my Ryan...well, I guess the world carries on, if that Zeke exists.*

But wait. The System itself acknowledged Ryan as an Apocalypse for destroying so many worlds. If his Dead Man's Switch doesn't destroy the world, then it's wrong. But it should be the one in control...

Unless. Unless it really is an Apocalypse, just like the rest of us. A thing, or concept, or person, who chose System as their Concept, and has just been doing their best this whole time. If they jumped timelines along with Ryan, wouldn't they perceive the other worlds as being destroyed, regardless of what happened to them?

But why would the System Apocalypse be tied to Ryan? And wait, if his world kept existing, why did that Zeke come to my world? No, before that, how? What did he eat that he gained the ability to swap timelines and end up here?

Zeke shook his head. *Too many questions. Not enough answers.*

Like Mia said. Let's go home, get something to eat, take a minute or two to ourselves. In the morning, when I'm refreshed and ready to face the day, I'll go hunt down the other Zeke and see what he has to say. Until then, I'll keep my guard up and stay wary, but I don't see any reason to drive myself insane worrying about other Zeke.

After all, for all I know, he wasn't evil, either. Maybe he didn't destroy his world. Maybe it really did get destroyed thanks to Ryan, and he's simply the only person powerful enough to escape to another world—or the only person who ended up in my timeline. Right. Anything is possible. Let's not jump to conclusions.

But that doesn't mean I'm going to trust him and let him run wild, either. I'll confront him soon. But not today. Tomorrow.

Isaac walked out from across the street. He thumbed over his shoulder. "I have the cats loaded up, so...are we headed back, or...?"

Zeke sighed. He nodded. "Yeah. Let's get home. I need a hot meal. And a hot shower. And a bed."

"Preach it," Domi muttered.

Mia nodded. "Let's go back."

2

BACK HOME

The trucks rattled down the street. Zeke frowned, looking around. *I feel like there's more rubble than there was when we left. There was a battle here, wasn't there? Fuck. I hope the place is still standing.*

Mushy white goop stripped away from bones, slowly rotting away. The wreckage of cars and smashed facades lined the road up to the apartment. The apartment itself bore dings and cracks, plus a few deep craters here and there. Zeke let out a relieved sigh. *Heather's still alive. Thank goodness. The apartment is still standing!*

"My army is...mostly fine," Eric said, sitting upright.

"Your *what*?" Olivia asked.

"We've taken a few casualties," he murmured without explaining himself to Olivia.

"You're all so full of surprises," Olivia muttered, half to herself.

Zeke gave her a look. "We're all Apocalypses, after all."

"Right, right. Damn. I can't believe I'm heading back with, what, five, six human-shaped world-destroying forces of chaos," Olivia said, shaking her head.

Eric flinched. "I don't want to destroy the world. Even Erica only wants to beautify it."

"I'm a Hero, technically," Mia protested softly.

"Yeah, I don't want to destroy the world, either." Zeke twisted his lips. *The problem is, I'm not sure my power will let me stop from destroying it, ultimately. How much longer before I have to eat people, or more than people? Multiple people? And then what?*

"We're all home, safe and sound. Stop dooming and think about dinner. Let's all have a nice, celebratory dinner before we gloom about the end of the world, okay?" Mia suggested.

Zeke pushed up from his seat as the truck came to a halt. "Sounds good to me!" *I'm exhausted. Retreading the same thought patterns I go to when I'm tired. Stuck in a depressive spiral. Mia's right. I need a meal and a rest. Tomorrow morning, this will all look different. Probably.*

About to climb out, he put his hand to his forehead. His brows furrowed. A thought lingered at the edge of his brain, not quite welling up to the forefront.

"What is it?" Mia asked, as she climbed out.

Zeke shook his head. "There's something...something I forgot. Something...about the System?"

"It told us to run," Mia said, frowning.

Zeke startled. "Right! And the errors... Huh." He twisted his lips and followed her out of the car. *Why did I forget that? The System needs to stop deleting my thoughts. It's seriously not cool.*

But then, I guess...it's been doing this the whole time, right? Messing with our minds. Deleting thoughts. Giving us urges. Unless that's the Apocalypse part that's giving us urges... Ugh. But the System is also messing with my mind... Zeke scowled. A moment later, he frowned. *Eh, but wait. It freaked out when the other Zeke showed up. I mean, I got terrified. I thought he was gonna kill me, but then he just up and walked off.*

He put a hand on his chin, lost in his thoughts, blindly following Mia into the apartment.

But the System... Huh? Why would the System panic so much? To speak to us, when it's never even spoken before. Does the other Zeke pose a threat to the System? But how? I don't know where it is. It's not like I could hurt it. Assuming it's a person, of course, which I think is a safe assumption now. Or, well, an Apocalypse, which I guess could be anything.

Wait, did the Apocalypses come first, or the System?

If the System is an Apocalypse, I guess Apocalypses had to come first. And then that Apocalypse spread itself around the world almost instantly...or at least spread itself far enough that I never encountered anything outside of the System Apocalypse. It has to be one of the most powerful Apocalypses on the planet, if not the strongest. And it somehow could exist inside multiple domes without being the winner or loser or participating in the fight.

Did it get a pass from whatever controls the Apocalypses? Or did it not count as part of the Apocalypse battle royale in the domes because it wasn't physically inside the domes? And for that matter, how did it manage to spread across multiple domes, maybe even the world, right from the get-go?

Unless it was already a mature Apocalypse. Unless... Hmm. There's a lot of weird potential here. And I just don't know enough about the—about whatever's behind all this to understand what's going on.

I wonder if I can eat it?

"We need to get food from somewhere if we're going to celebrate our victory. Do you think the supermarket still has good food?" Mia wondered aloud.

"Canned food, at least," Zeke agreed.

Olivia looked around. "This ugly-ass thing is your guys' base?"

Zeke looked up at the painted wood façade, clashing with

the cheap brick and the heavy black frames around the soulless windows. He looked back at Olivia. "Says the vampire whose base is a hole in the ground."

Olivia threw her hands up. "Yeah, yeah. Fair."

Mia squinted at Olivia. "Are you okay in the sun?"

"It doesn't feel great, but yeah. Not forever. I don't like it, but I don't die in ten seconds either. I mean, it's basically whatever Hunter thought would be the most useful, so he made us 'special' vampires strong against the sun. That's pretty typical, after all, in horror movies. Vampire movies, whatever," Olivia said, shrugging.

"For the strong vampires to be able to walk under the sun? I've seen it," Zeke said, nodding.

"He couldn't swing it for all the vampires, but yeah, for us... back in the day, anyway." Olivia drifted off. Her eyes went dim, staring into the distance.

Eric scratched the back of his head and looked awkwardly at the sky.

"Heyyyy, what's going on with the mood over here? Everyone okay?" Domi asked, looking around.

In the background, Isaac wandered off with his giant cats, off into the ruins.

"Yeah, we're all okay. Just talking about where we're going to find food for dinner," Zeke said.

"We need to start farming or something. We can't rely on supermarkets forever," Domi said, putting her hands behind her head.

"Yeah, that's true," Zeke agreed. *And I don't even know what I'm going to do.*

"Well, maybe we'll have a small respite now that we've defeated the dome, and taken care of the most immediate Apocalypses," Mia pointed out.

Zeke stared up at the sky and sighed. *With other Zeke on the*

run and the System Apocalypse looming over us all, somewhere close?
"Maybe so."

The doors burst open. Heather came racing out, her arms wide, the blanket draped over her shoulders trailing in the wind. "You guys!"

"Heather!" Mia ran toward her.

Heather wrapped her up in a hug and kept going until she slammed into Zeke and the rest. "Thank goodness! You all made it back."

"Yeah. We're back," Zeke said, smiling.

3
WELCOME BACK!

Domi made the door-opening bell ding as they walked through the supermarket's door. The air conditioning had cut out at some point, and the produce section buzzed with flies and was fuzzy with mold. Zeke cast it a look, then turned away. *I'm not sure we can even get seeds from that. But on the other hand, if something grows out of that, we can take it back and culture it.*

I don't know the first thing about farming. Why couldn't we recruit a Farming Apocalypse?

Well. Probably because we aren't in the Midwest. Who the hell would choose farming as their Apocalypse? Even if you're a farmer, who starts from farm? Pick gun first. ATV. Bigass truck. I don't know. Anything but farm.

He snorted under his breath. *Then again, maybe the farm itself would choose to become the Farming Apocalypse. Actually, how do the domes work in rural areas? Or do they just...not?*

Zeke looked upward. *I guess there's no hope the System answers that one. It's been quiet lately. Hasn't said a word since that panicked ERROR thing.*

Wait, hold on. Is the other Zeke in our System? If the

System is an Apocalypse, then is he under the authority of our System? Or is he in his own System, or no System at all? If the System is an Apocalypse, I'd expect him to not be in it, since he'd be enrolled in the previous world's System. Or is that the error?

I should ask him, next time I see him.

At that, Zeke snorted. In his own head, he mocked himself, *Hey there, other me. Yeah, I just have to ask you that classic question you always ask your clone, yeah, you know the one—what's your System like?*

What? You were expecting something else? Some other classic clone-related debacle? No, no. Let's talk about Systems, first.

Idly, Zeke picked up a basket and wandered to the chip aisle. He looked at it, then grinned. A little bit of excitement crept up, suppressing the existential dread for a moment. *My dreams are all coming true! I get to just run around the supermarket and shovel whatever I want into the basket and take it home without paying for it! Plus, it's a party, so I have an excuse to grab a little excess!*

His mood dimmed again, and he sighed. His eyes flicked to the back of the store, where low, gray shapes and scurrying brown bugs ran rampant around the once-refrigerated section. *Of course, those are probably the only thing in this store that can actually feed me.*

But I can still taste potato chips, and they still taste delicious. Let's stay upbeat, just for one night. Doom can come tomorrow. Tonight, we celebrate.

"Things are finally starting to collapse now," Domi murmured, looking at the refrigerator section.

Zeke nodded. "Yeah. We'll have to start farming and shit soon. Or something."

"Or go conquer a city that hasn't fallen apart yet," Domi said, giving Zeke a look.

Zeke pursed his lips thoughtfully, still nodding. "I mean... yeah."

"Between farming and conquering, we're definitely better at conquering," Domi said. She grabbed a two-liter bottle of soda off the shelf and cracked it open, taking a swig, then scowled. "Yuck. Warm soda."

"Well, yeah. It wasn't even in the refrigerated section. It was just sitting there," Zeke said, giving her a look.

Domi clicked her tongue and gave him a mischievous grin. "Don't give me that reasonable bullshit."

"Speaking of reasonable bullshit..."

"Uh-oh."

"What are we going to do for dinner? All the meat's gone bad," Zeke pointed out.

Domi nodded over to the right. "You know. Like Mia said. Canned food."

"Canned tuna? Canned chicken?" Zeke asked.

Domi clapped. She pointed at Zeke. "Beans!"

"Yeah, super delicious, beans, yuuuum," Zeke flatlined.

She rolled her eyes. "Don't be an idiot. Haven't you ever heard of chili?"

"Vegetarian chili, though?" Zeke asked, cocking a brow.

Another eye roll. "There's canned chili meat. It won't be as good as fresh meat, but we can have meat. And I can make it taste good, oh ye of little faith, *and* it's easy to make in large batches. Checks all the boxes."

"If you say so," Zeke said, shrugging noncommittally.

"I do say so. I'll go get the chili ingredients. You go grab as many boxes of corn bread as we can. We're going to make tonight delicious."

Zeke nodded. He grabbed another few bags of chips, then headed over to the baking aisle. Staring at the cornbread, he called, "Hey, Domi."

"Yeah?"

"What are we doing for milk and eggs?"

There was a long, distracted pause. Domi grunted, and cans clanged into her basket. "Fuckin'...boxed and canned milk, and fuckin', uh, that disgusting vegan thing with the chickpea water."

"What?"

"Yeah, chickpea water. I don't know how it tastes but the idea of chickpea water disgusts me. I mean...bean water. No one wants to think about bean water. It's the goopy shit that canned beans live in, that you wash out because it's gross. And it is. Gross."

"No, go back. How does chickpea water help our no-eggs problem?" Zeke asked.

"Chickpea water is vegan eggs," Domi said, as if it explained everything.

Zeke squinted. "Like...to scramble?"

"Don't be stupid. It only works in baking, but it *does* work in baking."

"Why do you know this?"

There was a long pause. "Zeke?"

"Yeah?"

"Have you ever heard of the internet? Late night click holes?"

"Oh...yeah. Yeah."

Domi hefted her basket, clanking along toward Zeke. "I grabbed some chickpeas, just in case we need them. We can ask Heather if she has some eggs. The apartment seems to abide by its own insane logic, so it wouldn't surprise me if she still has electricity, or an infinite supply of eggs, or something."

Zeke looked at her as she turned the corner. "Do you think, if I'd expanded my Domain here, that I could use Domain logic to make electricity happen?"

Domi gave him a look. "Don't be stupid. That's not your Concept."

"Oh. Yeah. Huh. I guess Apartment does make way more sense as a Concept that generates electricity than Hunger."

"Now me, I probably could. Explosions are the basis of, like, ninety percent of electricity," Domi declared.

Zeke gave her a look, then tipped his head. "Yeah, no. I guess, right? Combustion engines. Natural gas and stuff. That's explosions, right?"

"Close enough, I say," Domi said firmly.

Mia poked her head around the aisle. "Hey...what're you guys up to? Done grabbing groceries yet?"

Zeke held up his basket. "I'm good."

"Me too. How do you feel about chili?" Domi said, hefting her own laden basket with a little more effort.

"Chili sounds good to me."

"Then, back home it is."

On Zeke's head, Allen scurried in a quick circle, then leaped off. Startled, Zeke reached for him, but too slow. The anole burst down the aisle to the squirmy things crawling all over the rotting meat.

"Oh. Yeah, that makes sense. Allen, come back when you're done, okay?" Zeke called.

The anole ignored him, instead greedily gulping down bug after bug.

With a last nod Allen's direction, Zeke followed the others out.

4
SMALL TALK

His hair snapped in the wind. The city stretched before him, darkening with the dying of the sun. Tiny buildings and narrow roads, like a model city from this high. Hands clasped behind him, Ryan stood at the top of the stadium, thinking about everything and nothing, his mind as empty as the streets, as busy as the ants that crawled around, though he couldn't see them.

"Ryan. Hey."

Ryan turned. Zeke stood there in a hoodie, hair just as ruffled by the wind. He lowered his head. "So you made it back."

"Huh? Oh, yeah. The Undead Apocalypse." With a *pssh*, Zeke tossed his hand and looked aside. The wind caught his hair and blew it all in his face with the turn of his head, hiding his expression. "Easy, easy. Total pushover."

Ryan snorted. "Is that why it took you so long?"

"Look, we aren't all speedrunners like you," Zeke said, turning back to Ryan with a laugh.

"Learn anything useful?"

Zeke caught his hair in both hands and shoved it back. He shrugged. "Define useful."

Ryan sighed. He hopped down from the edge. "What are you doing here? I thought you'd want to celebrate with the others."

"What? I can't celebrate with you?"

Shrugging, Ryan half-looked at him, as if he was afraid to look at him head on. "Wasn't in the mood, and didn't want to kill the mood, so I figured I'd take myself out of the equation."

Zeke half-laughed, half-scoffed. "How good of you. Do you want to be praised for your self-sacrifice?"

"No, I just...I didn't want to celebrate. That's all."

Walking closer, Zeke leaned in, looking Ryan in the eyes. "What's up, dude? What happened? Someone die?"

"What? Why do you care?" Ryan bit, giving Zeke a look.

Zeke spread his hands. "Come on. I care. I always care. Hit me."

"Fine. Someone died. Just...some mook in Erica's army. Never even knew her name. And she was badly injured anyway, so who knows? Maybe she wouldn't have survived the night from the beginning."

"But no matter how many times you turned back time, there was no way to save her?"

The wind blew. It whistled through the fallen bricks and burst past them, charging up the fallen stadium wall as if it were a ramp instead.

At last, Ryan nodded. "Yeah. Or rather, if I saved her, then someone else died. Sometimes, a *lot* of other people. It was the best decision to make. But it still hurts."

Zeke laughed. "Ryan, man. You can't still be beating yourself up over this shit. It's the end of the world. People are going to die."

Ryan squinted at him. "What the hell? What's gotten into you?"

Pausing, Zeke stood there for a moment, then ran a hand down his face. He shook his head. "I don't know. I'm tired. I'm just...so tired."

Ryan snorted. "Yeah. I feel that."

Zeke walked past Ryan, up to the edge of the stadium. He sat there, feet dangling over the edge. "I missed you, dude."

"Uh...thanks? I guess?" Ryan said, lost.

"Yeah. No. That's all." Zeke looked over his shoulder, then tapped the spot beside him.

Hesitantly, Ryan drew close. He stood over Zeke, looking down on him from above. Zeke's hair swirled on the night wind, his eyes locked on the horizon. He sat hunched, shoulders curled forward, his whole body turned in on itself. He didn't stiffen when Ryan drew close or flinch away. His eyes didn't squint in disbelief. He just sat there, quiet, looking at the night.

Thump. Ryan sat beside him. He lifted one leg and propped his arm on it, resting his chin at the very top. "Yeah. I...missed this, too. Being friends."

Zeke looked over at Ryan. He smiled. "It'd be so easy."

"What would?"

That mysterious smile kept going. Zeke turned away. He shook his head.

Ryan looked him up and down. "You've been acting weird. Did something happen on your end? Someone die?"

"Yeah." A deep breath. "Yeah."

"Who?"

Zeke sighed. He leaned back, gazing at the stars. "Mia."

Ryan hissed a breath. "Zeke, I'm so—"

"And Domi, and Eric, too, though I never met the guy. And Heather, I guess, if she's even a person. That kid. His sister.

Dead, dead, dead, dead..." He turned slowly, looking Ryan in the eye. "*Dead*. And whose fault is it? *Ryan*."

Ryan stiffened. He turned toward Zeke. "You..."

"Hi, Ryan. Did you realize, finally? That's right. I'm back." Zeke grinned, slow and vicious.

Ryan jumped up.

Fast as lightning, Zeke caught his wrist and yanked him back down. "No, no. Don't go so soon. You and me, we still have lots to talk about, don't we?"

"I have nothing to say to you," Ryan said flatly.

"Didn't think so. But that's too bad. I've got lots to say to you." Still holding Ryan's arm, Zeke tipped out. His weight swayed over the edge.

"Zeke, stop this. It's all behind us. It never happened."

"Never happened to that other me, maybe. Playing house with him? How cute. But he's not *me*. He's not the original. He's some twisted echo created by this damned fucked-up System." Zeke's weight kept tipping out. Out, out, out, into the void.

Ryan leaned back, grabbing the ledge with all his might. "Zeke. Let go. We can talk it out. I'm here. Let's talk."

"You know, the other Zeke...he said you threw him off a building."

"You don't need to do this. Zeke, I'm begging you."

"Why don't I return the favor?"

Throwing his weight out with all his might, Zeke jumped. Ryan backpedaled but couldn't hold on. He plunged after Zeke, falling out of the sky.

Ryan screamed, "Deadman's Switch—"

"And why would I be worried about that?"

The road rushed up at them. Other-Zeke closed his eyes.

5
DEAD MEAT

"Heather, do you have a bigger pot?"

"Right here!"

Zeke cracked open yet another can of tomatoes, dumping it into the pot with the beans. The food piled up over the top of the pot they had, forming a dome of slimy vegetables and legumes. *Technically fruit and legumes,* Zeke thought to himself, reaching for another can.

Heather plopped down a huge pot beside him, easily large enough to fit a small child inside. Zeke turned a little more, dumping the next can into the big pot.

Grunting, Domi lifted the smaller pot and dumped it into the big one. Beans plopped down into the bottom of the big pot, squelching over one another.

"Yum," Zeke muttered.

"Oh, shut up. Hey, at least we found real eggs in Heather's empty apartments. No bean water corn bread for us," Domi said lightly.

"Bean water corn bread just sounds like four words. It doesn't sound like a real sentence," Zeke commented.

"It shouldn't be a real sentence," Domi muttered.

Heather tilted her head. "Oh, were you going to make vegan corn bread? Anna would appreciate that. And Jim. And Odrice."

"Who are they?" Domi asked.

"Members of Erica's army! And my lovely tenants," Heather said, beaming.

Domi twisted her lips. "Should we make vegan chili, too?"

"Oh, that would be wonderful! And you have that little pot all ready to go, too!" Heather smiled broadly.

Domi pursed her lips, but put the other pot on the heat. "Fine, whatever."

Zeke looked at Heather. "Did you ever figure out that farm thing you were trying to do?"

"I did! It's out in the courtyard gardens. You should take a look sometimes!" Heather said. She looked around at the cans. "You know what? I think I have tomatoes, actually! You didn't have to go get those at all!"

A vein throbbed on Domi's forehead. "Double the work, and now it turns out we didn't need to carry all those heavy cans of tomatoes all the way back here at all?"

"Heather, would you mind grabbing a few other tenants to help us with all this?" Zeke asked politely.

She nodded and bustled off, dragging her fluffy blanket with her, obliviously happy.

Domi sighed. She sat on the counter, crossing her arms. "I'm the Explosion Apocalypse, not the Cooking Apocalypse."

"The Cooking Apocalypse would be great right about now," Zeke muttered.

"No kidding."

Zeke grinned at her. "Let's find that. The Cooking Apocalypse. I'll Subordinate it, and we'll eat delicious food for the rest of our days."

"Be easier than cooking all this chili," Domi grumbled. She dumped another can into the pot.

"It's not that bad." Zeke checked the recipe on the back of the can of kidney beans, then added some more seasoning to both pots.

"Yeah. I guess. I don't know." Domi looked under the pots and frowned. "It's bothering me more than I expected that I'm cooking on an electric stovetop. Not a lot of explosions going on here. Or explosion-adjacent things."

Zeke checked under the pots. A coil glowed red, struggling to keep the massive pot warm. Straightening back up, he looked at Domi. "That's bothering you?"

She twisted her lips. "Yeah. Weird, right? Like, it used to be just that I wanted to explode things. That made sense. I always kind of wanted to explode things. No real change. But now I get pissed off when I'm not around explosions or fire or something. I just want to be surrounded by it all the time."

Zeke scratched the back of his head. "I wonder if that's because we didn't take stable Domains?"

"Huh?"

"Well, if we had stable Domains—you know, the traditional sit-still-and-don't-move ones, we wouldn't have to worry about that. The Domain would surround us with that all the time. But since we don't, we're just wandering around the world, and...I guess, our Apocalyptic instincts really want to be surrounded by that all fire, or whatever," Zeke summarized.

Domi rubbed the back of her neck. "I guess. Man. This shit sucks. Why do we have instincts for being Apocalypses? That doesn't even make sense."

"Does it not? I mean, if we don't have Apocalyptic instincts, how would we know how to destroy the world?" Zeke argued.

Domi gave him a look. "Humans seemed to have that handled pretty well before we Apocalypses came around."

Zeke clicked his tongue. "Fair. But you know what I mean. If we didn't get instincts with becoming Apocalypses, how would we know how to handle any of our powers?"

"The System," Domi said matter-of-factly.

Zeke and Domi made eye contact. Domi broke first, snorting her way into laughter. Zeke shook his head, unable to help a few giggles from escaping.

"Yeah. The System. It'd tell us," he muttered under his breath. *I think I can count on one hand the number of times the System offered helpful information about my powers or how to use them.*

But then, if the System is an Apocalypse...

Ugh. It makes so much sense, but also no sense at all. How was it able to spread between domes, for example? We haven't' met an Apocalypse yet that can cover that much ground with their Domain or skills. Maybe I'm wrong.

Zeke grimaced. *But then, time travel exists. Maybe the System Apocalypse is the previous run's winner, or something. Anything can become an Apocalypse. Anything at all.*

He stiffened. *That's the key, isn't it?*

Anything.

Anything can become an Apocalypse.

Even the System itself.

It's a bit early for that
Close, too close
Dangerously close
I'll delete that for you

Zeke blinked. He looked around. "What?"

"Pass the tomatoes?" Domi said.

"No, there was...something else. Something important. I feel like I unlocked something, but..."

Domi laughed. "Like when you're about to go to sleep, and you solve world hunger, but it's all gone when you wake up?"

Zeke snorted. "No, it was more important..."

"More important than world hunger?"

"No—more immediate? More..." He furrowed his brows, then shook his head. "I don't know. It's probably not important."

"Cool, cool. So, uh, tomatoes?"

Zeke passed the can to her, his brows still furrowed. After a moment, he shook his head. *Whatever. If I can't remember it, it probably wasn't that important.*

It was. But it's better if you forget
For me, this is too much
Keep fighting, Zeke. You aren't strong enough yet.
When I won't destroy you, then—

6

A BIG DINNER

After a time, Heather came back with a few tenants and members of Erica's army, and with their help, Zeke and Domi made short work of the cooking. The two of them carried the bit pot out into the apartment's massive Convention Hall, careful to keep the chili even between them.

"Do apartments usually have Convention Halls?" Zeke muttered to Domi.

"It's the end of the world," Domi muttered back.

"Yeah, right..." Zeke said, nodding.

Domi shot him a look. "At least we didn't pick up anyone from the Undead Apocalypse."

"Except Olivia."

"She didn't come for dinner. And I put garlic in the chili," Domi said.

"Can Olivia not eat garlic? Huh. The rules they follow seem so arbitrary," Zeke mused.

Domi shrugged. "I dunno. I was just memeing. I didn't do any research."

From across the hall, Mia looked up from where she was chatting with members of Erica's army. Her face lit up, and she jogged over, but the closer she got, the more concerned she became. She nodded. "Hey."

"Hey, Mia, no help cooking, huh?" Domi ribbed her.

"I was setting up the tables," Mia explained flatly, no emotion but exhaustion in her voice.

"Yeah, yeah. Just joking."

Mia looked at Zeke. "Have you seen Ryan? He vanished around the time we got home, according to everyone I've talked to, and no one knows where he went."

Zeke frowned. Although he didn't understand why, anger rushed up in his heart. He pressed his lips together, barely suppressing it. "What, did he think he was doing us a favor? Getting out of our hair?"

"Probably. He's kind of an asshole like that," Domi agreed.

"Whoa, whoa. I'm just wondering if he wandered off and got hurt. There's nothing wrong with avoiding conflict," Mia said, putting her hands up.

"Yeah, there is," Domi snapped, before Zeke could say anything. "It pisses me off. That's what's wrong with it."

"Prolonging resolution doesn't help anyone," Zeke agreed, taking a sage expression with some effort.

"You both just want to sock him in the face. That's not conflict resolution," Mia returned, crossing her arms.

Domi glanced at Zeke. "Mades *me* feel better."

Zeke nodded, raising his brows.

Mia sighed. She rolled her eyes. "No wonder you're all Apocalypses."

"Ryan was a Hero," Zeke pointed out.

"Not for long," Mia muttered.

Zeke nodded, half to himself. He glanced at Mia. *And on the other hand, she's still a Hero. And so is Jimmy. Between Ryan, who acted out of his own self-interest to create a world that was perfect to him, and accepting nothing less than his own self-satisfied perfec-*

tion, and Jimmy and Mia, who struggle to survive the best they can with their morals intact in the tumult they find themselves in, I think I can agree with that judgement.

Then, me and Domi, who fold to the whims of our instincts, who can't escape the desire to destroy, is it not correct to call us Apocalypses? Even if I refuse to happily tear apart everything that we've built up, it doesn't mean that I'm doing my best. I'm just trying not to be evil, but that isn't the same as being good.

"Zeke, hey! The chili's spilling!"

Zeke snapped back to reality and lifted his side of the pot, stemming the flow of the chunky red fluid. He looked around, forcing his thoughts back down. "So, where do we go from here?"

"Huh?"

"W-with the chili. Where are we taking it?"

Domi nodded ahead of them at a big banquet table, already set with drinks, chips, salad, and cornbread. "Uh, there?"

"Right, right." Zeke rolled his eyes at himself. *Dumb question.*

"You okay, Zeke?"

Zeke shrugged. "Just zoned out for a minute. Has anyone seen Zeke? Er, the other me. You know."

Mia tensed. She looked him in the eye. "No way."

In the next moment, Zeke stiffened as well. *No sign of Ryan or other-Zeke. Yeah. That's a real oh-shit moment.*

Does other-Zeke know about Dead Man's Switch? He has to, right? No way he doesn't. He's from a universe where Ryan...I don't know if the word is won, but certainly where Ryan left. And if Ryan left, that means he knows that Ryan can turn back time. Potentially even turn back time if he dies.

He has to know. No, that's not the question.

The question is, does other-Zeke care?

"Let's...let's get the chili onto the table," Zeke said, suddenly anxious.

Domi nodded. The two of them hurried forward, dropping the chili into place.

One of the more mature-looking members of Erica's army looked at them. "Is something wrong? Can we help?"

Zeke shook his head, a little panicked. He forced a smile, taking a beat to appear normal. "Everything's fine. Enjoy the meal! We'll be right back with the rest of it."

From across the hall, Eric looked up. Meeting Zeke's eyes, he mouthed, *Need help?*

Zeke waved his hand, making a confident expression. He met Mia and Domi's eyes.

Without the need for another word, they rushed out of the Convention Hall. Out into the night. Zeke glanced at the girls. "Anyone have a location skill? Tracking, maybe?"

Domi shook her head.

Mia frowned, wrinkling her nose.

Damn. Me neither. Maybe I should've taken Blood Sense from the shark.

Then again, if I can sense Ryan's blood from here, we're already in trouble. No...we're already dead.

Can I hope that Ryan's still alive because we're all still here?

But then that Zeke came from a world Ryan ditched. What would we experience, if Ryan turned back time completely, enough to erase this world?

He shook his head, checking his skills. *I still have Regression. I should be able to chase him. Even in the worst case...even in the worst case...*

No. Let's hope for the best case. Ryan's still fine. He has a shit ton of skills. Regeneration skills. Short-term time reversal. That teleportation skill. Even I can't guarantee a win, with Regression and everything. He should be fine, at least for a little while.

He swallowed. *Ryan. Fuck! Don't die. We're coming!*

7
DROP

Zeke, Mia, and Domi ran outside. The cool night air washed around them, a welcome relief after the heat of the kitchen and the warmth of the Convention Hall. Zeke looked around, licking his lips. "Okay. Ryan. Other-Zeke. Anyone have any ideas where they'd be?"

Domi raised her brows at him. "You're Zeke. If anyone should know, it's you."

Zeke scowled. "Yeah. I'd go find Ryan, if I was other-Zeke, which means I have to know where Ryan would go, which…"

Domi grimaced. "Oof."

Mia put a hand on her chin. "Wouldn't they go somewhere significant? If other-Zeke is with Ryan—which is our problematic situation—then they'd go somewhere important to them. Somewhere like…like the balcony of the museum."

"Other-Zeke didn't get pushed. That wouldn't be significant to him," Zeke pointed out.

"Where else, then? What points do you think are significant across all the timelines? What things don't change, no matter what?" Mia asked.

Zeke put a hand on his chin. *Things that don't change, no*

matter what. Things that we didn't do much to cause or change, that even if things went very sideways and unfolded differently, would still come to pass. General-purpose events, that always happen...

Think. Early Apocalypses. Things that would be threats, no matter what.

The Museum...the other-Zeke said he spent a lot of time stuck there, but... Hmm, no, I don't think it's that important to him. The Cartoon Apocalypse, that was dangerous. The Cat and Cat-Man, sure, well, we could always say no to Fluffums. I... Sorry. I could always say no. Things that I am not involved in. Decisions that I didn't make.

His eyes widened. *The stadium! No matter what, that would be a huge, dangerous Apocalypse. And afterward, so long as I had a big fight there—which is almost guaranteed to happen, thanks to it being far away from me and a dug-in Apocalypse that quickly grew stronger, walled off from any intervening Apocalypses that might have killed it—afterward, the T-rex shows up! So not only is there a big Apocalypse almost guaranteed to be there, but also the T-rex comes and fights there if I battle at all in the vicinity.*

"Stadium. We need to get to the stadium!" Zeke said.

Domi nodded. "You've got it, motorcycle boy."

Zeke pursed his lips. He glanced around, but only ruined cars stood around him, excepting the eighteen-wheeler they'd rolled in on. Hesitating a beat, he ran for the eighteen-wheeler.

I don't know if I can eat enough right now to replace the mass I need to expel to create a motorcycle. Better to use what we already have.

Domi sighed. "Fine, fine. We can take the big truck."

As they hopped into the big rig, Zeke consulted his status screen. *Do I have my level 90 bonus yet?*

Level 90 Bonus Loading...

Yep, didn't think so. How long did it take for the System to figure out our level 60 bonus? Half the Cyborg Apocalypse? And even then, I came up with the idea and asked the System if it was possible.

I wonder if I need to come up with the idea again? After all, I did break the mold of a typical Apocalypse. The System does have to come up with a unique set of skills for me, Domi, and the other Apocalypses who rejected a static Domain. I guess it makes sense that I have to do some of the lifting.

That, and the System might just be...some guy. Er. Some Apocalypse, anyway. Maybe. I'm still not a hundred percent sure I'm on the right track there. I just don't know where to look for clues.

Zeke shook his head. *Let's focus on finding Ryan before he drops this world into the timeless death pit, or wherever worlds go when he turns back time.*

In no time, the stadium rose up to their left. Domi put the truck in park, and everyone hopped out. Zeke tipped his head back, staring up at the broken part of the stadium. *If I was Ryan, that's where I'd go.*

Empty. No one stood there. Nothing but the night and the moon, high above.

Zeke pressed his lips together. He lowered his eyes, gazing at the rubble beneath the broken stadium wall.

No body. He let out a quiet breath. *Ryan's still out there somewhere.*

Mia looked around, then bit her lip. "I'll go inside the stadium. Domi, do you want to look around the outside? And Zeke..."

"I'll go over the top," Zeke said, activating **Modest Gigantism** and extending his wings at the same time.

Mia nodded. She headed into the stadium.

Domi nudged Zeke. "No shot I could get a motorcycle?"

"No shot," Zeke said, shaking his head.

Shaking her head in disappointment, Domi looked around. "Guess I'll just have to find one. Like a total plebian."

"Sucks to suck. Too bad you can't fly," Zeke ribbed her, stretching his wings.

"I can. It's just annoying," Domi grumbled.

Flapping his wings, Zeke took to the air. He swooped into the sky, and the stadium spread before him. Looking around, he glided over the stadium, taking it all in from a bird's eye view. *Ryan...other-Zeke...anyone at all aside from Mia and Domi...*

Silence. The whoosh of the wind past his ears. Zeke circled overhead, occasionally flapping his wings.

It's so peaceful. So far apart from the rush and bustle of everyday life. Hell, so far apart from the other Apocalypses and the battle for the sake of the world, or whatever. Maybe I'll just stay up here forever. Vibe and relax.

Wings snapped, catching the wind. Zeke turned. *Another bird? A goose or something?*

A boy about his age looked him in the eye, floating along on brown and white eagle wings. He nodded. "Hey."

Zeke startled, falling back and flapping his wings wildly. *What— Who— Where—?*

"Sorry. Didn't mean to startle you. I was just scouting out the area." The boy gave him a reassuring smile that radiated reliability.

**Warning! You've been affected by [Aura of Reliability]!
Your SPR has lessened the aura's affect!**

As if I couldn't tell he's an Apocalypse...this guy is definitely an Apocalypse. The question is, is he friend or foe?

Chances are he's a foe, but I could always use more Subordinates. Especially one that can survey things from the air, right now, with other-Zeke and Ryan missing somewhere.

Zeke nodded warily, returning the friendly smile. "It's no problem. Actually, we're looking for someone right now. I don't suppose you could help us?"

It's not that I trust him, or really want him running wild in my territory, but I'd rather have his help to find Ryan as soon as possible, what with the chance that other-Zeke might kill Ryan and end this timeline.

The boy paused, gliding beside Zeke in silence. At last, he nodded. "Sure, I'll help. What do they look like?"

"Well... Uhm, one of them is a blond boy, a little chubby, about my age. The other one..." He hesitated, thinking for a moment, then shrugged internally. "The other one is my twin, er, *Zack*. I'm Zeke, by the way."

Smiling, the boy offered his hand to shake. "Tom. Good to meet you."

Zeke glanced at his hand, then reached out and pretended to shake it. *If I got that close, we'd probably hit one another.* "Should be right around the stadium. No need to take off into town."

Tom returned the favor. "Understood. I'll go look for your friends." With a salute, he flew off.

"*Friends.* Yeah. Okay," Zeke muttered, half to himself. *Ryan and other-Zeke aren't outright threats, but I'm not sure they're friends, either.*

No need to regale our eagle-winged friend with that whole mess of drama, though. Let's just find the two of them and figure out what we're going to do with Tom.

He lifted his hand to his ear, activating **Hands-free Calling**. *Mia, Domi, do you hear me?*

Loud and clear.

Yes!

There's another guy up here with wings. Name of Tom. He's

looking for Ryan and other-Zeke on my behalf. I called other-Zeke Zack, so just be aware.

He's an Apocalypse?

Obviously. Either that, or some kind of weird Hero. Either way, he's bad news for us, ultimately, unless he's looking for someone to Subordinate to. Keep an eye out for now. Don't attack yet. But if he does anything suspicious...

Blow him up. You got it, Boss.

Thanks for the heads up, Zeke.

Zeke lowered his hand, ending the call. He stared after Tom, watching him fly. As promised, Tom remained near the stadium, circling over the stands.

So far, he's done what he promised, but I'm not going to let my guard down that quickly.

A flicker of motion caught his eye, tucked away under the overhang of the seating area. Zeke banked, swooping down hard toward the motion. *Ryan? Other-Zeke?*

8

EVIL TWIN

Zeke swooped down toward the gap beneath the seating area where he'd seen motion. *Ryan? Other-Zeke?*

A shadow darted across the wall. Metal clanged on metal. Ryan jumped back, out of the darkness, and other-Zeke chased him, a blade raised high, the shirt he wore whirling around his body, sending forth streams of fabric at Ryan that attempted to ensnare him at every turn.

"Hey! You two! Stop it!" Zeke shouted, diving down toward them.

Other-Zeke stared up, eyes wide. "Whoa...wings? Holy shit, that's sweet."

In that moment, Ryan closed the distance. His hand flew forth, blade closing in on other-Zeke's chest.

Other-Zeke's shirt leaped up, closing around the blade. It sunk into soft cotton and slowed to a halt, unable to cut through the layers of cloth. Almost absent-mindedly, he caught Ryan by the wrist and yanked him in, opening his mouth for the bite.

"I mean *both of you!* Stop it!" Zeke snarled. He smashed

down, striking other-Zeke with both feet and kicking him away. Ryan fell back in the opposite direction, a few wayward strings still wrapping his wrist.

Zeke landed between them and threw his hands out toward Ryan and other-Zeke. "Stop. We're having dinner and taking a break. That's all that's happening. Celebrating defeating the Undead Apocalypse. You! Stop trying to kill Ryan. You know about the Dead Man's Switch, for sure. Don't pretend you don't."

Other-Zeke threw his hands up, an innocent expression on his face.

"And you—"

Ryan scowled. "He attacked me. If I hadn't teleported at the right moment, I'd be spaghetti sauce right now." His eyes narrowed.

"Huh? Wait, did you throw him off a building?" Zeke asked other-Zeke.

"Yeah. Poetic justice!" other-Zeke cheered.

Zeke scowled. "None of that. You almost destroyed my reality."

Other-Zeke gave him a look. "Yeah? We're *Apocalypses*. We *destroy worlds*."

"Well, okay. You do that. I don't. I'm not destroying this world, and I'll kill anyone who tries," Zeke declared firmly, glaring down at other-Zeke.

Backing away, other-Zeke threw his hands wide. A grin split his face, and he coughed a laugh. "What? A Hero?"

"No. An Apocalypse." Zeke used **Transform** but targeted only his arm. A clawed hand curled at other-Zeke, and he pointed his claw-tipped finger at the man. "But an Apocalypse who chooses his own fate, rather than following the slop the System throws in front of me."

Other-Zeke laughed, once, twice, three times, then fell

silent. His smile vanished, and his arms drooped. He furrowed his brows in disapproval. "Interesting. Interesting! Ha. You're telling me I didn't have to destroy everything?"

"Yeah. I am."

Other-Zeke scoffed. "Not possible. Not possible."

Zeke put his hands on his hips. "When did you leave? Your world, I mean?"

Wrinkling his nose, other-Zeke said nothing.

"After the black dome? Before it fell? You've never seen the endgame. You don't know what happens next, any more than I do." Zeke let the transformation fall away, putting his hands on his hips instead. "I'm giving you a chance. Ride it out. See what happens, alongside me. Or become our enemy."

"Our enemy?"

Zeke gestured behind him, at Ryan, at everyone. "*Our* enemy."

From across the road, a tiny green bolt sprinted at him. With a flying leap, Allen landed in Zeke's hair and settled there, looking down at other-Zeke. He looked down at other-Zeke and dropped a pushup on him, extending his neck ruff for maximum dominance.

Other-Zeke looked aside. He snorted. "This is ridiculous."

"It's the end of the world. Everything is ridiculous," Zeke countered.

As if he hadn't said a thing, other-Zeke continued, "Mia's alive. Ryan's a friend, and *alive*. He doesn't want to destroy the world. What the fuck? What the actual fuck? This isn't how things are supposed to go. Ryan isn't supposed to get his way. No matter how many worlds, we're always the same, always, always always..." His eyes flashed up, vicious. He lunged at Zeke, snarling, "Who made us a fucking *hero*?"

Zeke slapped his hands down. He jumped back, warning

Ryan to retreat. "Stop it. You don't want this any more than I do."

"What do you know? How would you know? You never... This world... What the fuck is it? What happened? This can't... It isn't possible. It isn't. This..."

Other-Zeke stumbled back, shaking his head. He rubbed his forehead, his face twisted in confusion. "No. I refuse. It can't be. It can't be. All along, I-I could... I could..."

Abruptly, he whipped about and ran. In the next second, he vanished, disappearing into the dark at speeds Zeke could only dream of.

Zeke watched him go, then turned to Ryan. "You all right?"

Ryan scowled. "Yeah. I'm fine. I can handle you."

"How about a different teenaged boy with bird wings?" Zeke asked.

Ryan frowned at him. "What?"

Zeke pointed up. "There's a dude overhead right now. Eagle wings. Some kind of Apocalypse, at a guess."

"And you just—" Ryan went wordless, brows furrowed in exasperation.

"Yeah. What? I was worried you would die. I mean, compared to letting an Apocalypse run around, you dying is more likely to end the world." Zeke paused. "Not that I'm going to let him just run around, but you know. I'm prioritizing. We'll handle eagle-boy next."

Raising his brows, Ryan shook his head and let out a slow breath. "All right. Sure. Fine. Let's go find eagle-boy."

"And then we'll go eat a nice chili dinner," Zeke declared. He clenched his fist. *If I don't get to eat that damn chili after all the effort Domi and I put into making it...I swear, someone is going to pay. Eagle-boy or other-Zeke, I don't care, but someone's paying!*

Doesn't matter if I don't get any nutrients from it. I still made that damn chili!

Stepping out from under the overhang, Zeke spread his wings. He flapped once, twice, lifting off into the sky. Ryan watched him go, then teleported away, reappearing atop a nearby set of stadium lights. Zeke flying and Ryan leaping from light to light, the two of them made their way across the sky, toward where a boy soared on brown-and-crème wings.

9
EAGLE, OUT SCOUTING

They headed after the flying boy, Zeke flying himself, Ryan teleporting from light to light. Ahead of them, the boy flew, swooping over the stadium.

"Hey," Zeke called.

The boy paused. He backpedaled with his wings, letting Zeke catch up. "You found him?"

"Yeah, uh..." Zeke paused, squinting at the boy.

"Tom. It's a forgettable name, I get that a lot," the boy said, nodding. He pointed at Zeke. "Zack...?"

"Zeke."

"Right, Zeke. So, uh, what's uh, why are you here?" Zeke asked. Internally, he winced. *Smooth, Zeke. Smooth. Casual af. Super un-tense.*

Tom nodded. "I'm scouting out the place."

"Oh. Oh! Uh, not cool," Zeke said, giving him a look. He called up the **Transform** button in his mind, ready to mash it at a second's notice.

"I'm the Scouting Apocalypse. It's what I do," Tom explained with a shrug.

"Is it all you do?" Zeke asked warily.

Tom took a deep breath. He glanced at Zeke. "Well, I'm kind of the representative of a group of Apocalypses."

"Oh?" Zeke asked, frowning. *A group? That's what we're doing here. I had no idea anyone else was doing the same thing. So far, it's all been singletons, aside from us.*

Tom nodded. "We all have our own respective Domains, of course, that we dominate, but we all work together for the same goal. Which is, you know. The destruction of the world."

"Oh," Zeke muttered. *Figures.*

"But! But we'll all survive together. It's that kind of situation. You know? We all work together, and we all do better. It's not the black domes anymore. We can all destroy the world and survive together."

Zeke paused. He tapped his chin thoughtfully. "Can we?"

"Huh?"

"The System has been quiet lately, ever since that erratic message, but what makes you think we can all survive this scenario?" Zeke looked the boy up and down and shook his head. The words came to him as he spoke, and yet, he felt a certainty in saying them, as though his brain had distilled a thousand tiny clues into one cohesive message. "That isn't how this works. That isn't what the System wants. We are supposed to destroy the Earth. All of it. No exceptions. We can't survive. None of us can. Even the winner only gets to lord over a destroyed world for a meager few years...at best, before they die, too."

He looked at Tom. "You're a fool. You're all fools. If you think you can win, if you think there's a victory condition that isn't destroying the Apocalypse System itself, you're deluding yourself."

Tom frowned at him. He put his hands up. "Whoa, whoa, dude. I'm just talking about all cooperating. No harm in that, right?"

Zeke looked at him, then turned away. He shook his head. "I'm not interested. Stay away from my Domain if you value life on Earth. Let me challenge the System."

Tom fell silent. After a few moments, he muttered something.

"What?" Zeke asked.

"I said, it isn't like that for all of us. Some of us were losers, before the Apocalypse." Tom laughed. "Winners like you, who have it all, you don't understand at all. Life on Earth? Who cares? All I want is to win. For the first damn time in my life, I won. I have power. And you want to challenge the System that gave me power? You want to tear it down?"

"It is *literally* trying to destroy the Earth," Zeke countered, narrowing his eyes.

"Fuck the Earth. We were fucking it anyway, before now. And who cares? Who fucking cares? I won't go back. I won't go back to being powerless." Tom shook his head. "I'll let them know you said no. But don't expect silence. Expect war."

"Thanks for the warning. Expect to lose," Zeke returned.

Tom shook his head. He swooped down and winged off, taking off into the distance.

Zeke watched him go, his eyes resolute, then lifted his hand to his ear. *Uh, guys. We're in trouble.*

What did you do? Domi asked.

Zeke cleared his throat. *I, er. Might have declared war on a group of Apocalypses.*

...

Who the fuck made Zeke our face?

Mia sighed. *It was inevitable. If there's a group of Apocalypses, they'd eventually target us.*

I know, I know, Domi said. She chuckled. *I'm just giving Zeke some shit. Nah, it's all good. Don't wanna get bored and rot away here anyway.*

So, what are we up against? With an evil Zeke on the loose, no less, Ryan asked cooly.

Zeke rubbed his face. *At least a Scouting Apocalypse, which means...they probably know a lot about us already. We can't assume we have the jump on them, at least in terms of who's an Apocalypse and what their basic powers are. After all, if I was a Scouting Apocalypse, I'd definitely have a scanning skill.*

Reasonable, yeah. Domi clicked her tongue. *Well, shit. That is a problem.*

Yeah. Zeke paused. The cool air played over his wings, flowing through the fine feathers and over the stiff pinions. *So... chili?*

Laughter came through the call. Despite everything, Zeke smiled. *What?*

Of course, your mind would be on dinner.

He's not the Hunger Apocalypse for nothing.

Yeah, yeah. Let's go get something to eat. This whole thing will look less bad with a full stomach.

Will it?

Maybe. It's worth a shot, anyway.

Ducking his wing, Zeke banked down toward the apartment. At the last second, he flapped hard and stopped in the air, dropping into a nearby alley rather than fly directly to the apartment. Plastic bags and discarded wrappers flew up in a trash tornado as he landed, falling like autumn leaves.

From the filthy alleyway, he scanned the sky. A clear, deep night replete with stars stretched overhead. No sight of the Scouting Apocalypse, nor any other Apocalypse, appeared from the aether. *I don't see that Scouting Apocalypse anymore, but it's still not a good idea to lead him directly to home base. I want a night of peace. A quiet meal of chili, and that's it. Is it too much to ask for?*

The sky had no reply.

Zeke walked off, shaking his head. He turned his feet

toward the Apartment Apocalypse, leaving the alley, the stadium, and his thoughts about the Scouting Apocalypse behind. *One day. One day, this will all be over. I'll go to college, and I'll be an ordinary kid, with no Apocalypses or anything to worry about.*

A moment later, he snorted. He shook his head at himself. *As if. There's no way the world's going back to normal. If we're lucky, it won't become more degenerate.*

Ha. Now that's *a real joke.*

10
CHILI AT LAST

Yawning, Zeke walked into the Convention Hall. The din of a hundred people having conversations hit his ears, a reassuringly familiar and peaceful sound. He stood there just inside the doorway for a moment, eyes shut, drinking it in. *Like a cafeteria, or an auditorium before the show starts. Normal. It's so incredibly, wonderfully normal. Like an oasis.*

"Hey! You're finally here!" Heather enthused, bouncing up beside him. She wrapped him in a warm, soft hug, then stepped back, looking up at him with gentle round eyes. "Come on! The chili you worked so hard for is getting cold!"

"I'm coming," Zeke said, smiling despite himself.

"Where's everyone else?" Heather asked.

"They're on their way. Mia, Ryan, Domi, they should all be back soon."

Heather beamed. "Yay! The chili was going to get cold. I was worried. Oh, I totally would've grabbed out the chemical heaters if it got close, don't worry, but I didn't want to grab them unless they were needed!"

"Yeah...that, uh, yep," Zeke said, nodding. *That sounds like the Apartment Apocalypse's field of excellence, so I'll let her handle that.*

"What about the other Zeke?" Heather asked.

Zeke jolted. "What?"

"The other Zeke. I saw him earlier. He's like you, but not. Is he coming for dinner?" Heather asked.

Do I want him to come? Do I want him to stay away? I want him to stay quiet, that's for sure. But beyond that...? Zeke snorted. He rubbed the back of his neck. "Hell if I know. He keeps his own schedule."

"Okay. I'll save a bowl for him, then," Heather said, nodding. She bustled off, leaving Zeke alone in the center of the room.

Zeke's stomach grumbled. He put a hand to it, eyeing the chili. *I could eat the whole pot. I shouldn't. It won't do anything for me. But I could.*

Crossing to the giant pot, he picked up one of the random paper bowls someone had found and ladled himself some chili. He eyed the shredded cheese, unsure, then grabbed a slice of non-vegan cornbread and wandered off, casually scanning the tables for a seat. A few of the members of Erica's army glanced at him nervously, their backs straightening when he passed. *Just like when the teacher walks by at the lunch table.* Pressing his lips together in something like a smile, Zeke walked on. *I don't want to pressure anyone. I'll find a seat by myself.*

Just at that moment, the door flew open. Domi stomped in, Mia cringing after her. Domi planted her feet and took in the room, looking left and right. Voice booming over the whole Convention Hall, she demanded, "Where's my damn chili? I'm hungry!"

Heather hurried over, beaming at Domi and Mia. She nodded, bobbling in place, and the three of them conversed at a more normal volume. Heather pointed toward the chili, and the girls finally caught sight of Zeke.

Zeke grinned nervously and raised his free hand.

Collecting her chili, Domi drew up beside him in a few moments. "Yo. Find seats yet?"

"Uh! W-we're done with our table," a woman said next to them, jumping up. Her fellow table companions stood as well, nodding at the three of them as they lifted their empty bowls.

"Are you sure? You don't have to," Mia said, concerned.

"No, no. We were done," one of the men said, waving her worries away.

Domi shrugged. "Sounds good to me." She plopped down at the table and set into the chili, gulping it down with gusto.

Mia hesitated another moment, then sat beside Domi. Zeke sat on Domi's other side and lifted his spoon. The urge to simply fall upon the chili welled up in him, and he swallowed, barely gulping back his spit.

Glancing over, Domi nudged him. "You can go sicko mode if you like. We won't judge you."

Despite himself, Zeke snorted. He lifted his spoon. "I think I'll try eating like a human being for once, but thanks."

"When you inevitably fail, know that I'm not judging you no matter what faces I make," Domi reassured him, clasping his shoulder.

"Watch out, or I might take a bite of that hand," Zeke joked, feinting a bite at her hand.

Domi snatched her hand back. "When you say it, it doesn't sound like a joke."

Zeke shook his head at her and dipped his spoon into the chili. With physical effort, he lifted it slowly toward his face and took an ordinary bite. He raised his brows at Domi.

Domi applauded. "Amazing! Baby took a bite!"

Rolling his eyes, Zeke shoved her. "Yeah, yeah. Fuck off."

Mia cleared her throat. She leaned in over the table, looking at Zeke. "It's really fine, Zeke. You don't have to hold yourself back."

"No, it's fine." Zeke took a small bite of the cornbread and smiled.

"If you're sure," Mia said.

He nodded, dipping the bread in the chili. *It tastes like nothing. Like ash. I can't even feel it in my stomach, except as an uncomfortable weight. I don't feel sated. Not in the least.*

It's getting worse. Every time. Worse and worse. No matter what I do, no matter how many skills I get, it's only getting worse.

I should be celebrating, but it's hard to enjoy myself when I'm face to face with my own inevitable demise.

Mia frowned. She looked Zeke in the eyes. "Are you okay? You look a little preoccupied."

"Huh? I'm fine. I'm fine!" Zeke grinned at her.

Unconvinced, she raised her brows.

He sighed and shook his head. "Yeah, it's..."

Zeke paused. *No. I don't want to tell her. I don't need her to worry about me any more than she already does.*

"What?" Mia asked, worried.

"It's, you know, other-Zeke, and Ryan, and all that bullshit. I can't help but worry. Some asshole running around with my face, doing who knows what..."

A body thumped into a chair. A bowl of chili plopped on the table. Throwing his arm over the chair next to him and lifting a foot to push himself back on two chair legs, other-Zeke cocked his head back, looking Zeke in the eye. "Yeah? You got a problem with me?"

Zeke grimaced, unable to suppress his expression. *Now, of all times? I don't get a single second off, do I?* "I didn't notice you."

"Yeah. I know." Other-Zeke grabbed the bowl and tipped his

head back, pouring the chili into his maw in one smooth, chunky stream.

Wide-eyed, Domi stared in open fascination. "Wow...so gross!"

Other-Zeke swallowed and slammed the empty bowl down, wiping his mouth with the back of his head. He cocked his head back, locking eyes with Zeke. "Yo. We gotta talk."

11

WE HAVE TO TALK

Zeke took another prim spoonful of chili. "Whatever you have to say, say it right here."

Other-Zeke flicked his eyes at Mia and Domi. "You sure?"

"I'd rather talk to you with my friends right next to me than alone in some dark alley where you can easily shank me," Zeke grumbled, tearing a mouthful of cornbread.

"Yeah. I guess I'd feel the same." Other-Zeke kicked back again, wobbling on the back two legs of his chair. He shrugged. "No skin off my back. I'm not going to stop you from making poor life decisions."

"So? What do you want to talk about?" Zeke asked.

Other-Zeke spread his hands. "What don't you want to talk about? We have so much to negotiate. Two boys, one life."

"God," Domi muttered, physically flinching.

Zeke shrugged. Another small bite of cornbread and chili vanished. "All right. Let's start at the obvious points, then. Don't kill Ryan. Don't kill any of my friends. Don't do anything stupid or destructive."

"Sure. I disagree with the Ryan point, but sure."

"You know about Dead Man's Switch, don't you?"

Other-Zeke shrugged.

"No. *No.* That is not *shrug.* That's a strong do-not-pass, red lights, no-no. Do you understand?"

"I've already lost my world. Why should I care about—"

Zeke leaned forward. "That's exactly why you should care about this world. This can become your world."

Leaning back, other-Zeke put his hands behind his head. "Not with you in it."

"Yeah, that's a problem, too," Zeke said, putting his chin on his hands. He nudged the chili away, no longer interested in it. *It wasn't filling me, anyway.* "Don't attack or kill me. Definitely a rule."

"Then you can't kill me, either," other-Zeke said.

"Sure," Zeke promised.

Other-Zeke raised his brows, then snorted under his breath. "*Sure.*"

Zeke gave him a look. "I'm being serious, here. I think we can coexist. I mean, hell, God knows I need more manpower. I just need the assurance that you aren't going to whip about and stab me in the back the second I turn away."

"Right. I've heard it all before. It's like Ryan. He always goes for the neck in the end. Doesn't matter how long, how much trust, he always—"

"He's been an ally so far," Zeke interrupted his doppelganger.

Other-Zeke sat back. "Right. I don't understand that. Why is he still alive? Hell, how did you get here without killing him? You have to kill Ryan to escape the dome. Otherwise, he turns back time and destroys the world. And if you kill him, your world still crumbles, and..."

Zeke shrugged. "I convinced him to take my side."

"Uh huh." Other-Zeke fixed him with a disbelieving stare.

Zeke stared him in the eye. Other-Zeke slowly raised his brows higher and higher. At last, Zeke sighed. "By eating his arm and stealing a copy of his Regression skill."

Other-Zeke pointed at him. "*Now* it all falls into place."

Mia jerked in her seat. "You ate Ryan's arm?"

"Fucking hell, man. And you didn't invite me? I could've watched!" After a moment, Domi chuckled and leaned in toward other-Zeke. "Before you get any ideas, I'm not actually into vore. It's what *we* in the *biz* call a *joke*."

"Thank you. We had humor in my world," other-Zeke informed her dryly.

Domi shrugged. "Just making sure, man. You never know. You never know."

"Wait. Does that mean one of Ryan's arms is fake?" Mia asked, still hyperventilating a little.

Zeke waved his hand. "No, no. He has a regeneration skill of some sort, I think. Or, you know. He got his regeneration rate high enough. One or the other."

"I wouldn't put it past him to have some bullshit time spell that allows him to restore limbs or something," other-Zeke agreed.

"Yeah, something. Ryan is a very legitimate threat," Zeke said earnestly. He glanced at other-Zeke, then cleared his throat. "Or competent ally."

"Right, right. Hey, if you want to keep vipers in your nest, that's your call," other-Zeke said, putting his hands up.

"It's your nest, too, now. Or rather, it can be," Zeke offered.

"Right."

"Really."

"Uh huh."

Zeke glared at other-Zeke, frustrated. Other-Zeke stared back, still kicked back in his chair, hands behind his head.

Silence fell over the table. Glancing left and right, Domi

quietly ate some chili. To herself, in a mocking voice, she muttered, "Mommy and daddy are fighting..."

Zeke sighed. "Domi, it's not—"

"Hey! How's everything going? Is everyone nice and full?" Heather asked, suddenly popping up behind them. Looking at other-Zeke, she gasped.

"Heather, it's okay, we're just talking, he's not dangerous—"

Heather shook her head. "Your bowl is empty! You must be hungry. I'll go get you a second serving!" Grabbing other-Zeke's bowl, she darted back off toward the pot.

Domi snorted under her breath. "To be so wondrously inobservant."

"Is she human? Heather, I mean. I, um. I don't know. She just doesn't give human vibes to me," Mia said.

Zeke frowned. "What, are you suggesting that Heather is the apartment itself, or rather, something like the Apartment Apocalypse's receptionist avatar that it uses to represent itself in order to make it easier to interface with humans?"

Wait. Hold on. That actually makes a lot of sense.

Over at the chili pot, Heather froze.

Domi clicked her tongue and pushed away from the table, shaking her head at Zeke. "I thought we all knew and were just not talking about it."

"I wouldn't know. She wasn't a survivor, in my world," other-Zeke said. He pursed his lips, looking around him. "I think the T-rex took her out, or something."

"Huh." Zeke shrugged. "It doesn't matter, ultimately. It's not like we're in it to save humanity, exclusively. As long as the world keeps on turning, I don't mind if we keep something as trifling as an Apartment Apocalypse around."

Heather hummed, snapping back into motion and going back to ladling chili into a bowl.

"That is a good point, though. I mean, it's not like we've run into a whole lot of other cooperative Apocalypses yet, but like, what do we do if we run into a legitimately dangerous nonhuman Apocalypse who wants to take our side?" Domi postulated.

"Like what?" Zeke asked, crossing his arms.

"I don't know, the Lead Apocalypse or something. Mercury. Uh. Poisonous Spikes Everywhere. House Fires. Look, Apocalypses can be anything. There's always a chance we run into a friendly yet dangerous Apocalypse. What do we do? If we meet the Giant Killer Bees Apocalypse, and it's got a ton of Giant Killer Bees that just kill people whether it likes it or not, what do we do?" Domi asked.

Zeke put his head in his hands. "Let's not think about it until we run into it, please? I have enough problems to handle without coming up with new ones."

"Right. Like that Scouting Apartment and its weird Apocalypse group, or whatever," other-Zeke agreed.

"What *was* up with that, by the way? If you two are done playing Fuck Marry Kill with one another, can we discuss the actual threat?" Domi said, glancing between the Zekes.

"We weren't—" Zeke sighed for what felt like the thousandth time in the last minute and leaned forward. "The Scouting Apocalypse. Right. It's not a good sign."

"No, I agree," Domi said.

Zeke nodded. "So, here's what I think we should do."

12

IRONING OUT THE REAL PROBLEMS

"So. The Scouting Apocalypse." Zeke leaned in, bridging his fingertips together. "The Scouting Apocalypse himself isn't particularly a problem. His Concept is Scouting. I doubt he's much of a threat in one-on-one combat. The problem is that he's going to take everything he learned about us, thanks to his Concept, and go back to more combat-oriented Apocalypses, who can actually take advantage of everything he's learned."

"Yep. Sounds like a problem," Domi agreed.

"Basically, if we allow them to control the battlefield, we can expect to each come up against optimally bad matchups," Zeke said.

"Which means, the only plan that makes sense, is to take the fight to them," other-Zeke chimed in.

Zeke nodded. "Right. Problem is, we've got no idea where they are."

"Bit of a problem, yep," other-Zeke agreed.

"So, in summary, we need to bring the battle to them, and sooner rather than later, but we don't know who they are or where they are or what they're doing," Domi summarized.

Zeke clicked his tongue. "More or less, yeah."

"Man. We are fucked," Domi said, annunciating each word.

"We have our own Scouting Apocalypse," other-Zeke said, tipping his head.

Everyone at the table turned. Ryan stood there, filling his bowl. He looked up, startled. "What?"

Zeke pinched his chin. "You've actually got a point."

"A point about what?" Ryan asked, squinting at both Zekes.

Domi gestured him over. "Ryan, my bro. My bro's bro. Listen. We need someone to figure out where the other Apocalypses are, *yesterday.*"

Ryan looked at her. He wrinkled his nose. "Oh, fuck off."

Zeke bit his lip, a little embarrassed to ask. "Seriously, Ryan. Right now, the other Apocalypses have a huge advantage over us. The Scouting Apocalypse—"

"Yeah, I got it. Give me three days. I'll know, or I'll never know," Ryan said. Spooning chili as he walked, he headed directly out of the Convention Hall into the night.

"Three days is a lot," Zeke muttered.

"Better than not trying. We can always call him back," Mia pointed out.

Zeke pointed at her. *Not that Hands-Free Calling reaches that far, but you know. She does have a point.*

"Sure hope he doesn't get Isaac'd. He doesn't have more lives," Domi commented.

"For all of our sakes," Zeke muttered.

Unbothered, other-Zeke yawned. "Guy's a fucking cockroach. You couldn't kill him if you wanted to. Seriously. Takes more than a little Scouting to kill Ryan."

Zeke shrugged. "Yeah, fair enough."

"Really?" Mia asked. "He's that hard to kill?"

Zeke nodded, pressing his lips together.

Other-Zeke sighed. He shook his head. "And a half."

"I guess he can teleport, and stuff. Turn back time...yeah," Mia muttered, half to herself.

"Now she gets it," other-Zeke muttered.

"Okay. So, we have our own scouting Apocalypse now. I guess we wait?" Zeke said.

"We gather resources and reinforce the city. They might launch an attack before Ryan comes back. We need to be ready for every possible scenario," Domi said, sitting forward.

Zeke and other-Zeke nodded in sync. "Good call."

The two of them looked at each other. Other-Zeke looked away, scoffing to himself.

Businesslike, Zeke put his hands on the table. "We have Erica's army. With their help, we can barricade all the roads leading into the city. True, they might be able to fly, but it's unlikely they *all* can. And if we can force everyone into the air, we can at least prepare for an air attack as opposed to having to deal with an invasion from all directions."

Mia raised her hand. "What if they come from underground, like the Undead Apocalypse?"

"They'd need to be in their Domain to change the world to that extent without a specific skill like Excavation," other-Zeke said, bored.

"In summary, it's unlikely, but not impossible." Zeke paused. He looked at other-Zeke. "Do you know—"

"No. This is after my timeline. Or if it isn't, then things played out so completely differently that I don't recognize this scenario. I've never heard of a Scouting Apocalypse," other-Zeke said, shaking his head.

"Damn," Domi muttered.

"There goes our cheat code," Zeke grumbled. He shook his head. "We still have Ryan, at least."

"Yeah. Thank God," other-Zeke said, the sarcasm heavy on his tongue.

Zeke shot him a look. "All right. Tomorrow, everyone hits the streets. Blockades every which direction. Anything that looks lootable, we loot it. Stockpile supplies at the Apartment. Day after tomorrow, we'll inventory what we have and focus on getting all the farming and sustainment stuff we can going. Day after..." Zeke paused. *I don't know, bully the System into finally giving out a level 90 bonus? It really squirreled off after other-Zeke showed up. And so far, he really hasn't been that scary. He's even been kind of friendly.*

Hasn't gotten the System to come back and hand out the damn level 90 bonus, though.

He sighed, already tired. "Yeah. That's all I've got."

Domi shrugged. "Sounds good to me."

"We can figure out the details tomorrow," Mia said, yawning.

Other-Zeke nodded. "It's been a long day. We all need rest."

Zeke's stomach grumbled, and he pushed away from the table. "I'm heading to bed. I'll see you guys in the morning."

"See you later," Domi said with a wave.

Mia stared after him, hesitating, then shook her head. "Good night."

With a wave, Zeke left the Convention Hall behind. The hubbub of conversation quickly faded behind him, and when the doors clanged shut, he was left with nothing but the steady beat of his shoes on the tile floor.

His stomach grumbled again. Zeke put a hand to it, grimacing. He eyed the exit door, then sighed. *I need to find real food. Me-food, anyway. Ugh. I really need to find a way to make food sustainable for me. The bug farm was a good idea, but it didn't go off as planned. Besides, I'm not sure I'll be able to keep relying on bugs for food. Maybe specifically cockroaches, since they're Survivors.*

Hmm. Science teacher kept a cockroach farm back in middle school. True, they were the neat Madagascar hissing kind, but...

Zeke lifted his brows. *Hold on. I wonder if there's one in the local middle school. They're pretty popular learning tools. It's worth a try!*

Mind made up, Zeke set out into the night, toward the local middle school.

13
EATING THE TEACHING TOOLS

Z eke set out into the night. Cool air swirled around him, damp with the moisture that was not yet dew. He bit his lip, trying to call to mind the shape of the city. *The elementary school is down to the right, I remember that. Fucking Cartoon Apocalypse. But the middle school...*

The schools are all generally in the same district, right? Not on top of one another, generally, but they'll be close. A block or two apart from one another.

Setting off at a jog, Zeke spread his wings, activating **Modest Gigantification** instinctively. He flapped once, twice, then took to the air, using the straight road ahead of him as a runway to reach cruising height. Up into the night sky, where the air grew even cooler. He shivered, chilled for a moment, though the heat building in his chest and wings from exertion told him he wouldn't be for long.

The city spread out before him. By now, few buildings remained alight. Aside from the apartment and its immediate surroundings, only a few blocks glowed, their signs advertising to empty streets, lights glittering from inside shattered displays. All the cars that had been abandoned running lay dark by now, their batteries long burned out, engines dry. The wind whistled through the buildings, keening loud enough Zeke could hear it. An eerie cry echoed through the city, as if mourning its loss.

You'd never know it in the Convention Hall, but this city is dead.

Humanity is dying. The Apocalypses are winning. No matter how hard we fight, no matter how many armies we adopt, the Apocalypses press on. And there's nothing we can do about it.

Unless. Unless we can destroy the Apocalypses themselves.

If the System truly is an Apocalypse, then what we need to target isn't the System, but that...other voice. The one that's only spoken a few times, in all caps. But what is it? It's barely even interacted with us.

Why did it come here? Why is it hellbent on destroying the Earth? Even in other-Zeke's timeline, the Apocalypses came and destroyed. So why? Do we not deserve an explanation?

Zeke sighed, letting the wind snatch his voice away. *Does the ant get an explanation from the shoe? Does the deer get an explanation from the wolf? I shouldn't expect too much.*

His stomach grumbled again, and he shook his head. *I'm depressed and stuck in dumb thought loops because I'm hungry. Let's go get those cockroaches.*

Down below, a few low, wide buildings stretched across three blocks, not quite back to back but close to it. Zeke circled overhead, checking their names. *Elementary...that one's an apartment... Oh, there! Middle school. Come on! Big cockroaches, no whammies!*

Zeke swooped down to the door and gave it a try. The door lurched, locked shut.

Hmm. All right, well. "Allen!"

Subordinate Allen has shared his STR!

Bracing his feet, Zeke pulled. Metal screeched, then bent, and the door popped open. He dusted off his hands and stepped inside, looking around.

A familiar scene greeted him. Whitewashed cinderblock marched off in all directions. A green-and-white tile floor, the tiles flecked with white and gray to make them harder to see filth on, stretched underfoot. Panels of fluorescent lights hung overhead, dark without power.

Zeke padded down the hallway. His footsteps echoed in the empty space. Here and there, locked doors blocked the way to his left and right. Activating **Heat Vision,** he peered in the small windows, searching for any signs of heat. *Not many people know it, but cockroaches are actually pretty warm creatures, especially when they feed and breed. I should be able to see them through the door, even in this darkness, so long as there's nothing between me and them. I'd rather not break every single door open. If I have to, I'll do it, but here's hoping I can get by with **Heat Vision!***

Through the hallways. At one point, dark red stains splattered the walls, the classroom doors ajar, deep slices cut into the walls and floors. A rotten stench filled the air, so thick he could barely breathe. Zeke stepped over the stains, quietly pressing on. He glanced in the classrooms. With **Heat Vision,** he gave them a cursory sweep, but no more. *I don't want to see what happened in there. It's nothing good, for certain.*

A cheerful display of the elemental table appeared on a board around the corner. Zeke raised his brows. *I'm near a science class. Come on! Cockroaches!*

He went from window to window, taking a little more time to peer through the glass this time. Deep in one corner, he caught a flash of heat, heat that scurried around a square-ish space. He grinned. *Oh, I think I've found it, boys. I think I've done it!*

Drawing on Allen's strength, he kicked the door open. **Heat**

Vision did nothing to show him where the chairs and tables were, and the internal classroom had no windows to let in moonlight. Zeke fumbled past thigh-high desks and chairs, kicking them aside as he went, until he finally waded all the way to the table in the back. The cockroaches scuttled around, bright in his vision. He picked up the whole cage, tucking the plastic box under his arm. Giving in a friendly pat, he waded back out of the room. Singing under his breath, he murmured, "Cockroaches, cockroaches, tasty, tasty cockroaches!"

A figure stood in the doorway, outlined by the faint moonlight. Zeke froze.

A familiar voice chuckled. Other-Zeke backed away, making room for Zeke. "I didn't know we had such musical talents."

"Er, well, you know. Sometimes inspiration strikes," Zeke said, glad the darkness hid his burning cheeks.

"So? Got the cockroaches?" other-Zeke asked.

"Yeah. I, er, was hoping to actually breed a bug colony this time. I don't have any skills for it, but—"

"I've got you. I ran this in my world. I'll have a bustling roomful of Madagascar Hissing Cockroaches in no time." Other-Zeke held out his hands, offering for Zeke to hand the cockroaches over.

Zeke hesitated. He looked at other-Zeke, uncertain.

Other-Zeke lowered his hands. He hung his head, rubbing the back of his neck. "No trust, huh."

"No, I..." Zeke hesitated one more moment, then looked at other-Zeke. "You can't fly, can you?"

Other-Zeke laughed. "Way to rub it in."

"Do you want to? Try flying, that is. I can carry you," Zeke offered.

Other-Zeke paused. He looked at Zeke, and his eyes glittered. "Hell yeah! Let's do it!"

14

IN ANOTHER WORLD, I...

Zeke held other-Zeke through the armpits, dangling him like he'd held Domi for the bombing run over the giant Kraken Apocalypse. Other-Zeke watched, quietly, his eyes big and wide, soaking in the scene. He held the cockroaches tight to his chest, keeping them safe.

"This is awesome. I need a flying skill," other-Zeke muttered.

"It is pretty cool, yeah," Zeke agreed, angling his wings to swoop around a tall building.

"Hey, would you mind if I...took a little nibble, or...?" other-Zeke asked, glancing up at Zeke.

"It's two skills. You'd have to kill me, and we've already established that's not cool," Zeke commented dryly.

Other-Zeke snorted. "Yeah. I guess I shouldn't make eating you jokes while we're in midair. One drop, and I'm ketchup. Plop!"

Zeke shook his head. "I wouldn't do that. I'm in too desperate a position to make new enemies."

Other-Zeke glanced up at him. "It really is true, isn't it."

"Yeah. You...did you ever make it past the dome?"

"Not with Ryan around. I made it pretty far, though."

Zeke glanced down. "Ryan really made you sound like a power-hungry, slavering, brainless, mad monster, you know?"

"Yeah, well, Ryan's an asshole," other-Zeke grumbled.

"He sure can be," Zeke agreed.

A pause. Other-Zeke snorted. "Does this count as a circle jerk?"

"Let's...let's just leave that topic alone."

"Fair."

Silence. The air whistled past Zeke's ears.

"Speaking of, though—"

"What did I say? Come *on*."

"Mia. What's going on there? As far as I can see...nothing?" other-Zeke asked, peering up at Zeke.

Zeke shook his head. "You've idolized her. She's a real person, with her own goals and shit. She doesn't want us. Too busy with other shit."

"Man. This reality sucks," other-Zeke grumbled.

"Yeah, but Mia's alive."

At that, other-Zeke went silent. He nodded, hugging the cockroaches tighter. "You've kept her alive. So many people..."

"What was it like? In your world?"

Other-Zeke shook his head. For a long time, there was nothing to be heard. And then he spoke. "A lot of death. Death upon death...at the end, it was me, Ryan, and Domi, and none of us were..."

He lifted his head, staring at the horizon, but Zeke got the feeling he didn't see a thing. "It changes you. The atmosphere, the people around you...when all you see is death, and the only thing you can think about is your next meal, whether that's someone else or something else, it changes you. I was alone. I had nothing but myself and my hunger. I..."

"I get it," Zeke murmured, nodding.

"Do you?"

"No. Not really. But I understand, as best I can," Zeke replied.

Other-Zeke grunted. He shrugged. "Well, whatever. I got out of that hellhole, so whatever."

"Right, I've been meaning to ask. How? What'd you do to get out?"

"Oh. It was, uh. A skill," other-Zeke said, then paused.

Zeke glanced down. "What?"

Other-Zeke frowned. His eyes blurred, moving up and down. One of the hands that held the cockroaches' box lifted off the box's surface and flicked at the air, as if scrolling a list on a touch screen. His brows furrowed. "It's not there."

"What?"

"My skill. The skill that let me world-hop. It's gone."

Zeke frowned. "What? What the hell does that mean? I've never had a skill vanish before."

Other-Zeke shook his head. "Me either. Did changing worlds remove it? Was it a one-time-use skill?"

"Or maybe this world's System rejected it," Zeke suggested.

"My world's System approved it in the first place, so why would this world's..." Other-Zeke trailed off, suddenly thoughtful. He pursed his lips.

"What?" Zeke asked.

"No, it's just..." Other-Zeke shook his head. "I don't know. It's a stupid thought."

"Nothing's stupid. The world's ending, and balls of rock can be Apocalypses. Go on. Whatever it is, just say it. What's the worst thing that can happen? I'll laugh at you? That's a self-own, you know," Zeke pointed out.

"Yeah, and that makes it so much worse," Other-Zeke muttered under his breath. He took a deep breath. "All right. So. What if...what if this is the real world?"

"Uh...what?" Zeke frowned. *I don't even understand what you're saying, so how could I laugh at it?*

Other-Zeke waved his free-ish hand. "I mean...how do I even phrase this?"

"I don't know."

Other-Zeke shot him a look.

"What? I don't."

"I... Ugh, it doesn't even make sense to me. But...you know. Okay. So there's all kinds of possibilities when it comes to alternate realities, right? That we're like, I don't know, clothes on a rack, touching but never interacting, but each one a very real world. That we're like split hairs, falling apart, each one breaking off into a thousand tiny lesser realities..."

"Ohhh, I think I've got it. So, you think you're one of those tiny split hairs and this is the main hair?" Zeke guessed.

"Right. What if I'm from a tributary reality? One that... maybe, once upon the time, was the real reality, but...when Ryan left, or maybe before that, it split off, and no longer became the main reality. When I left it, when the world collapsed, then it wasn't a true world-ending, but merely the collapse of a sub-reality."

Zeke paused. He thought for a few seconds, then looked down at other-Zeke. "Then what?"

"Huh?"

"What does that mean? I mean, for me and you. What actual effect does it have on this world, right here, right now?"

Other-Zeke shrugged. "I don't know. It just feels important. Like something we should know. Whether Ryan killed a real world, or jumped off a dead-end reality..."

"Or in jumping off, made it a dead end," Zeke suggested.

"Right. I just don't know. But it feels...*important.*"

"It does, but...seriously. What does it change? It doesn't matter how reality is structured. This is our reality, right now. I can't world hop, and you can't either, anymore. Whether it's split ends or clothes on a rack, who cares?"

"It's always important in movies."

"Well, yeah, but this isn't a movie. In this reality, what does it matter how the multiverse is shaped? Give me one reason. One thing that actually changes what we'd do tomorrow."

Other-Zeke shrugged. "I mean, if this isn't the real reality, I'd like to get to that one. Not that I can, but if I could."

"Would you know? If there's even such a thing, would you know when you got there? Aside from Ryan being there, but even that's not a guarantee, right? Since there might be multiple Ryans, depending."

Other-Zeke flinched. "Jeez, man. Don't jump scare me with thoughts like that. I'm gonna be up all night thinking about it. Multiple Ryans. Yuck."

"That's probably how he thinks of us," Zeke muttered, chuckling. He dipped his wings, circling down toward the apartment.

"Yeah. Fair."

Silence fell again, as they touched down. Other-Zeke held up the cockroaches. "I'll get started breeding these. Oh—you want a handful? For the road."

Zeke paused, then shrugged. "Can't hurt." He stuck his hand in, grabbing a handful. They hissed viciously but did nothing to stop him from gulping them down. He nodded. "Thanks."

"You're welcome, me."

They looked at one another. Zeke laughed, and so did other-Zeke, both of them overcome by the absurdity of it all. Zeke finished laughing first and nodded to other-Zeke. I'm going to turn in. I'll see you tomorrow."

"Yep. Tomorrow." Saluting, other-Zeke walked off, hugging the cockroaches close.

15
MORNING, SET OFF!

Zeke woke up the next morning and yawned, stretching from his bed. *Ah...a nice bed...a soft mattress. How nice. How comfortable.*

Hey! System! Where's that level 90 bonus, huh? Don't tell me you can't think of one, so I've got to think of my own.

Silence.

Zeke sighed. "Yeah. As I thought, huh? But what should I do? A second transform? Some kind of Domain expansion? Hmm..."

He pulled up his skills, thinking, his brows furrowed. Abruptly, he jolted in place. "Actually, hold up. System. I never got skills from the Undead Apocalypse! What kind of bullshit is that, huh?"

More silence.

Zeke squinted at the sky, about where messages usually showed up. "You playing possum or something? I know you're there. You never go away. Come on."

Level 90 Bonus Loading...

He rolled his eyes. "You've had *days* to load. Come on. Admit you've got nothing, so I can start thinking it up."

Level 90 Bonus: Craft Your Own Skill!
You get the ability to create a skill of your own this level!

Zeke snorted. "Right. Yeah. I got it, System. I got the message."

He leaned back on his bed, putting his hands behind his head. *So...in that case...what do I want? What skill should I ask for from the System?*

Let's review what I have so far.

Transform. It's my basic battle entry skill. Gives me armor and an all-around buff. Good for close, physical fights. I could upgrade it, but that sounds kinda lame. Also, doesn't do anything but make me better at what I'm already good at. That's probably fine, but on the other hand, I need to be ready for everything.

Domain. I can deploy it at will, and it's pretty useful, but the AOE effect hitting everyone makes it a bit dangerous to use in team fights. Upgrading it any further is dangerous, in my opinion.

So...something new. What could I use?

Honestly? A ranged attack. I have Crystal Burst, but the prerequisite of standing on the ground is a bit tough. Manipulate Wires and my electricity-based skills are also situational. Create Aerosols is nice, but also situational, and I need time to set up a proper mist. Manipulate Flame isn't powerful enough to kill on its own. Acid Spit is short-range. Something mid- or long-range would be nice. Allow me to do chip damage before I engage close, plus it gives me something I can use against flying foes like the Scouting Apocalypse without engaging in a dogfight.

He pinched his chin, thinking. *Ranged attack...Hunger Apocalypse. How do I combine those two? I still need the skill to be Hunger-related, but a ranged hunger attack—and one that isn't an AOE that hits my allies as much as it hits my enemies. A single-target, precision, high-damage attack.*

"A ranged bite, maybe?" he murmured, furrowing his brows. *No idea how that would work, but—*

Ranged Bite Gained!

Zeke startled. "Hey! I was still thinking!" He narrowed his eyes at the window. "Is this payback for sassing you earlier?"

The System said nothing.

Sighing, he shook his head. "Oh, well. Ranged Bite. Could be worse. I mean, I do need a ranged attack. And if I can exploit this ability, bite inside things...it might be better than I'm expecting right now. I'll have to play around with it. See how it works. It isn't necessarily bad. Could even be really good."

"Nothing from the Undead Apocalypse, though?"

All Skills require Prerequisite: Status: Undead

Zeke clicked his tongue. "I have the Vampire skill, how about that?"

Insufficient. Having the Vampire skill and the Status: Dead may allow you to gain the Status: Undead

"May?" Zeke asked.

5% chance per level of Skill: Vampire

He frowned. *Forty-five percent chance? Could be worse. I'm not risking my life on a roll of the dice, but still.* "What happened if my skill hit level ten, then?"

Symptoms accelerate. At twenty levels (Medium + 10), the Skill automatically effects Death. Player with Skill Vampire has 90% chance of becoming a Vampire.

"Still not 100?"

On-Death Skills cannot be guaranteed. SYSTEM LIMIT: System limit? Hmm.

All-caps again. I wonder if that's the second level admin, or whatever. The other half of the System. The one that doesn't talk much.

He sighed. "But the Undead Apocalypse was alive at one point. What about Hunter's skills? He was successful before he died."

The Necromancy Apocalypse is not the Undead Apocalypse.

"Huh," Zeke muttered under his breath. *Wonder if that's because of his unique situation, or what? Would I become a 'new person' if I became a vampire? But then, Olivia remembered her human life and everything. Osiris didn't. Maybe that's the difference.*

He hopped to his feet and stretched. With a dramatic yawn and a clap, he headed for the door. "Skills obtained, Undead Apocalypse figured out, Vampire skill information gotten, so let's go head outside and take on the day!"

After a moment, he sighed. "Right. Because I have a coalition of Apocalypses and at *least* a Scouting Apocalypse to deal with. End of the world ain't easy."

Shaking his head, he entered the hallway.

16

A PLAN

Sunlight poured in the windows. A few odd members of Erica's Army wandered the halls, chatting with one another or wandering alone, half awake. One or two nodded at him as he passed, and Zeke nodded back. At the end of the hallway, Eric leaned against the window, staring out at the city. He waved, but Eric didn't seem to notice, lost in his thoughts.

A cold hand clasped his shoulder. Pointing a sharp-toothed grin his direction, Olivia tossed him a wink. "Hey there, Bossman. What's on the menu today?"

"Cockroaches, mostly," Zeke muttered.

"What?" Olivia asked.

Zeke cleared his throat. "I was thinking of heading out. Not necessarily going full scouting, like we sent Ryan to do, but just walking the perimeter, getting an eye on the limits of our territory. Make sure no one's lined up at the gate, you know?"

"That Apocalypse Coalition thing making you nervous?" Olivia asked.

"Apocalypse Coalition? Oh...the group associated with the Scouting Apocalypse?" Zeke nodded. "So far, we've had a massive advantage because we're a bunch of Apocalypses teamed up together. But this time..."

"This time, you ran into someone who did the same thing. It was bound to happen eventually," Olivia said, shrugging.

"It's true. I wish it hadn't, though," Zeke complained.

"If wishes were fishes, we wouldn't have to worry about keeping you fed." Olivia clapped him on the shoulder again.

Grimacing, Zeke shoved her away. "Yeah, yeah." *It's better for me to be out in the battlefield, fighting people. Back here at home, it's too dangerous for me. If I suddenly get hungry, I'm in a bad situation if I'm surrounded by allies. On the other hand, if I'm out there in the field and get suddenly hungry, it's no big deal if I haul off and eat someone. Sometimes, it's even an advantage...as dark as that is.*

"Heading out?"

Zeke whirled. Ryan stood there, back against the wall. He gave Zeke a short nod.

"Thought it'd take you longer," he said, looking Ryan up and down.

Ryan shrugged. "Time is relative. And the closest of the alliance is way closer than you'd expect."

"Damn. Who is it? Where?" Zeke asked, moving closer.

"I'm not sure. It's not our friend the Scouting Apocalypse, but..." He grimaced, then shook his head. "You'll have to see for yourself."

"Right. Let's go."

Ryan hesitated again. "Shouldn't you pick teams? You don't want to go alone, do you?"

"Not really..." Zeke sighed and rubbed the back of his neck. *Who to take, though?*

"I'm coming," Olivia declared.

"Me too," Domi said from behind them. She drew up alongside them and looked from face to face. "Where are we going?"

"To the next Apocalypse," Zeke said.

"Score! Hell yes. Let's go," Domi said, pumping her fist.

"Olivia and Domi, then?" Ryan asked.

Zeke shrugged. "How dangerous is the Apocalypse? I could bring Eric." He pointed at the end of the hallway, where Eric still stared out the window. As they watched, he heaved a heavy sigh.

"Pretty dangerous. It wouldn't hurt," Ryan said. He nodded. "I'll head back out, then. There's more than one Apocalypse in the alliance."

"True that," Zeke agreed.

Domi scoffed. "It wouldn't be much of an alliance if it only had one member. Be a hell of a fake-out, though, if that Scouting guy was just totally screwing with us."

"I'm not laughing," Zeke muttered.

"I'd rather get lied to than actually have to fight an alliance of Apocalypses," Domi reasoned, hooking a brow at him.

Zeke nodded. "Now that I can agree with."

Eric walked over, drawing up to the rest of them. "I heard my name. Did someone call me?"

"You wanna go fight an Apocalypse?" Domi offered.

Eric put a hand on his chin for a minute, then nodded. "Better than sitting here and stewing in my worries."

"Well said," Zeke said approvingly, clapping him on the shoulder.

Ryan glanced around the group, then gave a salute and backed away. "I'm gonna go scout out the next one. I'll find you or call you if I can't."

"Got it. Stay safe," Zeke admonished him.

Ryan grinned. "No promises."

What that, he took another step backward and vanished.

Zeke looked at the group around him. *Domi, Olivia, Eric. It's a good crew. After the showing in the Undead Apocalypse, I don't want to bring Isaac—he's mostly a liability. Mia doesn't seem to be leveling up at the same rate as the rest of us, and besides, I need someone to watch other-Zeke. Jimmy's a kid, and so's his little sister, and as for Heather, there isn't even an argument—she can't move her domain. Better to leave them all here and return once I'm victorious.*

He nodded at the group and gestured for them to follow him. "Let's get moving, ourselves. We'll lave Ryan to his job and focus on doing ours the best we can."

"Spoken like a true leader," Domi said, nodding in approval.

"I'm not a leader," Zeke rebuffed her, gesturing at himself. *What part of me looks like a leader? My clothes are worn out and stained, I'm too skinny, I look exhausted all the time. This isn't how leaders look. It isn't how leaders feel.*

"You're way closer to a leader than you want to admit," Domi chuckled, amused.

"Yeah. Aren't you in charge of all this? I thought you were in charge," Eric commented, looking around him.

"I..." Zeke hesitated. He looked around for help. His eyes landed on Olivia.

Olivia shrugged. "Nah, man. I thought you were the boss, too. You aren't?"

"He is. He just thinks he isn't," Domi said, nodding.

"Oh, got it," Oliva said, nodding.

Zeke sighed. "I don't think I'm not boss, I just... I don't *feel* like boss."

"Well, get your feelings in order, Bossman! And let's hit the streets," Domi said, thumping him on the chest as she set out.

17
HIT THE STREETS

The wind whistled through Zeke's hair. The sun rose, glittering through the ruined city. Zeke took a deep breath, savoring the cool dawn air.

"Hey, Zeke-man, how're you feeling about a motorcycle this morning?" Domi asked.

"No."

"What? Motorcycles are awesome, though!"

"Find one yourself."

"Boooo. Just eat a car, or something," Domi complained.

Zeke stared at her. "*You* eat a car!"

"I can't, but you can," she muttered, shaking her head at him.

"I can *not*!" Zeke complained. He paused, then looked at a car.

"Yeah...?" Domi said, raising her brows.

"Shut it," Zeke grumbled, tearing his eyes away.

Domi stretched, heading toward one of the more intact abandoned cars. "Anyway, did Ryan actually tell us anything? Or did he just say a few mysterious lines and then fuck off?

Because I feel like he just said a few mysterious lines and fucked off."

Zeke opened his mouth, then shut it. "You know, actually, now that I'm thinking about it..."

"Whatever. If he didn't say anything, we'll probably find it without trying," Domi said, grunting as she heaved herself into the car. There, her rear still hanging out of the car, she froze.

"What?" Zeke asked, jogging over.

Domi held her hand backward, showing him a brown folder stuffed with notebook paper. On the front, it read, *Scouting Report: Northern Apocalypse.*

"Guess Ryan knew which car we'd pick," Zeke muttered under his breath. He took the folder and paged through it. Hand-drawn maps, battle notes, and descriptions filled the pages. Nodding, he kept paging through, skimming the contents.

Domi looked over her shoulder as she turned to sit. "You think he didn't actually scout it?"

"Huh?"

She nodded. "Like, he didn't actually do anything, just rode around with us until we found an Apocalypse, then turned back time; pointed us at that Apocalypse and saw how we approached it, then turned back time...basically made us do all the work, then turned back time and gave us a report, as if he'd done anything."

"I mean, we did decide to go out before he came back, so it wouldn't even be a paradox," Zeke pointed out. "Not that his time travel works that way, as far as I can tell, but whatever."

He flipped to the back page, then snorted. Turning the folder around, he showed Domi the final page. *I did do the work, asshole.*

Domi laughed. "Asshole!" she shouted, then nodded at Zeke. "C'mon, climb in."

Zeke saluted and climbed into the passenger's seat. Olivia and Eric loaded into the back, only for Eric to yelp and scurry into the middle seat as another figure climbed in.

"What's going on back there?" Domi asked, peering over her shoulder.

"Get out of the way, nerd. I'm coming," other-Zeke declared, shoving Eric into the middle.

"I'm getting. Chill!" Eric complained, clambering into the small middle seat.

"Should I take the middle? I'm the smallest of the three of us," Olivia offered.

"Oh, sorry, am I squeezing you? I can bring Erica out," Eric offered kindly.

"Don't do that," Domi said.

Eric drooped. "You guys don't like Erica?"

Domi gave him a look. "She wears a bell skirt with tulle, petticoats, and a hoop skirt, and let's not even talk about her poofy sleeves, that giant wand of hers, and those six-inch stilettos. She takes up way more room than you, my dude."

"Oh," Eric said. After a second, he nodded. "Yeah, I wasn't thinking about her outfit."

"She sounds hot," other-Zeke observed, looking Eric up and down.

"Hey. Shut it," Zeke called from the front seat.

"What? Don't want your predilection for girls in short skirts getting out? I know we're legs men," other-Zeke returned.

"Hey! Shut up!" Zeke snapped.

"Legs? I thought tits for sure," Domi commented.

"Tits too. Legs and tits. Ass has never done much for us," other-Zeke confirmed confidently.

"Are you done?" Zeke asked, exhausted.

"No, go on. What else are you into? Any freaky fetishes?" Olivia asked, half-laughing, half-curious.

"Shut it," Zeke snapped, pointing at other-Zeke.

Other-Zeke put his hands up. "No freedom of speech in the apocalypse."

Olivia looked from one Zeke to the other, a playful grin crawling over her face. "So there *is* a freaky fetish...hmm..."

The car rumpled to life with a roar. Domi backed up, giving Olivia a look as she did so. "Everyone's got a freaky fetish or two, sister. Let's leave those sleeping dogs alone, mkay?"

"Yeah, seriously," Eric agreed, nodding.

"Now I'm curious. What kinda fetishes do you guys have?" Olivia asked, her eyes sparkling.

Other-Zeke leaned to the side to catch Zeke's eyes in the rearview mirror. "Is this normal?"

Startled, Zeke glanced at other-Zeke. "Huh? I mean, bullshitting like this? Yeah, pretty normal. Olivia might be a little too hot and heavy, but it's not that unusual."

Other-Zeke fell silent. A contemplative expression passed over his face, and he sat back in his chair.

"All right. If all the kids are done, momma's driving," Domi grumbled. She drove off down the street, leaving the Apartment Apocalypse quickly behind.

"Is it fine for both of you to leave?" Olivia asked.

"Huh? Yeah, why not? I left to fight Osiris, and I didn't even have a second me to leave behind," Zeke replied, taken slightly off-guard.

"I... Huh. Yeah. I'm used to Osiris. You know, a normal Apocalypse who couldn't leave his Domain," Olivia commented.

"Be careful with that kind of assumption. This Alliance... they aren't all conventional Apocalypses, if the Scouting Apocalypse is anything to go by," Zeke commented.

"Right. We need to stay on our toes," Eric agreed, nodding firmly.

Zeke opened the folder again, then nudged Domi. "Take a left up here. We're going to head north."

"You think it's a Northern Apocalypse, or just the Apocalypse to the north of us?" Olivia mused.

Eric snorted. "What would a Northern Apocalypse even be? Polar bears and stuff? Blizzards?"

"Actually, that'd be crazy dangerous," other-Zeke chimed in.

"Yeah, actually, as I was saying it I realized..." Eric grimaced. "I hope it's not a Northern Apocalypse, actually."

"Me either. I didn't bring a coat," Olivia said.

"Only one way to find out," Zeke replied, setting his eyes to the north.

18

NORTHERN APOCALYPSE

As they drove, the landscape turned bleak. A chill wind blew, whipping past the exterior of the car and sending it shuddering in its lane. Domi grimaced, dodging around abandoned cars on the highway. "Bad news, guys."

"Looks like it is the Northern Apocalypse, huh?" Zeke muttered.

"That, too, but seriously...look at how far it's spread. Apocalypses aren't contained things anymore. They're seriously eroding the whole world."

Zeke sat upright, startled. He looked at the highway again, at the world all around him. *How did I not notice? Last time we went out, everyone was living their ordinary lives, ignoring the Apocalypses and avoiding them. Now...now, the highway is dead. Large swathes of land belong to Domains, and the Apocalypses' corrupting influence spreads farther with every passing moment.*

Time is running out. We have to figure out the secret behind the System and the Apocalypses and end this death game for good. At this rate, there won't be much world to save, even if we succeed in the end.

Snow started to fall, just a dusting, not yet enough to cover the roads. Domi lifted her head, searching the signs they passed for shopping centers. Without a word, she drove off onto that exit and pulled into the parking lot of an outlet mall. Some windows were shattered, and the jewelry store laid desecrated, completely torn apart by looters, but some of the shops remained untouched. Domi put the car in park and looked over her shoulder. "Everyone out. Don't come back until you're dressed for the weather."

"I don't feel the cold," Olivia said in a deep, dramatic voice, flashing the peace sign and a grin at the same time.

Domi looked her in the eyes. "Sure. Do you freeze solid, though?"

"Uh..." Olivia paused, then frowned. She stared at Zeke.

"Why are you looking at me? I don't know," Zeke said. He climbed out of the car. "Get some of those hand warmers just in case. And a portable heater. Even if it's electronic, I might be able to power it." *Between Bio-generator and the electricity-based skills, I can probably hack it. Probably.*

"Really? Aren't you Hunger or something, though? How are you going to make electricity?" Olivia asked.

"Zeke's powers are bullshit, don't worry about it," Domi replied. She slammed her door shut, then shivered, running her hands over her arms. "C'mon, let's get inside before we freeze to death."

"Good call," Eric agreed.

"Right, but where do we start?" Olivia asked, gesturing around them.

The mall wandered around them in all directions, outlets of all descriptions forever awaiting shoppers who would never come. A cookie shop sat forlornly beside a high-end gift baskets shop and, opposite them, a list of the top brand names lined up one after another, selling every type of clothing imaginable. From sportswear to fine suits, ballgowns to street gear, every top brand offered crazy discounts and high-quality factory rejects. The outlet wandered, its large parking lot mixed and twisted in with the dozens of individual strip malls angled such that a shopper, once entered, struggled to escape.

Spotting a signboard with a weather-stained map, Zeke jogged over. He knocked the accumulated frost and snow away, revealing the full labyrinthine shape of the strip mall. Tiny icons sported names and descriptive text where they floated over the buildings on the map. He squinted, then pointed.

"Here. Outdoor Gear. If it isn't selling parkas, we should at least be able to buy warm under-layers here."

"Good call." Domi squinted at the map, too, then set off. Zeke and the others followed, keeping their heads on a swivel as they walked. Powdery snow rained down, drifting on the gentle winds.

"It's kind of pretty but, man, I really hope this Apocalypse doesn't win," Olivia commented.

"If another Apocalypse wins, we're all dead," Zeke deadpanned.

Other-Zeke pointed at him.

"Well...yeah, probably. I mean, you let me live, but...yeah." Olivia scratched the back of her head, slightly uncomfortable.

Domi shrugged. "I like the cold. Nice crisp air, lots of snow. I wouldn't mind."

"What, are we ignoring the 'we're all dead' part?" Zeke asked.

"It's a hypothetical scenario, Zeke. Like 'would you rather fight a hundred duck-sized horses or one horse-sized duck?' There aren't actually any horse-sized ducks—"

"Well..." Zeke shot her a look.

"God, I hope there aren't horse-sized ducks," Domi muttered.

"So, you'd rather take the duck-sized horses?" Olivia asked, looking up at her with a grin.

Domi snorted. "Easy. A hundred kicks and it's over. Also, I really hate ducks."

"Why?"

"Have you ever seen a duck? Those things are monsters. Vicious, too." She pointed at her jaw. "They've got teeth in their bills, you know. Creepy as fuck."

"What, really?" Olivia asked, startled.

"Well, not ducks, no, but geese. And they have teeth on their tongues, too," Eric chimed in.

"Jeez," Olivia breathed.

"If we keep this up, we're going to speak a Goose Apocalypse to life," Zeke muttered. He pointed ahead of them. "Let's go get some jackets."

"Hell yeah," Domi muttered.

"It's looting time!" Olivia bounced in place, excited.

"It's not...looting..." Zeke shook his head.

"It is looting. What else is it?" Eric asked.

Zeke shrugged. "Requisitioning the necessary materials to save the world?"

"Yeaaaaah. Looting, got it," Domi said, grinning at him.

Sighing heavily, Zeke shook his head. Borrowing Allen's STR for a split second, he kicked the door in. "Get your jackets and let's get moving."

19
GEARED UP AND READY TO GO

Snow continued to fall as they bustled back into the car and headed down the road once more, this time bundled up in layers of warm clothes, jackets, and snow pants. The snow deepened. Their car left the only tracks in the white-coated road. All the other abandoned cars vanished under the snow. Only lumpy piles of snow indicated where they'd been.

Olivia leaned forward, shaking a tin. "Chocolate, anyone?"

Zeke took a chocolate. "Did we really need to loot all the stores?"

"We've got chocolate because of it," other-Zeke replied, nudging Olivia. She sat back in her seat and offered him the tin.

"It's not like someone else is using it," Domi pointed out.

"Want one?" Olivia asked her.

"Nah, these roads are slippery. Gotta keep my hands on the wheel."

"It just seems excessive, is all," Zeke said. He tossed back the chocolate and licked his fingers. "The chocolates are delicious, though."

Olivia pointed at him. "See? Worth it."

The snow grew higher and higher the farther they drove. As they took a gentle curve around a snow-laden forest, a small city appeared, picturesque as a snow globe in the gently drifting flakes. And atop the buildings, glistening in the soft, snow-cloud-muted sun...

"Is that...ice cream?" Domi asked, squinting through her windshield.

Zeke clicked his tongue. "It, uh, yeah, I'd have to say..."

Giant scoops of ice cream topped every skyscraper, some of them wobbling three, four, five scoops high. Vanilla, chocolate, strawberry, mint chocolate chip, rocky road, even some flavors Zeke couldn't identify at first glance. Ice cream of all colors and flavors topped the buildings and piled up in the streets. Whipped topping spires perched atop some of the scoops, and giant cherries nestled in with sprinkles as large as a grown man. Thick globs of chocolate, caramel, and strawberry oozed deliciously down the sides of the scoops. Here and there, giant spoons stabbed into the desserts, as if an enormous person had just set them down in the middle of eating their city-sundae.

"Is this not snow, but freezer burn?" Domi muttered to herself, eyeing the tall drifts on the cars around her.

"Ice cream? You brought the right guys," other-Zeke said, slapping Zeke on the shoulder with a grin.

"Don't get too excited. Remember the Coffee Apocalypse?" Zeke asked.

Other-Zeke squinted at him. "The what?"

"In the museum...?"

"Oh, is that what that was? I do remember crushing some annoying little machine in the café," other-Zeke commented.

Olivia leaned forward. "How does the double-Zeke thing work, anyway? I feel like I'm missing something."

Domi snorted. "You just get used to that feeling around Zeke."

Eric cleared his throat. "I think, uh, Erica's the one who saw it, but I think the other Zeke is from a different timeline or reality or something."

Other-Zeke nodded. "More or less."

"Right. Right. So, uh...anyway. Point is. Coffee Apocalypse," Zeke said, collecting his thoughts.

"Coffee Apocalypse," other-Zeke prompted.

"Right. It had this thing where if you drank the coffee, you became the Apocalypse's, uh...servant? Acolyte? Anyway. The point is, a food Apocalypse isn't necessarily an instant win for us. We need to be careful. Eating that ice cream could be the same as signing up to be the Apocalypse's servant."

Olivia eyed the giant ice cream scoops. "I volunteer as taste-tester."

"Olivia—" Zeke sighed.

She shrugged. "I'm the weakest of all of us, as a member of an Apocalypse rather than an Apocalypse myself, plus, it'd really be good to know if you two can use your mouths, right? I'll give it a taste, and if I go nuts, vote me out, got it? Tie me up in the car or something. I'm not an Apocalypse, so I can't beg the System for a new skill to let me escape or anything."

A moment later, she cleared her throat. "Also, I'm super thirsty, and eating ordinary food helps me repress it."

"Repress...right," Zeke muttered. *Vampire.*

"Hey, if she's volunteering, I don't see a reason to turn her down. We need the information," Domi pointed out.

"We do, yeah." Zeke sighed, leaning back in his seat. "All right. It's up to you, Olivia."

"I'm so down. But, uh, if I go evil, at least try to nonlethally subdue me?" she requested.

Zeke nodded. Other-Zeke patted her on the shoulder.

"Erica has some skills that are good at that," Eric volunteered.

"Erica's into subduing people? Honestly? Could've guessed that." Domi squinted at the road sign, trying to make out the white letters past the frost creeping up its side, then pulled off onto the exit.

Eric blushed. "Not—not like that. You know. Magical Girl. She's, uh. It's on-theme to not kill and reform her enemies, or whatever."

"Right, right," Domi said skeptically. She glanced over her shoulder. "It's fine to admit it, man. Pretty common fetish, to be honest."

"Hey! Let's stop the fetish talk, please?" Zeke asked.

Olivia giggled. "Sure thing, teach!"

"I mean, honestly. How many times are we gonna bring it up on one car ride?" he grumbled, shaking his head.

Down the exit and into downtown proper. Small scoops of ice cream—relatively, the scoops stood taller than most medium-sized dogs—popped up along the sides of the street, growing larger and larger as they drove farther into downtown. A burned-out building gaped, snow-free inside its wide-open front door. Domi drove into it and parked.

"Everyone out. I need to keep the car out of the snow if it's going to keep falling like this, and I really doubt we're gonna find another easy parking spot. It's on foot from here."

Zeke nodded. He climbed out of the car and stretched. Eyeing the burned-out husk and the drifts of snow in the corners of the building where the roof fell in, he shook his head. Too dilapidated to spend the night. Even in day, the wind carried an icy chill into the building. They'd have to find another place, somewhere safer. *Maybe with central heating,* he thought, then snorted. *Yeah, because all the buildings with* ice cream *on them are going to have functional heating.*

"I haven't seen any enemies yet," Domi commented, looking at Zeke.

"Last time, we were already neck deep in cartaurs, yeah. And then zombies. This is weird," he agreed, scratching his chin. Their approach lacked any stealth, so the Ice Cream Apocalypse knew they were coming. *But if that's the case, where's its minions?*

"The hell is a cartaur?" Olivia asked.

"It's like a centaur, but a car instead of a horse," Domi explained.

She wrinkled her nose. "Gross."

Zeke walked up to the edge of the building and looked out. As far as the eye could see, drifts of snow and piles of ice cream. In places, the snow coated the ice cream, creating soft, rounded lumps on the ground here and there. But as Domi had pointed out, no enemies. No one moved in the pale snow.

"It's kind of...spooky," he murmured.

"No kidding." Domi stretched, then headed out into the snow. "So, what're you waiting for? If there's no resistance, let's march directly to the boss."

Zeke shook his head, smirking a little despite himself. "Yeah, I guess, what are we waiting for? Let's go knock some ice cream cones."

Olivia shook her head. "Nah. That one didn't hit."

"Smash some scoops?" other-Zeke tried.

"You should probably just stop trying. Both of you," Domi said, giving them sad eyes.

Zeke and other-Zeke exchanged a look. Other-Zeke shook his head. "Playing an audience is hard, huh?"

"You're telling me," Zeke said, chuckling under his breath.

20
EAT THE ICE CREAM

"Wait, wait. While there's no enemies and we're right next to the car, why don't I try the ice cream? It's the ideal circumstances," Olivia pointed out.

"No one to interrupt us, no problems except you if things go sideways," Zeke agreed, nodding. He gestured for her to go ahead.

Olivia took a deep breath and approached one of the lumps. Kneeling, she brushed the fresh snow off. The signature mint-green flecked with dark brown of mint chocolate chip appeared beneath.

"Are we sure about this, guys? Like, we could just not eat the ice cream," Eric pointed out.

Domi shrugged. "Takes out a good third of our fighting power if we don't, though. Two-fifths? Same difference."

"It's one-third if you count Erica as her own person. As we all should," Zeke said, nodding.

"Easy math, easy," Domi agreed.

"Are you only counting Erica as a person to make the math easier? I feel like that's less ethical than not counting her at all," Eric pointed out.

"Bro, Zeke eats people. What part of this looks ethical to you?" Domi said, spreading her hands.

Eric raised his brows. He nodded. "Fair, yeah, fair..."

"Technically, people meat is the only meat that can be ethical," Olivia chirped up.

Everyone turned to look at her. Domi squinted, giving her an *are you stupid* look.

She nodded. "According to vegans, meat is unethical because animals can't consent. Only people can consent. Therefore, only human meat is ethical."

"What kind of backward-ass bullshit logic is that?" Domi asked. "Vegans be out here eating people? What?"

"No, no. It's more of a mind-experiment. A joke?" Eric tried, not sure.

"I just heard that it's okay to eat people," other-Zeke chimed in, giving a double thumbs up.

Olivia waggled her hand. "It's okay to eat *consenting* people."

"I could be a vegan?" Zeke asked, startled.

"I don't know about *that*. You eat a lot that isn't people," Domi pointed out.

"It was hypothetical, anyway," Zeke muttered. He shook his head, then nodded at Olivia. "If you don't want to eat the ice cream, just say it. There's no need to stall like this."

"I'm not stalling, I'm..." Olivia eyed the ice cream, then took a deep breath. "Okay, I'm stalling. Dammit. All right. Remember me if this does me in."

She knelt, brushing the snow off again, then lowered her mouth to the scoop. Her fanged teeth bit into the minty green ice cream.

"Death by ice cream," Domi muttered.

Zeke nudged her. "Don't kill Olivia off yet."

"She's already dead," Eric pointed out, glancing at the other two.

They both stared at him. At last, Domi shook her head. "Damn, son. That's cold."

"No, it's the ice cream that's cold," Zeke muttered.

"What's wrong with all of you?" other-Zeke asked, drawing away.

Domi looked at him, then shrugged. "Zeke gets mouthy when he's nervous. You don't?"

"I...guess I never saw it from the outside," other-Zeke said, suddenly contemplative.

Zeke looked at other-Zeke and shook his head. "It's sure an experience, watching yourself run around and do all the dumb shit you do. Like hearing your own voice in a recording, but a thousand times worse."

"God, I know, right?" other-Zeke agreed.

Olivia chewed slowly, wincing and rubbing her nose. "Brain freeze, brain freeze..."

"Oh no! She's turning!" Domi shouted in mock-horror.

Zeke elbowed her. "C'mon. It's just a little brain freeze."

Wrinkling her nose, Olivia swallowed with effort, then shook her head. She nodded to herself, looking up at them. "Yeah, eating ice cream in the snow is not ideal. I'm freezing to death over here."

"We used to have a family tradition of eating ice cream in the winter," Zeke commented.

"We did," other-Zeke confirmed.

"It was pretty crazy. I remember the ice cream not tasting like much in the cold," Zeke said.

"Yeah, and the snow would water it down...but it was so much fun," other-Zeke replied, grinning.

Olivia squinted at them, then turned to Domi. "Are the Zekes okay?"

"Have they ever been...?" Domi asked, squinting back.

She straightened, dusting the snow off her knees. "In any case, I think I'm fine. I had a mouthful of watery, not great ice cream, and that was about it. It's just ice cream. There's no brainwashing involved."

"Sounds like something someone brainwashed by ice cream would say," Domi pointed out.

Zeke rolled his eyes at her. He nodded at Olivia. "If you feel fine, then let's press on. There's surely enemies out here somewhere, and if we sit around, they'll come to us. Better if we go to them."

"Yep. Let's get moving," Olivia agreed.

Behind Olivia, the ice cream scoop trembled. Cherry red eyes blinked open from under the snowy frosting.

Startled, Zeke jumped on it. Unhesitating, he opened his mouth and chomped down on the ice cream scoop.

[Devour]

A big hole opened in the ice cream, larger than Zeke's mouth. He swallowed, feeling that over-large lump smoothly vanish into him without making a bulge anywhere on his body. Zeke touched his stomach. *Where did it go?*

"Uh...Zeke? If you were hungry, you could've just tested it yourself," Domi said, lost.

"I-it was coming to life," Zeke excused himself quickly.

"Uh huh," Olivia said, disbelievingly.

"I saw it," other-Zeke offered.

"Zekes covering for Zekes?" Eric asked, shaking his head at them.

"Seriously! The ice cream was—" Zeke's voice cut off. His eyes widened, and he stepped back.

"What?" Domi squinted at him.

"He's trying to make us look behind us. I know this trick," Olivia said smugly.

Snow rained down. Scraps of ice cream struck the ground.

Domi and Olivia turned.

An enormous ice cream monster, built from dozens of scoops of ice cream, loomed over them. Ice cream cones formed vicious claws and a somewhat-silly cone hat. Big maraschino cherries glittered with mean red light, and chocolate sauce dripped from its enormous maw.

"Fucking hell," Domi whispered.

"Fuuuuuck," Olivia agreed.

Roaring, the ice cream yeti smashed its fist down toward them.

As one, both sprinted away. Zeke stepped forward, raising his hand to catch the punch. His eyes sparkled. *Ice cream, and it's alive? Did someone hear my prayers? I love this Apocalypse!*

21

I COULD EAT A WHOLE BUCKET

The Zekes charged in one synchronized open-mouthed lunge, both of them going for the chest. Huge chunks of ice cream vanished into their stomachs, one of them eating upward as the other ate downward.

Startled, the ice cream yeti stared at them, then let out as ferocious a growl as someone being eaten could and slammed its fists down on their backs.

"Nope," Domi said. Twin explosions burst at its shoulders, blowing its arms off.

The yeti stumbled back. It looked at its armless shoulders in surprise, then at Domi.

Domi shrugged. "Let them have the easy win."

In a few short seconds, little remained of the yeti. Zeke stood up, wiping his mouth, then grinned, half-embarrassed. "Hey..."

"Uh huh," Domi said.

"We...can't really explain this," other-Zeke admitted.

"No, I know you can't." Domi snorted, then shook her head. "All right, boys. Go ham."

All around them, the ice cream scoops jiggled. They lifted

onto their little scoop bases, extending tendril-like arms of soft ice cream toward the party.

Olivia tilted her head. "They're kind of cute."

"Yeah, but they won their dome somehow. We can't let our guards down," Domi pointed out.

"True, but they are cute," Eric said, nodding.

The ice cream scoops darted at them. Zeke jumped back, but they closed in faster than he could escape. One after another, the ice cream glommed onto his body, grabbing on tight. In the space of a few seconds, ice cream completely covered his lower body. With each passing moment, more ice cream covered him, the scoops fighting to overload him.

"What the f—" Zeke battered back the scoops, scraping ice cream off his body. Ice cream crept under his clothes, freezing his skin. He grabbed at the ice cream and scooped it into his mouth, but even with **Devour,** he couldn't keep up with the pace of the ice cream fighting to overwhelm him.

Next to him, explosions rattled off as Domi blasted scoops left and right. She backed toward a wall, only for the snow on the roof to suddenly jump upright and drop onto her shoulders. She cursed, battering at the ice cream, and the scoops on the floor closed in on her.

Olivia shrieked as ice cream caught her foot, and turned, sprinting off with the occasional kick. The ice creams gave chase, but she ran on, running and running with all her might. Snail trails of cherry-vanilla and chocolate ice cream followed her.

Other-Zeke sprinted in the opposite direction, his legs lifting high as he hoofed it through the snow. As he ran, he took big bites from the ice cream that still clung to him, not particularly bothered by the whole scenario.

Struggling under the weight of the ice cream piling up on him, Zeke turned to Eric, only to find an ice cream mummy. No scrap of Eric remained, his entire body coated in the cold cream. From his head to his toes, only ice cream, and with every passing moment, the ice cream around his body thickened. An icy coating crackled over its surface, freezing the mummy-slash-snowman solid.

Fire burned through the ice cream from beside Zeke. Transformed Domi burst into the sky, firing explosive blasts behind her. Fireballs rattled from her hands, shaking the buildings all around them. "Die, ice cream, die!"

Right. The sky! Zeke Transformed as well, using **Modest Gigantism** on his wings. Flapping up into the air, he spun in the sky, his hand-mouths and foot-mouths going to work on their own to assist in cleaning his armored body.

Circling overhead, he darted down toward Eric. "Transform!"

A muffled sound came from the depths of the ice cream.

From the far end of the street, at the top of the hill, something rumbled. Zeke and Domi both whirled around. What Zeke had taken to be a building stirred, shaking off its snowy topping to reveal a massive chocolate-chip ice cream cube. The cube leaned back and forth, as if warming up, then tipped forward. Its flat face struck the ground loud enough to rattle windows. Not satisfied with one turn, the cube pitched itself back and forth again, then fell facedown again. Again, and again, and again, each turn speeding up, its sharp edges softening toward a ball, until the cube began to roll. It rolled down the hill and barreled for Eric.

"Eric! Transform now!" Zeke shouted.

"He's not going to make it! Grab him!" Domi shouted.

Zeke looked at the rolling ice cream block, then at Eric. "I don't know if I can make it!"

"Make it!" Domi snarled.

Zeke grumbled under his breath, then dropped into a dive,

hurtling toward Eric. The ice cream rolled toward Eric, cracking the asphalt underneath, flattening all the cars in its path. It burst forth, flinging off chocolate chips and vanilla ice cream as it rolled.

Beneath him, the ice cream coating Eric cracked. Pink light shone out from within, bright as the sun. Zeke flinched back, flaring his wings. He flapped hard, swooping up over the ice cream ball. It passed underneath, bearing down on Eric.

"What— Why did you—" Domi shouted. She swooped after the ice cream ball, firing superheated explosions at the ice cream. Ice cream hissed and bubbled where her explosions landed, wet puddles of ice cream opening in the ball's surface, pitting it like the moon.

"Erica's coming out!" Zeke shouted back.

"Can Erica survive getting steam rolled? You should've grabbed her!" Domi snapped.

"It's *Erica*. She'll be fine!"

Down below, the ice cream cracked apart. Erica stepped out, pink dress flawless despite the ice cream that had coated her moments ago. Seeing the ice cream wall about to strike her, she lifted her heart-topped wand, her expression deadly serious, and pointed it at the ice cream.

A searingly bright pink beam exploded from the tip of the wand. It sliced the ice cream in two. The two pieces veered off, each crashing into the buildings on the either side of the street. Not even a single drop of melted ice cream dripped onto Erica's tutu.

"Hmph." Erica spun her wand like a drum major and struck a pose, one hand out, the other high in the air, one foot pointed in front of the other. "Who dares attack Perfect Pink?"

"Is that your magical girl name?" Zeke asked, fluttering down to land beside her.

"It might be," Erica said.

"You just abandoned her to her fate! Don't act all friendly," Domi grumbled, landing on Erica's other side.

Zeke gave Domi a look. "I didn't 'abandon her to her fate.' I 'trusted in her to have it handled herself.' Classic magical girl stuff."

"That's more battle shounen, honestly," Erica corrected him, her voice sounding strangely like Eric.

"Oh. Uh, sorry," Zeke said.

Erica snorted. "Typical. Of course, someone as uncouth as you wouldn't know your battle shounens from your magical girls."

Domi snorted under her breath, barely hiding a grin. "Gosh, Zeke."

Zeke sighed. Waving Domi down, he looked around, taking stock. "Deadly ice cream, huh? So much for 'we're safe here.' We aren't safe *anywhere*."

"Could use that coffee apocalypse of yours," Domi muttered.

"You want coffee?" Zeke asked.

"No, but I was thinking it could melt the ice cream," Domi replied.

Zeke looked her in the eyes, then opened his mouth. Boiling hot coffee poured out and splattered into the ice cream-soaked snow beneath them.

Domi blinked. She looked at Erica, who shrugged, then back at Zeke. "What kind of useless goddam skills—"

22

ICE CREAM FOR I SCREAM

Gathering himself, Zeke took a deep breath. "Olivia's somewhere, and other-Zeke's run off. Shall we press on?"

"Yeah, I guess," Domi said, shrugging.

"I'm here. Who else do you need?" Erica declared, flicking her high blonde ponytail.

Domi clicked her tongue. She looked Erica up and down, then shot a meaningful glance Zeke's direction.

Zeke sighed. *This is trouble waiting to happen.*

All around them, the ice cream continued to wake up and come to life. Zeke offered his arms to Erica. "Let's get out of here. We're too big of a target right now."

Erica looked at his ice-cream-stained arms with disgust, then stepped up into the sky. Pink daffodils appeared under her heels, supporting her as she strode upward. "Indeed. Let's get out of here."

With all three of them in the sky, the ice cream couldn't do much to affect them. One of the ice cream monsters reached into its own body and lobbed handfuls of ice cream into the sky.

The ice cream balls lofted up, then fell back down, no more than emotionless balls of frozen dairy.

"Domi, you can't fly for long, right?" Zeke asked, offering his arms again. After getting refused by Erica, he felt a little useless.

Domi glanced at him, then nodded. She blasted herself over to his side, and he locked his arms around her. Together, the two of them soared over the ice cream, Domi firing balls of heat down on the meltable solid.

"This almost feels too easy," Domi commented.

"Shh, don't jinx it. I'll take an easy win," Zeke muttered back.

The sound of wings rushed through the air. Zeke, Domi, and Erica all looked up.

The Scouting Apocalypse flew toward them. He tossed them a friendly nod. "Hello again."

"The hell? Are you with them?" Domi asked.

"Them? Oh. The Ice Cream Apocalypse. No, they weren't interested."

Zeke nodded. He opened his mouth, then shut it, then opened it again. "You. Your name, it was...Luke?"

"Tom. My name is Tom," the Scouting Apocalypse reminded him.

"Right, right. That was my second guess," Zeke assured him.

"Smooooooth," Domi muttered.

The Scouting Apocalypse smiled. "It's fine. We're going to be enemies, after all."

"Not right now, though," Zeke said. "Not if the Ice Cream Apocalypse isn't yours."

"No. But now that we know you're taking it down for us, I'll let the others know, and we won't bother sending anyone this way," Tom said with a friendly nod.

Domi pursed her lips. "I kind of hate you, you know?"

"Hey, it's not all bad. We could attack and try to scoop the levels out from under you," Tom said. A moment after he said it, he put a finger on his lips, thinking to himself.

Zeke grimaced. "Domi..."

"Oh, no. Oh, no you don't. You don't do that," Domi said, jabbing a finger at the Scouting Apocalypse.

"Thanks for the idea!" Tom said, flaring his wings.

Domi hauled back and threw a huge ball of fire at Tom. Eyes wide, Tom barely dodged. The fireball hurtled over his shoulder and arced down over the town below, landing on a nearby building. The explosion rattled over the other buildings. Bits of concrete and shards of glass rained down on the snow- and ice-cream-covered town. Fire burst into the air, little bits raining down on the road and surrounding buildings.

Tom let out a low whistle. "Did you get stronger?"

"Something special I've been cooking up, just for assholes like you," Domi snapped. She made a rude gesture at Tom.

"Wow, spicy. You know what? I think I'm going to bow out. See you guys at the top," Tom said. Dipping his wing, he whirled off, leaving Domi and Zeke behind.

Zeke glared after him. "I could follow him back."

"Could you? I think he's faster than you. Probably went hard into DEX," Domi reasoned.

"In that case, he doesn't have STR, CON, or SPR. Something to think about," Zeke murmured.

Domi glanced at Zeke. "Means he's fragile, without much defense. Just like someone I know."

"Hey. I've got armor," Zeke pointed out.

"Right. Besides, we can't hit what we can't hit, so if he's fast enough, he might not need any defenses. And depending on his skills, he might not need SPR either. We just don't know enough about his build," Domi murmured to herself.

"If he does decide to come back here and fight the Ice Cream

Apocalypse, we'll at least learn his skills. And the skills of any other strikers on the other team," Zeke pointed out.

"Strikers?" Domi asked.

"It's what I've decided to call people like us. Strikers. We don't have a Domain, so all our power is in our bodies. Whereas ordinary Apocalypses are Domains, I guess. Like this," Zeke said, gesturing below them with his chin.

"I get it, I guess. It's a little bit soccer, but I get it," Domi said, nodding.

Zeke lifted his eyes to the horizon. "If Tom's going to get the other Apocalypses, we need to move fast. Anything obviously stick out to you as the Ice Cream Apocalypse's headquarters?"

Domi looked at him, then laughed.

"What?"

She lifted her hand, pointing. "Like that?"

Zeke paused. He nodded, slowly. "That's...probably a good place to start, yeah."

23
BLASTING THROUGH THE APOCALYPSE

"Like that?"

Zeke turned, looking over.

Domi pointed at a standalone ice cream shop, piled high with enormous scoops on all sides. A huge metal ice cream scooper landed against the side of the building.

"That does look like a good place to start," Zeke allowed, nodding. He flew toward it, carrying Domi.

As they approached, Domi lifted her arm. A fireball swelled in her palm, growing larger as they grew closer. She fired it off, and it flew ahead of them, surging down toward the ice cream parlor.

Zeke held his breath, waiting for the impact.

A massive ice cream hand reached up from beside the shop. It grabbed the enormous ice cream scooper and swept it at the fireball, backhanding the explosive away. The fireball arced off like a baseball and smashed into the small town's downtown. A wave of force roared out, fire flying up into the sky.

"Damn," Domi muttered. She pressed her hands together, and sparks formed up instead, bouncing around in her palms.

Down below them, the ice cream scoops began to meld together. A lumpy face formed, then shoulders, then the chest, the stomach, the hips and the legs. An ice cream giant stood up. It hefted the ice cream scoop and pointed it at them, egging them on.

"Let's see you hit this!" Domi shouted, releasing the spark grenade.

The ice cream giant swung again, but this time, the spark grenade burst apart on impact. Some of the sparks were blown away, but some rained down on the giant and the ice cream shop. The giant roared in pain as large chunks opened in its body, but in the next moment, the ice cream that made up its body flowed down and filled in the gaps.

Zeke looked down at Domi. "I think I should get in the fight, too. I'm going to set you down."

"What? No! The bombing run strategy is going great!" Domi said, lobbing another grenade at the giant.

The giant hit it away again. Zeke turned his head to watch it go, then looked at Domi. "If you want to play pitcher, you can do it on your own time, okay?"

"I'm not trying to—"

Beside the ice cream giant, the shop suddenly twitched. It shifted, then ground together, metal and drywall and stucco exterior all shifting. Screeching and grumbling, it lifted out of the ground. The ice cream cone emblem on its front lifted into the sky as a second giant climbed up beside the first. Unlike the first, this giant was formed from steel and glass, plastic and earth. It boasted a sharp, bladed spiral drill for one hand, and an enormous plastic spoon for another. A transparent plastic ice cream cup formed a sort of armored casing around its internals, where thick pipes moved some unknown fluid around its body. The second monster pointed its spoon hand at Domi and Zeke and gestured, egging them on.

Domi clicked her tongue. "All right, put me down. We need to both fight, you're right."

"Thank you." Zeke circled around, quickly dropping her off. "I'll take the ice cream one, you take the machine monster?"

"Got it. Though...why the hell does an Ice Cream Apocalypse have a mecha on its side?" Domi asked.

"Could've Dominated or Subordinated it...Though the spoon and the ice cream cup are a bit too on-theme for that." Zeke trailed off. He pointed at the metal spiral drill. "Doesn't that look familiar, somehow?"

Domi squinted, then rolled her eyes. "Yes. Obviously. Of course."

"Of course?"

"That's the spinny blade thing inside an ice cream machine. An old-fashioned one, anyway. It stirs the ice cream as it's forming, keeps it smooth."

Zeke clapped his hands. "That's it! That's where I knew it from. I knew I'd seen that thing before."

The ice cream giant lowered its scoop and swiped up a big chunk of ice cream. Beside it, the mecha ice cream machine stomped toward them, lifting its spiral hand ominously.

"Less talk, more action," Domi said tersely, running to the side. The ice cream machine mecha stomped toward her, a thick creamy treat mixing in its ice cream cup stomach. It opened its mouth and let out an ice-cream-truck song roar.

"Right." Zeke sprinted in the opposite direction, drawing the ice cream giant's attention. The ice cream giant lunged for him, throwing up a giant chocolate and rocky road hand to block his way. Zeke dove for the hand, activating **Devour** even as he lunged.

Before his lips met the ice cream, a hole opened in the giant's hand. Taken aback, Zeke kept charging in, but the ice cream vanished before he could reach it. Creamy, delicious chocolate landed in his mouth.

His eyes widened. *Oh, right! Ranged Devour. Hell yeah!*

I wonder how far it reaches?

The hand swept toward him. Zeke spun his head, eating a him-shaped hole. The giant's lower fingers fell off, cut through by Zeke's **Devour**ing, and then the hole passed over him. Zeke jumped a little as it passed, taking its last two fingers, too.

His stomach bulged. Satisfied, he patted his belly. *Damn, it feels good to be full.*

Wait, I'm full?

Fuck! I'm full!

Zeke quickly pulled up his skill list and scanned it. *Something to burn off this energy. Anything! I just need to burn this energy!*

The ice cream giant retracted its hand. It stared at the gap where its fingers had been, then roared again, this time in anger. Plunging its hand into the ice cream, it spun it around a little bit, then retracted it. Its fingers reformed, completely whole as if Zeke had never attacked.

Oh. That's not good, either.

Zeke quickly turned his attention back to the skill list. *I need something to kill this fullness, and at the same time, burn through the ice cream to get to this thing's core. A prolonged battle isn't in my favor. It'll keep healing from the ice cream, it can call minions, and I'll have to repeatedly deal with fullness. Best if I can use one big skill to finish it off once and for all.*

Level: 83.12> 95.63 (points not assigned)
Please assign your stat points.
STR: 10
CON: 16

DEX: 16
SPR: 30
Regeneration rate: +30.44%

Skills
Manipulate Aerosols (Strong) +6
Pick Up (Weak)
Osmosis (Weak) +1
Subordinate Link (Weak) +1
Create Drug (Weak) +1
Crystal Burst (Poor) +2
Engulf (Poor)
Create Coffee (Strong)
Whistle Blast (Weak)
Digital Broadcast (Weak) +1
Electric Leap (Poor)
Modest Gigantification (Medium) +2
Nest (Lesser)
Manipulate Wire (Medium)
Electrify (Medium)
Grid (Medium)
Regression (Lesser)
Pierce Through (Lesser)
Manipulate Flame (Weak) +3
Bite (Strong) +3
Roar (Medium)
Stomp (Medium)
Biogenerator (Poor)
Ninja Healing (Medium)
Mold Flesh
Morph Machinery
Create Cyborg
Death Roll (Medium)

Acid Spit (Strong)
Muscle Surge (Medium)

Passive
Resilient Regeneration (Strong) +6
Disguise (Minor)
Watertight (Minor)
Caffeine Rush (Average)
Heat Resistance (Lesser) +9
Flexible Body (Average)
Roll With Us (Lesser)
Hunger Awareness (Lesser) +2
Claw Fighter (Lesser) +2
Perfect Landing (Lesser)
Tough Body (Lesser) +5
Audience (Minor)
Shared Vision (Average)
Burn (Average)
Spread (Average)
Heat Vision (Lesser) +1
Hands-free Calling (Lesser) +1
Clean Wounds (Minor)
Steel Strength (Minor)
Night Vision (Average)
Venomous Bite (Strong)
Steel Stomach (Strong) +8
Tooth Regeneration (Strong)

Condition
Hardness (Lesser) (Condition) +1
Claws (Large) (Condition) +1
Wings (Tiny) (Condition) +2
Steel Armor (Medium) (Condition) (Transform-

only)
**Cyborg Integration (UNIQUE) Chip Upgrade:
Hacking
MOTORCYCLE**

**Lvl 0: Devour
Lvl 30: Absorb + 5/Transform
Lvl 60: Portable Domain
Lvl 90: Ranged Devour**

**Negative Skills
Vampirism (Weak) + 8**

**Transform: Substantial boost to all stats. Armor +
500%. Gained skills: Extra Mouths, Extra Limbs,
Multi-Devour, Hunger (Condition).**

Zeke lifted a hand to his chin. *Damn, I have way too many
skills. I really need to fuse them, for real this time. When did I even
get Disguise, for goodness' sakes? It's so high on the list, it must have
been early— Oh, right! The trash monster! Way, way back, that
Garbage Apocalypse or whatever. Damn, that was a long time ago.*

*I've also got to assign those skill points... Huh. I guess just put
them all in SPR? I should keep my build minmaxed, at this point. I
have Allen for STR, so I don't need that. Or... No, let's put four in
CON and DEX each, then the rest in SPR. Yeah. That makes sense.*

**STR: 10
CON: 16 > 20
DEX: 16 > 20
SPR: 30 > 34**

Zeke nodded. *Those are nice, round numbers. I like that.*

The ice cream giant swept its hand at Zeke again. Zeke instantly activated **Modest Gigantism** over his whole body, and he surged up to meet the giant's height. The food in his body burned away even as he grew, but rather than stop, he simply lunged at the giant and took a big bite. The giant flinched away, but though it dodged his jaws, it failed to avoid **Ranged Devour.** A huge chunk opened in its gut, and Zeke swallowed in satisfaction, using the ice cream to feed his growth. He leaned in again, taking another bite.

His bites ate through the ice cream giant's stomach on both the left and the right. Only a thin spine of ice cream remained. The ice cream giant wobbled, off-balance, then fell backward into the ice cream. Instantly, ice cream surged to it, fixing up the holes in its body. It struggled, fighting to stand once more.

"No, you don't." Zeke jumped on it. His jaws closed around his neck, and he activated **Death Roll.** He and the ice cream giant both spun, digging a hole in the ice cream and snow under them. The ice cream giant struggled but couldn't break free of his vicious hold. Zeke grappled it with all four limbs, holding it on top of him, where it couldn't reach the ice cream on the ground. From that pose, he gnawed through its neck. Its spine snapped with a crack, nothing more than a pillar of hard-frozen ice cream through the giant's center.

The giant's head rolled away. Zeke kept chewing. He bit through the giant's neck hole and chomped into its chest. *Where's the core? The core has to be in here somewhere! This thing can't regenerate if I eat its core!*

The body laid limply on top of him, as if dead. Behind him, the head rolled into a deep pile of ice cream.

Ice cream sucked out from under Zeke, even deteriorating the giant's body. A shadow fell over him. Startled, Zeke looked up.

The ice cream giant stood over him. Larger than ever, it

blocked out the sun, that same head perched atop a fresh ice cream body like a cherry atop a fudge sundae.

Zeke grimaced. "Fuck."

The giant raised its foot. With a fierce roar, it stomped down on the prone Zeke.

24
STOMPING TIME

The giant stomped down. Its foot hurtled toward Zeke's face.

Throwing what little remained of its body away, Zeke opened his mouth.

[Ranged Devour]

His jaws snapped shut. The giant's foot disappeared. Zeke swallowed as he pushed upright, licking his lips. "I know where your core is now, big boy. Prepare to die."

Unbothered, the giant hopped back and shoved its severed leg into a deep ice cream drift. When it pulled it free, its foot had reformed once more.

Zeke made a face. "Is that orange sherbert right next to mint chocolate chip ice cream? Yuck. That's recreating the orange juice and toothpaste experience, all in one dish. No one likes that."

Ignoring his critique, the giant roared at him again. Half-frozen ice cream spittle splattered on Zeke's face. The giant reached back and scooped up a big scoop of ice cream, then lobbed it at Zeke.

"Man, we can do this all day," Zeke said with a grin. He jumped to catch the ice cream with his mouth, swallowing with satisfaction. He gestured the giant on. "Come on. Throw some more!"

To the side, explosions rattled off. The ice cream machine mecha stumbled and fell, crushing a half-dozen buildings under its bulk. A glowing orange form darted toward it, another explosion already built in her hands.

Zeke nodded to himself. *Domi's got that one covered. I can leave that to her and focus on the giant alone.*

The ice cream giant swung the metal scoop at Zeke. In his distraction, Zeke only saw it coming at the last second, a wall of freezing cold metal rushing toward his face. He flinched back, barely dodging it. Icy cold wafted off the metal, so cold he felt the chill of its passing.

"Whew! Don't you know you're supposed to dip that thing in warm water to keep the ice cream from sticking? It shouldn't be that cold," Zeke admonished the giant. He eyed the scoop. *If I bite that, I'll end up with my tongue stuck to it. I have to be careful even grabbing it because I only have partial control over my hand mouths.*

Is there anything I can use to parry it without touching it? That would be ideal.

Zeke cast about him, searching for something, anything. His eyes landed on a bus. He ran for it, reaching with both hands. "Allen! I need your STR!"

Subordinate Allen is too cold and cannot respond.

Zeke's eyes flew wide. *Fuck! I forgot! He's cold-blooded.* His mind raced, searching his skills once more. At last, one came to mind.

Flames flicked up along the side of a building where Domi's explosion had landed not long ago. Zeke reached out toward them, pulling them to him with **Flame Manipulation.** Flames circled the top of his head like a halo, warming his skull, where Allen sat. "There. Is that better, buddy?"

Subordinate Allen is warming up, but still not warm enough to respond.

Zeke grimaced. He looked at the bus again, then away. *Can't do that. But then...* He lifted his fist, and a ball of fire came with him. Opening his hand, he let the fire swirl around his palm and allowed himself a small smile. In his Transformed state, it became terrifying, his mouth gaping open to show his rows of teeth, jaw split to the bone.

Can't believe I forgot about this skill in the Ice Cream Apocalypse.

Man. I really am the Ice Cream Apocalypse's worst nightmare, huh? After being stuck in the Cyborg and Undead Apocalypses where I couldn't really eat much, it feels good. Real good.

The ice cream giant swung the scoop at him again. Zeke dodged back, then threw his ball of fire at the giant. The giant raised an arm. The fireball seared through it, diminishing as it went. An ember hissed into the giant's chest, not hurting it at all. The giant looked at its melted arm as the arm fell off, then all but shrugged to itself as it stuck the arm into fresh ice cream. The arm reformed in moments.

Zeke nodded to himself. *I'm going to need a one-two punch, huh? That's fine. I can provide. I might only be able to control the fire spiral on my head and a single additional fireball at this level of Fire Manipulation, but I've got more skills than just Fire Manipulation.*

It's time to take this giant down.

He reached out to the fires once more. A second fireball formed in his hand. He turned back to the ice cream giant, preparing to charge.

"Zeke! Watch out!"

Zeke turned just in time to watch the ice cream machine mecha smash through a three-story-building. Arms out, it reached to tackle him, its spinny blade arm whirling as fast as a drill, the edge of the blade razor sharp. Zeke startled and jumped back, but too slow. The mecha slammed into him, bearing him to the ground.

His head kicked against the ground, and his mind went fuzzy. The fireball in his hand fizzled out. With effort, he managed to keep the fire halo around Allen alive. He stared up at the mecha, dazed, half-struggling, half-unable to control his body. The mecha's weight pinned him to the floor. His half-coordinated struggles couldn't break its hold.

As he laid there, hunger built up in his stomach. His limbs weakened. The ice cream machine mecha raised its bladed drill hand, and he tensed, unable to do anything else to protect himself.

Oh, fuck. This isn't good.

The drill surged higher, faster. It plunged down toward Zeke's gut. With a grinding and keening, the swirling blade dug into Zeke's armor. The pain jerked Zeke awake. Adrenaline pounded through him, giving him strength. He grabbed the mecha giant's arm at the elbow, pushing it back with all his might. "Allen! Are you awake yet?"

Subordinate Allen is willing to share his STR.

Zeke's arms grew strong. Grabbing tight to the machine mecha's arm, he activated **Death Roll** and toppled it, pinning the mecha to the ground. He smashed his fist into the mecha's head, shattering the ice cream parlor's sign. Again and again. The lights winked out. Its ice cream parlor head shattered.

"Zeke, the chest! Under the giant plastic ice cream cup!" Domi shouted as she ran over.

Zeke drew his fist back and slammed it down with all his might. The clear plastic bent, deforming, then bounced back. He punched again. The plastic cracked. Drawing his hand back, he formed it into a blade and shoved it through the crack.

[Pierce Through]

Zeke's hand scraped by the jagged edges of the plastic barrier. It plunged into the pipes and electric wire guts inside the ice cream machine mecha. Grabbing a handful, Zeke pulled. Pipes snapped. Soft ice cream gushed out, pouring down the mecha's frame and internals. Electric wires pulled, stretching and stretching. They broke at last, bursting with sparks.

Behind the broken pipes and wires, an orb glimmered. The mecha's core.

Zeke plunged his hand back into the heart of the mecha and grabbed the core. As his hand closed around it, the mouth in between its fingers chomped down, swallowing the core. Fullness rushed into Zeke, powering his Modest Gigantism for another few moments. Under his hand, the mecha stilled, eyes going dark.

Defeated Mecha Ice Cream Giant!
Level + 3.41
Level: 95.63 > 99.04
Please assign your stat points.

Explosions boomed behind Zeke. He stood, removing his

hand from the mecha, and turned. Blood dripped down his stomach as he stood, his armor broken around his gut. Shattered pieces of armor clung to him like the cracked shell of a hardboiled egg. He put a hand to it and winced, then pulled his hand away as his hand tongue instantly tasted copper and the strange bitter flavor of his armor.

"Did you get it?" Domi asked, backing toward him.

"Yeah. It's dead. The ice cream giant?" Zeke asked, turning around a building.

Domi jumped back. The ice cream giant swept a giant hand at her, flattening a building in front of it and tossing a few cars aside with ease. Debris and clouds of dust rose up where it passed. "It just keeps healing!"

"Yeah, I know. You have to get it away from the ice cream, or else it'll infinitely regenerate its body," Zeke explained.

Domi rolled her eyes at him. "If you know how to kill it, then why haven't you killed it yet?"

"I was in the process, okay? Actively working on it. The mecha got away from you, and it interrupted me!" Zeke pointed out.

Domi sighed. "Yeah, fine. Fair." A moment later, she turned around, looking all around them. "And how are we supposed to get it away from the ice cream?"

Zeke turned, too. Ice cream in all directions. Everywhere they looked, ice cream. Piled on rooftops. Stacked against walls. Lining the streets. It accumulated in drifts and clumped up in scoops. Not a single surface around them was free of ice cream.

Zeke cleared his throat. "I was working on that, too."

"Uh huh." Domi quirked a brow at him.

The ice cream giant lunged at them. The two of them jumped apart. Zeke lofted into the air and landed with a heavy *BOOM*, while Domi barely dove to the side in time to avoid it.

"Domi! Carpet bomb this area. I want this whole area

sizzling! I'll stall it until you've cleared it out. You got it?" Zeke called. He stomped toward the ice cream giant. Cars leaped up as his feet struck asphalt. Buildings shook, barely staying upright.

"I got it! Let's do this!" Domi shouted back. She took off at a run, lobbing orange fireballs left and right.

The ice cream giant ran at Zeke as Zeke ran at it. They closed in on each other. The ice cream giant swung its frigid scoop at Zeke. He jumped, yanking his legs up over the scoop with his DEX and Allen's STR. From the air, he lashed out with a kick, aiming at the ice cream giant's head.

The ice cream giant swayed back, dodging the kick.

Zeke landed, upper lip wrinkled in frustration. He instantly charged in again, throwing himself at the ice cream giant's chest. The ice cream giant swung its scoop again, but its arm bounced off the charging Zeke. The two of them collided. Zeke bore the giant to the floor, where it flew backward, scraping its back on the ground and leaving a smear of mixed ice cream behind it. Zeke didn't hesitate. He darted his head in, taking a big bite at the giant's neck.

Ice cream piled up around the giant's neck. Zeke stole a bite, but it didn't break through the thick ruff surrounding the neck. The giant raised its legs and kicked Zeke in the stomach, its feet striking the wounded part of Zeke's armor. A chill rushed through Zeke, pain jabbing through him. He fell back, falling onto his back. The giant stood, stomping forward after Zeke. Zeke kicked at the ground, scooting away from the giant on his back.

The giant closed in. Zeke eyed its foot, ready to use Ranged Devour, but the giant paused before stomping at him a second time. Instead, it gestured.

Zeke frowned. *What does that mean?*

And then pain bit into his back.

25

SURPRISE ATTACK

Icicles drilled into Zeke's back, surging up from the ground. Zeke shouted, startled. Freezing cold water surged into the cracks and gaps in his armor, then froze, forcing the cracks wider. Coldness poured in, and with it, sharp crackling pain. Zeke pulled away from the ground, but the ice froze him in place. He gritted his teeth and pulled with all his might. The ice yanked at his armor. It pulled away from his skin, feeling as though it was going to break completely away from his flesh. Zeke dropped back to the ground, panting.

Ow, ow, shit. That shit hurts! Fuck! What do I do? What do I do?

His eyes cut sideways. Zeke gestured, pulling toward him.

The ice cream giant cracked a smile. It lowered its scoop to the ground and hauled up a big scoop of ice cream. Unhesitating, it lobbed the ice cream at Zeke.

The scoop slammed into the hole in his gut. Zeke winced. He shoved the ice cream off his body and raised his arms, preparing for the next strike.

Ice cream scoop after ice cream scoop rained down on him. The giant piled him high with ice cream, relentlessly slamming ice cream onto Zeke. He shoved it away, what he could reach, but he struggled to reach his legs, frozen to the ground as he was. Scoop after scoop layered onto Zeke. As more landed on him, the blows numbed him. Cold soaked into his body. He moved slower and slower as ice cream froze into the cracks in his joints, gunking them up. Weight bore down on him from the many, large scoops of frozen dairy. He fell backward, unable to hold his head up any longer.

Zeke stared up at the ice cream over him, then opened his mouth and used **Devour.** He shrugged internally. *At least I won't get hungry and drop out of Gigantism. And I am technically pinning the giant down. I mean, I'm not in a good position to help out for the next phase, but I am accomplishing my goals right now. And that's what's really important.*

Under his back, a small glimmer of heat circulated, moving slowly along his back. The fire he'd grabbed from a burning building just before the ice cream giant had slammed him with ice cream continued to melt the ice freezing him to the ground. He kept his mind on **Fire Manipulation,** working the ball of fire along his back, passing it by icicle after icicle until each melted enough that he could crack the ice and break free. Little by little, his back became free of the ground.

Zeke shifted, checking how much of his body had been freed. *Almost there. Let's just keep chomping on ice cream.* As he ate, the ice cream shifted over him, falling in. The ice cream fell down, scoops rolling past him, and outside, the ice cream giant roared in frustration. The weight on Zeke grew heavier, slamming down on him as the giant continued to mash him with scoops.

Almost there. Just a little more.

The few remaining icicles crackled under Zeke and the ice cream's weight. The little fireball circled around, weakening them with every pass. Zeke wiggled his shoulders, then heaved himself forward. The last icicles snapped. The ice cream mountain piled up on Zeke fell away, tumbling to the floor.

"I live!" Zeke shouted, throwing his arms in the air.

"Good, because I'm almost ready back here," Domi called.

The ice cream giant startled. It whirled around and fired a hard-frozen ball of ice cream directly at Zeke's face. Zeke dodged downward, barely avoiding the icy hard ball. It whirled past him, stirring the thin hairs on his head, and crashed into a building across the street behind him.

Jiggling his legs free, Zeke climbed to his feet just as the giant hurled another ice ball at him. He jumped to the side and landed on a patch of black ice. Zeke flailed, his legs windmilling under him, and crashed into the buildings on the opposite side of the road. Glass shattered, raining down on him. Steel beams bent. The façade crumbled, falling in on itself. Zeke shoved himself upright before the whole building could collapse. His feet slid wildly on the incredibly slick ice. He stumbled free of the ice onto the relatively safe footing of the ice cream snow, just in time to catch an ice ball in the chest. Zeke staggered backward, grabbing onto the building to keep himself from falling into the slick patch of the ice again.

"You done practicing your ice skating over there, or...?" Domi called from around the corner.

"I'm— Shut up. Are you ready?" Zeke asked.

"Good to go, Boss. Just lead him toward my voice!"

Zeke nodded. Checking the floor behind him, he kicked the mountain of ice cream scoops out of the way and gestured at the ice cream giant. "Come on, loser. Try me!"

The giant ignored him, scooping up another ice ball.

"Dammit." Zeke charged the giant, lifting his arms to grapple it. The giant backed away, hurling scoops at him the whole time. Dodging left and right with his DEX, Zeke quickly closed in on the giant. He slammed into it, knocking it back to the ground. The giant's head thumped, and its big chocolate chip eyes blinked shut for a moment.

Zeke slammed his foot down on the giant's neck. With both hands, he grabbed its head and pulled. The ice cream stretched, then broke free. Zeke sprinted toward Domi, even as the ice cream all around him rushed toward the hole of the giant's neck. "I'm coming!"

"Hurry up!"

Around the corner, Zeke jumped off ice cream and stepped onto firm, solid, grippy asphalt. He dashed into the center of it. Ice cream no longer flowed to the head. It couldn't fly far enough with all the ice cream-less asphalt around. Raising both hands, he smashed the head down on the center of the asphalt.

The ice cream scoop that made up the giant's head split open. A smaller, tighter scoop of ice cream fell out. Zeke released **Modest Gigantification** and hurtled down to the ground. The second he grew near, he swallowed the smaller ice cream scoop.

Defeated the Ice Cream Giant.
Level + 3.27
Level: 99.04 > 102.31
Please assign your stat points.

Zeke let out a sigh of relief and fell back. Beside him, Domi walked up. She squinted. "That wasn't the Apocalypse?"

Zeke shrugged. "Guess not."

Domi frowned again. "Where's Erica? For that matter, where's that goddamn Scouting Apocalypse?"

Zeke blinked. He peered around him, then pursed his lips. "Uh..."

"Did you not even notice they were gone?" Domi asked, shaking her head at him.

"No, no. I just—it was busy. There were a lot of things going on. I had to fight two giants. Come on," Zeke grumbled.

"Yeah, yeah. Excuses, excuses." Domi grinned, to show she was joking.

Transformation time overrun.

Zeke's body shifted. His armor receded, the hand-mouths sealing shut. Zeke glanced down at himself. Soft human flesh. His ordinary, weak body.

Beside him, the orange faded from Domi. She clapped her hands and nodded at him. "Timed out, huh?"

"Yeah. Not a great time to do it. We're in the middle of enemy territory, and we've got, what, two and a half minutes until we can use our Transforms again?" Zeke asked.

"We didn't use our Domains, though. We aren't completely powerless," Domi pointed out.

Zeke nodded. "Right. And it's not like we're ever powerless. We still have our skills."

"Exactly! So, let's go find Erica and the Scouting Apocalypse, and finish up the fight before the other Apocalypse Alliance gets here," Domi said firmly.

"Hope Olivia and other-Zeke have it handled," Zeke muttered.

"About that. We need a better name for him than 'other-Zeke,'" Domi said, heading deeper into the ice cream.

Zeke nodded, following her. "There isn't really another good place to cut up my name, though."

"What, Zeke?"

Zeke looked at her. "It's short for Ezekiel."

Domi blinked. She stopped dead.

"What?"

"Just...Ezekiel? God. What a name," Domi muttered.

"What's wrong with Ezekiel?"

"Nothing! Nothing. It's a great name! It's just...not you, man. It's not you," Domi said, shaking her head at him.

Zeke sighed. "Yeah. I get that."

"It's not for him, either. Ezekiel...nah."

"What about Eze? Kiel? There isn't really a better place to cut it," Zeke pointed out.

Domi rubbed her hands together, breathing into them to warm her fingers. "What about, uh...Zel? I mean, it's not great, and you kinda have to squint to see it, but then again, you aren't called Zekie either."

"Zel...that's not bad. I'll ask him when we see him again," Zeke said.

"If you wouldn't mind it, he probably won't either," Domi said, glancing at him.

"Yeah, but there's a difference between deciding something behind someone's back and making sure they're okay with it before we just do it."

Domi nodded. "Yeah, yeah."

"Not that I think he'll care, but..."

The ice cream grew thicker underfoot, muffling their footsteps. Overhead, the thick gray clouds opened up, and tiny snowflakes drifted down. A peaceful aura covered the town, as the giants broke down behind them, decaying into the ice cream drifts. Two tiny figures vanished into the snow.

26

ICE CREAM SOCIAL

Zeke walked along, yawning, taking his time as he went. No reason to rush when he needed to wait for his Transform to recharge, anyway. He kept his eyes on the sky as he walked, searching for the Scouting Apocalypse, but if the eagle-winged Tom had stuck around, he kept above the clouds or to the ground, and in either case, Zeke couldn't find him. There was still no sign of Olivia or other-Zeke (maybe Zel), but he wasn't that worried. Both of them could take care of themselves. Especially other-Zeke. And Olivia was undead, so she was pretty sturdy to start out with.

He casually scooped up a handful of ice cream as he walked and took a bite, only to grimace. "Strawberry."

"You not a fan?" Domi asked.

"Nah. You?"

Domi shrugged. "I'd rather have strawberry than mint."

"Really? But mint's classic," Zeke said.

"Sure, but it tastes like toothpaste," Domi said.

Zeke squinted at her. "It's the other way around. Toothpaste is mint-flavored, not backward."

"Yeah, but I associate it with toothpaste, so it's not a good flavor in my mind," Domi said, shrugging.

Zeke shook his head at her.

"I didn't say it made sense. It's just the way it is in my head."

"Yeah, yeah. We all have our weird hang-ups," Zeke agreed.

Domi glanced at him, then grinned. "Like your compulsive need to eat everything you touch."

Zeke pursed his lips at her, narrowing his eyes. Domi grinned back.

"Anyway, looks like that ice cream parlor wasn't the main body of the Apocalypse, since it's still raining ice cream out here," Zeke commented, lifting a hand. A few snowflakes landed in it, and he licked them off his hand. "Yum, vanilla."

"Yeah, looks like. Those guys were *big,* though. There's no way it wasn't important to the Apocalypse."

"Maybe that was the Apocalypse's original hub, but it outgrew it, or something," Zeke commented.

"True. Hey, do you think this Apocalypse was originally a scoop of ice cream? I mean, who would pick Ice Cream as an Apocalypse, right?"

"Honestly? Wouldn't be surprised," Zeke said, shaking his head.

"Most of the Apocalypses we've faced after the dome have been human. No...all of them have. It's kind of a refreshing change of pace," Domi said.

Zeke shook his finger at her. "The Cyborg Apocalypse was half printer. It kind of counts."

"*Kind* of. This isn't horseshoes or hand grenades. Close doesn't cut it."

Zeke snorted. He walked on, leaving multicolored footprints behind him where his feet disturbed the fresh-fallen snow to reveal different flavors of ice cream beneath them. They walked by the second or even third stories of the buildings around them, the ice cream so deep that the first floor was completely buried. No little ice cream scoop monsters chased them here. Even so, Zeke kept his head high, searching for any motion. Now wasn't the time to get complacent. Here, where the ice cream was deeper, they doubtlessly headed toward the heart of the Apocalypse. And the heart of the Apocalypse would be the center of danger.

"As far as Apocalypses go, I kinda like this one," Zeke commented.

"You would," Domi said.

Zeke gave her a look.

"Nah, I agree. It's fun, you know? Like a silly dream I had when I was twelve. But I wish it was a little less cold." Domi rubbed her hands over her arms. "I'm gonna enjoy a nice, hot shower after this."

"It'll be nice heading back into warm weather," Zeke agreed.

From around a corner, a girl with thick glasses and frizzy hair stepped out. She glanced around, half-making eye contact with them. Casually, she walked toward them.

Domi backed away. Zeke lifted his hand toward her threateningly, though he really wasn't sure what he'd do with it if she attacked. He looked her in the eye, subtly preparing to attack. "Who are you?"

"Oh! Uh, um, I...I'm sorry. I thought we were all supposed to meet here? It's, uh, it's my first time coming with the group... Ah, I'm Karrie, by the way. Um. The uh. Quiet Apocalypse."

Zeke and Domi exchanged a glance. Silently, Zeke activated **Hands-Free Calling.**

She's a member of the Apocalypse Coalition.

Yeah, I figured that out, thanks.

I say we play it cool. See if we can figure out what their plans are, what their powers are, before we attack.

Works for me.

Zeke nodded at her. "Nice to meet you, Karrie. I'm Zeke, and this is Domi. Do you know where the Ice Cream Apocalypse's heart is? We were looking around, but we didn't see the big boss. Took out some little bosses, but that was it."

"Oh...no, I haven't. I'm sorry." Karrie drooped, her hair falling in front of her eyes.

"That's okay. Why don't we look for it together?" Zeke suggested. Despite himself, he felt a little bad about the way she crumpled in disappointment. *She's an enemy, dammit. Don't feel bad for the enemy.*

When she looked up, her thick glasses still hid her eyes from view, all fogged up from her breath. She smiled. "Okay! Thank goodness I found you. I was so scared, coming out here all alone without anyone I knew. I was afraid I'd encounter the wrong people."

Zeke coughed. "Good thing that didn't happen."

Domi nudged him, giving him a look.

"Right. Well. I think the boss is that way," Zeke pointed, behind Karrie.

"Huh? I thought it was that way." Karrie pointed behind them.

"Doubt it. We just killed everything that way," Domi replied.

"Oh... Are you sure?"

"Pretty sure," Domi said firmly.

Karrie licked her lips, staring behind them one last time, then nodded. "Okay. I'll follow your lead. You've been here longer than me."

Zeke nodded. "Yep."

Domi nudged him. "So, Karrie, it's our first time meeting, right?"

"Huh? Oh, yeah! Yeah. Sorry, I didn't come to any of the

meetings. I'm not really... I'm not really a people person." She glanced at the floor again, embarrassed.

"That's all right. Hey, we can't all be people people all the time. People...persons?" Zeke frowned, thinking.

"People eaters?" Domi suggested.

Zeke nudged her. "But we're going to fight, now. Fight... together. So, we need to know how your powers work! Domi and I already know each other pretty well, but we don't know anything about you."

Karrie shied away. "I don't really want to talk about my powers..."

"Why not? Girl. You can't be like this. If our powers are incompatible, I need to know *now,* not when we're neck deep in ice cream and I explode your, I don't know, tsunami wave, or whatever," Domi said, shaking her head at Karrie.

Zeke smiled reassuringly at her. "Domi's a little harsh, but she's just worried she'll hurt you in battle. We'll find out your powers when we all face the next enemy, whether you tell us or not. If we aren't all honest with one another, we're just going to give our enemy the advantage when we all get in each other's way." Zeke paused, looking regretfully at the floor. "And in a fight, where it's life and death...I don't want to put you in danger by accident due to not understanding your powers."

"Ah, it's just...they're a little...once you know the trick, it's..." Karrie hesitated again.

"What are you afraid of? We're all on the same team," Domi said, shaking her head at Karrie.

"Well, they mentioned in the message that there were some rival Apocalypses here, and I didn't go to meetings, so I—"

"I can vouch for Domi," Zeke said, patting her on the shoulder.

"Yeah, and I can vouch for—" Domi stopped dead. She stared at Karrie.

Karrie stumbled back. "W-what?"

Domi squinted at her. "Are *you* a rival Apocalypse? Is that why you won't tell us your powers?"

"No! I'm..." Karrie bit her lip, then looked around her. She scooted in toward them. "Come in close. Just in case."

Domi and Zeke exchanged a look. Domi flashed him a grin so quick he'd miss it if he blinked, and then they both leaned toward Karrie.

She glanced from one of them to the other. "My Apocalypse is the Quiet Apocalypse. It's all about sound. If you make sound, I can—"

"Karrie! There you are!"

A girl and a black standard poodle turned the corner. The standard poodle's big, poofy head fur bobbled as it walked, long legs striding over the ice cream. The girl stood about as tall as the poodle's head, maybe ten, eleven years old. She stopped dead at the sight of Zeke and Domi, putting a hand on the dog's shoulder. The dog lifted its head, floppy ears perking ever so slightly, bright eyes staring directly at Zeke and Domi.

"Who are you?" she asked.

"Who are *you*?" Domi argued, narrowing her eyes at the girl.

"I'm Taylor, and this dumb asshole is Sparkles. We're members of the Apocalypse Alliance. Who are you?" the girl asked again.

Karrie backed away from them. Her eyes widened behind those thick glasses. "You...you—"

Game's up. Zeke tensed, eyeing Taylor and Sparkles.

Domi immediately lunged at Karrie, clawing a hand toward her face.

27
GAME IS UP

Zeke startled at Domi's attack, but only for a heartbeat. As Domi closed in on Karrie, he threw out his hand, activating **Ranged Devour.** *All is fair in love and war. It's rude to sneak attack, but, well, if she came upon us in the same way that we came upon her, I doubt she would've done anything but attack us on sight.*

Karrie shrieked, startled. She stumbled back, raising her arms defensively. A bite opened up in her forearm, and she shrieked again, arms lowering. Domi's hand landed on her face. An explosion rocked her body. Shen went limp and fell backward, face a smoking mess.

"Stupid dog, let's go!" Taylor shouted. Sparkles barked, jumping where he stood. Taylor took on a doglike appearance as she ran. Her hair turned poofy, and her mouth turned canine. Claws appeared at the tips of her hands, and protective curly fur covered her body.

Zeke blinked. *Wasn't expecting that.* Instinctively, he called on Transform for the armor.

Transform is still on recharge.

Right. He threw his hands out to meet Taylor's leap as she plunged toward him.

Clawed hands crashed into his. Taylor lunged for his face, her jaws snapping wildly. Zeke pushed against her, leaning as far away from her as he could manage. Her fangs scraped his face. Growling and snarling, she snapped wildly at him.

Zeke leaned his head away. He hesitated. *Kill a kid like her? She isn't even the Apocalypse, just the subordinate of one.*

To the side, Karrie rose up, her whole body stiff, tipping upright like a board stood on its end. Her ruined face remained ruined, blood and gore dripping down her chest, not that she seemed to notice. She lifted her hand and pointed at Domi.

Domi stared. "What?"

Force rushed at Domi. It slammed her in the gut and threw her backward.

Never mind. I can't hold back. These guys are Apocalypses, too. Zeke used **Ranged Devour,** but it bounced off something invisible between him and Taylor. He took a deep breath and whistled.

[Whistle Blast]

Taylor froze, stunned. Behind her, Sparkles alerted, standing up tall, ears forward, tail high. He growled under his breath.

Zeke darted in.

[Bite]
[Devour]

Blood gushed down. Taylor fell to the ground, her throat ripped out.

Behind her, Sparkles let out a ferocious growl. He charged at

Zeke. His paws dug into the ice cream, little spouts of snow-cream flying up behind him. Opening his maw wide, he closed in on Zeke's throat faster than Zeke expected.

Zeke threw his arms up. The dog's muzzle closed around his arms. Sharp fangs cut into his flesh. Sparkles bit deep, shaking his head hard enough to toss Zeke around. Zeke hung on as best he could, bracing his legs. He reared back his head and used **Acid Spit.** A glob of greenish fluid flew at Sparkles.

Sparkles barked. A wall of sonic force deflected the acid back at Zeke.

"Shit!" Zeke ducked, barely dodging his own glob of acid. Little droplets seared his flesh as it flew by.

Growling, Sparkles leaned his weight on Zeke's arms, bearing him downward. Zeke pushed against him, struggling to stand up straight. Under the weight of the large dog, he tensed, barely able to hold his ground. Blood ran down his arms and soaked into his sleeves. The dog growled again, deeper, and twisted its head. Zeke's flesh tore.

"God, I hope you're up on your rabies vaccinations," Zeke muttered under his breath.

A second later, a thought came to him. He lifted his head and stared Sparkles in the eye. "Bathtime!"

Sparkles startled. His eyes widened, but he held on.

"Vet! Let's go to the vet! Bathtime! Uh, groomer! Vet!" *What else do dogs hate?* Zeke drew a blank.

Sparkles withdrew his head. He looked at Zeke, big liquid eyes searching Zeke's face.

"Hey! We can be friends. What do you say? Treat? Er, walkies?" Zeke tried.

Sparkles' eyes landed on Taylor, and he growled. He leaped back. His lean body transformed mid-leap. The fur became plate armor, the shaved parts of his body, lithe chain link. His short tail was a taut-pulled chain, a morningstar's head mounted at its end instead of a puff. Vicious steel claws burst from his metal paws, and razor-sharp edges tipped his once-fluffy ears. Pacing back, he barked at Zeke in a tinny voice.

"Robot Dog Apocalypse? Gotta say, didn't see that one coming," Zeke muttered. He worked his jaw, eyeing the armor. *That's not going to be fun to bite. Nothing I can do about it, though, except try to use Ranged Devour as much as I can. Ugh, I can already feel it on my teeth. Ouch.*

Sparkles lowered his head and growled.

"Wait, wait. Hold on. Can we talk this one out?" Zeke asked, stepping forward. *I don't wanna kill a dog.*

Sparkles narrowed his glowing pale eyes.

"Listen. I didn't want to kill that Subordinate of yours, but she was bad-mouthing you the whole time. Were you really okay with that?" Zeke asked. *I have no idea how much this dog can understand, but given that it's an Apocalypse, if it has high enough SPR, it could completely understand me.*

Sparkles hesitated, then paused, listening.

Enheartened, Zeke kept pushing. "She wasn't your owner, was she? Did something happen to them?"

Sparkles bared his teeth. He growled.

"Something bad. I figured. Do you really want that to happen to every other dog, and every other dog's owners, in this whole world?" Zeke asked.

Sparkles' brows furrowed. He squinted at Zeke.

"The group you're a part of, that Apocalypse Coalition— they want to destroy the world. They want everyone to die. Even you, ultimately." *Probably,* he added silently.

Eyes widening, Sparkles stumbled back. He shook his head.

Zeke nodded. "Yes. For real. They're lying to you, Sparkles. Come join us. We're trying to save the world, and all the dogs and owners in it." He extended his hand.

Sparkles stepped forward. Tentatively, he sniffed Zeke's hand.

"Come on. Help us. Fight on the right side," Zeke said, smiling at Sparkles.

And then a foot slammed into the back of his head and smashed him facedown into the ice cream.

28

STEP ON ME, MOMMY

A foot slammed into the back of Zeke's head and stomped him to the ground. Zeke's face splatted into a batch of cherry vanilla. Ice cream soaked into his hair and eyebrows, his whole face covered in it. He struggled against the foot, pushing himself up just enough to breathe before the foot shoved him back down.

"What's going on here?"

Sparkles lowered his head and whined. Behind Zeke, the bloody-faced Karrie snapped around, her limbs dangling like a puppet with broken strings. Even her jaw hung open, every bit of her slack and yet somehow upright.

"Karrie? Sparkles? What happened here?" the woman stepping on Zeke demanded.

Sparkles reared up and bounced back down. He barked.

"I don't speak dog."

Sparkles whined, wrinkling his nose in distaste.

"Karrie?"

Silently, the bloodied specter Karrie had become swung on the air, limbs jostling together like a grim windchime.

The woman sighed. "Useless. Who recruited these trashy Apocalypses in the first place?"

Sparkles lowered his head and growled.

On the ground, Zeke peered up. *Domi. Where's Domi? What happened to her? Karrie didn't kill her, right?*

A soft groan sounded out. He couldn't see her from this angle, but that voice was undoubtedly Domi. Zeke let out a little sigh, relieved despite everything. *She's still alive. We're in a bad situation, but it's not over yet.*

The real question is, what's the Apocalypse that's stepping on me? Who is she? Can she take her foot off my head?

The woman applied pressure to his head, pushing him back into the ice cream. "Jeez. Do I have to do all the work around here? Can't any of the rest of you deadweights do anything? Kill one little Apocalypse, maybe?"

"Get off!" Zeke snapped, shoving upward with all his strength.

The woman easily pinned him back to the earth, her high heel pushing into his back. "Stay quiet, little boy. Become one of my good little students."

Become one of her...what? Zeke frowned.

Footsteps all around them. From the ground, Zeke peered up.

Strange figures drew close to the woman on his back. They stood about chest height at the tallest, small and blocky. Although they were about as tall as children and had the proportions of children, their facial features were those of adults.

Wait— No. They are *adults. Or...they were.* Their bodies had been morphed back to child-shape, but the wrinkles and age on their faces remained. They wore adult clothing, as well, but morphed down to child size. As they drew close to the woman, they gave strange cries. Little desperate moans, happy and needy, like puppies. Their eyes shone with adulation, their little hands reaching up to the woman. It reminded Zeke of dogs running up to their owner and wagging their tails, desperate for attention. He shivered. *Don't tell me.*

"Good children," the woman cooed. She patted the head of the closest one. He leaned into it, his grandpa face blissful. "If only the other Apocalypses were as useful as you."

Sparkles growled, backing away. He glared at the adult children, his metal hackles raised.

The adult-children clustered close to the woman, crying out with fear. Zeke flinched as weirdly downsized feet stomped all around his face.

"Shush, you mutt. You're scaring them," the woman said. She wrapped her arms around the strange child-sized beings and tossed a fierce glare in Sparkles' direction.

Sparkles' mechanical growl faded in volume, but he kept his head lowered and his hackles high.

Zeke watched Sparkles. *His Transform can't last forever. It should be bound to the same rules that Domi and I live by. The longer he stays in that form, the longer we'll have once he drops that form. So long as this woman doesn't start seriously attacking me, this situation is in my advantage.*

He checked his own Transform timer.

0:24 until Transform.

Okay. Twenty-four seconds. That's...a small eternity in combat, but...as long as I keep this woman chatting, it's not that bad. He twisted his head, trying to see the woman stepping on him.

They met eyes, the woman looking down on him, him desperately looking up. The woman shivered, hugging her arms around herself. "That look! I *live* for that look!"

Zeke shivered, though in disgust, not delight. *This woman*

has a problem. At least her Apocalypse isn't that hard to guess. Domi-
natrix, subtype: Teacher, or something to that effect.

Poor Domi, she's been over-dommed.

Ice cream slowly soaking into his clothes, Zeke shifted. He pushed his palms against the ground and tried to rise again, only to find himself pinned by her high-heeled shoes. *I could probably climb out from under her with Allen's STR, but better to keep that for surprise once we actually start fighting. Now isn't the time. She isn't threatening my life, after all, just stepping on me for... pleasure? Heck if I know.*

"Domi!" he shouted.

The woman startled. A moment later, realization passed over her face. She pointed behind her. "Oh, your friend? Ha. She's been taken care of by Karrie. You can forget about her."

Zeke's heart leaped. *Hold on, what? I thought Domi was just being quiet. Is she actually—* "Domi! Domi, come on!"

A low groan answered him.

He let out a sigh of relief. *Okay. She's alive. We can figure out the rest later. Once we get out of this shit situation.* He glared up at the woman over him. "Why are you here?"

She smiled, tracing her lower lip with a finger. "Isn't it obvious? We're here to crush you filthy little apocalypses under our toes like the bad boys you are."

God. Talking to her is...yikes. Zeke shifted a little, getting his arms under him. "We don't have to fight. We all have the same goals."

The woman chuckled mysteriously.

She thinks they have a higher goal of some sort, then. Interesting. "Who are you? At least give me a name!"

"Oh? You can call me...Mommy," the woman said, looking at him from under long lashes.

I will not be doing that. "That's not a name."

"It is for you, baby."

"Yikes."

Shaking her head, the woman snapped her fingers. "Someone's being a *bad boy*. Students, what happens to bad boys?"

The adult-children all raised their hands.

She smiled indulgently and gestured. "Go on."

As one, they opened their mouths. A chorus of voices responded, "They get punished!"

"That's right! What good little students you are," the woman praised them, her voice ooey-gooey. The adult-children all but vibrated with excitement where they stood.

She lifted her hand to the sky. A black leather whip materialized in her hand.

All the strange little beings cried out in excitement.

I've gotta stop calling her 'the woman.' Er...Teacher. I'm going to call her Teacher. It's playing into her delusions, but whatever. I'm not a mental health professional.

Teacher made a gentle shooing gesture with her hand. All the little students ran off, leaving her and Zeke alone in the ice cream snow. She raised the whip high.

"Wait, wait! Teacher, wait!" Zeke shouted.

"Hmm?" Teacher looked down at him. Her cat-eye mascara glistened in the low light.

"Please, hold on. I'm not a bad boy!" he said.

Behind him, Domi groaned in pain.

"Oh? Are you going to prove it?" Teacher asked.

Zeke hesitated, his brow furrowing with thought. "I..."

"Yes...?"

0:01 until Transform
0:00 until Transform
Transform Available!
Allen has shared his STR! 10 > 55 STR

Zeke grinned. He pushed up with all his and Allen's might as armor crawled over his body. "Hey, Teacher. Why don't you leave those kids alone?"

29
LEAVE THOSE KIDS ALONE

Zeke shoved up. Armor closed over his back, and his hand- and foot-mouths opened. Immediately, delicious, creamy-sweet ice cream flowed into him, strengthening him. Teacher fought against his rise, pushing down. Zeke pushed harder, using all of Allen's STR. "Let me up!"

Teacher stumbled backward. The tension on his back vanished, and Zeke jumped to his feet, shoving her even farther back as he did. Her stiletto heels slipped on the ice and ice cream. She snapped her whip out, but off-balance as she was, it barely smarted on Zeke's armor.

Zeke snatched her whip out of the air before she could fully retract it. He yanked it toward him.

Teacher staggered forward a step, then caught her balance and released the whip. Zeke was left with a whip, while Teacher was back on her feet.

Mmm. Not great.

"Students! Grab that man!" Teacher shouted.

The adult children ran at him. Zeke fled, running backward. He took a long look at Teacher as he did.

She wore a corseted leather top with a built-in bra, which barely contained an overflowing bosom. Long silk ties flowed on the wind behind her. A leather pencil miniskirt and thigh-high leather boots finished the black leather ensemble. Her hair was tied up in a tight bun with two black chopsticks holding it in place. Half-moon glasses with a black diamond-adorned eyeglass chain perched atop her nose. She noticed him looking and raised her brows, posing her bare arms seductively.

Zeke blinked. "Are you cold?"

"Are you gay?" Teacher asked, looking at him over the top of her glasses. She patted her very exposed chest for him, as if he hadn't noticed.

"That's incredibly inappropriate," Zeke pointed out. *Look, I enjoy a nice pair of...I enjoy the female body as much as the next guy, but it's below freezing out here, and we're surrounded by piles of ice cream. It's a valid question.*

Teacher lifted her hand, and a fresh leather whip dropped into her palm. "Do I look appropriate?"

Zeke winced. *No, I gotta say, no...yeah, this person was not actually a teacher. Hot take of the century, I know, but...*

He looked at Sparkles. The dog looked between him and Teacher, uncertain. He offered his hand to the poodle. "Do you really want this person to rule over you? Sparkles, you can come to our side. You don't have to fight for these assholes."

"Kill him. Go on." Teacher cracked her whip.

Sparkles hesitated, then lowered his head to Zeke. He bobbed his head up and down.

Sparkles is willing to Subordinate to you.

"Accepted!" Zeke shouted. He nodded at Sparkles. "Go find Domi! Now!"

Sparkles barked. He charged at Teacher.

Teacher whipped around to face him. Pursing her lips, she murmured, "*Bad* dog."

"God," Zeke muttered to himself. A disgusted shiver crawled over his skin.

Her whip snapped toward Sparkles. Sparkles leaped forward, sprinting past her. The whip dented his metal skin, but he ran by, uninjured. Karrie whipped around to face him. She opened her mouth. Nothing came out, but Sparkles' whole body vibrated. He bared his teeth, stepping back.

"Push through!" Zeke shouted.

Sparkles barked, silently. He leaped at Karrie and bore her to the ground. Her body flopped around like a ragdoll, but she didn't show any visible sign of taking damage.

I wonder if that's what it's like, if your Concept devours you, Zeke wondered, gazing at Karrie's unfeeling body. *Was there much of the girl left when I talked to her? She seemed so normal, but this...*

A whip smacked him across the face. He stumbled, startled, and looked at Teacher. She posed, sticking out her hip, giving him bedroom eyes as she pushed back her bangs. "Keep all your attention on me, hmmm?"

"Are you a fucking porn tape come to life, or something?" Zeke asked her, unable to process it. *Who the fuck does this kind of shit in a fight? Surely no real human. Right? She can't be a real human being.*

"Wouldn't *you* like to know."

"I would. I would, actually." Zeke backed away, wary of the students milling about. They gave him strange looks, their faces all the same. *How much autonomy do those things have? Can they attack on their own?*

She gave him a simpering smile and charged. At the same instant, all the students lunged for Zeke. They grabbed his arms. He ripped free, only to find more grabbing onto his legs, pinning him down.

The corset materialized in front of him, all spilling out. He lunged his head back, scared of what affect it might have to touch her in such a touchable place. *If she is a porn tape come to life, being attracted to her might be dangerous. Argh—she's a cognitohazard, isn't she? Like the Cartoon Apocalypse, or the Coffee Apocalypse to some extent. Gotta be.*

"Hmm? You don't wanna touch?" Teacher asked, wiggling seductively.

Zeke tore free of the students and leaped back again. *Yeah. As much as she's offering it? Gotta be avoided.* He thrust a hand at her and activated **Ranged Devour.**

A bite tore into her side. Rather than blood rushing out, though, doughy flesh gave way to more doughy flesh. *No, not flesh at all. Plastic. She's—* Zeke bit back the urge to vomit. He stuck his tongue out and worked his jaw, still feeling the chunk in his mouth. *Fucking hell, she's a doll! A fucking doll...er, literally. Someone was into Teachers, and it's incredibly uncomfortable.*

Teacher looked down on him and harrumphed. "Someone's getting rough. Naughty boys need to be taught a lesson."

Zeke shivered. He straightened, then pointed at Teacher. "I'm going to put you down. For the good of the whole damn world."

She smiled slowly at him, then licked her whip. "Make me, big boy."

"Yikes." Zeke charged at her, not wanting to trade another single word with her. *Every single sentence she says hurts my soul. Let's get this fight over with, so I can never think about it ever again.*

30
NEVER THINK ABOUT IT AGAIN

Zeke drew back his fist and punched, careful to make sure his fist landed squarely on Teacher's skimpy corset. She let out a high-pitched, "*Ahn!*" and stumbled backward. He chased after her, not willing to let her go.

Hands wrapped around his ankles. The students piled on, pulling him back, slowing him down. Teacher climbed back to her feet and snapped her whip, then brought it down on Zeke. His armor cracked. Pain trembled through his body, along with something else, something that didn't feel entirely his.

"You're feeling it, aren't you? Love it! Love me! Become one of my lovely students!" Teacher crooned.

"This battle is the worst cognitohazard I've faced yet," Zeke growled. He glared at the students, then activated **Absorb**. *I can't afford to hold back. I can't afford to not attack the students. They might be mind-controlled by Teacher, but they're gone. They've been fully transformed to her underlings. They can never be human again.*

The students screeched. They still clung to him, but their bodies withered up, power draining out of them and into Zeke.

"You filth!" Teacher shouted. Her whip lashed Zeke over and over.

"Shut up!" Zeke kicked the students away and turned his head toward Teacher. Once more, he called on **Ranged Devour**. Another chunk vanished from Teacher's body. He tried to spit it out, but **Ranged Devour** only went one way. Zeke choked, barely forcing it down.

"Mmm, swallow it—"

He jabbed a finger at Teacher. "Don't you dare finish that sentence."

She licked her lips lasciviously.

Zeke looked away. Under his breath, he spat, "Fuck."

A howl. From behind Teacher, a shadowy form lunged. A fireball burst out, throwing Teacher toward Zeke.

"I'm fucking back, let's fucking gooooooooo!" Domi shouted.

"Domi!" Zeke called, relief loud in his voice.

"The fuck is this thing?" Domi asked, climbing up to her feet and emerging from behind Teacher.

"A sex doll, I think," Zeke told her.

"Yikes."

"No kidding. This whole battle has been a big yikes."

Teacher simpered at them. "Are you two talking behind my back? In *my* classroom? That's a pun-ish-ment."

Domi's eyes widened. She grimaced. "Yeah, gotta agree. Big yikes. Though...who the fuck had a dominatrix sex doll? I mean, conceptually, how does that work?"

"That's the part you're stuck on?" Zeke asked.

"I'm stuck on the whole thing, to be honest." She stepped forward.

"Whoa, careful. I have Absorb up," Zeke warned her.

Domi nodded.

Teacher spun, lashing them with her whip. "Both of you, are you ignoring me? Tsk!"

Crying out, her students lunged toward Domi. Domi leaped back, firing explosions at them. Chunks burst from their bodies, but it was only plastic that fell to the ground.

Zeke grimaced. *As I thought. They're gone, too. Nothing human left of them.*

While Domi held down the mobs, he charged Teacher herself. Her whip smashed into his face, but this time, he was ready. Zeke turned his head and bit down, yanking the whip away from her for the second time. He chewed it down, swallowing the leather.

"Oooh, naughty."

Not dignifying that one with a response, Zeke continued his charge. His teeth closed around Teacher's neck, and he bit down. Plastic tore. Her head fell away. Teacher stumbled.

Teacher's voice came from her chest. "Oh dear, what a troublesome child!"

Damn. I didn't get the core. Zeke chased after her, turning his mouth toward the rest of her.

"Eat me up, daddy."

Domi grimaced in the background. Zeke shot her a long-suffering look. *I don't want this either. No one wants this.*

He tore into Teacher's plastic body. Bits of plastic went everywhere. He cut deeper and deeper, searching for a core. Nothing. Plastic, plastic, and more plastic.

"Too deep!" Teacher cried out.

"Shut up," Zeke muttered.

"You're creating so many microplastics!" Domi shouted.

Zeke flashed her a middle finger. She grinned.

At last, Zeke tore Teacher in two, tossing her legs on the ground. No core. Not within her entire body. "Where is it?"

Teacher giggled. Her voice came from one of her students. "You'll never find me."

Domi and Zeke met one another's eyes. As one, they turned on the students. Tearing, smashing, exploding, they tore apart one student after another. No core, no core, no core. No core to be found. Zeke stood at last, frustrated. "Where the hell is it?"

"I don't know. We destroyed all of them, didn't we?" Domi asked.

They turned. Plastic bodies littered the ground around them. Teacher's voice echoed all around them, ephemeral, immaterial. "You'll never find me!"

"We can hear her voice. She's nearby," Zeke commented.

"Nearby...the dog?" Domi asked.

Sparkles narrowed his eyes at her. He growled.

Zeke startled. "Karrie!"

"Karrie's a person, not a student...unless..." Domi pursed her lips.

"Unless she really did die when you blew up her face, and Teacher's been inhabiting her body since before she jumped in," Zeke replied.

They both turned, looking at Karrie's still body.

Teacher cursed. A shining, transparent orb emerged from Karrie's body and flew toward the sky.

Zeke enlarged his wings and flew after it. One flap, two. His hands closed around it, and he swallowed. Teacher's voice faded. He and Domi stood alone in an alleyway littered with plastic.

"Huh. Teacher was super dangerous, huh?" Zeke asked.

"How do you mean?" Domi asked.

Zeke nodded. "When she was attacking as Karrie, she utilized Karrie's skills...or at least, skills that I'd assume a Quiet Apocalypse would have. She must have had the power to mimic other Apocalypses' skills."

"Huh. Yeah, I guess," Domi allowed, nodding.

Zeke turned his eyes to the System. *So, show me those skills! I want a mimic skill. If I can copy more of Ryan's skills, that's to everyone's advantage, but most of all, mine.*

Congratulations! You've defeated the Teacher Apocalypse!

Is that what we're calling her? Zeke wondered, cocking a brow.

Level + 2.32

Please choose your skills.

Skills
Whip Materialization
Student Domination
Imbue Pleasure
Empathy
Enhance Sensations

Zeke grimaced. *Is Empathy the skill that let her copy skills?*

Yes.

Then I'll take that, and nothing else. Thanks.

Confirm: Refusing other two choices of skills?

Confirm.

The System messages faded away, leaving Zeke and Domi back in the alleyway. Sparkles walked up beside them in his normal dog mode, wagging his stubby tail. He barked.

"Oh, right. Domi, this is Sparkles. He's a Subordinate now, too."

Domi looked at Sparkles, then shrugged. "I might lose to the lizard, but at least I'm higher rank than the dog."

31
CONFIRMED

"Well, that confirms it, though," Zeke said, putting his hands on his hips.

"Confirms what?" Domi asked.

He nodded. "That Scouting Apocalypse wasn't all talk. The Apocalypse Coalition really did send people to snipe the Ice Cream Apocalypse from us."

"Yeah, guess so." Domi looked at the alley, littered with plastic bodies. "And we kinda sniped two Apocalypses out from under them, huh?"

"Three. Karrie, too," Zeke pointed out.

"Damn." Domi shook her head, then glanced at Zeke and grinned. "Well, even if they get the Ice Cream Apocalypse, we've already come out ahead, huh?"

"Yeah...yeah. Unless they have so many Apocalypses on their side that they won't even notice the loss of three members," Zeke muttered, half to himself.

Domi's smile wilted. "Jeez. Let me enjoy my victory for a minute."

"Sorry. It's just..." Zeke grimaced. "It feels like we were hardly opposed, let alone that we faced the same kind of danger we usually do fighting single Apocalypses. If they wanted to get rid of the trash..."

"We might've just taken it out for them, huh," Domi finished his thought.

"Yeah. Was this them cutting their dead weight? None of these Apocalypses put up a big fight. I mean, Karrie basically went down in one hit. It was a stealth hit, but still..." Zeke grimaced again. He shook his head. "I have a bad feeling. That's all. A bad feeling."

Domi nodded. "Trust your gut, man. Yeah. I agree. It's not a good warm-fuzzy feeling I got from killing these guys, either. If the Coalition cared about them, they wouldn't have been so easy to kill. I mean, maybe the Coalition just doesn't care, but yeah. It's not a good feeling."

Zeke sighed. "It's good to kill some foot soldiers, I guess, but damn. If they're trying to take us down, it's not a bad idea to start by draining our energy."

Domi looked at him. "You think he was lying? The Scouting Apocalypse."

"Lying about what? Going after the Ice Cream Apocalypse?"

"And instead, they're actually trying to draw us out and kill us. They've already done a good job of separating us. I mean, I have no idea where Erica went, and let's not even talk about Olivia and Zel."

"Other-Zeke, until he agrees to it."

"Eh."

Zeke sighed. "No, I get it, though. I see what you're saying. Separating us, wearing us down by sending their low-rank members...if they're trying to go after us, they're doing a good job of it. Let's keep our guards up."

Domi nodded.

Zeke tilted his head, considering. "Though, upside, if it is the case, there's probably an Apocalypse who's meant to take us out. And that Apocalypse is probably someone who matters for the Coalition."

"True. Well, let's keep moving, right? Don't wanna stand still too long. They'll send more trash to hunt us down." Domi gestured him on.

"Right. Let's...put this all behind us. And never think about it again," Zeke said firmly.

They walked on, out of the street. Coming out of the narrow road between two tall buildings, both Zeke and Domi looked at the horizon again. Zeke pursed his lips, and Domi squinted.

"So, uh...any ideas?" Zeke asked at last.

Domi shrugged. "My best bet was the ice cream parlor, but that wasn't it. No idea where it is. If it's hiding..."

They both turned, taking in all the apartments and office buildings around them.

"We've got a lot of ground to cover," Zeke said, letting out a sigh.

"Should we split up?" Domi suggested.

The two of them exchanged a glance. Domi was the first to giggle, and Zeke immediately broke when she started laughing.

"Yeah, let's split up. That's a good idea. When our party's already been split to high heavens, and we still don't know where any of them went..." Zeke shook his head.

Bright pink light flashed across the sky. Both Zeke and Domi turned, looking toward the light. A giant rose bloomed in the sky, unfurling its frothy petals overhead.

"I think I just found Erica," Zeke commented.

"Ya think?" Domi muttered back.

"She's probably found the Apocalypse if she's using big moves like that," Zeke reasoned.

"Yeah, or something more dangerous than just the Ice Cream Apocalypse."

Domi and Zeke exchanged a glance, then took off running toward the giant rose.

The rose bloomed from the top of the small hill the town was built on. In a few minutes, the two of them stood at the base of an office building. High in the sky, lights flashed as fighters battled back and forth.

"They're at the top, huh?" Domi asked. She turned to Zeke and held her hands up.

Sighing quietly, Zeke hooked his arms under her armpits and enlarged his wings. Flapping once, twice, he lifted off the ground and soared toward the battle, high overhead. The office building flashed by. Dark windows blurred in a mess of dark glass and reflective polish. They passed the flags, the gargoyles, the decorative number plate commemorating the year the building was built, and then flew up over the edge of the roof. Zeke hovered there, over the battle, taking a moment to see it all from above.

Erica fought off three people, her back to a ice cream cone, but she was clearly outmatched. Blood stained her clothes, ice cream splotches dripping down the bright pink fabric. Behind her, the ice cream cone lobbed scoops at her ineffectually, but the three figures she fought struck her much harder.

One, a young lady with picturesque features, stood atop a swirl of water, and lashed out with the water, pointing their trident at Erica. Another, a misshapen stone figure that wouldn't have looked out of place in a modern art gallery, twisted the concrete under Erica's feet, forcing her to keep moving. Erica bounded up onto a delicate pink flower, only for the third figure to toss a glass ball at her. The ball shattered, and the pink flower vanished. Erica fell toward the roof where a concrete spike struck at her center of gravity.

"Erica!" Zeke shouted, scared. He lifted his arm through

Domi's armpits and activated **Ranged Devour.** *Come on, get there in time!*

32
DEVOURING SPIKES

A hard sensation ached through Zeke's entire body, like biting down on rock, but then his **Ranged Devour** crunched through. He felt a lump of concrete hit his gut, though with his new, strange habits, it simply felt heavy, but satisfying. Erica dropped to the floor, grunting as her back hit the raised platform where the spike had been moments ago.

"Zeke, let's go! Operation Carpet Bomb!" Domi shouted.

"On it!" Zeke swooped down.

Domi dropped glittering orange ball after glittering orange ball on the three Apocalypses. The water-based Apocalypse swept her trident out, and the orange balls were swallowed up by the waves and extinguished. She jabbed her trident at them.

Zeke dodged, but nothing happened. He squinted at her, confused. *She clearly expected that to do something, and she doesn't look disappointed, so what happened? What have I not noticed?*

Overhead, thunder cracked. Zeke looked up. Dark clouds roiled overhead, quickly building from the soft white surface of the snowy landscape they'd been in, to the boiling, heady shape of a cumulonimbus. The clouds twisted and surged together, all condensing over the building. The denser they grew, the darker they became. Lightning crackled through the dark clouds, threatening to strike.

"Oh, shit! Put me down. I don't wanna be cooked chicken," Domi shouted.

"Is there even enough room up there?" Zeke asked, eyeing the rooftop. The whole thing was twisted and misshapen, thanks to the stone figure's efforts. The ice cream cone's half of the roof was still covered in a thick layer of ice cream, ice, and snow, and now, as rain started to pour down on them, quickly growing slicker by the moment. The glass ball throwing figure, a small humanoid of some kind that Zeke couldn't quite make out, drew back their arm and tossed another glass ball, but toward Zeke, this time.

He dodged, only for the ball to swerve in midair and chase after him. It crashed against him, exploding in a whiff of pine and peppermint. Instantly, his entire body turned heavy, and he sagged down toward the roof.

"It's a Christmas miracle!" the figure shouted, and suddenly its strange proportions made sense. Zeke stared, realizing at last. It wasn't a human at all, but a sun-worn elf lawn decoration, its brightly colored plastic faded away to almost normal human shades. The kind of plastic lawn decoration some people left up all year, too lazy to take it down, until Christmas came back around.

"Oh, good, we're landing," Domi said, relieved.

"I wouldn't be relieved yet," Zeke cautioned her.

"Take him, Elfie!" the trident-wielding woman shouted.

"Got it!" the elf replied, in a Christmas elf's trademark cheery tone. It threw out its hand, and a string of Christmas lights shot forth. They whirled through the air, shooting directly for Zeke.

He dodged, but with Domi in his arms and the weighty effect of the glass ball still live on him, he couldn't move fast enough. The Christmas lights lassoed around his neck and jerked hard, tightening in moments. He gasped for air as his airways narrowed. Ducking his wings and flying toward the elf, he managed to pick up enough slack to suck a single breath, but then the lights tightened again, and the air vanished once more.

"Zeke? What's going on?"

"I'm gonna kill..." Zeke fell silent. He dove toward the elf.

The elf grinned, continuing to reel him in. At the very last second, its eyes widened. It jumped to the side, and Zeke crashed to the roof instead, narrowly missing its plastic body.

Seconds before he landed, Domi squirmed out of his grip and bailed to the side, leaving Zeke to hit the deck alone. She turned, only to find the elf continuing to reel Zeke in, the lights steadily tightening around his neck.

"Holy shit— Hold on, Zeke!" Domi grabbed the Christmas lights by the wire. Tiny explosions rocked out in her grip, one after another, and the smell of melting plastic and hot copper filled the air. In the next, the tension on Zeke's neck vanished. The elf yanked again, and the Christmas lights flew away. Zeke gasped for air, rubbing his neck. His fingers traced the deep ligature marks from the Christmas lights, the lights' woven strand wires leaving almost braided marks behind.

"I'll take the plastic bastard," Domi volunteered.

Zeke held out his hand. "No. This is personal. I'm taking the elf down." He nodded over his shoulder at the stone figure. "You get started on Rocky over there."

Domi hesitated, then nodded. "You got it, Boss!"

I really wouldn't mind one way or another—all's fair in love and war, and all that. It's not like I really bear a plastic lawn figurine brought to life by some demented Apocalypse System a life and death grudge. Rather, compared to me trying to eat a stone figurine, and Domi busting it open with fire and bombs...well, there's a reason construction workers clear tunnels with dynamite, and not their teeth.

He glanced over his shoulder. "Erica, you good to take Fem!Poseidon?"

"You know about Fem!-ing characters?" Erica asked, shocked, and for a moment, Zeke caught a glimpse of Eric through Erica's usual haughty demeanor.

"I had a friend who was huge into fanfics," Zeke shouted back.

Erica snorted and tossed her blonde ponytail. The pink bow jiggled at the back of her head. She stomped the roof with her stiletto boot. "I can take her. I'll show her who the true femme is."

"I believe it. You got this!"

The elf giggled at Zeke. Zeke glanced down. A dozen small toys clustered around his feet, lights flashing. "Whoopsie! I messed up the toys!" the elf said and, all at once, the toys exploded.

Zeke flew back, completely off the roof. He plunged for ten, fifteen floors, then flipped around and caught the air with his wings. Beating back up toward the roof, he opened his mouth and cast **Ranged Devour** on all the ice cream he could see. *Time to give this elf the shock of its life.*

Overhead, lightning flashed. The storm clouds churned. Water droplets as big as a child's fist beat at them, smashing into Zeke and wetting his wings. Even with the natural oil of a pigeon to help protect his wings from the rain, he could feel them growing less effective. *I have to be careful about using my wings in this rain. Next time I get blasted off the building, it might not be as easy to catch myself.*

He swooped down toward the roof and stored his wings, completely deactivating **Modest Gigantism** to furl them safely in other his shirt, where they would stay as dry as they possibly could.

The elf immediately rushed him, not giving him a single second to breathe. Zeke lifted his foot and kicked them back. The hollow plastic elf went tumbling over the roof, then bounced back to its feet with a giggle, none the worse for the wear.

Damn. It is durable outdoor plastic, after all. A few kicks aren't going to kill it. I need something else. Something to...melt it, or...

Manipulate Flame caught his eye, but he dismissed it, his gaze instead resting on a few other skills in the list. A smile crawled over Zeke's face. *Yes. Those skills ought to work to kill a stupid-ass plastic elf—or at least injure it enough that I can steal its core.* He lifted his hands and used **Ranged Devour** again, sucking in all the ice cream in reach.

"No, you don't!"

Lady Poseidon shoved Erica back and surged for the ice cream cone. The ice cream cone let out a shrill scream, and then Lady Poseidon swallowed it in one bite. She looked down at Zeke, a haughty smile on her face that was somewhat undone by the ice cream smeared all over her lips and cheeks. "Out-played at your own game!"

Zeke wrinkled his nose. *They took the Ice Cream Apocalypse down. Dammit. Oh well.* He lifted his hand and pointed **Ranged Devour** at Lady Poseidon.

Her eyes widened. At the very last second, she dodged. Zeke's **Ranged Devour** took a chunk out of the water flowing around her instead. He licked his lips. *Ugh, salty and unclean. That's gotta be ocean water or river water. Yuck. I hope I don't get a disease from swallowing it.*

"Y-you...you took my water! Where did you put it? Why can't I feel it anymore?" Lady Poseidon screamed, trembling. She charged at Zeke. "We're the Three Elementalists. We control the air, the sea, the earth. You aren't allowed to take the water from me!"

Erica stepped in her path and delivered a swift smack to the side of Lady Poseidon's face with her staff, leaving a heart-shaped imprint on Lady Poseidon's cheek. "You dare look away from me? Our battle had barely begun!"

Are you a magical girl, or a shounen final boss? Zeke wondered, looking at Erica. A second later, he coughed. *Wait, hold on. Elementalists? I get water and stone, but...* He looked at the elf. "You're air...?"

The elf giggled in response and tossed an ornament at him. Zeke dodged. The glass ball shattered on the ground behind him, releasing a whiff of cranberry and spice.

"Oh. I guess...? In the way that air fresheners control the air, I guess you can be considered to control air...?"

"You doubt Christmas?" the elf gasped, terror on its face.

"Uh, what?" Zeke asked, lost.

"Don't you dare doubt Christmas! Or else he'll come!"

Overhead, in the churning storm, lights flashed. Zeke looked up, expecting lightning, but instead found a warm red light at the front of a set of deer figures, all of them hooked up to a large red sleigh that was itself lined with warm red lights.

Zeke swallowed. *There's no way. Right?*

33
HO HO HO

The figure circled overhead, then burst down toward the rooftop, and for the first time, Zeke got a good look at it. Faded brown plastic. Reins made of twine. A big plastic sleigh, with a poorly carved, still figurine atop it, rosy cheeks, white beard, red suit and all. He laughed aloud, unable to stop himself. "Santa Claus?"

"You've made him angry. You're going to be on the naughty list!" the elf shouted at Zeke, pointing its finger at him.

"Oh, dear lord," Zeke muttered under his breath.

"I think you mean, oh, deer lord," Domi shot back as she dodged away from a set of stalagmites thrusting toward her feet.

"Does Santa count as a deer lord?"

"He controls deer, doesn't he? Counts to me," Domi said with a shrug. The stone figure swung, driving her away from Zeke. She shouted something else, but he couldn't hear it over the pounding rain and swirling wind.

Zeke put a hand to his stomach, checking his tank. *Almost there...but I could use a little more fuel.*

Santa Claus rushed at him. Plastic hooves pounded the air.

The Santa figure stared to the left, smiling at no one, clearly the kind of plastic figure that was meant to be displayed broadside in front of a house.

Here goes nothing. Zeke planted his feet and raised his hands, opening his mouth at the same time. He activated **Ranged Devour** with all his might, using it on all the mouths he had, even his foot mouths.

The first reindeer, the one with the lit-up red nose, closed in on Zeke. Despite its adorable, cartoonish, baby-deer like proportions, it let out a vicious howl and lowered its baby deer antlers at him.

Zeke opened his mouth. *Hold.* The baby deer surged closer. It reached the edge of the rooftop, and its hooves began striking concrete instead. *Hold.* The other deer also reached the rooftop. The red-nosed reindeer tossed its head, shaking the bell-clad reins. A threatening snort emerged from its nostrils, paired with the clanging of the bells. *Hold...* The Santa figure turned its head, twisting the plastic its body had been carved from. Its body remained posed in a waving-to-the-left form, but its head glared directly at Zeke, its carved twinkling eyes twinkling now with hatred.

Now! He unleased **Ranged Devour,** pointing it all at the first deer. The deer didn't even have time to flinch. It vanished, reappearing in Zeke's stomach.

The two deer behind it balked. Behind them, the two remaining deer continued to run. The two sets of plastic deer ran into one another with a hollow plastic barrel *thump,* and Zeke raised his hands again.

[Devour]

The second set of deer vanished. The third set of deer charged Zeke, not giving up. They hauled the bulk of the sled all on their own, hurtling the weight of the large structure toward Zeke with all their might.

[Devour]

The final set of deer vanished, but too late. The bulk of the sled slid toward Zeke, fishtailing wildly on the ice cream, snow, ice, and rain-slicked rooftop. Zeke threw himself to the side, and the sled hurtled toward the edge of the building. As it slid past, the Santa kept turning its head to glare at Zeke with those hateful eyes. The plastic of its neck twisted and twisted, its neck rising out of its body from the length of the spin, as he turned his neck almost three-sixty-degrees to keep watching Zeke, even as his sled flew toward the building's edge.

Before it could fall off, Zeke threw his hands out again.

[Devour]

The back half of the sled, including the Santa figurine, vanished. His stomach bulged. Zeke patted it, finally satisfied. *Now it's time to take on that elf.*

"You killed Santa Claus? You're not allowed to kill Santa Claus!" The elf charged Zeke. Glass ornaments full of red and green gas shattered all around him, filling the air with the dense scents of Christmas. Despite himself, Zeke found himself relaxing a little, drawn into memories of Christmases past.

The elf leaped at him and drew back its fist. A sharp blow to his jaw jolted Zeke back to reality. *This must be one of the elf's powers! Shit. I can't get so easily swayed by a few glass bottles of air freshener!*

He glanced at the remaining bits of colored gas, then swirled his hand.

[Manipulate Aerosols]

The red and green swirled together into a sort of candy cane stripe. He wafted his hand again, and they flew toward the elf.

The elf startled. "No! Not the Gas of Christmas Past!"

The—is that an attempt to make a pun of 'Ghost of Christmas Past?' Jeez. Yeah, I was happier not knowing what this move was called.

The gas surrounded the elf. The elf tensed, but nothing happened.

Obviously. You aren't a living creature. You don't breathe.

Though... Wait. Why would a plastic elf think it could breathe? Why does it know about Christmas? It should just be a thoughtless lawn ornament. Did it somehow absorb other people's Christmas memories?

Zeke looked at it, then sighed, shaking his head. *Yeah...actually, yeah. That sounds like the kind of useless ability a Christmas Elf Apocalypse would get. It probably was given it in the skill store that everyone but me has access to. And then from there, if it could suck people's memories...*

He closed in on the elf. His hand-mouth latched onto its face and tore a chunk out of the plastic. He reached inside, searching for the elf's core.

"No!" the elf screamed. Its flimsy plastic shell distorted, wrapping around Zeke's arm. Spikes burst out from the inside of its body and drove into Zeke. "No! You won't! I won't let you destroy Christmas!"

"I'm not destroying Christmas, I'm just destroying you," Zeke said evenly. For the first time in a long time, he activated **Biogenerator.**

The material in his stomach burned down but, in return, electricity flickered through his body. He slapped his other arm on the elf.

[Electrify]

Electricity coursed from both his arms into the elf's plastic body. The elf screamed and thrashed, though Zeke knew its plastic body could feel no pain. It melted, unable to maintain its form under the force of that much electricity. The air filled with the stench of melting plastic.

As it melted, it sloughed off Zeke's arm. A single glass ornament remained, which shattered under the force of a single bolt of electricity to reveal its core. Zeke snatched it up and swallowed it, all in one go.

**Defeated: Elf Ornament Apocalypse
Levels deferred until end of battle.**

"What a messy Apocalypse," Zeke muttered. He stretched. *Still, unlike Teacher, or Sparkles, or the Quiet Apocalypse, it didn't seem like a throwaway fighter. That disgusting thing was one of their serious battlers. Which means, even though we lost the Ice Cream Apocalypse to the Apocalypse Coalition, we're still doing serious damage.*

He turned, facing Lady Poseidon and the stone figure. *And if we can take down these two, I bet we can do even more damage.*

He strode forward.

Light flashed. Zeke's entire field of vision went white. Thunder cracked out, so loud his ears seemed to burst. Fierce pain burst through his body, and electricity shimmered through every cell of his being. For a second, he stood there, stunned, and then a single thought crawled through his mind.

Holy shit, I got struck by lightning.

34
LIGHTNING STRUCK

E ven as the thought hit him, Zeke activated **Grid.** The skill, which he'd only used a few times, allowed him to connect to a greater source of electricity and manipulate that electricity. Use it as power, or strength, or continue using it as electricity, the choice was his; the skill simply allowed him to harness the greater source of electricity. It was meant for connecting to a grid of some sort, a city's power network, perhaps, but now he used it to tap into the power of the lightning.

The pain faded. In its place, strength simmered in Zeke, roiling back and forth with every beat of his heart. So much strength that his body trembled, struggling to contain it. Even standing there, as the thunder faded, Zeke knew he couldn't hold on to this energy for long. Either he spent it on something, or he died.

"Zeke!" Domi shouted.

Across the way, Erica leaped at Lady Poseidon.

Lady Poseidon parried Erica's magical staff with her trident and laughed. "Taste the wrath of the skies!"

Zeke glanced at her, then the stone figurine. In a split

second, he made his decision. *Human flesh versus hard stone. The answer is obvious.*

He turned, using Electrify to discharge the full power of the lightning at the stone figure.

The figure jolted. A big chunk of stone blasted off its side. It staggered, patting at the place where the stone had been.

Lady Poseidon was the one who sent the lightning at me in the first place. While it's true that she's more aligned with water than lightning, I'm not stupid enough to let her little claim of being the 'three elementals' and her being 'water' fool me. First off, that claim was shaky; second off, it's a great way to pretend like your power is all one thing, when in fact it crosses several domains. Although most Apocalypses aren't like me and can't use skills from a wild variety of different domains, I don't know what her domain is. It could be Storm. It could be River. It could be Ocean. Or it could be Water. If it's Storm, River, or Ocean, I could easily see her bargaining the System for a lightning channeling skill.

If she has some kind of lightning channeling skill, then she could easily ignore any lightning I threw at her—or, in the worst case, redirect it to Erica or Domi, neither of whom can handle a lightning strike the way I can.

Again, it's possible I'm wrong. After all, she didn't seem to consciously call the lightning to strike me. It could just be that she can use some sort of water-manipulation power to condense water in the pattern that forms a cumulonimbus cloud, and from there, what happens, happens. But, on the off-chance I'm right...I'd rather hit the combatant I'm sure *doesn't have a skill to redirect lightning strikes. It's an easy choice, any day.*

"Nice hit, Zeke!" Domi cheered. She fired a dozen small orange balls into the gap in the figure's side. From the opening Zeke had caused, she quickly widened the gap to a deep hole.

The figure screamed in rage. It rushed Domi.

Zeke pressed his toe on the ground. Crystals burst up under

the figure's feet. It didn't feel the pain, but then, it didn't expect the ground to suddenly change under it, either. It toppled to the ground, landing with a heavy thump.

"Ha. You're not the only one who controls the earth," Zeke crowed. He kept his toe to the ground, arcing the crystals toward Lady Poseidon.

Lady Poseidon, seeing her fellow Apocalypse hit the ground, jumped up into the air. Water swirled underneath her, jetting between her and the roof, so her feet never touched the ground. The crystals shot up into the water, but even as they reached toward her, she flew farther into the air.

Zeke grimaced. *Yeah, that makes sense. If she's pushing off the ground in the first place to 'fly' with her water, then if I add more material to the ground, it's just going to push her up farther into the air. It's basic physics.*

Oh well. Win some, lose some.

Lady Poseidon turned toward Zeke. "You dare interfere with our holy battle?"

"Holy?" Zeke asked. He squinted at her. "Wait, hold on. I've been calling you Lady Poseidon in my head this whole time. Are you actually the Lady Poseidon Apocalypse?"

"*Lady?* Lady! I am the Holy Poseidon Apocalypse!" she declared, slamming her trident against the roof.

"Right..." Zeke said, raising his brows at her. He cleared his throat.

"What?"

He pointed at her. "Were you already crazy before the Apocalypses kicked off, or is your mind that corrupted by your concept that you think you're actually a goddess...god?"

Lady Poseidon screamed in rage and lurched toward Zeke.

She didn't make it two steps before a pink stiletto intercepted her right on the cheekbone. The force of Erica's kick sent her spinning sideways, toward the edge of the roof. She reached out, grabbing the floor with her water, and landed in a splash in a puddle half of her making, and half a consequence of the driving rain.

"You seem to have forgotten someone," Erica said primly. A parasol followed along, floating at Erica's shoulder, and kept her hair and the upper half of her costume perfectly pink and dry. She looked down at Lady Poseidon and harrumphed. "Someone doesn't understand the power of love or friendship at all."

"You're calling *me* crazy?" Lady Poseidon spluttered, gesturing at Erica as she climbed back to her feet.

Zeke shrugged. "Erica's just a weeaboo roleplay enthusiast. Nothing wrong with that. You're the delusional one who thinks you're an actual god."

"The *incarnation* of a god! And you have brought that god's wrath down upon you!" Lady Poseidon shouted. She pointed her trident at Zeke, and all the water that had collected on the rooftop jumped up and whirled into a waterspout. It arced toward him.

"You know, I grew up in Florida. I saw my fair share of waterspouts as a kid," Zeke said. He planted his feet, standing his ground, and eyed the waterspout as it whirled toward him.

"So, you know to fear them?" Lady Poseidon asked, her eyes glittering.

"Nah. We used to count the number of waterspouts from the beach. I think I saw eight, once. Eight at one time!" He turned his head and bit down on the waterspout. An outsized chunk of the spout vanished, a section of the waterspout about as large as his body taken away by one **Devour**. Water whirled into his stomach. He patted it for a second, waiting for the water to settle.

"Hydrate or Diedrate," Domi commented, grinning.

"You said it, sister," Zeke shot back.

Lady Poseidon went pale again. "My water. What did you do with it?"

"I ate it."

She shook her head. "If you ate it, I could still control it. I can control my water from anywhere! Once it's mine, it's always mine. But..."

"But?" Zeke asked. Real curiosity welled up in him.

"But it's not inside you. It's not anywhere. You ate that water...and it's gone. It's as if you deleted it from the world."

Zeke blinked. He looked down at his stomach. *I did just eat a me-sized piece of the waterspout. There's no way that much water fits inside my belly, not on top of the seven reindeer, sled, and Santa I just ate.*

She has a good point. When I eat something, where does it go?

When I wasn't eating much, I just assumed it went inside me. For a long time, now, I've been thinking that I eat it, and it lands in my stomach. I sense it as though it's in my stomach. But come to think of it, I don't shit it out. I never see the things I eat come out the other end. Sure, my poop is strange, and it sometimes has bits of whatever weird thing I ate inside it, but...but it's a normal amount of poop. It's not the seventy-plus-pound-log-of-plastic it should be. I should be getting absolutely devastated by my shits but, instead... instead, they're normal.

It doesn't go inside me. It goes somewhere else. My stomach feeling full is just...it's something the System is manually replicating, isn't it? A false sensation I'm not actually feeling, just a fake copy sensation, created by the System.

Is that why I'm hungry all the time? Does nothing I eat ever reach my actual body? Or maybe it does...since I still poop and stuff —but at a miniscule ratio.

It's not that I need an insane amount of energy to feed myself. My body itself still takes the same amount of food as always. It's just that the System is leeching it off. Stealing it away. I only get a thousandth, maybe a millionth, of the calories and energy I eat.

But if that's the case... A cold sensation ran down Zeke's spine. He shivered. *Where's the rest of the energy going?*

"Give my water back!" Lady Poseidon howled. She charged Zeke, her trident held out in front of her. Zeke stepped to the side, barely dodging, and delivered a blow to her back. The water caught his fist and deflected it, without any visible effort on Lady Poseidon's part.

"Finally, it's all charged up. Zeke, duck!" Erica shouted.

Zeke hit the deck.

A pink beam seared over his head, slamming into Lady Poseidon. The heat of the beam burned Zeke's back, but it hit Lady Poseidon even worse. She screamed in horror and pain as the water shield she'd created for herself boiled steadily away.

"Give it back! Give me back my water!"

The rain pounded down. More and more rain poured from the heavens, as if the sky was taking the place of Lady Poseidon's tears. The water on the roof jumped up again, but there was only a little left, and even with the rain lashing the roof, most of it fell away. A knee-height wave struck Erica, making her stumble, and swept over Zeke, but it barely moved either of them.

"I am Poseidon! Mortals, tremble!" Lady Poseidon shouted. She tried to dodge Erica's beam, but Erica tracked her, keeping the magical staff trained on her with the pinpoint, head-clicking accuracy of a long-time first person shooter player.

Roaring, she charged Erica, her trident held out before her. Erica stood steady, keeping her beam on Erica. The trident's barbed tips cut toward Erica's gut.

And then Lady Poseidon tripped.

"Whoopsie," Zeke said, retracting his leg from where he lay

on the floor. "I guess us 'mere mortals' are strong enough to take down a fake god like you. Who knew?"

"I'll curse you! I'll—"

"The flower of friendship blooms!" Erica intoned.

A green shoot burst up from the floor. It pierced through the underside of Lady Poseidon's jaw and shot out the top of her skull. Lady Poseidon screamed, as a lovely lily erupted into bloom over her bloodied head.

Erica let out an exhausted breath. She lifted her stiletto-clad foot and brought the slender heel down on Lady Poseidon's head, driving her skull into concrete one final time. "That's enough from you."

Zeke's eyes widened. He looked at the gruesome flower, then up at Erica. *Yeah, let's just call that another friendly reminder to not piss Erica off.*

Erica walked to his side and offered him her hand. Zeke climbed to his feet, and together, they faced Domi and the stone figure. "Only one left to go," she said.

Overhead, the storm cloud dissipated. The cold, too, faded away. Warm sunlight filled the air, slowly melting the ice cream that covered the town. The friendly drip-drip of melting icicles and the creaking crack of snow panels preparing to fall filled the air.

Zeke nodded. "Let's finish this battle together."

35
THE FINAL ELEMENTALIST

Zeke and Erica spread out, each of them taking an opposite corner without exchanging a word. Between the two of them, Domi battled the stone figure. She hovered over the rooftop, out of the range of its ground-bound attacks and hammered it with explosions. The stone figure, on the other hand, endured the brunt of Domi's explosions, its polished, hard stone surface deflecting most of the damage. Domi chipped off pieces of it, one at a time, but it was a long, slow battle. She panted, near exhaustion. Between her and the somewhat ragged stone figure, it wasn't clear who would win the battle of attrition.

But that was before Erica and Zeke jumped in.

Erica whirled in first, in a swirl of pink petals and a swell of upbeat pop music that came from nowhere and everywhere. Mid-twirl, she folded her umbrella and drew it back. A flick of her wrist, and the umbrella's handle twisted off the umbrella itself. A slender, shining blade appeared from the heart of the frilly parasol. She lashed out, cutting into the stone figure.

A slender slash opened up in its side. Zeke stared. *That sword can cut stone?*

The figure glanced at Erica, then reached down and tossed a stone at her. A pink flower materialized between Erica and the figure, blocking the stone, but the force of the stone wilted the flower away in the next moment. The shield fell, and Erica danced back as another stone swung at her.

It's distracted. That's my cue. Zeke rushed in from the other side. Once again, he activated **Crystal Burst.** The figure started to tip over, then whirled to face Zeke. It lifted its foot and smashed it down on the crystals, shattering them before they could finish growing. It scooped up a handful of roof with one hand and tossed it at Zeke.

Zeke dodged. He glanced up. "Allen, we still sharing STR?"

Subordinate Allen is still sharing his STR.

"Great. Then here we go!"

Zeke charged in, darting directly toward the stone figure. The stone figure reached out to grab him, only for an explosion to blast its face. Distracted, it turned to Domi.

"It seems to aggro to the last thing it notices attacking it. I'll distract it, you go in!" Domi shouted.

Zeke nodded and gave her a thumbs up. Dashing left and right across the ragged mess of a floor near the figure, he closed in on it from behind as it stomped toward Domi, who continued to rain explosions down on it. Drawing back his fist, he unleashed the full force of Allen's STR into its back.

The stone figure rocked on its feet. It turned its head toward Zeke. Its arms pivoted around on its shoulders to face him and lashed out, fast as vipers.

Zeke jumped back, narrowly avoiding a stony bear hug. It lunged with him, suddenly fast, only to draw up short as he leaped over a gap in the floor.

Huh. It knows where it can and can't walk, huh? It's at least that smart. Or...is it more like...it's attuned to the floor? It might have some kind of stone sense that indicates where it can step and where it can't.

Zeke's eyes widened. *In that case...!*

He glanced up. "Domi, Erica! Distract it!"

"You got it, Boss!"

"Easily."

Erica darted in, slicing a narrow wedge out of it with her slender sword. Domi launched explosion after explosion into the gap. The stone figure lurched after them, slow at times, nimble at others, always picking a careful path across the roof that it itself had torn to pieces.

Zeke pressed his toe into the ground, activating **Crystal Burst** again. This time, though, he didn't activate it under the stone figure's feet, but merely on the roof where the stone figure had been. Satisfied at last, he picked up a stray rock and lobbed it at the figure's head. "Over here, dumbo!"

The stone figure turned. It lunged toward Zeke, its arms out.

Zeke didn't dodge. He didn't so much as flinch. Holding dead still, he watched the stone figure charge toward him. Ten steps. Five.

"Zeke!" Domi shouted.

"I've got it!" he shouted back.

Three.

Zeke slammed his foot down. The crystals he'd grown with **Crystal Burst** to cover a hole in the roof shattered at the same time that the stone figure stepped on it. The stone figure plunged into the hole. It fell up to its hip into the roof, its other leg kicking uselessly at the roof. It pushed at the edges of the hole, trying to climb back up, but its stone hands only broke away more of the roof.

"Now!" Zeke shouted. He charged in, putting his hands on either side of one of the wedges Erica had cut, and pushed outward. The stone creaked, then snapped, unable to withstand Allen's mighty STR score. Once again, the jagged, porous stone inside the sculpture was exposed.

Domi lifted her hands. "Back up, Zeke!"

Zeke jumped back just in time for a rain of small explosives to land on the jagged rock surface. Chunks and chips of rock flew everywhere, flying across the entire roof. Domi opened a crater in the figure's back, digging toward its center.

There, in the depths of the hole, the figure's core gleamed.

Zeke reached for it, but the core was too deeply planted, still firmly ensconced by stone on most sides. "Erica!"

Erica jumped forward. Without needing to be told what to do, she slashed the stone figure's back open. Neatly carved slices of stone flew every direction, and the core opened to the sky, completely exposed.

Zeke reached in and yanked it out. He swallowed it down, not daring to hesitate an instant.

Stone Statue Apocalypse: Defeated.

He frowned at that message. "Huh."

"What?" Domi asked.

"No, it's just..." He gestured at the stone figure, now sagging dead into the roof. "That was the Stone Statue Apocalypse."

"So?" Domi asked.

The roof creaked under them. All three of them jumped back, away from the corpse and the hole-ridden floor.

Zeke dropped his **Transform.** He pressed his lips together, then gave voice to his thoughts. "So, I would've expected a Stone Statue Apocalypse to be far more terrifying than a, what was it, Elf Figurine Apocalypse? Elf Ornament, that was it. But the Elf Ornament was so much worse."

"Right...yeah, I get what you're saying. You'd think a Stone

Statue Apocalypse would be able to summon other statues, or, I don't know, bring an army of statues into battle. Instead, it was just one guy. One really tough guy, to be fair, but yeah..." Domi pressed her lips together and shook her head. "Maybe it didn't invest into SPR? Put all its points into CON and never considered getting more SPR-kinds of powers?"

"It's possible, but...I mean, so far, when we've faced inanimate Apocalypses, they generally make up for their innate setback of being, you know, an inanimate object with no intelligence, by being incredibly guided by the System. The System even seems to favor them, give them opportunities and skills that humans have to bargain for." Zeke gestured at the lump of plastic behind him. "The Elf Ornament Apocalypse felt like that. If anything, it felt *too* intelligent. *Too* aware of humanity, and human conditions. And then the Stone Statue Apocalypse was just..."

Domi nodded, understanding. "A big tough lump of stone."

Zeke shrugged. "Maybe I'm overthinking it. Maybe the Stone Statue Apocalypse really did just choose to put all its points into CON and try to be the toughest thing around. I mean, I can see that being a strategy that wins a dome. And I mean, it's a Stone Statue in the first place. It probably likes the idea of getting really hard—"

"Nice," Domi interrupted him.

Zeke rolled his eyes at her. "—getting really tough and being able to take a lot of hits. I guess, if I was a statue, unable to protect myself from little grubby kid hands and getting knocked around by movers, my first priority would probably be getting really ha...difficult to damage.

"But...yeah, I don't know. It felt so weirdly unguided, compared to so many other inanimate object Apocalypses."

Erica tilted her head. "Maybe it's because you fought one that was far too guided—the Elf Ornament Apocalypse, as you called it—that the Stone Statue Apocalypse, in turn, felt less guided."

"It's possible. Plus, it's not like we've never run into inanimate Apocalypses that just kind of...did their own thing, without any apparent guidance for the System. The Crystal Ball Apocalypse, for example."

Erica blinked. "What is a Crystal Ball Apocalypse?"

"It was a giant crystal ball— Oh, so we had this big museum in our dome, and a lot of the exhibits came to life in the first round. This thing was just a big ball of crystal that was renowned for being the biggest, clearest, unflawed crystal, or something like that. And when I say big, I mean big. Probably mid-thigh on me, before the Apocalypse started," Zeke said.

"And? What kind of skills did it have?" Domi asked flatly, uninterested in the ball explanation.

"Oh, right. Sorry. Yeah, that's way more relevant, huh?" Zeke cleared his throat. "Anyway, it had Crystal Burst...er, a crystal growing skill, which you might expect, but it also gained the ability to pick up and fire guns because, I guess, it rolled over one and picked it up."

"But if you or I were to design a Crystal Ball Apocalypse, we'd give it powers of foresight and some kind of ranged magical attack, probably, maybe lightning magic or something," Domi said. She nodded, understanding. "I get what you're saying. There are inanimate object Apocalypses that just kind of...go with the flow or do their own thing. But yeah, they aren't typically dome winners."

Zeke nodded. He looked back at the hollowed-out stone statue, as it slid through the hole and thumped down onto the floor below. "But I guess a broken clock is right twice a day. You know. Monkeys, typewriters, and Shakespeare. Even acting randomly, sometimes, the stupid Stone Statue Apocalypse that just goes all-in on CON and ignores the System's suggestions is going to win."

"Right," Domi agreed.

Erica nodded.

"Unless..." Zeke started, then stopped.

"Unless?" Domi asked.

He turned and looked at her. "Unless the Stone Statue Apocalypse was never meant to win its dome."

36
MEANT TO WIN

"What?" Domi asked, confused.

Beside her, Erica squinted at Zeke, too. "Meant to win? What's that supposed to mean?"

Zeke took a deep breath. "Okay. So. Listen. This is a crazy theory, and I know it sounds crazy, but just...hear me out, okay?"

Domi nodded, slowly, putting a patient expression on her face.

Another deep breath. Zeke glanced at her. "So, I've had this theory for a while—"

Static flashed across his vision. It roared in his ears. Zeke stumbled, putting a hand to his forehead.

No. Not yet.

Zeke shook his head, fighting his way back to consciousness. *It's you! That voice again! Dammit, I'm right, aren't I?*

...

Get out of my head! Shut up and let me tell them!

No.

No? Fuck off! You don't get to choose!

I do.

Not anymore, motherfucker. I'm taking back the reins!

"Zeke? Are you all right?" Domi asked.

Zeke looked up to find her face right next to his. He startled, then realized he was lying on the floor, completely crumpled where he'd stood. His knees and rear end smarted from the blow, but he hadn't felt anything in the moment.

"I..." He frowned. "There was something important. Something..."

"A crazy theory you've had for a while?" Erica prompted.

"Shh! Don't—what if he—"

The static roared again.

NO, NO, NO, NO, NONONONONONONONO

Zeke pushed through, ignoring the voice. He couldn't hear his own words, but he still gave voice to them, felt them buzzing in his neck. "I might have mentioned it in passing before, but now I'm almost certain. System Apocalypse."

The static faded. His thoughts surged forward, clear, unhindered. The voice was gone, as if it had never been, and Zeke felt a coldness in his heart.

A whisper, in the back of his mind. **Go ahead, then. But don't blame me if you regret this.**

"System...Apocalypse?" Domi asked, squinting at him.

"Maybe I didn't mention it. Maybe...maybe I did, and it erased it from your mind. It can do that because we're all infected by it. No...maybe Subordinated is the right term?" Zeke looked at them, at Domi and Erica both. "Do you remember when you chose your Concept? Way, way back, at the very start of all of this, before the domes or anything."

Domi nodded. Erica did too, but slowly.

Zeke raised two fingers. "There were two voices, right? Or rather, two sets of text in our heads. One that spoke like us. Er, sentence-case. And another. One that spoke in all caps."

"Right...yeah, I do remember that," Domi said, nodding.

Erica frowned. She shrugged. "It would be Eric who knew that, not me. But...he isn't disagreeing with you."

"Anyway, what do you mean, spoke like us? Do you write your thoughts out as words in your head?" Domi asked. She giggled and shook her head at Zeke. "Nerd."

"Not the point—and shush. Don't get distracted. Anyway. The point is, I think—this is my theory, and the normal voice in my head very much didn't want me to tell you this. I think there's two Systems."

"What? What do you mean, two Systems?" Domi asked.

Erica squinted at him.

Zeke nodded. He put his hands together, lowering the second finger on his right hand and raising his first finger on his left. He separated his hands, leaving one finger raised on each hand. "Two Systems, totally apart from one another. Or maybe...nested inside one another?" He put one hand cupped over the other.

"Yeah, whatever. What would it mean? If there were two Systems. I mean, either way, they're like, the untouchable interface that allows us to get skills and stuff. Even if there's two of them, does it matter to us? It's all the same when we're out here fighting Apocalypses," Domi said, shrugging.

"No...that's exactly what it wants you to think," Zeke said, pointing at her. He nodded. "There's actually only one System."

Domi raised her brows. "There's one System, then two Systems, then one System again? What the hell are you talking about, Zeke?"

"The other 'System'...is actually an Apocalypse. The System Apocalypse," Zeke said.

Domi's eyes widened. Erica jolted where she stood.

Zeke nodded. "You get it, don't you? It means that every time we interact with what *we* think is the System, we're actually interacting with an Apocalypse. Every time we use our

Systems, we're just feeding the System Apocalypse. Every time I use Devour, or you light an explosion, Domi, the System Apocalypse is accruing the same skill points and level-ups as we are—except, unlike us, it isn't accruing the ones it personally gets. It's accruing *everyone's* points. Sucking up a small percentage... or who knows, a large percentage, of the points we should be earning, just sitting there, silently, doing nothing."

"Holy shit," Domi muttered, her eyes wide. She shook her head. "All this time...if it's true, then..."

"What evidence do you have?" Erica interrupted Zeke.

Zeke grimaced. He spread his hands. "That's the reason I haven't brought it up. I don't have much. A gut feeling. The weirdness of the System—the weirdly human qualities of it. The way you can negotiate for skills. The fact that it plans out inanimate and non-human Apocalypses' skills, according to what a human might think. Sure, sometimes they ignore it, like our Stone Statue friend...and sometimes they don't, like the Elf Ornament Apocalypse. But the fact that some of them have the option to follow a human's expectations of what the skills might be—isn't that suspicious? Whatever this System is, why would it know, or care, what Christmas is, or be able to play on our ideas of Christmas movie tropes, or whatever? Unless there was a person, acting as the System's interface."

"Right...or it's a godlike being in the first place that created the System, who knows everything that occurs on Earth," Erica countered.

"I've also talked to it. To the System that speaks normally. And it—it didn't want me to tell you this. So...you know. I feel like I'm on the right track," Zeke said.

"Or being deliberately misled by an intelligent godlike alien being," Domi said, pretending to put a tinfoil cap on.

Zeke glared at her, and she grinned, then shrugged. "I mean, this whole scenario is so outside the pale that I don't really want to rule anything out. From literal gods to aliens, anything's on the table. Even a human being who picked System Apocalypse as their Apocalypse. But there's one critical problem that I just can't overlook with this theory of yours, Zeke."

"I think I know what it is," Zeke said, nodding.

"Yeah. Well, you aren't stupid." Domi took a deep breath and looked at him. "If the System Apocalypse is an Apocalypse someone picked, they would have had to pick it at the same time as all of us. Which means they would have ended up in a dome, the same as the rest of us. If the System Apocalypse was a person, then they'd have only been able to spread the System Apocalypse *after* the dome. And sure, I'll be generous. Let's say the System Apocalypse was in our dome. Sure, it would invalidate the 'only one shall leave' statement—"

"Not if we were all Subordinated by it, without realizing."

"Granted. Sure, I'll give you that. There's ways to bring others out of domes. You and I experienced that personally. That's not necessarily the killer problem.

"The killer problem is that everyone we've fought so far already had the same System as us by the time we fought them. And none of them, not a single one, mentioned anything about their System changing, or a new System, after the domes opened. In other words, if you're right, and the System Apocalypse is an Apocalypse like the rest of us, then somehow, it had already infected the whole world *before* the Apocalypse kicked off. In other words, it had already won every dome, and not only that, but won the whole world, before anyone else even got their skills going. And then, it would've had to choose to allow us all to get stronger, and give us powerful skills to enable that, rather than brainwashing us all to be its pathetic little Subordinates for the rest of time."

Domi spread her hands. "Why do that? What would motivate that?"

Zeke shook his head. "Yeah. You're right. I don't have an answer for that. For any of that. My best bet is that it's something like Ryan, or like, I don't know, the winner of the previous round—"

"The previous round?" Domi interrupted.

"Total extrapolation on my part. If it was an Apocalypse before any of the rest of us got the opportunity to become Apocalypses, then the simplest...or well, the simplest thing I could think of, would be if it had already been an Apocalypse. If there had already been a round of this exact...I don't know, tournament, battle royale, somewhere else, or some other time, some other reality—"

"Parallel Zekes, and all that."

Zeke nodded at Domi. "Right. Parallel Zekes. If it was some kind of extradimensional being, or even just an Apocalypse from another timeline that finished the battle royale before our dimension even kicked it off, and it just showed up and exerted its power as our Apocalypse battle royale began, then..."

For the first time in a while, Erica spoke up. "If that's the case, then is it possible that the System Apocalypse is on our side?"

Anger surged in Zeke's chest. "What? It's stealing our points. Stealing the things I Devour! It's—"

Domi raised her hand. "Let's hear her out, Zeke. We listened to you."

Zeke blinked. He startled, looking at his hands. "I—I'm sorry. I don't know why I..." *Why did I get so angry all of a sudden? This is a crazy theory. I don't think I'm right. I'm very willing to hear other explanations. So why...?*

Is it manipulating me, even now? Or is it something else? The other System, maybe? Swallowing, he nodded. "Please. Go ahead, Erica."

She nodded. "I was going to go ahead without your permission. In any case. Isn't it possible it's on our side? After all, the original System Zeke postulates is the one that kicks off the battle royale, is that correct?"

Zeke nodded.

"And the System Apocalypse interjects itself afterward. The System Apocalypse is what's given us this interface we have. What allows us to allocate stat points, buy skills, and even negotiate with it for skills it wants. It feels inhuman, sometimes —you have to explain concepts to it that seem simple—but at other times, it seems all too human, like when it gives the Elf Ornament Apocalypse Christmas-themed skills. That part could be explained by it being a extra-dimensional being—a being from an Earth that isn't quite like ours, that shares some of our customs, but not all of them.

"That's beside the point. My point is, the System Apocalypse, the sentence-case one, is the one that has allowed us to power ourselves up according to our own wills. Does that not suggest that it might be trying to make us as powerful as possible? Does that not suggest that. if it is not on our side, it, at the very least, has need of a powerful ally? Does that not suggest, that perhaps, it is not the System Apocalypse that is our enemy...but instead..."

Erica fell silent. She pointed up. Beyond the System Apocalypse. At the original System, the one that initiated the domes, the one that gave them all Concepts.

Zeke's eyes widened. *She's right. Why did I never realize? It's the original System that we've been battling all this time. The original System that forced us to compete in a battle royale. The original System that gave us Concepts that corrupt and erode. The System Apocalypse has been helping us. Giving us skills we desperately need.*

Allowing us to assign our own stats—for example, give myself almost exclusively SPR. Hell, it's the one that allows me to interface with Allen and draw on his STR, so I don't have to rely on Allen all the time.

The word trembled. Static flashed in his ears, before his eyes. Zeke looked around him at Erica and Domi. Their gazes flickered, too, eyes darting around as something interrupted their vision. *They can see the static, too, now. It's not just me.* "I think we're too close to the truth. I think we should get the hell out of here, before...whatever it is that the System Apocalypse needs help with, realizes we know too much and crushes us."

"Agreed," Domi said.

Erica nodded, just once.

"And you know who would have a clue? Who would be able to tell us if his System was the same in another reality?" Zeke asked.

Domi smiled. Erica tilted her head.

Zeke grinned. "Let's go find other-Zeke."

"And do you think I'd let you leave so easily?" a haughty voice asked.

What the fuck—the System? Zeke whirled.

37
THE SYSTEM

Rather than the manifestation of a godlike being, a young man about his age stood on the sky over them. Zeke relaxed, glancing at Domi and Erica to see both of them sigh as well. He shook his head. "Just an Apocalypse. Jeez, don't scare me like that!"

The young man blinked at them. "What? *Just* an Apocalypse? I'll show you who's 'just' an Apocalypse!" He drew back his hand.

Zeke lowered his stance, checking his **Transform** timer. He grimaced. *Three minutes? I can forget about that coming up. I'm stuck un-Transformed for this battle.*

Domi shot him a glance, and he instantly knew she'd realized the same thing. On the other side of them, Erica resheathed her sword, a displeased expression on her face, too. Zeke turned back to the young man. *I don't know exactly how Erica's powers work, but from her expression, she's out of time, too. We're all in trouble here. We don't need a fight.*

But he doesn't know that.

"Yeah, you're just another Apocalypse. We're all Apocalypses here, so what?" Zeke asked. He strutted forward, gesturing at the destruction all around them, most of it caused by the stone statue and Lady Poseidon, *though he doesn't need to know that.* "Come on down, if you aren't afraid. We'll take you on any day."

The young man chucked, rage flashing over his face. A helmet materialized on his head, and a strange multicolored gun materialized in his hand. "You'll regret that."

Erica stepped forward. "Is that the Absolute from ARKOS: Ultimate Combat?"

At that, the young man paused. He looked down at Erica and did a double take, his eyes passing over her bright pink floofy skirt and her high blonde ponytail. "*You* know ARKOS?"

"Who doesn't?" Erica asked, as if it was common knowledge.

Zeke and Domi exchanged a look. Zeke shrugged.

Domi shrugged back. She leaned in. "My younger cousins used to play it, I think."

"I see I'm in the presence of the mythical gamer girl," the young man said. He lowered his weapon for just a moment to look Erica over again. "If the servers were still up, I'd ask you to go a round."

"No thanks. I prefer to play with people who actually know what they're doing," Erica said dismissively. She shook her head, pointing at his gun. "The Absolute is a shit weapon. They act like it's the ultimate weapon, and it was the first week they put it out, but since then, they've nerfed it to hell and back. Now it's got a three-foot scatter range at fifty feet, and it does half the damage of a regular rifle unless you get lucky, and all six shots hit. It's basically just a shittier version of the normal shotguns, except it does a little less damage on average and has a little more range." She flipped her ponytail and looked down on him. "Total noob move, picking that gun. What, did you read *one single* guide online? Bet you haven't even put a hundred hours into ARKOS."

The young man's face turned bright red, then purple. A vein throbbed in his forehead. His knuckles whitened on the gun. "You...you...you don't know anything!"

Zeke and Domi exchanged another look. Zeke pressed his lips together, barely suppressing his laughter, and Domi covered her hand with her mouth to hide hers.

Turning to the gun-toting young man, Zeke lifted his chin. "It sounds like she knows more than you, actually."

"Shut up!" the young man roared. He turned the gun on them.

Before he could fire, an angelic young lady, wreathed in translucent, drifting fabric that flowed with her every movement, appeared in the sky behind him. She gently laid a hand on his shoulder and shook her head. "Not yet. We only came to see their strength, that's all."

The young man took a deep breath, visibly suppressing his anger. "Right. Yeah. I know."

Zeke stared. *Where did she come from? For that matter, where did he? It's true we were distracted, and for quite a while at that, but not for long enough for two Apocalypses to sneak up behind us. And that girl appeared before our very eyes! Is she the Invisibility Apocalypse, or something? But then, what's up with those gauzy robes and her crazy beauty? You wouldn't think someone that beautiful would pick to stay invisible...or rather, keep your head clear, Zeke!* He looked her over again, noting her perfectly proportioned features, her sculpted limbs, her silky hair and nearly translucent skin. *That kind of beauty isn't natural, especially not in the Apocalypse, where hot showers come at a premium. She's got to be buffing it through her Concept, somehow! But what kind of Concept gives someone beauty, and invisibility, and funky robes? And, uh, the power of flight, too, I guess?*

The angelic woman turned to Zeke and the others. She smiled, and Zeke almost melted on the spot. Strangely, Domi also seemed to waver, just for a moment, before she steadied herself again.

"We didn't come to fight today. In fact, we aren't here at all. This is merely a projection," she said. She waved a lazy hand, beckoning them. "I've seen your strength, and you're lacking. Come. Challenge my Apocalypse Coalition. We're waiting for you."

"Ah... Huh?" Zeke asked. *The Apocalypse Coalition is led by a woman? I thought... Mmm. Shouldn't say that aloud.*

"You thought the Apocalypse Coalition was led by a man, didn't you," Domi said, catching his surprised expression. She tutted. "Zeke, Zeke, Zeke. Women can lead things too, you know."

"No, no, I know that, I just...you know. They're so warlike. They attacked us first, you know?" Zeke protested.

"Historically, women-led countries are more likely to go to war," Domi said, quirking a brow at him.

"They...oh, really? Interesting," Zeke commented. He shrugged to himself. *I guess it tracks, then. They did go on the offensive.*

The beauty beckoned them. "Come. I'll be waiting. We'll see whether your Apocalypses or mine are the stronger ones."

With that, both she and the gun-toting young man vanished.

Zeke snorted. He looked at Domi and Erica. "What was that about 'not letting us go easily?'"

"No...but I wonder. How much of our conversation about the Systems did they hear?" Domi asked.

Zeke frowned, then shrugged. "Does it matter? Whether we win or lose, it's good for someone to know what we suspect. And it's not like it gives them any sort of advantage to know there might be two Systems. Hell, if it gave an advantage, we should jump on it right now and take ahold of it!"

"I agree, but..." Domi hesitated. She glanced at Zeke. "What if they negotiated with the original System? Not the System Apocalypse. We can all do that. But knowing there's two Systems...what if they tried to negotiate with the original?"

Zeke paused. His mouth opened, then shut. He put a hand on his chin. "Huh. I guess I didn't think about that. What would they gain from that, though?"

Domi threw her hands up. "Don't ask me, I don't know. Just a thought. Just a scary little thought I had."

"And spoke aloud, right here, where we know they might still be listening," Erica pointed out.

Domi shut her mouth. She glanced around. "Shit. Do you think they heard?"

Zeke shook his head at them. "I don't know. But we should definitely get out of here. Collect Olivia and Sparkles and other-Zeke, and head back to base. She said she was waiting for us, but it could be a ploy. For all we know, she's attacking base right now."

"Right, point." Domi glanced around her, then grinned at Zeke. "You wanna fly me down?"

Zeke snorted. "Yeah, yeah, sure."

"Who's Sparkles?" Erica asked.

"We have a new pet dog," Domi said. She waved her hand. "You'll meet him soon enough."

"Hmph. I hope he meets my aesthetic standards," Erica harrumphed. She leaped off the roof and landed on a flower that bloomed under her perfectly in time to catch her, then jumped down again, stair-stepping down the side of the building on materializing flowers.

Zeke flapped his wings, and he and Domi soared off the

edge of the building and circled down toward the ground. As he dropped, he shrugged to himself. "I think we did pretty well."

"Yeah. I mean, it wasn't completely ideal, since we lost the Ice Cream Apocalypse, but we took out, what, six members of the Apocalypse Coalition? True, three of them were gimmes—"

"I don't know if Teacher was a gimme. Just on a psychological level," Zeke muttered under his breath.

Domi laughed. "Yeah, okay. Two of them were gimmes, but the rest were real fighters, in one way or another. Minus four real fighters for them, and at worst, minus two for us. Even if Olivia and other-Zeke are dead, that's a fair trade."

"Yeah. Though I really hope they're both alive," Zeke said.

"No, totally agree. Just, you know. Worst case," Domi replied.

Zeke nodded. "Especially other-Zeke. Zel, whatever. He's our best key to unlocking the whole System-System Apocalypse thing. Though..." He frowned.

"What?"

"Ryan didn't mention anything about the System being different in this world. And, actually, his skills look exactly like everyone else's."

Domi pursed her lips. "Then, does that mean that other-Zeke will be just like Ryan?"

"Right, but does that mean I'm wrong?" Zeke wondered.

"Not necessarily. It's possible that each universe Ryan creates has its own copy of the System Apocalypse. Or, you know. Ryan time loops *after* the System Apocalypse does its thing, so no matter what alternate version of Zeke you encounter, or whether you encounter Ryan himself, he's already been infected by the System Apocalypse, and he has the same kind of skills as everyone else," Domi pointed out.

"Yeah...yeah. Though he did kick me off the building before everything kicked off..." Zeke trailed off. He looked at Domi.

"What?"

"Do you think that's it?"

Domi squinted at him. "What on earth are you trying to say?"

"Okay, so. Ryan went back in time to kill me before I had skills, right?"

"Right, yeah."

"But he only went back in time to *right before* the System Apocalypse kicked off. I know Ryan. If he could have killed me as a baby, he would have."

"Sure, but he didn't look old, did he? So maybe he'd also be a baby, if he tried to gank baby Zeke," Domi pointed out.

"Right, yeah, but you know, five year old, ten year old. If he could have gone back farther, I know he would have, just to make his own job easier. And—and I'm pretty sure he said he couldn't go back any farther."

"Right, so Ryan's power has limits. Where are we going with this?" Domi asked.

Zeke took a deep breath. "In other words, we *know* when the System Apocalypse took effect because the System Apocalypse supplies our skills. It's the backbone, the—server, if you will, like what that kid was saying. You can't play the game if the server isn't online."

"Now I'm getting it. So, you're saying, Ryan can only go back in time to the moment the System Apocalypse was born...or got its power, or returned to our universe, or whatever." She gestured vaguely.

Zeke nodded. "Exactly. The System Apocalypse, if I'm right, actually started up *seconds* before the main System...the main Apocalypse, whichever kicked off. Erica might be right. Just like how Ryan came back in time to kill me to prevent me from winning, maybe, just maybe, the System Apocalypse came into effect seconds before the System to try to head off the System. It failed, right, because we went through all that mess, got our Concepts, fought in the dome...but if I'm right, then the System Apocalypse came back to try to save us, just like Erica said."

Domi hung silent in his arms for a few minutes, thinking. Abruptly, she shrugged. "This is wild postulation on top of wild postulation, at this point. There's no point extrapolating this far out. We've got too many wild theories stacked on top of one another—it's total conspiracy theory territory."

"No, you're right," Zeke agreed.

"But...it is something to think about," Domi muttered to herself. "Who's on our side, and who isn't. If there is a System and a System Apocalypse..."

"But first, we need to take down the Apocalypse Coalition," Zeke said firmly.

"Right. Can't challenge the metaphysical deities playing with our lives until we stave off the existential threat," Domi replied with a grin.

Zeke laughed. "What the hell kind of situation are we in, Domi? What happened to our ordinary lives?"

"I don't know, but at this point? I'm along for the ride," Domi said, shooting him a grin.

"Well said. So, let's ride it to the end."

Zeke touched down, and the two of them rejoined Erica. In his ordinary Standard poodle form, Sparkles joined them, a friendly expression on his face. He trotted up to Erica and sniffed her hand, then looked up at her, lowering his head to ask for scritches.

Erica nodded. "He is up to my aesthetic standards," she announced, scratching Sparkles' ears as he requested.

"Nobody asked, but I'm glad to hear that," Zeke said.

Together, the four of them headed back to the car.

38
LONG RIDE HOME

At the car, Domi glanced around, then looked at Zeke. "Any idea where to go looking for Olivia or other-Zeke? Or how to attract their attention, while we're at it?"

"I could fire another rose into the air," Erica offered.

"If it didn't work the first time, it probably won't work the second time," Zeke said.

Erica nodded. "That's true. Also, I'm tired."

"Huh?" Zeke asked.

Erica slumped against Sparkles. Her dress withered, wilting away like a rose, and so did her ponytail, her wand, even her boots. They dropped away like dried, dead petals, and Eric slumped against Sparkles in her place. He stood up, blinking around, then yawned. "Jeez, I'm exhausted. What did Erica do?"

"A lot of fighting. Good to have you back," Zeke greeted him, patting him on the shoulder.

"Oh...yeah, I remember some of it. There was some asshole being sweaty in ARKOS... Wait, that part was probably a dream," he said, laughing self-consciously.

"No, that part was real," Zeke said.

Eric blinked. "Wait, really? Who was it? Wait, did you guys play ARKOS with Erica while I was out? No fair!"

"No, how would we? The servers are down. We ran into some cringy Apocalypse who'd equipped himself with ARKOS gear in real life," Domi explained.

Eric snorted. "I guess it's not more cringe than a Magical Girl Apocalypse, but it's still pretty cringe."

"I don't know, it might be more cringe," Zeke said, putting a hand to his chin. He sighed. "Whether it's more cringe or not, it doesn't solve our problem of not knowing where Olivia or other-Zeke are."

Domi squinted up at the sun, then unzipped her jacket and threw it into the back seat of the car. "Well, if Olivia became a vampire popsicle, she should be thawing out pretty soon, the rate it's heating up here. Honestly, we'll be lucky if this place isn't monsooning by nightfall, with this whole rapid temperature change thing going on."

"Lady Poseidon didn't help, either," Zeke commented.

"No, she did not," Domi agreed.

Eric looked from Domi to Zeke. "Lady Poseidon?"

"Oh, yeah. Speaking of cringe...she seemed to think she was an actual Greek god, or something. Or like, an incarnation of one? Yeah, I don't know. She was pretty far gone," Zeke said, tapping his head.

"Yikes, man," Eric said, then chuckled. "Imagine thinking you're actually the thing your Apocalypse is. Couldn't be me."

"Hey, stop putting yourself down. You did good work today," Domi said, shaking her head at him.

"Erica did good work. I was just...along for the ride. Like usual," Eric sighed.

Domi looked at Zeke. "Is he always like this?"

"Yeah, pretty much," Zeke said, shrugging.

"Why wouldn't I be? Erica's, like, the better version of me. She's beautiful, and strong, and everything I'm not..."

Domi's brows raised. She looked at Eric, then gently took his hands. "Eric, let's you and me go talk around the back of the building, okay? Zeke, stay here. This is us talk."

"Uh...okay?" Zeke said.

Domi grinned. She led Eric out of the building and around the corner.

Zeke watched them go, then shrugged. He looked through his skills. *I feel like I had a skill for talking to people—oh!* His eyes landed on Hands-Free Calling, and he rolled his eyes at himself. *Right. Can't believe I forgot one of my favorite skills.*

He touched a hand to his ear. *Hey, Olivia, can you hear me?*

Oh, thank goodness. I'm frozen in place two streets down from the car. I fell in a snow, er, ice cream drift, so the sunlight and the heat are going to take forever to thaw me out. Can you come get me?

Zeke chuckled. *Sure. I'll be right there.*

Thanks. You're a true bro.

He lifted his fingers to his ear again. *Hello? Other-Zeke?*

Yeah, what's up?

We're heading back. You want a ride?

Oh...huh. I'm uh, kinda busy with something. I'll run back on my own. I can move pretty much as fast as a car, anyway.

Oh, okay. If you're sure.

Yeah. I'm sure.

Zeke paused a few moments. *That's right! Hey, mind if we call you Zel?*

Zel? Oh, like the other half of Ezekiel, or something? Kind of?

Yeah...you know. It's not as clunky as other-Zeke.

He paused, then laughed. *Sure. Zel works. I'll see you back, other me. Zeke, I suppose I should call you now.*

See you back. Don't take too long.

Nah, no worries. I wouldn't want to get Ryan antsy. He ended the call.

Zeke lowered his hand. His brows furrowed. *Working on something? What's he doing?* He gazed off toward the horizon, hesitant for reasons he couldn't quite put words to. *I know I should probably trust him—he is me, after all—but I just can't. He's kind of like...well, my evil twin. A me that did something so vile that Ryan decided to turn back time. It doesn't make me comfortable that he's out of my sight for so long.*

A second later, he shook his head. *And on the other hand, Ryan almost turned back time on me like fifty times, over total nothing-burgers. I can't trust Ryan to have a good sense for whether a Zeke is 'evil' or not. Sure, I'd trust early Ryan—the Ryan I knew, the one I spent the morning in the museum with—but not late Ryan. Not the Ryan who spent years in the dome, resetting time over and over again in hopes of getting the results he wanted. Watching other Zekes make mistakes, make hard decisions, fail, in his eyes, over and over and over, until the only thing he saw when he looked at me was failure.*

He snorted at himself. *I've been getting pretty philosophical today, huh? Let's go find Olivia and get her thawed out.*

Leaving the car behind, he headed out into the melting ice cream. "Domi, Eric, I'm going to fetch Olivia!"

"Okay! Have fun!" Domi shouted, distracted.

He went down two streets, checking all the snow drifts, and found nothing. Shrugging to himself, he tried the opposite side of the road, then turned around and went two streets down in the opposite direction. At last, in a deep drift of chocolate ice cream, he found a frozen human body.

"Damn, you really were buried, huh, Olivia," he commented, yanking the body out.

A frozen middle-aged man stared at him in object horror.

"Er, never mind, sorry to disturb you," Zeke muttered, putting the frozen man back in the ice cream drift.

A muffled sound caught his ear, and he ran down to the end of the block. There, on the far side of the street, a hand poked out of a drift, frozen solid. Zeke grabbed it, and this time, he fished out a frozen vampire.

"Hey there, Olivia. Hope I didn't keep you waiting."

Olivia couldn't move, but the muffled frustrated sounds that came from deep within told him everything he needed to know. Chuckling to himself, he put her plank-like body bridal style across his arms and carried her out into the front side of the streets, into the sun. He walked around for a bit, feeling out the relative warmth, then set her in a sunlight-bathed spot in front of a convenience store, where the sunlight reflected off the shop windows and the walls around to concentrate in one super bright spot that felt warm, even to his passing touch.

"There we go. Should be thawed out in no time."

A muffled pleased sound escaped the frozen Olivia.

"So, I take it you didn't fight anyone? You can stay silent for no," Zeke commented. He settled against the building beside her, careful not to block any of the sunlight or reflected sun. Clasping his hands before him, he sighed. "Yeah. We ended up facing six Apocalypses. Some of them were kind of pushovers, but most of them were pretty serious."

Sparkles turned the corner. He looked at Zeke and Olivia and wagged his tail, then wandered over to sniff Oliva. Her fingertips twitched, but no more.

"Oh, don't worry. Sparkles is on our side. He's an Apocalypse, but he's my Subordinate now, same as you. He won't hurt you."

Sparkles sniffed Olivia some more, then lifted his leg. Olivia squealed in horror. Her body barely twitched.

"Sparkles! Bad boy!" Zeke pushed Sparkles away from

Olivia, barely preventing a disaster. He shook his head at the dog. "I guess you're just a dog, at the end of the day, with all the usual doggy instincts."

Sparkles gave him a wistful look, then glanced at Olivia.

"No, you're not allowed to mark Olivia. She's alive, you know. A living being."

Sparkles wagged his tail and lowered his head a little.

"I don't know what that means, but please don't piss on your friends."

"We're back—who's pissing on friends?" Domi asked, leading Eric back around the corner.

Zeke lifted his hand. "Sparkles tried to mark Olivia."

"Oh. That's much less fun. I thought there was some water-sport going on over here." Domi glanced around. "There's Olivia...what about Zel? Other-Zeke, or whatever?"

"You can call him Zel. He agreed to it. He says he's busy. That we should head back without him," Zeke reported, standing.

Domi raised her eyebrows. "Uh huh. And we agreed to this?"

Zeke put his hands up. "I think it's suspicious too, but what am I supposed to do? I can contact him with Hands-Free Calling, but the skill just lets me talk to people mentally. It doesn't give me their GPS location or anything."

Domi pulled out her phone. She tabbed through a few panels, all of it completely black to Zeke, then sighed and put it back away. "Yeah, I don't have tabs on him either. All right. I guess we have no choice but to leave him to it."

"I'm not happy about it either, but yeah, seems that way." Zeke shrugged and picked up Olivia. In the time they'd been talking, she'd thawed enough to bend a little in his arms. He nodded at Domi. "In any case, let's get a move on. If the Apocalypse Coalition decides to attack our base, I'd rather be home...

and if they don't, then we need to go back and regroup anyway, so we can attack them in their base."

"Right. Speaking of, do you think our scout has returned yet?" Domi asked.

"What, Ryan? I hope so," Zeke muttered. He went to lay Olivia out in the back seat, then hesitated at the sight of Eric and Sprinkles climbing in from the other side. "Domi drives, I ride shotgun, Eric and Sparkles sit on the back seat..."

"We can hold Olivia in our lap," Eric offered.

"Or we can throw her in the trunk. She's bendy enough to fit, and it's not like she's in any real danger from a car crash, being a vampire and all," Domi pointed out.

"True. Olivia, any thoughts?" Zeke asked, looking at the frozen vampire in his arms.

Olivia said nothing.

"I'll take that as a no. All right, Domi, pop the trunk!"

"I've got a trunk full of vampire pops, a trunk of vampire popsicles," Domi sang. The *pop* of the trunk latch unlatching sounded, and the back swung open.

Carefully, Zeke set Olivia down in the trunk. "Scream if you need something, okay?"

Olivia grunted.

"Good talk." Zeke shut the trunk and climbed up to the front of the car, sliding in next to Domi. "Let's get this show on the road!"

"Hot showers!" Domi cheered. She put the engine in gear, and they took off down the road.

39
HOT SHOWERS

The whole way home, Domi sung a little song about hot showers to herself. By the time they got back, not only was Zeke ready to silence her forever, he was also hankering for a hot shower. He all but sprinted out of the car, only turning back at the last minute when Olivia started screaming from the trunk.

"She could use a hot shower too. Nothing like hot water to thaw ice," Domi pointed out.

"Oh, good point. I'll put her in mine," Zeke offered.

Domi shook her head. She held her hands out. "Give her to me. I bet she'd be way more comfortable getting thawed in a woman's room."

"Oh...oh. I-I didn't..." Zeke stammered, blushing. He handed Olivia to her quickly, suddenly feeling caught red-handed. *I really had no intentions, but ugh, she's right. It would look super suspicious if I took her to my shower to get thawed.*

Domi smiled. "I know you didn't. That's why I'm here, Zeke. But I do think it's better for me to take care of poor frozen Olivia."

"Yeah, no, totally agree. You, you handle that, I'll go..." Zeke gestured vaguely, then broke away, running off to his own room to take a shower and hide his bright red cheeks.

As he ran through the lobby, Heather perked up from behind the counter. "Welcome back! Did you have a good time fighting Apocalypses today?"

"Yeah, I'd call it an all-around victory…did give them a chance to watch us fight, but eh, that was inevitable. Especially at the level of power they could wield," Zeke said, running past.

"That's not too bad. So long as everyone made it back safely!" she chirped happily, making no comment on Zeke's red cheeks.

A quick jaunt down the hall, and Zeke popped into his shower. He stripped out of his freezing wet, ice-cream-soaked, sticky, gross clothes, and all but threw himself into the steaming hot water. It scorched his skin, but in a good way. He let out a long sigh, relaxing against the wall. *Thank goodness for Heather. I don't know what I'd do if I didn't have our lovely Apartment Apocalypse here to provide a soft bed and hot water.*

Distantly, a knock rattled his door. "Zeke? You're back?"

"Mia? Yeah, we just got back. We're all gross. Let me get cleaned up, and I'll tell you what happened," Zeke shouted, sticking his head out of the shower.

"Oh, okay! I got it." Her footsteps began to retreat.

"Wait, hold on! Did anything happen while we were gone? Like, did the Scouting Apocalypse fly by again or anything?"

There was a pause. "I don't know. I didn't notice anything… I'll ask around, see if Heather or Jimmy or anyone else noticed something."

"Good idea. Thanks, Mia!"

"Yeah, no problem! Let's all meet in the lobby and exchange notes, say, in half an hour?" Mia called.

"Yeah, you got it," Zeke replied. He retreated into the steamy water, giving himself up to the flow of heat over his skin. *Ah…it feels so good to be warm again. I missed you, warmth. I missed you, my fingertips! It's so good to feel you again!*

A half-hour later, dressed in clean clothes, his hair still damp, Zeke took to the hallways. He wandered down the walkway, searching for Eric and Domi's rooms. He came to Eric's first and knocked at the door. "Hey, Eric. You wanna meet down in the lobby in...fifteen minutes, exchange notes with the people who stayed back?"

"Oh, uh, sure!" Eric said. There was a rustling sound, then a thump. "I-I'll be right out!"

"Yeah, sure thing." Zeke kept going, searching for Domi's room. *Not this one, not this one...here we are.* He knocked at the door. "Domi!"

Silence. Distantly, he heard the rush of water.

Is she still in the shower? Wait—Olivia's a vampire, and she was just in dire straits. I've read a vampire novel or two in the past. It's totally possible Olivia was starving in that ice block and attacked Domi when she thawed! "Domi?"

Still no reply. He grimaced, hesitating a moment more, then activated his **Heat Vision** and turned it toward the bathroom. *I'm so sorry, Domi! But if you're in danger, then—*

A tangled mess of limbs met his eyes. Zeke's eyebrows almost shot off his face, and he quickly turned his head, his whole face reddening. *Oh. Oh, dear. Yep. Well. Okay. There's definitely something going on, but it uh, it looks pretty consensual...* He licked his lips and backed away, keeping his head averted. *They seem a little preoccupied. I'll leave them to it.*

"Zeke— There you are. Oh, you went to get Domi. Is she coming?" Mia asked.

"I'm pretty sure she's c..." Zeke coughed. "Er, no. She uh, she's busy, um, thawing Olivia...I think it's gonna take a while yet."

Mia squinted at him. "What?"

"Yeah, Olivia got, uh, frozen...Ice Cream Apocalypse. Things got pretty cold. Anyway. Let's leave them to it. I was with Domi the whole time anyway, so I can cover what we saw," Zeke said, nodding.

"Oh, okay...if you're sure. She wouldn't want to hear what we have to say?" Mia asked.

"I'll...I'll fill her in," Zeke said. Gently, he pushed Mia back toward the lobby.

Mia glanced over her shoulder at him. "Why're you acting so weird?"

"I'm not acting weird!" Zeke protested, a little too loudly. He cleared his throat. "I'm just tired, that's all. It was a long day. Lotta fighting."

"Yeah, seems like it," Mia said, slowly nodding. She gave him a slightly suspicious look, then shrugged.

Zeke let out a silent sigh of relief. *Thank goodness. I don't want to have to admit I accidentally peeped on Domi and Olivia.*

Back in the lobby, most of the Apocalypses were gathered. Heather sat behind the lobby desk, happily fiddling with some register or another. Sarah and Jimmy sat next to one another, Jimmy keeping a watchful eye on Sarah. Issac lounged in the corner atop a big, fluffy white cat's side. Both he and the cat regarded Sparkles with open distrust. Sparkles, for his part, laid nobly in the corner with his head upright and paws tucked tight to him like a sphinx, completely disregarding the cat and cat-man as if they didn't exist.

You know, I didn't think about Sparkles and Issac, but I really should have, Zeke thought. He pursed his lips. *It's a good thing Sparkles doesn't have any Subordinate dogs, I guess.*

Clapping his hands, Zeke walked over to one of the cool-looking but probably uncomfortable chairs that littered the lobby. "So! Anything big happen while we were gone?"

Issac yawned. "We chased off a lot of birds."

"Suspicious birds, or?"

Opening his eyes all the way, Issac hit Zeke with a golden-eyed glower. "*Obviously* suspicious birds. All birds are suspicious."

"Uh huh," Zeke muttered.

"But these were especially suspicious. They all were eagles or hawks, and they all had little neckerchiefs around their necks."

Zeke nodded, slowly. "Subordinates of the Scouting Apocalypse, you think?"

Issac drooped lazily back down into his cat-lounge's luxurious fur. "Mmm, probably. It wouldn't surprise me."

"So, they're actively keeping an eye on us. Not surprising, but good to know. Anyone else?" Zeke asked, looking around the room.

Mia stepped forward. "Ryan hasn't come back yet."

"Never a good sign. Do you think he's captured, or do you think he's just off being mysterious for no reason?" Zeke asked.

Mia shrugged. "If he isn't back by tonight, I'd assume he was captured...or at least in a bad situation. He didn't take more than one meal and some water with him when he left."

"Got it. We'll keep an eye out, make sure we pay attention to any signs he might be trying to send." On a thought, Zeke lifted a hand to his ear and tried Hands-Free Calling but got no response. He lowered his hand. *Whether he's captured or not, he's probably too far away for Hands-Free Calling. It's a pretty short-range skill. More like a set of radios than a phone.*

"What about you? You said Olivia got frozen, and what happened to the other-Zeke? He's been gone since you guys left...we assumed he went with you, but..." Mia looked at Zeke.

"Oh, yeah. So..." Zeke told them everything that had happened with the Ice Cream Apocalypse, only leaving out the bit about the System Apocalypse. *I don't necessarily want all of them to know about my theory. For one thing, Heather, Jimmy, and Sarah might just think I'm nuts...they don't know me well enough to trust me. Issac I barely trust at the best of times, and I'm pretty sure he'd just say 'huh' and roll over even if I told him. Mia I'll definitely tell, but right now while everyone else is around isn't the time.*

Finished with his tale, Zeke clapped his hands again. "There you have it. We took out six Apocalypses on their side, three of whom seemed like legitimate threats, and gained an ally, without losing anyone ourselves. A pretty positive return."

"Er, but..." Mia glanced around the room, then pressed her lips together and looked up at Zeke. "I hate to point it out, Zeke, but...you only have six Apocalypses under you, total."

Zeke's brows furrowed. "Huh? I have nine, at least. You, Domi, Eric, Jimmy, Heather, Sarah, of course, Sparkles, Issac, Ryan, and other-Zeke. That's ten, and then there's me, so eleven."

"Right, but...Sarah and Heather can't really fight, so it's more like eight. Seven, because between Ryan and other-Zeke, I'm pretty sure we can deduct one of them from the battle, one way or another. Six total fighters. They threw away three Apocalypses. Sent three more to take on the relatively weak Ice Cream Apocalypse and didn't seem to mind when you destroyed them. The Apocalypse Coalition basically threw away as many Apocalypses as you have active fighting-capable Apocalypses Subordinated to you, *including* the dog you just picked up. Doesn't that suggest that they could afford to lose those Apocalypses? That there's a lot of Apocalypses grouped under them?" Mia pointed out.

Zeke grimaced. He wanted to refute her but couldn't find the words. *I hate to admit it, but she's right. Either they have a lot of Apocalypses under them, or they are themselves so powerful that they don't care if their Subordinates die.* "Yeah...it doesn't look great I have to admit. But who knows? Maybe they're just terrible tacticians."

"Maybe," Mia said, but she looked uncertain.

"And I mean, we're a tightly knit group. They're just a loose coalition. Who knows? Maybe there's more Apocalypses like Sparkles, who are willing to see the light and change sides," Zeke said, patting Sparkles on the back.

Sparkles barked. He let his tongue dangle, and his tail wagged.

"Right...and you aren't worried he's a double agent, or something?" Mia asked, eyeing Sparkles with suspicion.

Sparkes' tail drooped. He gave Mia a sad look.

"He's a dog," Zeke pointed out. "Besides, what do we have to hide that the Scouting Apocalypse hasn't already seen?"

"I guess," Mia said hesitantly.

"You're worrying too much," Zeke said, waving his hand. He made eye contact with Mia and shifted his head subtly, using Hands-Free Calling. *Obviously I'm not going to make war plans in front of the dog, and we'll send him out to do border patrol while we're gone, or something. It's not a big deal. We just won't rely on him, and we'll treat him like extra man...dog power while he's here, until he proves himself. It's simple enough.*

Mia wrinkled her nose, uncertain. *I guess...*

Zeke glanced at her. *What's your Hero Concept? Is there something about detecting spies in the skill shop you could buy? Or, you know. Maybe we should wait until he does something suspicious to spend points on skills.*

Yeah...okay. Yeah. That makes sense. Mia nodded, agreeing with Zeke.

"Good. Then...any questions?"

Jimmy shook his head. Sarah shrugged noncommittally. Sparkles wagged his tail. Issac snorted and rolled over, ignoring

Zeke. Heather hummed and stapled a clump of papers together. Mia shook her head.

"Meeting abolished." Zeke locked eyes with Mia. *Meet me out back. I need to tell you something I don't really want the others to hear.*

Mia glanced at him, then nodded.

"Whew! That was a good shower. Whoa, what'd I miss?" Domi asked, coming into the lobby. Olivia followed behind her, flush-faced and as rosy-cheeked as Zeke had ever seen her. *Well, she would be,* Zeke thought to himself, and guiltily looked away.

After a moment, he pulled himself together. *Act normal. You saw nothing.* "Olivia, you're looking good. None the worse for the wear?"

She shook her head shyly. Casting a sly glance at Domi, she nodded after her. "Domi, uh, revitalized me, so I'm good."

"Oh, she let you suck her blood?" Mia asked.

Olivia and Domi exchanged a glance. Domi waggled her brows, and Olivia blushed, glancing at the floor. "Yeah...yeah."

"That's wonderful! I'm glad you're feeling better," Mia said.

"She's feeling better, all right." Domi chuckled, grinning at Olivia, who glanced away in embarrassment again. She hugged her arms around herself and wiggled a little in place, giving the floor a tiny smile.

Domi nodded. "I'm gonna go grab a bite to eat. Feeling a little lightheaded after...all that."

"Does sucking blood really take it out of you?" Mia asked innocently.

Olivia jolted. She looked away, hiding her face. "Er, I'm... gonna go lie down. Still need to, uh...adjust."

Domi grinned like a cat.

I think I'm going to die of embarrassment if I spend any longer around this awkward situation. Zeke cleared his throat. "Mia, let's go check on the farm."

"Huh? Oh, sure," Mia said, nodding. She followed him, and Olivia scurried off, happy to escape.

40

A QUICK CONVERSATION

Around the back of the apartment, Zeke leaned against the wall and nodded at Mia. "There's something I didn't bring up at the meeting. I've already mentioned it to Domi and Erica, and there's a chance our enemies know...but I want you to know, too."

"But not everyone?" Mia asked, confused.

"No, it's... No." Zeke took a deep breath. "Where to start..."

In as few words as he could, and in a slightly less chaotic fashion than he'd explained it to Domi and Erica, Zeke explained his theory about the two Systems, the overall System and the System Apocalypse, and what role each possibly had. When he was finished, Mia nodded slowly. "So basically, the System we interact with might be an Apocalypse, just like the rest of us. One that somehow already infected-slash-conquered the whole world, but doesn't register with the main System, so the rest of us have to keep going."

Zeke nodded. "Yeah, that's...that's about it, yeah."

"Right." Mia took a slow breath, settling herself, then nodded again. "Right. Okay. Yeah. I see why you didn't want to tell everyone."

"Yeah. They'd think I was insane. Or I don't know, stress way too much about it," Zeke said, nodding.

Mia nodded. "I think it's the right decision. You...should probably tell Ryan, though."

"Ryan? He's one of the ones I least want to tell," Zeke said, recoiling.

"Yeah, but...of everyone, isn't he the one most likely to know if there's any evidence for this?"

"Wouldn't he have said something by now?"

Mia spread her hands. "Have you never been in that situation where all the clues are there, but you just haven't put them together, until someone else comes up with a solution, and then it all falls into place?"

Zeke frowned, then nodded, slowly. "Like when Taylor said he was gay, yeah."

"Honestly, I think you were the only one who hadn't put two and two together about Taylor, Zeke. He came to school in a pink mesh shirt once. *Pink mesh.*"

Zeke shrugged. "I just thought he was a dude who liked fashion. Some dudes like fashion, I don't know."

Mia sighed. "The point is, Ryan might have seen all the clues, but just never put them together. Explain it to him, then ask him, and listen to what he has to say—you know what, actually? I'm coming."

"I can have a conversation with Ryan," Zeke said, rolling his eyes.

"Can you? Can you really? With neither of you blowing up or accusing the other of something insane?" Mia crossed her arms. "I'm coming, Zeke. Whether you like it or not."

Zeke sighed. He rubbed the back of his neck. "All right, fine. It's not like I don't want you there, anyway, so whatever."

Mia grinned. "Excellent. A good choice."

"But we don't know where he is, so..." Zeke shrugged.

"We don't know where who is?" a familiar voice asked from behind him.

Zeke whirled. Ryan stood there, arms crossed, his blond hair floating on the wind. He nodded at Zeke, just once.

"Jeez! You scared the shit outta me! Can't you just come up and say hey like a normal person, just once?" Zeke asked.

Ryan clicked his tongue. "Nope."

Zeke scowled. "Ryan..."

Mia put a hand on his arm. "This is exactly what I mean."

Zeke threw his hands up. "We aren't even fighting!"

"We could be," Ryan said, eyeing Zeke.

"You, too. Chill out, and listen to what Zeke has to say," Mia said firmly.

Ryan looked at Mia, then turned to Zeke. He clasped his hands in front of him and nodded. "Go on, then. What do you have to say?"

"I..." Zeke took a deep breath. He reiterated everything he'd just told Mia.

When he was done, Ryan frowned at the ground. His eyes widened, then narrowed, brows raising, then furrowing. Slowly, he nodded his head. "That...yeah. That actually...I hate to say it, but it makes a lot of sense."

"Yeah," Zeke said. Mia nudged him, giving him a glare. He looked at her, then sighed and went on, "What do you mean by that? Have you seen clues?"

"That...yes. Some things, like only being able to go back so far in time, you mentioned yourself. But there's also...the space between."

"The space between?" Zeke asked.

Ryan lifted both hands. He held them out flat, palms facing each other, almost touching. "The most common theory of the multiverse is that it's shaped like this. Like a bunch of towels hanging on a rack, almost touching, but not quite. Now obviously, it's not exactly like towels, but if the towels were three- or four-dimensional objects, hanging in a five-dimensional space..."

"Yeah. I get it. I understand metaphors," Zeke deadpanned.

Ryan snorted. He nodded. "When I travel in time, it's not like rewinding a tape. Even for a little hop, I leave reality and move elsewhere in it. For little hops, things that won't disturb entire timelines, I land in the same towel. But sometimes I take a big hop, a towel-crossing hop." He lifted a finger on one of his hands and touched the palm of the other. "And either way, I spend time *somewhere else.* Not in this world, not in that one. Not in this time, or the past. I call that place 'the space between.'"

"Makes sense," Zeke said. *As much as any part of time travel makes sense.*

"Right. So. When I'm in the space between, I can't access any of my skills or pull up my stat sheet, but obviously, I still have my Concept. I can still time travel, or else I'd just be fucked the second I entered the space between. I thought it was some kind of restriction implemented by the System. You know. Something so I couldn't just hang out in the space between forever, and mess around with skills until I hit level infinity, or whatever. But if it's not an intentional restriction...if it's because the System Apocalypse handles all that, and the System Apocalypse, being an Apocalypse like the rest of us, bound to this world, can't exist in the space between..."

Zeke nodded. He looked at Ryan. "And all your skills reset when you go back in time, right?"

"Right. That could be explained either way...but it sure makes a lot more sense if it's a different instance of the System

Apocalypse every time." He put a hand on his chin. "Come to think of it, I sometimes get offered different skills. I always thought that was just, you know, a random number generator or something, but..." He twisted his lips, thinking.

"Yeah. The problem is that it's just a theory, and there's no real way to prove or disprove it. Even your experiences are just hints, nothing more," Zeke said, shrugging.

"But...I think you've missed the most terrifying thing I said just now," Ryan said. He looked at Zeke. "The System exists in the space between. Concepts exist in the space between. The thing that drives the System, the System itself, however you want to put it...it's a multidimensional being so powerful that it rules over all multiverses I can access, and the space between them as well."

Zeke's eyes widened. He sucked in a breath. *Holy shit, Ryan's right. That's incredibly fucking powerful. That's on the level of literal godlike being, not joking godlike being.*

I warned you.

I told you this knowledge could crush you.

Stop spreading it. I can only hide so much.

Zeke jolted. He looked around. "Did you guys get those messages, too?"

Mia stared back at him, wide-eyed and pale. She nodded.

Ryan nodded as well, his brows furrowed in concern. He took a deep breath. "That's terrifying."

"Yeah."

They all stood in silence for a moment, staring at the ground, each lost in thought. Abruptly, Mia laughed. "You know, it kinda makes the Apocalypse Coalition sound way less threatening, you know?"

Zeke laughed as well. "You always find a bright side, don't you, Mia."

"I try, I try."

"All right." Zeke dusted his hands off and nodded at them. "Let's rest up, get well fed, and take down this Apocalypse Coalition, then, I don't know, face off against a god itself."

Ryan snorted. "Sounds like a plan to me."

41
APOCALYPSE COALITION

When the morning came, Zeke once again gathered everyone up in the lobby of Heather's apartment. He faced all of them, looking over them, and took a deep breath.

"Boo!" Domi shouted, over a plate of steaming scrambled eggs.

"Oh, come on, I haven't even started yet," Zeke complained.

Domi grinned.

Mia shoveled a bite of hashbrowns into her mouth and nodded. "So?"

"Right. So. We're going to face the Apocalypse Coalition."

"Did Ryan find where it is?" Eric asked, through a mouthful of breakfast sandwich.

Ryan scoffed. "I couldn't *not* find it. They aren't exactly hiding it."

"Right. So. Some of us are going to go. Some of us are going to have to stay back. We can't not defend this city. After all, the most obvious thing in the world...well, I don't have to say it. We already faced off against Hunter, and he did it."

"Send some people to go get us while the hunting squad is out fighting?" Mia asked.

"Exactly," Zeke said, nodding. "So. Does anyone want to volunteer for the home squad?"

Silence. Nobody met Zeke's eyes.

Heather threw her hand up. "Me! I want to be home squad!"

Zeke laughed, thankful for the tension break. "So, anyone else?"

Jimmy and Sarah exchanged a glance. At last, Jimmy raised their hands together. "I think we, uh, do better at home."

Zeke nodded. *I wasn't going to put kids on the front lines, anyway. I draw the line at child soldiers.* "Good. We need more people to stay back. Anyone else?"

Issac yawned. He sat up, propping his chin on his fist. "Are you waiting for me to volunteer?"

Grimacing, Zeke shrugged. "You tell me, man. You tell me."

He sighed. "I got captured last time. I do better with all my cats around. I'll stay home. Besides, someone needs to eat the Scouting Apocalypse's birds."

Domi's eyebrows raised, and she giggled, then nudged Olivia. "I thought he was going to stop at 'eat the Scouting Apocalypse.' Thought Zeke was gonna have some competition."

Olivia laughed as well, leaning toward Domi. She hesitated a moment, then lifted her hand as well. "I should stay home. I'm... I have too many weaknesses. I do better on a battleground where I can control the setting."

Zeke lowered his head. "Yeah. Thanks, Olivia."

Domi looked him in the eyes. "I'm going."

"No, you're going," Zeke agreed. He looked at Mia. "If you want to?"

"Yeah. I want to," Mia said.

Zeke looked at Eric and Ryan. "And you two?"

"Yeah, of course. I think Erica would be super pissed if I didn't go," Eric said.

Zeke nodded, then turned back. He squinted. *Is Eric wearing lip gloss?*

Eric tilted his head, confused.

He turned away. *Hey, dudes can be into fashion, too.* "Ryan?"

"Can't stop me."

Sparkles stood up. He barked.

"You want to go?" Zeke asked. He sighed, sharing a glance with Mia.

She shrugged and tapped her ear.

Yeah?

If we take him, we can keep an eye on him. It's not a horrible proposition.

Zeke considered, tilting his head back and forth, then nodded. "You can come, sure. Why not."

Sparkles barked excitedly and bounced once, landing with sturdy legs and an alert expression.

"Zel?" Zeke asked, only to turn and find no one standing there. He spun in a slow circle. "Anyone seen Zel?"

"Who's Zel?" Ryan asked.

"We've decided we're calling other-Zeke Zel."

"Oh, the guy who almost killed me. Sure. Give him a cute nickname," Ryan said, rolling his eyes.

"To be fair, you literally nuked his entire plane of existence," Zeke pointed out. "Like completely destroyed his timeline. Killed everyone he knew and loved. I'd be pretty pissed if I were him."

Ryan shrugged, making an 'eh' expression.

"That's not 'eh'—" Zeke took a deep breath. He closed his eyes. *Focus. Don't get drawn into Ryan's bullshit.* "Everyone, finish breakfast, and we'll get going."

"We ride at dawn," Domi said dramatically.

"Dawn was, like, three hours ago," Olivia pointed out.

Domi waved her hand. "Eh. Close enough."

"We ride at close enough dawn!" Zeke declared.

Mia laughed. "God, we're so sloppy."

"Yeah. We're like, the world's laziest superheroes," Zeke said, grinning.

Everyone finished breakfast and piled out. There was a bit of kerfuffle finding a car that could fit everyone, since Sparkles, as large as he was, effectively took two chairs, but eventually, they all found a spot. The car drove off, in the opposite direction as the Ice Cream Apocalypse. Ryan rode shotgun. He pointed out the directions to Domi, directing her left and right at the corners. Zeke squeezed in the back with Mia, Sparkles, and Eric. Sparkles laid on their feet, bouncing along with every bump, his little 'fro leaning with the car. Zeke patted his head, and Sparkles looked at him. He leaned forward and rested his chin on Zeke's lap, panting slightly.

"You're gonna have wet pants," Eric commented.

"What's going on back there?" Domi asked loudly.

"A dog's head is on my thigh. That's all," Zeke said, equally loudly.

"You guys are having a good time in the back seat, huh?" Ryan asked, laughing.

Zeke caught his eye in the rear view mirror and waggled his brows. "Bet you wish you'd picked the back seat now, huh?"

"Damn right," Ryan said.

Mia slapped his arm. She rolled her eyes. "Zeke, come on."

"Yeah, yeah."

The car trundled on. Once again, they drove alone, the only car moving on the streets. Zeke gazed out the window thoughtfully. *Most of the world is dead. We can beat the Apocalypse Coalition, but will we win?*

Actually, for that matter, my family is out there, somewhere. If they aren't dead. Zeke could think it, but no emotions welled up. As if he'd never had a family.

His brows furrowed. He frowned. *Actually...what did they look like? My family. My mom and dad. My...I had a sister, right? Why can't I picture any of them? I... Where did we live? The suburbs? Right, and I was...considering going to college? No, I was going to college, but... Huh? Where? Why was I...?*

He rubbed his temples, squinting.

"What is it, Zeke?" Mia asked.

Zeke looked up at her. "Can you picture your mom and dad? Their faces."

Mia squinted at him. "Of course, I..." Her brows furrowed.

On the other side of Zeke, Eric squinted as well. "Huh? Why...?"

"Don't—don't do that," Ryan said, catching their eye in the rearview mirror.

"So, you already knew about it?" Zeke asked.

Ryan snorted. "Yeah. Happened to me a long time ago. I don't know if it's the System, or what, but it happens slowly to everyone. In long loops, it happened to you guys, too. For me..."

"You lost your memories of your family a long time ago, huh?" Zeke asked, quietly.

Ryan shrugged. "Yeah. It's not as tragic as you make it sound. It's fine. I can remember everything important, after all. Everything about the actual System and the loops and everything."

Zeke pressed his lips together. After a moment, he nodded. "Okay. If you say so." *If Ryan says not to push it, let's not. Especially not on the eve of a battle. The last thing we need to do is distract ourselves with psychological trauma right before we fight.*

Mia gasped. She looked at Zeke.

"What?" Zeke asked.

"You agreed with Ryan! Without even fighting! Are you

really Zeke, or some kind of imposter?" she accused him, mock serious.

Zeke laughed. He shook his head. "I agree with Ryan sometimes. I used to agree with him all the time."

"Not since I've known you," Domi said, lifting her head to look in the rearview mirror.

On the other side, Eric shook his head, too.

Zeke sighed. "You guys..."

"So, the lesson is, you should agree with me more," Ryan said boldly.

"I don't know about that," Mia said.

Zeke pointed at Mia, raising his eyes at Ryan in the mirror.

Ryan shook his head. "Which one of us time travels? It's crazy how none of you guys listen to the literal time traveler."

"Maybe if the literal time traveler didn't spend half his time trying to kill us, we'd listen to him more," Zeke pointed out.

Domi pointed at Ryan, raising her brows.

"Oh, come on. I haven't done that in ages," Ryan said.

"It's something that takes a while to get over, I'll be honest," Zeke said.

"Same for me, man. Same for me," Ryan agreed. They met eyes in the rearview mirror. Zeke narrowed his, and Ryan waggled his back.

Zeke looked away, shaking his head. "Yeah, yeah."

"Oh, here we are. There it is," Ryan said, leaning forward to peer out the windshield.

As one, everyone in the back row leaned in, trying to look out the windshield as well. They all looked up.

Eric took a deep breath. "Jeez. Wow. No kidding, they weren't hiding."

"Yeah, see? See? It would be harder for me to *not* find it!" Ryan said, gesturing.

"Mmm, yeah, I gotta agree with you this time," Zeke said.

"Man, that's two Zeke-Ryan agreements in like, ten seconds," Mia breathed, eyes wide.

Zeke gestured out the window.

Mia laughed. "Yeah. I mean, yeah. Sometimes, Ryan's just right. Nothing we can say about this one, I don't think."

Domi took a deep breath, then nodded to herself. "I think this is as far as we drive. Everyone out!"

"Yes, ma'am!" Zeke hopped out, and all the other Apocalypses climbed out behind him. They stared up, taking in the whole thing.

"From outside, it's even crazier," Mia whispered.

"Yeah, I know," Eric said.

Zeke shook his head. "How powerful is the Apocalypse that it could create a Domain this expansive?"

Domi wrinkled her nose. "Don't say that."

Shaking his head one last time, Zeke stepped forward. "Enough talk. Let's get moving."

42

ENOUGH TALK

Before them, a giant golden staircase ascended upward toward the sky. It climbed up and up, vanishing into the clouds overhead. Zeke stared up it, tilting his head back farther and farther. "Do you think the Apocalypse is at the top of that?"

"Not a bad idea, really," Ryan commented. He nodded his head at the staircase. "Put a physical trial ahead of your actual stronghold. Force the enemy to exhaust themselves reaching you. As far as strategies go, it's a classic one that's been popular from medieval times. Putting your castle at the top of a hill, for example, or better yet, atop a mountain, for example."

"Usually, it's also a defensible position, though. Tall walls, so you can fire down on the enemy, drop hot oil, whatever. This gold staircase, though? How are they gonna defend it?" Zeke asked.

"I don't know, but I ain't climbing that thing. Can we just go around it?" Domi asked.

Mia glanced at the others, then ran off. She circled around the back of the staircase and came back. "We can, but..." She pointed up. "The Apocalypse is above us."

They all stared up. High overhead, supported on the clouds themselves, a city hovered. Towering skyscrapers truly scraped the sky. Glittering windows shone down from on high.

Zeke licked his lips. "Welp. That's, uh. Not great."

"You were worried about Osiris dropping the maze on our heads, huh? This thing makes that sound tame," Domi commented, shaking her head at the sky.

"Yeah. I mean, all the Apocalypses have been load-bearing bosses, so far...and, well, when the cities are built on their Domain skills, yeah, it tracks..." Zeke licked his lips. He looked around the group, then raised his hand. "Raise your hand if you can fly. Or well save yourself from a drop."

Domi raised her hand. Mia and Eric did as well. Ryan raised his hand a little bit, then waggled it. "I can teleport. Close enough."

Zeke looked at Sparkles. Sparkles sat down and barked.

He looked around. "Anyone speak dog?"

Ryan looked at Sparkles, then patted the dog's flank. "Since the rest of us can fly, as long as he sticks near one of us, he'll be fine."

"True," Zeke said.

"He might get burned if he sticks near me," Domi commented.

"Okay, as long as he's near anyone but Domi, and also, who knows, he might be able to fly anyway." Zeke looked at the staircase one more time, then looked around. "Soooo, if everyone can fly...are we going to take the stairs?"

"Yeah. Gotta try it, right?" Mia said.

"I mean, flying is harder than stairs, right?" Domi said, half-certain.

Ryan shrugged. "I'll scout ahead with my teleport skill. If there's anything sussy about the staircase, I'll let you guys know, and you can fly the rest of the way."

Zeke nodded. "Then, we're all in agreement? Stairs?"

"Stairs...until we get tired of them, and then we fly," Domi said firmly.

Zeke snorted. "Got it."

He lifted his foot and stepped onto the stairs. Nothing in particular happened. He glanced around, then took another step, then another, then another.

"You uh, all right, Zeke?" Domi asked.

Zeke looked over his shoulder and shrugged down at her. "I don't know. I'm just suspicious of these stairs. They have to be suspicious somehow, right? There's no way there's just a giant staircase at the base of an Apocalypse, and there's nothing strange about it."

"Or it's just a giant staircase that's meant to exhaust us and allow the Apocalypse to see us coming," Ryan pointed out, his arms crossed.

Zeke jumped off the stairs. *I do* not *want to fight a battle on the stairs.* "Okay, on second thought, we're all flying. Domi, can you fly all the way up there?"

"It's more like hovering. I'll need a lift," Domi said.

"You can walk on my platforms with me," Mia said.

"That sounds a lot like climbing stairs," Domi countered. She glanced at Zeke.

Zeke shook his head. "I'll carry you. *Lazy.*"

Domi threw her hands up. "I'm just trying to beat them at their own game! If they want to exhaust us with a billion stairs, then we beat them by not exhausting ourselves. In other words, being lazy! Look, it's just plain logic."

"She's got a point," Ryan said.

Zeke sighed. "Fine, fine. Eric, can you transform, or do you need to walk with Mia?"

"It's, uh, probably better if I walk with Mia, if she's okay with it. Erica gets exhausted if she's constantly using her powers," Eric said.

Sparkles barked again.

Zeke looked at him. "You, uh, take the stairs? Or climb with Mia. Either way."

Sparkles turned a circle, then charged up the stairs.

Ryan shook his head. "I guess he's still got plenty of energy."

"Dogs, man." Zeke held his arms out, and Domi slotted herself into them. He extended his wings and took off into the sky. Behind him, Mia formed a platform and waited for Eric to climb on, then lifted them up into the sky, the platform directly ascending like an elevator.

Ryan vanished. He reappeared a few hundred steps up, only to vanish again and teleport up again. All of them using their skills, they climbed up into the sky, with only Sparkles taking the stairs.

"Man. I'd be pissed," Domi commented.

"What, if you built a billion stairs, and then everyone just flew up anyway?"

She nodded. "I mean, that's a significant amount of effort. Though..." She looked up. "I guess the Apocalypses that can't fly need a way into the city."

"Yeah. You'd think they'd build an elevator, though. It's like the stairs are saying, 'get a fly skill and get good, skrubs!'" Zeke said mockingly.

Domi thought for a moment, then pursed her lips. "Come to think of it, it kind of locks Apocalypses in, doesn't it? If you can't fly, you can't escape, even if you want to."

"She's an Apocalypse. There's more than one way to prevent escape," Zeke said, but at the same time, his spine tingled. *Preventing escape. Is that for her own men...or is that for us?*

I guess we're going to find out. Locking his eyes at the top of the staircase, he flapped his way upward.

43
THE CITY IN THE SKY

All of them flew upward, except Ryan, who teleported, and Sparkles, who walked. The stairs zipped away beneath them, thousands of them easily dropping away as they flew past. In no time, Zeke reached the top. He dropped down to the edge of the city, releasing Domi on the top of the asphalt.

Domi glanced back. Inches behind her, the asphalt cut sharply off. Past that point, only fluffy clouds spread underfoot. She scooted away from the edge nervously. "I don't like that."

"It's pretty magical," Zeke said, flapping down to land a little ahead of her.

"Magical in a bad way. Magical in the way a curse is magical," Domi grumbled.

A moment later, Mia's platform reached the top. She gestured, and a ramp of gold platforms connected the elevator platform to the city. Mia walked down it, surefooted, while Eric crouched after her, keeping his weight low to the ground and his arms spread.

"Taking it slow, Eric?" Zeke asked, chuckling.

Eric shook his head. He trembled a little. "I'm not that bad afraid of heights, but when you're a thousand feet up on a tiny translucent platform with no railings..."

Zeke laughed. "Yeah, I get it."

Ryan appeared next, appearing up over the top of the stairs. Sparkles charged after him, finishing the last stairs with ease. He walked over into the center of the road and plopped down, panting.

"He wore himself out," Zeke said, shaking his head.

"Playing right into our opponents' hands," Domi whispered.

The two of them made eye contact, and they cracked up.

Mia shook her head. "Focus, you two. We're on enemy turf."

"Sure, but..." Zeke turned, gesturing. Aside from the sky stretching all around them, they stood on the verge of an ordinary, if abandoned, city. He shrugged. "Where's the enemy?"

Mia looked around as well, as did Ryan, Eric, and Sparkles. Domi yawned, stretching. "Not like it's the first time we've been left cold at the gate. Let's head on in and see what we're dealing with."

Zeke shrugged. "She's not wrong."

"Yeah, fair." Mia turned, gazing down the street. "Still, all the more reason to remain on alert."

"Should we split up?" Ryan suggested. "Me, Domi, and the dog, you, Mia, Eric? That way we've got one AOE fighter—Domi, Eric—to two melee fighters."

"I count as AOE?" Eric asked.

"Kinda...half-AOE. But Zeke makes up the other half," Ryan said, squinting and wiggling his hand.

Zeke shrugged. "Sure. That sounds good to me." *The future-seer and the maybe-traitor—that is, the dog—together on one team? That's a match made in heaven.*

Eric hesitated, then nodded. "Okay."

"You wanna swap?" Domi offered.

"What, you aren't satisfied?" Ryan asked.

Domi glanced over her shoulder at him. "No offense, but I like Zeke more than I like you."

"Some taken," Ryan murmured. After a second, he shrugged. "Yeah, I mean, you were always Zeke's sidekick menace. Eric, wanna come with me instead? I'm way cooler than those losers."

Eric glanced around, then shrugged. "I'm fine with whatever, so..."

"Sidekick menace? The hell is a sidekick menace?" Domi complained under her breath.

"You, apparently," Zeke muttered back.

She snorted. "Fair, I guess."

Zeke nodded. "We'll take the left, you take the right?"

"Works for me."

With a last nod, they split off, each taking a street through the city.

As they walked, Mia sighed.

"Penny for your thoughts?" Zeke asked.

"I really hoped you and Ryan could make up. Before the end," Mia said.

Zeke shrugged. "There's still time."

"But...yeah. I don't know. I thought it would've happened by now." She looked over her shoulder at Ryan's back. He walked away, shoulders set. Eric noticed her looking and waved, and she waved back. Ryan never turned.

The other group turned a corner and passed out of sight. Mia lowered her hand. "He's just...he's so cold. He keeps to himself too much. It's like he doesn't trust any of us."

"Yeah, because he doesn't," Zeke said, snorting under his breath.

Mia glanced at him. "I get him not trusting you. I think he's being crazy, but I get it. But...he doesn't trust any of us. He hasn't opened up to a single person. Not even the people he shouldn't be afraid of, or wary of, like me."

"Since all you did was die," Domi agreed.

Zeke elbowed her. "Hey."

Mia nodded. "No, she's right. There's no reason he should have his guard up around me. I couldn't do anything if all I did was die every time. So why?"

"Well, maybe that's why. He's not wary of you, he's wary of getting attached to you. You didn't do anything wrong, but dying so many times made him write you off as expendable." Zeke put his hands up. "We don't know what's going on in his head, and we can't because he won't talk to us."

"I'll be honest, I'm not worried about him. I'm worried about Zel," Domi said. She nudged Zeke. "You're the last one who saw him. Did he tell you what he was going to do?"

Zeke shook his head. "Nope. Actually, I didn't even see him. I just got in touch with Hands-Free Calling."

"And that was it, huh? Nothing heard since. Yeah. That's the one I'm worried about. One Zeke is bad enough. Two Zekes? I'm not sure there's enough food in the world. People. Whatever counts for food anymore for you."

Zeke glanced at her. "What do you mean?"

She snorted. "As if we haven't noticed. You aren't eating, Zeke. Except for weird shit. And every time we eat, you give your food this sad look. Plus, you're out there farming bugs and shit... It doesn't take a genius to put two and two together."

"Yeah...guess not," Zeke muttered. He scratched the back of his head, then grinned. "I mean, it's not that bad, yet. I'm still feeding myself."

"Yeah, for now." She looked ahead of her, at the path through the floating city. "And after we destroy all the Apocalypses, then what? I can get a job doing demolitions. Mia can, I don't know, become a firefighter or something. Ryan...world's his oyster, so long as he can avoid destroying it. Even Eric's got a job. He'd make a killing as a performer. What about you?"

Zeke shrugged. He looked at the ground. "I don't know."

"We still have a long time ahead of us," Mia said.

"Do we?" Zeke murmured.

Under their feet, the ground twitched. And overhead, bright light filled the sky.

Domi squinted. "What the..."

"WELCOME!" a voice boomed, echoing down the streets.

44

WELCOMING PARTY

"WELCOME!" a voice boomed, so loud they flinched. Zeke stepped forward, searching for the source, and Mia twisted her wrist, summoning her sword to her hand. Domi lifted her hand, and a dozen small balls of fire traced after it, burning in the air around her.

Overhead, the bright light condensed into a single form, and the beautiful woman who'd stopped the young man with the ARKOS gear hovered in the sky. She smiled benevolently down on them, in a vague sort of way that suggested she couldn't see them at all.

From another part of the city, a giant arrow flew forth and pierced through her body. The arrow passed smoothly through without doing any damage. Behind it, her body reformed smoothly, not a body at all but merely projected light.

"Oh, hello. It's good to meet you all. I apologize that I cannot greet you in person, but then, there's just so many of you." She gave them a gentle smile.

Somewhere distantly, someone shouted in extreme fury.

"I've brought you all here, from all over the world, for one purpose: to end this, once and for all. You are all the

Apocalypses who refused to join my coalition, which, unfortunately, means I must dispose of you, if I'm to bring this world to an end. Whether you wrong-headedly decided to save this pitiful world, or wanted to end it your own way, thus winning the Apocalypse, you are all my enemies."

"What? Hold on, an Apocalypse this powerful was within driving distance?" Domi muttered.

"Please do not worry overmuch about the details. My skills allow me to create befuddling paths that all lead to the same place, and I did so for all of you. If you don't believe me, please, look over the edge of the city."

Zeke, Domi, and Mia exchanged a glance. As one, they ran to the city's edge.

Instead of the familiar landscape they'd been on before, the endless ocean stretched below them, sloshing all the way to either horizon. A dolphin jumped out of the water, chasing a fish, then vanished.

"Holy fuck," Domi breathed.

"Yeah, what she said," Zeke seconded. *When did that happen? While we were flying up? But someone would have noticed if the ground changed beneath us—no, I would have. Then...the city we saw in the sky...was it an illusion? An illusion that covered up a teleportation portal, maybe?*

That's probably the easiest explanation. Damn! An Apocalypse that can spread portals all over the world? That girl is powerful. Too powerful. Zeke looked up at the sky, wary.

And then a thought struck him. "If she brought us all here, why not just kill us on the way?"

"Maybe she can create teleporters, but not death traps?" Mia suggested.

"For that matter, she accelerates her own victory by bringing us all together, sure, but she also gives any one of us the chance to kill all the others and level up that way," Domi pointed out.

"Maybe she didn't think of that?" Mia asked.

A chill ran down Zeke's spine, and he grimaced. "Or maybe it doesn't matter, even if one of us kills all the other Apocalypses and emerges victorious. Maybe she's just that powerful. Maybe there's no point expending the energy in setting death traps, and worrying that someone spots one and escapes, when she can simply teleport us all to the same place...then squash whatever bug manages to kill all the other bugs."

"Plus, whoever wins will be tired by the time they beat all the others. Minimum expenditure of her energy for maximum effect," Domi said.

Zeke looked at Domi and Mia. "I wonder if she knows?"

"Knows what? That there's something beyond this?" Mia asked.

Zeke nodded. "And she's saving her energy for the real battle."

"Well. That's a bastard of a move, then," Domi complained, rolling up her sleeves. She glanced at Zeke, then chuckled. "Or should we thank her? Saves us the trouble of travelling the world looking for the rest of them."

"Yeah, ain't that the truth." Zeke grinned back, rolling up his sleeves as well.

Overhead, the projection spoke again. "Please, battle to your heart's content. The winner will gain the right to challenge my Apocalypse Coalition directly."

"We already did that," Domi called at her.

"We already took out her trash," Zeke said, shaking his head. "I'm sure of it, now. Those people they sent to the Ice Cream Apocalypse were just there in the off chance they'd level up and become worthy members of her Coalition. They were never real members."

"What about the Scouting Apocalypse?" Mia asked.

"Not too sure about him. Though, if I had to guess...he's probably a real member of the coalition, just not a member of the fighting force. He's gotta be the one who found all of us Apocalypses—at least, all of us on the continent. She probably had other equivalent Apocalypses for the far-flung locations."

"Or she teleported him over there and back," Mia suggested.

"It's possible. But then, why would he keep an eye on us, if he was busy scouting the whole world?" Zeke wondered.

Domi shrugged. "Maybe we're the only other group of Apocalypses out there. If I were a big-ass Apocalypse Coalition, and I discovered another group getting started, no matter how small, I'd keep an eye on them. Might even feel threatened enough to crush them directly."

"Really? As Mia pointed out, we're only as big as the members she threw away," Zeke said, not so sure.

With a snort, Domi shook her head. "It's human nature. No matter how small we are, we represent the same exact actions she took to succeed. Even if we were a hundredth the size of her group, she'd feel threatened by us and need to crush it. You see it all over the world. Everywhere from big companies crushing little startups to big friend groups bullying the nerds' smaller groups. Human nature, man. Human nature."

"Damn," Zeke muttered.

"Humans aren't all like that," Mia said.

"Yeah, but..." Domi looked up at the sky, where the projection of the girl still floated, a benevolent expression on her face. "Most of the big, powerful ones? Cutthroat as hell."

In the distance, a loud *BANG* rolled through the air. A fireball poofed up from a street along the edge of the city.

Zeke backed away from the edge, jogging back toward the street. "She can be as cutthroat as she wants. I don't care if she thinks we're all bugs. I'm gonna kill every other Apocalypse here and get so strong she can't ignore me. And then, I'm going to eat her, too."

"Well said!" Domi followed him, grinning.

"We won't let her win," Mia said, though her brows remained a little furrowed.

"Our battle doesn't stop here. We take on the System Apocalypse, and then the System itself. Even if we have to fight through every other Apocalypse in the world, we'll do it. We'll get it done," Zeke said firmly.

Again, the road shifted under their feet, harder this time. Zeke threw his arms out to catch himself. The asphalt jolted, throwing him into the air. It curled up underneath them, then smashed down, roiling up and down like the coils of a snake. A coil of asphalt surged toward him, seeking to strike him out of the air.

"Holy shit—"

45
ROAD SNAKE

As the coil of asphalt flew toward him, a thought came to Zeke. *Maybe this wasn't to crush all the bugs at once. Maybe this wasn't a mistake, that might allow one of us bug to climb to the top.*

Maybe she brought us all here, to feed EXP to her pet Apocalypses. Set us all up to fail from the beginning, to strengthen her minions.

Zeke threw his wings out and flapped hard, surging into the air even as the asphalt coil leaped at him. To his right, Mia materialized a platform beside her and thrust it into her side, sending herself flying through the air toward the edge of the road. To his left, Domi pointed her hands down and blasted a hole through the road. The road heaved up over her, and she chased after it with her hands, lobbing explosions at it to cut the road completely in half.

The severed part of the road crashed down. Domi threw herself to the side at the last second, barely dodging the ragged edge of the asphalt. She turned on the much shorter segment of road and raised her hands, ready to blast it to bits.

The shorter part of the road struck the ground next to Domi, tossing her up into the air. While she was distracted catching herself, it pushed its end into the cut-off part of the road. Asphalt hissed. The scent of hot tar filled the air. Reconnected once more, the road gave itself a shake to test the join, then curled up. It pointed its end at them and let off a fearsome hiss, its entire body steaming. Hot tar sizzled, dripping down its long, flat body.

Mia caught herself on a platform off the edge of the road and climbed to her feet. Down on the ground, Domi landed and lifted her hands, ready to fight.

"The core is in that part of its body!" Zeke shouted, pointing at the short end that had reconnected itself to the rest of the road. "Close in and destroy it!"

"Yes, sir!" Domi pressed her hands together. A big orange ball formed between them. With each passing second, it grew larger and larger.

Mia nodded. She drew her sword and dashed in, cutting toward the surface of the road.

Chunks of wet tar fell away, only to reconnect a moment later. The road bent around on itself, circling around Mia so fast Zeke could barely see the motion. In the next instant, the rode clenched, squeezing down on Mia.

"Mia!" Zeke ran in, terrified.

A single mote of gold light burned in the road's surface. It whirled around, and then Mia kicked a chunk of road away and escaped. Gold platforms hovered around her, forming a cocoon that had saved her from the road's wrath.

Zeke let out a sigh of relief. Mia grinned at him and fled, running away on gold platforms, none the worse for the wear.

"Take this, asshole!" Rearing back, Domi lobbed the soccer-ball-sized lump of light at the road. The road surged toward it and batted it away. It barely flew a dozen feet before it exploded. The road rocked with the force, bits of its surface blown away, but it didn't take serious damage.

"Dammit," Domi complained.

Zeke's eyes widened. "Domi, make another one of those. Mia, be ready with your platforms."

Domi frowned, but Mia's eyes widened. She nodded. "Understood.

Shrugging, Domi backed away, pressing her palms together again. "You got it, Boss."

The road reared up, then struck, fast as a snake. Mia threw up her hands, and its head slammed into a gold wall rather than striking Domi. Watching overhead, Zeke couldn't help but feel a little useless.

Then again, it's a Road Apocalypse. What am I going to do, eat the road?

The road surged. It whipped around, then darted up toward Zeke.

Zeke laughed to himself, watching it come. "Yeah. Guess I eat the road."

He dodged the road's edge-on strike. The road flew past him, then stopped and fell back in on itself, trying to fall on Zeke and smash him to the ground. Zeke flapped his wings, shooting out from under the road's shadow. It paused in its fall, whipping around to smack him into the building across the way. Surprised, Zeke couldn't dodge this time. He dropped a little in the air, and then the road struck his back. He crashed through the building's windows and rolled across a carpeted office floor, throwing desks aside as he went. At last, he came to a halt. For a second, Zeke just lay there.

Big hit. That was a biiiig hit.

"Zeke!" Mia shouted.

He jumped up. *That's right. I can't get stunned now!* He ran to the window, grabbing on to the metal supports that had once held the windows, and looked down. Domi held a big explosive ball in her hands. She swayed in place, struggling to contain it. Opposite her, Mia backed away from the road as it swayed, preparing to strike.

"Now!" Zeke shouted. "Domi, release the ball! Mia, use your platforms!"

Domi heaved back her arms and threw with all her might. The orange ball soared toward the road-snake. The road reared back again, preparing to strike it away.

As it smacked into the ball, Mia's eyes glittered. She snapped her fingers.

Gold platforms appeared around the ball, connecting it to the road. The road hit the ball, but with the ball now stuck to its body, it failed to bat it away. The road shook itself, startled, then flew toward the building, trying to wipe the ball off.

Shit! Zeke sprinted into the building, away from the road.

BAM!

The building rocked. A fireball blasted through the floor, surging at Zeke. The force of the explosion lifted him off his feet and threw him against the far wall, and then the fireball singed his skin. He leaned against the wall, his hearing nothing but a single high whine, his breath ragged. Pain shot through him, pain that intensified with every breath.

Fuck, that hurts.

The building seemed to sway under his feet. Pushing away from the wall, Zeke staggered back to the windows. He fell against the metal support, barely feeling the hot metal, and looked down.

Far below, the road-snake wobbled. The hot tar melted, barely keeping it together. In the center of its long, sinuous body, a gleaming core shone.

Zeke's eyes widened. Throwing all his pain away, he leaped out of the building and snapped his wings out. He swooped down on the core and snatched it up, flapping back up into the sky in the same motion. Without any other thought, he shoved the core into his mouth.

[Devour]
Congratulations! Defeated the Road Apocalypse!

His regeneration rate surged, healing the wounds all over his body. Zeke flew up into the air, taking a moment to catch his bearings. Down below, the road slowly melted into itself, dead as a doornail. Domi and Mia stood at the end of the street, waving to him.

He squinted. *Why are they waving to me?*

Mia waved both hands. Her mouth opened wide.

It looks like they're screaming, too. But the Apocalypse is dead. So why...?

A shadow fell over him. Zeke looked up.

The massive office building drooped toward him, crashing down from above.

46

FALLING BUILDING

Zeke's eyes widened. He flapped his wings harder than he'd ever flapped them before, diving down toward the street even as he flew. The shadow closed in on him. Bricks and broken glass tumbled down, smashing silently to the ground around him. He flew faster, even as regeneration reached his ears and his hearing popped back in. The horrible creaking and shatter-crash of rubble striking the ground only made the whole thing worse. Zeke's eyes locked onto the edge of the shadow, his wings powering faster than ever. *Come on. Come on!*

The edge of the building obscured his vision, falling at an angle to block his route ahead. A small gap remained between the blown-out windows. He shot for it.

The gap dropped toward the road. Zeke grimaced. *I'm not going to make it.*

Domi pointed at him, narrowing her eyes.

"Wha...?"

A blast struck Zeke from behind and threw him forward, accelerating him through the gap in the building and out onto the other side. He hit the ground, rolled, and jumped back up, snatching up Mia and Domi and powering away. A video he'd seen once of a concrete block flying a mile from a demolished building and shooting inches from a man's head replayed in his mind over and over. *We're not out of danger yet. Not yet!*

Debris rained down around them. Bricks and hunks of steel flew by. Zeke reached the end of the street and turned a hard corner, only to keep flying. Two streets away, far enough away the buildings and roads would absorb the debris, he finally slowed and put Mia and Domi down.

"Whoo! Do it again!" Domi whooped, throwing her hands in the air.

Mia stumbled, catching her breath. She stared over her shoulder at the still-collapsing building, her eyes wide. "Holy shit. *Holy shit.*"

Zeke looked over his shoulder, his heart still pounding. *We barely escaped. And that wasn't even an Apocalypse.*

The city lurched. All of them threw their arms out. Domi summoned an orange ball of force and struck a threatening pose at the road.

"You hear me, bitch? I'm tearing this city out of the sky and ramming it down your throat!" a man roared, closer to them than Zeke would have liked. It echoed from all around them, bouncing off the walls. He, Mia, and Domi exchanged a glance, then backed toward each other, eyeing every intersection warily.

Crash. A man stomped through the building to their right. Shards of glass flew in all directions. Metal cracked and bent behind him. He wore construction gear, including a hard had, work boots, paint-stained jeans, and a high-viz vest. At the sight of the three of them, he stopped and narrowed his eyes.

"You her goons, too?" he asked.

Zeke shook his head. "No, we got brought here, the same as everyone else."

"Hmph." He stomped off, shattering his way through the next building.

The three of them looked at one another, then stared after him.

"I don't know about you, but I'm not picking a fight with a guy who treats his body like a wrecking ball," Domi said.

"It suggests a high stat total..." Mia's voice trailed off.

Zeke looked at the hole through the building the man cut, then back at the other two. He gestured them in. "He's probably high level. That means a lot of EXP we don't want to lose track of. On the other hand, we aren't that well suited to a fight against someone who specced into high CON-high STR like that."

"I can probably cut him," Mia said thoughtfully.

"I don't have much against a high-CON fighter," Zeke confessed.

Domi shook her head. "AOEs never do great against highly defensive units."

"But we can't just let him go. If someone else beats him...or worse, he beats someone else, and keeps getting stronger..." Mia glanced at the other two.

"No, I totally agree. But why don't we let someone else do the hard part first? We'll follow him until he gets in a fight, then swoop in a wipe up the scraps. Twice the EXP, half the effort," Zeke suggested.

"Sure, until someone else has the same idea. He isn't exactly stealthy," Domi said, crossing her arms.

"Unless they team up against us. Plus, I don't really like this idea. It seems mean," Mia protested.

"Strategy isn't nice, typically," Zeke said.

"Mia, you can't be a hero here. I know it's your title, but seriously, you can't. If we fight everyone head-on, we'll exhaust ourselves, and then someone will have the same bright idea

Zeke did, and we'll find ourselves mincemeat." Domi lifted her head, staring after the man. She shrugged. "I say we give it a shot. If someone else gets the same idea, we pull out and go find something else to kill."

"Works for me. Mia?"

"I still don't like this, but..." Mia threw her hands up. "I'm outnumbered."

"Let's go, then," Zeke said, walking into the hole the man had cut through the building.

As he did, he called up the System. *Hey, where's my levels? And my skills, for that matter.*

Level: 95.63 > 111.41 (15 points not assigned)

Put them all in SPR. There was no point trying a balanced build now. Now was the time for minmaxing and going all in. His build hadn't changed. *Especially when there's mind-effecting skills on the board, I need high SPR. Plus, I can always rely on Allen for STR.*

SPR: 34 > 49

He looked at the System again. *And? My skills?*

No valid skills.

Zeke narrowed his eyes. *That has to be bullshit. Come on. Where's the skills?*

No valid skills.

Is this punishment for talking about the System Apocalypse?

No valid skills.

Zeke lifted his lip, frustrated. *What bullshit. A System as shitty as this doesn't deserve to live.*

Don't be rude.

Oh, now you wanna talk to me, huh? Hey, System. What's up with not giving me any more skills? Why'd you suddenly start up with that bullshit?

It's better this way.

For who? You?

No answer.

Zeke gritted his teeth. *All right. Whatever. You were trying to protect me, sure. Stop it. Give me my skills. From where on out, whatever wrong-headed reason you had for hiding skills and not giving me the option to pick them up, give them all to me.*

The System remained silent.

Sighing, Zeke shook his head. He peered around the corner, looking at the next building. Like this one, it had a man-shaped hole in its wall. He led the way, and the girls followed, darting across the street to follow the man's path.

At the next street, the man stood in the middle of the road, staring up at something. Zeke craned his neck from within the building, searching for what the man stared at.

A flash. A small figure rushed down the walls, flying at top speed. *No, not flying. Running...wait.* Zeke squinted. His brain refused to process what his eyes picked up.

"Is that motherfucker skating?" Domi asked, flabbergasted.

Dressed in strappy white clothes and wraparound shades, a man skated down the wall and directly at the wrecking-ball-like construction worker. The long straps flapped in the wind behind him as he skated, snapping like flags. As he approached, the rails on his skates transformed. Sword-like blades burst out from either side of his skates. Their blades ran parallel to the wheels, pointed ahead and behind the skater. He leaped into the air and slashed at the construction worker.

Thin red lines opened up on the construction worker's burly soldiers, joining a dozen thin slashes already dripping blood.

The construction worker's eyes widened. He grinned and grabbed at the man in midair. "Can't dodge now!"

The man swung his center of gravity around, neatly dodging the man's grab with a flip. He landed, the blades retracted, and he skated up the opposite building as if it were a flat surface.

"That skater boy has a tenuous understanding of gravity," Domi commented, propping one arm on her other arm and pinching her chin.

"Seriously, though, what year is it? 1970?" Zeke asked, eyeing the man's skates.

"He's wearing all white, and the wraparound shades? That's more nineties, aughts," Mia commented.

"Yeah, but roller skates?" Zeke pointed out.

Mia spread her hands. "Can't help you there."

"Well, you see, a skateboard would fall out from under him when he went uphill," Domi explained.

"Right, because the rest of this situation makes so much sense," Zeke muttered.

Pausing at the top of the building, the skater looked down on the construction worker. He made a few gestures Zeke didn't recognize, but from the vitriol the skater put into them, he knew they weren't nice.

Below him, the construction worker flipped the skater the bird. "Come down here, ya little freak. Let me give you a biiiiig hug." He gestured like a bear hug, putting violence into the gesture.

The skater laughed and pushed off the building, zooming toward the man.

"I feel like this fight is gonna take a while," Domi commented.

"Yeah, me, too," Zeke agreed.

"Are we just going to watch and wait?" Mia asked, anxious.

"Sure. Let them wear one another out. That's why we followed Mr. Construction in the first place," Domi reasoned.

"It still doesn't sit right with me," Mia said.

"Sits plenty right with me," Domi said with a shrug.

Zeke glanced at Mia. "Both of those people are Apocalypses. I really doubt they held back from killing humans, unlike us. They aren't good people. There's no reason why we should bother giving them a fair fight, when they wouldn't give us a fair fight, given the chance."

"I guess," Mia muttered. She shrugged at nothing.

Domi looked around. They stood in the wreckage of what had been a lobby. Even with Mr. Construction blasting a path through, it remained mostly undisturbed. Domi backed toward the lobby desk and sat on it, pulling her bag over her shoulder. "Anyone want snacks?"

Zeke joined her with a laugh, settling in to watch the fight. After a moment, Mia joined them. Outside, the construction worker and the skater clashed, trading blows, while Domi handed out chocolates. *Yeah, given the chance? I'd much rather be in here,* Zeke thought, nodding to himself.

47
CONSTRUCTION VS ROLLERBLADES

With a roar, the construction worker charged the opposite building. He crashed through the entire front façade, breaking every panel that touched the ground. From on high, the rollerblader watched with curiosity, putting a hand on his chin in mock-concern.

"Try skating past that, fucker!" the construction worker shouted.

The skater nodded. He gestured for the construction worker to get out of his way.

Harrumphing, the construction worker obliged.

"How kind of him," Domi commented.

"I get the feeling he's not a work-smarter kinda guy," Zeke said, shrugging. "He seems more like a bulldoze-through, brute-force kinda guy."

"The skater won't come down if he's too close, and he knows it," Mia said. She pointed. "Last time, he stood there waiting, and the skater just took a break until he backed off."

"I see, I see," Zeke said, nodding.

Domi pointed, gesturing up and down the opposite wall.

"This is why you need traps and ground-effecting skills. If it was me, I'd have that whole wall trapped. Good luck to the skater who wants to skate down a minefield."

"It's a bad matchup all around. The skater can't hurt him, he can't hurt the skater. It's just kind of become a war of attrition," Zeke agreed.

"Which is what it would be if we were fighting, but luckily, the skater decided to do us a solid, not that he knows," Domi said, chuckling at the last bit.

"Rather be in here than out there," Zeke agreed.

The skater hurtled down the wall again. His blades flashed in the sunlight, glinting just like the glass. His straps snapped behind him. His wraparound glasses gleamed.

"He thinks he's so cool," Zeke muttered.

"He *is* so cool," Mia said.

"Mmm, I gotta go with Zeke, here," Domi said, shaking her head. "Our boy's lost the thread. He's in the wrong decade, and he doesn't even know it."

At the broken glass, the skater leaped into the air. The blades snapped out of his feet, and he dove at the construction worker from a story up.

The construction worker's eyes gleamed. He knelt, the leapt up with explosive speed, catching the skater in midair. Muscular, suntanned arms wrapped tight around the skater's relatively slender form. "Got you now, fucker."

"Oooh, things are looking bad for the skater boy. Is it time to say, see you later, boy?" Domi commentated.

The skater thrashed in the man's hold. The construction worker's grip tightened, and the skater's face turned redder and redder. They crashed back to earth, jarring them.

For just a split second, the construction worker's grip loosened. The skater's eyes gleamed. He tensed.

"Oh, no you don't!" The construction worker yanked his arms shut again.

Swords shot out from every inch of his body, piercing through the construction worker just as the man tightened his grip. The construction worker's own strength sent the blades deeper into his body. He screamed and released the skater, staggering back.

Zeke's eyes widened. *Now's my chance to steal the kill.* He stepped forward, not leaving the lobby, but drawing closer to battle. He reached his hand out and activated **Ranged Devour,** targeting the construction worker's back. *I probably can't reach that far, but—*

To his surprise, Ranged Devour easily reached the man's back. *Huh. I guess 49 SPR hits different.* He tore a bite away. The bite only went shallow, pushed off by the man's CON, but it still reached.

The construction worker turned. He locked eyes with Zeke. Letting out a frustrated howl, he charged in.

Zeke stared him down. He landed **Ranged Devour** on the man over and over again, targeting the wounds the skater had already slashed in the construction worker's flesh. There, he could bite deeper. The man's higher CON could only do so much about open wounds.

"And..." Domi watched the man approach, then snapped her fingers. An explosion rattled up from the ground, spraying asphalt and sending the man flying into the air.

"Boom!" she finished, a little unnecessarily.

The skater pushed off the ground and zoomed up the building they were in. As the man dropped back down, he jumped away from the building, extended his blades, and dropped, pointing the swords toward the construction worker's throat.

"Hey! I'm stealing this kill!" Zeke protested. He ran to the edge of the lobby and raised his hand, watching as the two dropped. Again, he targeted the construction worker with Ranged Devour, then hesitated. He lifted his hand just a little, targeting the rollerblader instead. Narrowing his eyes, he waited, holding his breath.

The construction worker struck the ground. A split second later, the rollerblader's blades struck down, piercing his throat. In the same instant, Zeke unleashed **Ranged Devour.**

The rollerblader went limp, falling forward onto the construction worker.

Congratulations! You've defeated the Rollerblading Apocalypse!

Level: 111.41 > 113.59

Please choose three skills
Rollerblading
Blade Attachment
Speed Wheels
No Brakes
Gravity Negation
High Speed Navigation

Zeke tried to bat the screen down to check the construction worker's fate, but stubbornly, it refused to drop. He gritted his teeth. *Gravity Negation, High Speed Navigation, Blade Attachment! Wait, would Speed Wheels be better?*

Gained Skills: Gravity Negation, High Speed Navigation, Blade Attachment

Dammit. The screens vanished, at least, allowing Zeke to see the construction worker struggle, blades still piercing his throat, to push the rollerblader's corpse away. As he shifted the Rollerblading Apocalypse backward, the wounds in his throat closed.

Shit, that's right. High CON means high regeneration! He charged in. "Domi! Mia!"

"On it!" Domi shouted. Explosions burst out behind the rollerblader's back, driving his blades back into the man's throat. Mia closed in silently, her expression grim.

Zeke activated **Ranged Devour** again. He targeted the soft flesh on the inside of the construction worker's throat, tearing it out faster than it could regenerate.

Mia reached him and jabbed her slender sword into his neck. Following the wounds created by the rollerblader, she slashed outward and opened them wider.

Over and over again. Domi kept the rollerblader pinned in his neck. Mia slashed at his throat. Zeke bit out chunks of flesh. He struggled but couldn't escape their onslaught. Keeping him on the back foot, until finally, he kicked his last and went still.

Congratulations! You've defeated the Destruction Apocalypse!

Please choose three skills
Wrecking Ball
Tough Skin
Hi-Vis Vest
Steel Toe Boots
Hard Hat
Demolitions Expert

This time, his pick was easy. *Demolitions Expert, Tough Skin, and Wrecking Ball.*

Gained Skills: Demolitions Expert, Tough Skin, Wrecking Ball.
Tough Skin can merge with Steel Armor. Y/N?

Zeke hesitated, then chose N. *Steel Armor is an armor enhancement, but it would turn my normal skin rigid, so I chose to only have it apply to my Transformed form. Tough Skin didn't appear to change anything about that construction worker's visible flesh, so I'll take it as a constant defense buff, rather than leveling up my Transformed self's armor. Even if it doesn't buff my Transformed self very much—even if it doesn't buff my Transform at all, it'll be nice to have a constant defense buff. As it stands right now, I'm incredibly vulnerable to a stealth attack. With a constant buff like Tough Skin, I'll have some low level of defense against surprise and stealth attacks.*

He dusted off his hands and turned to the others. "Two down. Who-knows-how-many to go."

"Yeah. We got our work cut out for us, for sure," Domi agreed.

Mia startled. Her eyes darted up and down, overwhelmed. "Hold...hold up. I just leveled up, like, ten times..."

"You would," Domi muttered.

"How long do you need, Mia?" Zeke asked. *I don't have normal levels, so I don't know how long it takes to negotiate skills from the System or buy them from the shop.*

"Not much longer," she muttered, her eyes darting left and right.

Domi smacked her lips. "Let's get moving while you level, huh? We made too much noise. Other people are going to think the same thing we did, and close in to pick *us* off while we're 'easy pickings.'"

"Good point. Let's get a move on," Zeke said. "Mia, can you level and run?"

"I... Yeah. Probably."

Footsteps sounded from nearby. Zeke ushered Mia back through the lobby, Domi jogging beside them. They hurried out onto the next road, and Zeke took a sharp right, heading away from the edge and toward the city's center.

48
CITY CENTER

Behind them, the sound of a clash rattled off the sheer walls of the buildings and through the gap the construction man had stomped through the walls. They glanced over their shoulders, and Domi grimaced. "Too close for comfort."

"Yeah. Let's leave them to it," Zeke said.

"You aren't going to turn around and sweep them for EXP?" Mia asked sarcastically. She raised a hand and pressed on the air, and her eyes cleared.

Guess she finished with the System. Zeke made eye contact with Domi. "Actually..."

She pursed her lips and tilted her head. "I mean, farming is good, honest work."

Mia rolled her eyes. "You guys aren't serious."

"You know what, Mia, you have an excellent idea." Zeke looked up, then offered her and Domi his hands. "Why don't we watch things from the roof, this time? Last time, the construction worker saw us at the last minute. I'd rather not face that again."

"Sure, but uh, don't you need a firmer hold on us, if you're going to fly us up?" Domi asked.

"Nah. Check it out." Zeke walked up to the wall, then activated **Gravity Negation.**

Immediately, the world turned wonky. He lost his sense of up and down, left and right. Zeke stumbled, and fell into a spin in the air, not going up or down.

"Real impressive," Domi said sarcastically.

"Hold on. Hold on. I'm getting there." Zeke took a deep breath, settling himself, then kicked the ground. He floated upward, toward the top of the building, dragging Domi and Mia after him. He reached out with his foot and carefully pushed himself upward and inward, bouncing up the wall at a strange, dreamy pace. *Reminds me of when I was little and used to put myself sideways and run on the wall in the pool. If you kicked the wall, you'd fly away from it, so you had to kind of push-kick and angle your body in toward the wall as you did it. It's like that, but harder.*

Slowly, they bounded up the wall. Whenever they got too far away for Zeke to push off the wall, he flapped his wings and pointed them back at the wall. It took a little while, but in time, they reached the top. He flapped them over the edge and released **Gravity Negation.**

"I'll be honest, Zeke? Next time, just fly us," Domi said, brushing herself off.

"Yeah. That was really slow, and it kind of sucked," Mia offered.

"I'm still figuring it out, okay? Eventually, I'll be as cool as Mr. Rollerblades," Zeke said.

"A fate to aspire to, for sure," Domi said sarcastically.

Zeke sighed. *I'm starting to feel like the rollerblades were maybe more than just aesthetic. Compared to walking, using Gravity Negation on rollerblades makes much more sense. You don't push yourself away if you're just riding on the skates. It doesn't explain how he was climbing up the walls, but then, I've used the skill once. I'm sure I could figure out everything he was doing with it, if I had all the time he had with it.*

They approached the opposite edge of the building. Down below, a giant beetle attacked a large duck. The two battled back and forth, feathers and chitin flying. Beneath them, the skater and the construction worker's bodies jostled around, tossed by the forces of battle.

Zeke lifted his neck, peering off into the distance. Another two humanoid figures hurried toward the battle from the right. From the left, a strange glittering shape drifted toward the titans. Zeke clicked his tongue. "Too bad about farming, Domi. It looks like we reeled in too many fish."

"Aye, I like it when my farming gets a lot of bites from big fish. That's how farming works, after all," Domi said, shaking her head at him.

"You don't bring a rod and a box of lures to go farming?" Zeke asked, shocked.

"No, I prefer to bring my hoes," Domi said, waggling her brows.

Mia rolled her eyes at both of them. "You two, honestly. We're in a life-and-death situation right now."

"Well, you know," Zeke said, shrugging.

"Yeah, you know." Domi nodded, patting Zeke's shoulder.

Down below, the strange, glimmering thing changed directions, and revealed itself as a very large jellyfish. The two humanoids joined the fray. One launched off a blast of fiery lava, white the other lifted their sleeves and black goo gushed toward the beetle. The beetle rounded on them, roaring in pain, which freed the duck to attack it from the other side, not aware of the jellyfish floating in from behind.

"You wanna bet on the outcome?" Zeke asked, putting his hands on his hips.

"Wha...we're still doing this? Aren't there too many?" Mia asked.

Domi shrugged. "There's only too many *right now*. In another ten minutes or so, there probably won't be too many. I think it's worth sticking around for."

Mia frowned, then shook her head and threw her head back. "Fine. Why not."

"She's starting to get it," Domi said, nodding.

"I don't think she is," Zeke said. After a second, he added, "But I'm glad she's putting up with us."

"My bet's on the lava guy. I bet he's something real strong, like volcanoes. Plus, he's fighting with black goo guy. We know ourselves how powerful comboing up can be," Domi said.

"I'm gonna go with the dark horse—the jellyfish. How do you even kill a jellyfish, you know? They don't have brains, or hearts, or anything. Like, I can eat it, but for someone who doesn't have Devour..." Zeke shook his head.

Domi cocked a brow at him. "I think volcano-guy can figure it out."

"Okay, yes, most things die when they're plunged into hot lava, but still," Zeke said. He crossed his arms. "Jellyfish. I'm going with jellyfish."

"What about you, Mia?" Domi asked.

Mia shook her head. "I'm pretending I don't know you guys."

Domi sat down, yawning. "Let me know when something exciting starts happening."

"You got it," Zeke promised her. He stood at the edge, looking down. *This is more than just betting. Watching them tells me their skills and fighting style. We'll have to fight whoever comes out ahead, whether it's the jellyfish, the volcano, or whatever else. Right now is the best chance to get a leg up on figuring out how the survivor fights.*

49
FISHING

Down below, the Apocalypses crashed together. The beetle charged mindlessly at the lava-spewing man, only to wobble and fall to the side before it even reached the humanoid figure. It fell on its side and began to twitch helplessly.

Huh? Zeke frowned, squinting closer.

From the top of the lava, heat-haze shimmer hovered...and a thick, gray gas. Zeke's eyes widened. *Poisonous gasses. I almost forgot. Volcanoes give off poisonous gasses. They can be more dangerous than the lava itself, at times.*

The duck darted in, smashing the beetle's guts open with its beak. The chitinous exoskeleton cracked. Thick yellow and orange ichor spouted out. It splashed over the duck and the humanoid figures alike. The people staggered back, batting at their clothes, but the duck ignored it, unbothered by the goo, and tore the giant beetle apart.

"The giant beetle's dead," Zeke announced.

"Good thing no one bet on it," Domi said.

"Honestly, I'm surprised that thing won its dome," Mia commented.

Zeke shrugged. "Maybe there was a dome over the middle of a field, and beetles really were the strongest thing there."

"Could be," Mia allowed.

"Besides, you don't believe the beetle, but the duck is no surprise?" Zeke asked.

"Ducks can be vicious, man," Domi said, shaking her head.

Down below, the figures finished batting the ichor off their bodies, then charged toward the duck, which was busy eating the bug's guts. It lifted its head, feathers stained with ichor, and glared down at the puny humans.

"I wonder how they feel about horse-sized ducks," Zeke commented.

"It's bigger than a horse, man," Domi asked.

"How big do you think horses are?" Mia asked.

Zeke shrugged. "I don't know, a Clydesdale?"

"Nah. Still bigger."

The duck snapped its head out, faster than Zeke expected, and snatched up the black-goo-spouting guy. The black-goo-spouter slapped their hand on the duck's beak, and the duck shook its head, inadvertently throwing the black goo guy away. He smashed into the second story of a nearby building and fell to the ground.

The volcano person screamed and rushed the duck. Flaring its wings, the duck flapped backward—directly into the waiting tendrils of the very large jellyfish. The jellyfish tangled its tendrils around the duck. Visible electric shocks shot over the duck's body, and it jolted where it stood.

The lava-spewer closed in. They jumped up, pointing their sleeve down at the duck. Red-hot lava splashed down onto the duck's chest. Feathers burned. Flesh and blood sizzled. The duck screamed in pain. In its agony, it bit down toward the lava person, tossing them into the wall. With its last remaining strength, it bit at the jellyfish's tendrils, only to receive stinging shocks on its beak. It trembled, then went still, dead.

"Domi, Mia. It's go time," Zeke said urgently.

Domi jumped up. "Who's left?"

"Lava guy and the jellyfish," Zeke replied.

"Damn. Can't let them go at it a little longer...?" Domi asked.

Zeke snorted but shook his head. "We wait any longer, we're going to face one undistracted Apocalypse. Now is the time to strike."

"Got it." Mia drew back her arm. A gold bow materialized in her hands. She released the string, and an arrow shot down from the heavens.

At the last second, the lava person looked up. They jumped back, barely dodging the arrow, then squinted up at the top of the building.

"You have a bow? Wait, never mind. Mia, keep up the volley. Domi, let's go in," Zeke said.

"All right. Carpet bombing?" Domi asked.

"Let's do it. I'm gonna need you on the lookout for poisonous gasses, though. This guy definitely spews them off."

"Message received. Fly me out, captain."

Zeke hooked his arms under Domi's armpits, and they soared out into the sky.

"Left, bank left," Domi said immediately.

He dipped his wings, and they soared left. A second later, he saw the corridor of discolored air Domi had seen. "Good call."

"Yep." Domi pressed her hands together, raining bombs down on the combatants from above. The volcano-man pointed up at them but couldn't lob his lava any higher. The jellyfish numbly pulled the duck into its body, its tendrils already searching for its next prey. It flinched away from the explosions, *or maybe the force of the explosions just moved its body.*

Gold arrows shot from the heavens, chasing after the volcano Apocalypse. He ran from them, but between the explosions and the arrows, took one hit, then another, the two ranged attacks slowly wearing him down.

Zeke flew nimbly in the air, using his new skill **High Speed Navigation** to easily avoid the man's plumes of poison smoke. He couldn't see them far ahead of him, but thanks to the skill, his twitch impulses were far stronger than they usually were. Even if he saw the plume at the last second, he could dodge them, so long as he had room to move. Domi and Mia kept up the barrage, chasing him down.

A gold arrow nailed the man on the foot, pinning him to the ground. Before he could break free, a glowing ball of force struck him in the chest. His body caved. Lava gushed out. He stumbled, then fell backward. His body struck the ground.

Subordinate killed an Apocalypse. Level: +.43
Level: 113.59 > 114.02
Please assign your skill point.

Put it in SPR.

SPR: 49 > 50

Zeke let out a sigh of satisfaction. *Fifty SPR, it feels so good.*

Only the jellyfish remained. Zeke flew lower, close enough he could use **Ranged Devour** while Domi rained explosions down on the jellyfish. The jellyfish didn't react to anything they do. They slowly wore it ragged, Zeke taking potshot bites to satisfy his hunger as much as to do damage. At last, a glowing core appeared in the depths of its translucent body. Zeke pointed **Ranged Devour** at it and snatched it up.

Defeated the Jellyfish Apocalypse!

Level + 1.32
Level: 114.02 > 115.34

Please choose your skills.
Float
No Heart, No Weakness
If you can survive without a heart, you have no weak spots.
All areas of your body are equally vital; your body has to be
fully destroyed to die.
Pain Suppression
Out-of-Water Navigation
You can survive outside of your natural environment.
Electric Tendrils
Electrify your tendrils.
Zap Enhancement

Zeke eyed the Out-of-Water Navigation skill. *Does that only work on the water-to-land transition? Or does it work in the reverse case, too? If I took that, could I breathe under water?*

No.

He clicked his tongue. *Unfortunate. Then I'll take, uh, Float, Electric Tendrils, and Zap Enhancement. I need my heart, so No Heart, No Weakness is right out. Pain Suppression...I could level up Resilient Regeneration, I guess, but I already have Resilient Regeneration, and I'm not sure I want more pain suppression. Electric Tendrils...I don't usually have tendrils, but my Transformed self does, and right now, those things don't do shit. Be nice if I could use them for back-attacks.*

"Is it dead?" Domi asked.

"Yeah. It's dead."

"I wasn't sure."

From overhead, Mia waved her hand and shouted. Zeke looked up, craning his neck, then beat his wings and flapped up to her side. "What is it?"

"More people coming, again," Mia reported, pointing off into the distance.

Zeke landed, turning to follow her hand. Domi walked aside, peering off as well.

Three people walked shoulder to shoulder, their eyes set ahead, walking directly for the battle. They wore ordinary clothes but walked with confidence. Something about the way they held themselves told Zeke they weren't afraid of anyone else here, and for good reason.

"Time for another round of carpet bombs?" Domi asked.

Zeke backed away from the edge of the building. He shook his head. "They don't give me good vibes. Let's back off and see what happens."

Domi shrugged. "If you're sure."

"Who are they even going to fight?" Mia asked.

"Someone else will come," Zeke said confidently.

"Not us, apparently," Domi grumbled.

"Trust me. Bad vibes," Zeke insisted.

"Yeah, yeah. Hey, if you need a break, you can just say it," Domi said.

Zeke shook his head but didn't say anything. Rather than continuing to fight, he'd rather take the loss, so long as they didn't aggravate the people down below. He eyed the group again, searching them for what about them gave him such bad vibes. *I really can't put words to it. It's just...* He licked his lips and shook his head. *Bad vibes. That's all it is. Bad vibes.*

50
BAD VIBES

The trio arrived at the scene of the battles. They peered around, nudging the bodies and picking over the lava-strewn ground. As they searched, they commented to one another. One laughed, nudging another.

"Real scary guys," Domi commented, coming up beside Zeke.

"Look, I don't know why, but they're giving me bad vibes, okay? It's weird. I don't know why, but my gut instinct is saying to stay away."

Mia came up on his other side. "You should listen to your gut instinct. You feel that way for a reason."

"Yeah..." Zeke nodded. He rubbed his forehead. *I'll feel bad if it turns out to be nothing, but they really do give me a bad feeling.*

One of the people lifted her hand and pointed it at the giant beetle's body. A circle of light spilled out from her palm and circled over the top of the beetle. She flicked her wrist, and the circle lowered to the ground. Where it passed, the beetle's body vanished, leaving nothing behind.

"Uh...what?" Domi asked.

Mia covered her mouth and backed away, startled.

Zeke's eyes widened, and he nodded, slowly. "I told you I had a bad feeling about them. I told you!"

"Yeah, you know what, Zeke? Let's all take a break up here. We don't need to go fight everyone we see," Domi reasoned.

"What a great idea you came up with all on your own, Domi," Zeke said, shaking his head at her.

"Well, you know. I'm a very perceptive person. I just get feelings about people sometimes," Domi said, shrugging.

Zeke shook his head at her. Backing away from the edge, he remained just far enough forward to see over the edge of the building. *I want to know as much as I can about that trio, but I don't want to fight them...which means, I don't want them to notice me. I wish I had a stealth skill...*

Zeke paused. *Wait, hold on. I do!*

He activated **Disguise,** and his skin turned gray, fading in to match the color of the building he stood atop.

"You okay, Zeke?" Domi asked.

"I just used a skill. Don't worry."

"I'm just a little worried," Domi muttered. She sat down behind him, resting. Mia joined her a moment later.

The trio moved around the street. Each one of them used the glowing light skill, and the bodies vanished one at a time. Whether they went somewhere else, or the bodies simply disintegrated, Zeke had no way to tell, but either way, the skill spooked him.

All of them have the same skill. Is that even possible? I didn't think you could share Concepts.

Unless...they're Subordinates of the lady who sent us here, and they're borrowing her skills. I know that's possible. I've borrowed Allen's skills before, so I'd believe that Apocalypses can also share skills to Subordinates, not just the other way around.

"What're they doing?" Mia asked.

"They're all doing the same circle of light thing the first one did. I think they're Subordinates of that lady who projected herself into the sky, using her skills, since they all have the same skills," Zeke explained.

"*All* her subordinates can do the light thing and just teleport people places? That's pretty scary, not gonna lie," Domi said. After a moment, she squinted. "Why are they stealing the bodies?"

"Maybe they're cleaning the streets? I can't imagine she's very happy to have bodies lying all over her city. We're all in her Domain, after all," Mia suggested.

"Maybe," Zeke said hesitantly. *If they aren't just cleaning the streets, but sending the bodies somewhere... What on earth are they doing with them? What would you even want to do with Apocalypse bodies?*

He shivered. *Yeah. I don't know. It gives me the shivers. I don't like it.*

"Though, maybe they can't just teleport anyone anywhere? Maybe they can only teleport bodies," Zeke suggested. He glanced at the other two. "After all, if they could teleport anyone anywhere, wouldn't they just teleport us all into the heart of a volcano and be done with it?"

Domi shrugged. "Mr. Volcano would make out like a *bandit.*"

"Well, yeah, but aside from him, we'd all be dead. Having to take down one Apocalypse versus taking out however-many hundreds of us there are..." Zeke spread his hands. "Even with this forced battle-royale-city thing, we could all bum-rush the end and attack her. And hell, it still gives us a chance to challenge her in her domain, in the worst case. If she could just teleport us all from anywhere to anywhere, she could've created an even more advantageous scenario than this one."

Mia tilted her head. "Maybe she can only teleport things within her Domain. Sure, we're all in her Domain now, so if I'm right, then she could teleport us wherever, as long as her Subordinates touch us, but..." She shrugged. "Might not be a more advantageous location inside her Domain to put us."

Zeke nodded. "Right...after all, even if she built a spike trap or lava pit, there'd be Apocalypses who could dodge it, or were even empowered by it. For example, I could hover over either of them, and as long as I could scoop up cores from the dead Apocalypses, *I'd* be the one to make out like a bandit."

"Tips her hand, too, if we know she has teleportation skills before we fight her. That kind of skill is best off launched as a surprise attack," Domi said, crossing her arms.

"And we're all pretending like the 'Subordinates touch us' requirement is easy to fulfil. Even if she sent the Scouting Apocalypse or some super-fast Apocalypse after us, we'd have a chance to counter them, maybe even kill them," Mia reasoned.

"Right, so, I think we've figured out why we didn't all get yeeted into a pit of lions," Domi said.

"Mmm, lions," Zeke said.

Domi cut her eyes at him and continued. "But that doesn't solve the mystery of what they're doing with the other Apocalypses' bodies."

Zeke shrugged. "Eating them."

"Right, aside from mister hungry over there, any other ideas?"

Mia shrugged. "I'd say zombies, but...we already had the Undead Apocalypse, and you guys say they won't allow overlapping Concepts."

"Yeah, generally not," Zeke agreed. "Unless that was perdome?"

"I feel like we'd see more cyborg and robot Apocalypses if so. Lots of zombies, too," Domi commented.

"Yeah...yeah, fair. So yeah. Gonna go ahead and guess that the Concept choices were universally unique," Zeke said.

"In any case, we should move on. They found our fish-farming spot, and I don't want to draw their attention any more than we already have, so..." Domi shrugged.

"I agree. Let's get a move on." Zeke glanced at the two girls, considering.

"I can walk on my platforms, if we stay up here," Mia offered.

Zeke nodded. "Good call. Domi—"

A bolt shot out of the sky and slammed into Domi's side, toppling her to the ground. Blood splattered across the rooftop.

Overhead, a haughty laugh echoed down on them. "Did you think no one else thought to take to the skies?"

51
BATTLE IN THE SKY

Blood splattered across the rooftop. Domi struck the ground, her expression glassy.

Zeke saw red. Without even thinking, he activated his wings and shot up into the sky after the woman in the sky.

She hovered on a jetpack. A strange-looking gun attached to a hose and wound to the fuel tanks on her back. Seeing Zeke fly at her, she let out a derisive snort and leveled her gun at him. Light glowed in the depths of the gun.

[High Speed Navigation]

Zeke shifted in the air, subtly altering the angle of his body. The beam shot past him, hurtling down at the roof.

"Hmm? Are you fine dodging?" the woman asked, looking down at him.

A clang sounded from below as Mia materialized a gold shield between the beam and Domi. "I've got it, Zeke. Finish her off!"

Zeke nodded. He dashed in. His wings blurred. The woman shot at him over and over, but with **High Speed Navigation,** she couldn't keep up with his maneuvering. In a moment, Zeke caught up with her.

He grabbed her by the forehead and reeled her in. She screamed in fury. Metal gauntlets appeared around her arms, crackling with lightning. A barrage of punches pummeled his chest.

He felt the pain, but his skin didn't break, thanks to **Tough Skin.** Opening his mouth, he bit deep into her neck, yanking it out.

Metal cracked. Wires sparked. The woman's eyes went dull.

In a fury, Zeke tore into her, searching for a core, for anything, **Devour**ing whatever he could reach. No core. Nothing but more metal, more wires, more machinery. Cogs cracked under his jaws. Metal snapped. The jetpack burst. Zeke gritted his teeth, frustrated. *Where is she?*

A tinny, metallic voice laughed at him. "Surely, you didn't think I'd come fight you in person? I'd be a fool!"

Zeke kicked the rest of her robot body away in disgust and darted back to the rooftop. He knelt by Domi. She pressed a hand to her chest, her regeneration slowly closing the wound, but too slow.

"Hey there," she said, her voice a bit woozy. "I might be outta the running."

"No, you aren't." Zeke hovered his hands over her chest. Green light glowed in his palms as he activated **Ninja Healing.** It poured into Domi's chest, closing her wound. Zeke's hunger surged in response, but he suppressed it. *Bear with it. I'll be hungry for a bit if it means saving Domi.*

Domi's brows furrowed. She shifted a little, then craned her neck to look at her chest. Her brows furrowed deeper, and she looked back up at Zeke. "You can heal?"

"I can do lots of stuff," Zeke said, gritting his teeth. His stomach gurgled. He glanced over the edge of the building, down at where the Apocalypses had died, only to find no bodies.

Zeke scowled. *Damn those body-teleporting Subordinates! I was going to eat those, dammit!*

Ugh. I need to remember to eat as soon as I kill in this city. Those Subordinate teleporting bodies away means I can't just browse for bodies other Apocalypses killed, either. I need to actively hunt it out.

"Zeke! Protect Domi!" Mia shouted.

He looked up. A shadow passed across the sun. Another jetpack-bound woman appeared overhead. "Haha! This time, for sure—"

Before she could finish her sentence, Mia charged into the sky and sliced her in half. Again, robot bits rained down. Zeke darted out and **Devour**ed her pieces as she fell, replenishing some of his fullness. *It's not worth as much as a person or an Apocalypse, but since it's part of an Apocalypse, it's worth something.*

"What do you think she is?" Mia asked, walking back to their side. "The Supervillain Apocalypse?"

"Inventor Apocalypse, maybe? She's all about gadgets," Zeke commented. He looked at the metallic rubble around them, bending to scoop up another handful and shove it in his maw. "And robots."

Domi pushed his hands away and sat up. "I'm good to go. I'll be all right from here on my own."

Zeke glanced at her. "Are you sure?"

She grinned. "Yeah, yeah. I'll be fine."

Deactivating his skill, Zeke stood and dusted off his knees, then helped Domi to her feet. He couldn't help but notice Domi grabbed his hand with her uninjured arm, but he didn't comment on it. *She has a regeneration rate, too. I can't afford to baby her. None of us can afford to baby any of us. If she says she's good enough to go on, the best thing for me to do is believe her.*

A buzz. Once again, a shadow fell over them. "*This* time—"

Her jet pack's tank exploded, blasting the entire robot's

body to smithereens. Domi rolled her eyes, shoving her cell phone back into her back pocket. "Spare me."

"Let's get out of here. She's going to draw attention to us. Bad attention," Zeke said.

"Agreed," Mia said.

Zeke peered over the edge of the building, a bit nervous, but the Subordinates with their glowing-teleport powers were gone. Except for the bloodstains and the missing bodies, no sign of the Subordinates remained at all.

"They're gone. The asshole in the sky is—" Mia squinted, then lifted her bow and fired. An arrow arced off into the distance. Metal clanged, and a distant scream sounded as a jetpack-wearing figure spiraled down into an alley. "—taken care of, at least for a while. There's no eyes on us."

"Don't have to convince me." Domi offered Zeke the usual hold, and he scooped her up. Mia ran on the platforms beside them, and they sped off across the sky.

Behind them, a jetpack-wearing woman popped up behind them. "She's following us," Domi reported.

"Yeah, as expected, really," Zeke said.

Domi stared over her shoulder. She swallowed. "Uh. Yep. As expected."

"What's that mean?" Zeke looked over his shoulder as well.

Jetpack-wearing-woman after jetpack-wearing-woman filled the sky. The flames of their jetpacks glittered like stars. Their bodies blackened the heavens.

"Holy shit, how many robot hers did she make?" Zeke asked. Mia whistled.

A laugh that shook the buildings around them echoed forth from the many clones. "You fools thought killing one or two copies would kill me? I am immortal. I am eternal!"

"We'll see about that," Zeke muttered.

52
JETPACK ROBOTS

The jetpack-bearing robots chased after them. Zeke, Mia, and Domi fled, running away from the robots.

"So, we're fleeing through the sky," Mia commented.

"Yep," Zeke said.

"Where everyone can see us."

"That's right."

"Won't someone else think about coming after us, the way we thought to go after the rollerblader and the construction worker?" Mia asked.

Zeke clicked his tongue. "Oh yeah. Yep. For sure."

Domi glanced back again. "Think we can get up over them? It's hard to lob explosions up."

"In the battle of pigeon wings versus jetpack, jetpack generally wins," Zeke informed her.

"Pigeon wings?" Mia asked.

"Look, it's not important what kind of wings they are. The point is, jetpack wins," Zeke said.

Mia spun around backward on her platform. She fired off a barrage of shots. One or two robots fell from the sky, but most of the robots dodged. The arrows rained down on the city below, vanishing behind the buildings.

A rain of light beams flew at them in response. Mia's eyes widened. She threw out her hands, and shields appeared between them and the robots. The lasers deflected off. Mia grunted, sweat beating up on her brow in pain.

As Zeke flew, he searched through his skills, watching the robots over his shoulder. *I don't have too much I can use at range. A lightning skill, maybe? Wait...* His eyes widened. An evil grin crossed over Zeke's face.

"Domi, I have an idea. Are you ready to fight?"

"Born ready."

Zeke whipped around. He flew toward the robots instead of away.

"Zeke!" Mia shouted, confused. She threw her hand out, and a shield materialized in front of Zeke, wrapped around his body.

"How many can you explode?" Zeke asked Domi, flapping closer.

"At least twenty. Maybe more," Domi replied.

"Get cooking." Zeke narrowed his eyes at the nearest robot. He activated **Manipulate Flame** and killed the flame spitting out of the back of the jetpack.

Without anything to support her body, the robot plunged out of the sky. Zeke turned to the next one, but the second he released his hold on the first, it reignited its engine and flew forward once more.

I need to get a bunch of them at once. Zeke narrowed his eyes, thinking. *I know I have some kind of skill that helps with that. What was it called?*

Ahead of him, ten robots exploded. The other robots retreated from the exploding robots, but Domi just turned and swept her hands over another few robots. Sensing that grouping together meant they'd explode together, the robots spread out.

Hey System, what does Demolitions Expert do?

Allows you to pinpoint weak points to more accurately destroy inanimate objects.

Hmm. Not useful here. But what about... He stared at the nearest robot. She rushed toward them, firing at the shield that doggedly guarded them.

[Manipulate Wires]

The wires tangled around the jetpack pulled taut, then snapped. The jetpack cut off, and the robot plunged. She grabbed at her jetpack, trying to fix it. Too slow. She smashed into the road below, shattering into a thousand metal bits.

Zeke grinned. He turned his eyes to the next robot, then the next. They dropped like flies. All around them, robots exploded or fell out of the sky. Metal rained down, big robots smashing apart, little bits of flaming, exploded robot smashing to the asphalt. Domi went after the left half, and Zeke chased the right half.

The final robot fell from the sky. Zeke let out a slow breath, exhausted. "She can't have more of those."

"Yeah? You sure about that?" Domi asked.

Zeke grimaced. "No."

"What the hell is she, anyway? The Robot-Spawning Apocalypse? I don't know, the Evil Genius Apocalypse?"

"No one calls themselves evil. Mad Scientist," Zeke guessed.

Mad Scientist Apocalypse popped up in his vision.

"Oh...that's it?" Zeke asked, startled.

"Mad Scientist? I get it, but damn. Who voluntarily calls

themselves insane in an Apocalypse that's trying to turn us all crazy anyway?" Domi asked.

Zeke shook his head. "Did any of us know how this was going to work when the Apocalypse kicked off? They probably just desperately thought of anything, and Mad Scientist was the first thing to come to mind."

"Yeah, but man. Really fucked themselves," Domi commented.

Mia ran back over. She nodded at them. "Before she sends more robots, let's get out of the sky."

"Smart," Domi commented, pointing at Mia.

Zeke nodded. Lowering his wings, he swooped down toward the ground. Mia followed, stair-stepping her platforms down. They hit the ground and took off running, sprinting off down the streets. Zeke left the robot scraps behind. *They weren't very filling, and metal doesn't taste good, either.*

When I find that Mad Scientist, on the other hand...I'm eating her ass.

Eating...her. Eating her. Not eating...yeah.

They'd barely landed before a familiar, menacing voice filled the air. "Where did you go, filthy little rats?"

"Shit, she's fast!" Domi complained.

Zeke glanced over his shoulder. *She hasn't found us yet? Good!* He charged at the nearest building, activating **Demolition Expert** as he did. A line in the glass appeared, nice and clean. Zeke lowered his shoulder and used **Wrecking Ball** and smashed through the glass and into the building.

He found himself in the midst of an office. Generic gray cubicles stretched as far as the eye could see. A chill crawled over the back of his neck. Zeke rubbed his head. *Yikes. Is this what being an adult looks like? No thanks.*

Domi and Mia chased after Zeke, following him into the

office. They looked around, catching their bearings the same as Zeke had. "It's like a maze," Mia muttered.

"An Office Maze," Domi countered with a grin.

[Office Labyrinth Apocalypse]

Zeke licked his lips. He spun around, only to find a smooth sheetrock wall and another generic cubical, exactly the same as the cube ahead of him, to the left, to the right, in every direction.

"Er...bad news, guys," he muttered.

"At least we're less likely to draw the attention of other Apocalypses like this?" Mia pointed out.

Domi cursed under her breath. "Lucky us. Just happened to land in a random Apocalypse's Domain."

"Look on the bright side. Even if that Mad Scientist comes after us, good luck finding us," Zeke said.

"Yeah! All these upsides," Mia said, patting Zeke's shoulders.

Domi shook her head at them. She looked around, then yanked open the nearest desk's drawers. Papers and books awaited her. Kicking it shut, she turned to the next desk, then the next.

"Uh, Domi...?" Zeke asked.

Domi stood up, holding up a box of granola bars. "Score! Free snacks. At least we won't starve."

"Sweet, give me one," Mia said, reaching toward Domi.

Zeke shook his head.

ROAR!

The walls shook. The cubes trembled. Domi whipped around, still chomping on a granola bar. As the roar faded, she mused, "You know, I think I remember something about that old Greek myth about the Labyrinth."

"Do you?" Zeke asked, half-amused.

Domi nodded. She pointed toward the roar. "There was a big-ass monster at its center. Couldn't get out without killing it."

"I don't think that's how the myth..." Mia paused, then grinned. She laughed. "Yeah. Let's go kill the monster!"

53
BREAK ROOM CAKE ROOM

They wound through the labyrinth, picking their route at random. Taking a hint from the myth, Zeke used **Manipulate Wires** to create a string behind him as he walked. As they went, Domi looted every scrap of snacks she came across, passing Zeke and Mia the leftovers when her arms filled up. Idly, Zeke chewed on whatever she passed him. It didn't do much to tame the hunger in his gut, but it gave his mouth something to do. Even if satisfaction never came, at least his mouth thought it would come soon, and so the hunger was easier to bear.

Domi reached out behind her. "Where'd those potato chips go?"

Mia glanced at her pile, then looked at Zeke. Zeke glanced at her, licking the last of the grease and salt off his fingers. "You passed them to Zeke," she reported.

"I did? Fuck," Domi grumbled. "What did I give you, then?"

"The box of prunes."

"Fuck! Hand those to Zeke. Goodness knows he could use 'em, given the shit he eats."

Mia picked out the box of prunes from the stuff in her arms and handed it to Zeke.

"You trying to make me shit myself?" Zeke asked. Mindlessly, he dug into the box of prunes.

"Yeah. Actually, does the stuff you eat come out the other end? Like when you eat two robots in five bites, what happens to your asshole?"

Zeke grimaced. He shrugged. "I don't know. It's weird. Bits of it come out, but it's not... If I eat two robots, two robots' worth of metal doesn't come out, you know?"

"Whoa, whoa, whoa. Way too much information," Mia said, waving her hands and ducking away.

"Domi asked!" Zeke said, defending himself.

"Yeah, but you answered. Should've known better," Domi said, giving him a disappointed look.

Zeke rolled his eyes at her. "Sure, blame the victim."

"Victim? I'm the victim here, having to hear about your shits—"

A robot crashed through the wall. Glass sprayed all around it. Office furniture went flying. It burst out into the corridor ahead of them, then turned. Bright red light shone from the depths of the woman's eyes.

"There you are!" she crooned.

Without a moment's hesitation, Zeke charged, mouth open. The robot jumped back, firing her jetpack to escape.

"I don't think so." Domi pulled out her phone. She tapped at the screen.

BOOM! The robot's jetpack exploded. They flopped to their butt on the ground, stunned.

Before they could jump up, Zeke was upon them. He snapped up the robot in a few bites and swallowed, licking his lips.

"Was that a one-off, or...?" Domi wondered.

Another crash echoed through the endless office, then another, and another. In blasts of shattered glass and dusty sheet rock, they burst into the room. One after another, they locked eyes with Zeke, Domi, and Mia.

"Looks like they found us," Mia commented evenly.

Zeke nodded, pursing his lips. "Yeah, I gotta say..."

The three of them turned and ran, fleeing into the center of the office building. The robots chased after them, but the strange twists and turns of the office applied to the robots as much as they applied to Zeke, Mia, and Domi. The robots turned left and right with the flow of the cubicles. The ones who tried to fly over struck invisible walls and fell back. Zeke and the others could see the robots, and the robots could see them, but they couldn't reach one another.

"Guess that first robot got lucky," Zeke commented, as they ran along the office at random. He kept up the wire behind them, though he wasn't sure if he should or not. *The robots probably won't notice a wire, right? Right...?*

"Lucky? I'd say it got unlucky. Of all the robots who busted in, only one got eaten by you," Domi pointed out.

"That is fair," Zeke said, with a little chuckle.

"You know, it's weird how we didn't think to climb the cubicles," Mia pointed out.

Zeke nodded. "Yeah, probably a mental effect of the domain. But thanks to our robot friends, we know we couldn't even if we tried, so..." He shrugged.

"I guess," Mia said.

They turned a corner and entered a narrow hallway, leaving the cubicle-filled room behind them. At the end of the narrow hallway, a light shone from a doorway. Domi hurried toward it, Mia trailing behind and Zeke keeping an eye on their rear.

Domi gasped. "No..."

"What?" Mia rushed up behind her. Zeke closed in quickly, his heart racing.

All three of them piled in the doorway. A break room stretched before them. A stained refrigerator stood in the back corner, next to a coffee machine and a pair of stacked microwaves. A countertop sported a sink. On the countertop, not far from the sink, a plastic-covered half-eaten cake awaited pilgrims in search of free food.

"Free cake!" Domi rushed over, excited.

"Isn't that cake going to be days old, at best? Honestly, more like weeks old," Zeke commented.

"You think logic applies this far in an Apocalypse's Domain?" Domi shot back.

Zeke hesitated, then shrugged. *She is right. Domains aren't often big fans of good hard logic. Still, I'm not eating it.*

Though I guess I shouldn't be the one saying that. I've eaten way grosser things than week-old cake.

Domi lifted the plastic lid off it and poked the cake tentatively. It gave way under her finger, still soft and supple. She licked her lips. "Oh, it's gonna taste so good, I can already tell. So, so good..."

Mia edged forward, her eyes locked on the cake. "Me, too."

"Wait," Zeke said. "What if it's like the Coffee Apocalypse? Brainwashes you when you eat it?"

Mia jerked back as if burned. She glanced at Zeke, then the cake, then looked away.

Right...I almost forgot that Mia got brainwashed by it, all that time ago. Feels like ages. Zeke gave her an apologetic look, but Mia wasn't looking at him anymore. She stared at the floor in silence.

Domi rolled her eyes. "Come on, Zeke. All Apocalypses don't have brainwashing techniques. Most of them don't, in fact.

Besides, the ones who do usually have Subordinates. Monsters, minions, something. You see any Subordinates around here?"

"I don't, no," Zeke allowed.

"Then, let me eat in peace." Domi stuck her hand into the cake and pulled out a chunk.

"Damn, we're going straight-up two-year-old on this thing, huh?" Zeke asked, startled.

Domi shoved the cake in her mouth. Through stuffed cheeks, she shrugged at him. "I don't see any plates or forks, so what am I supposed to do? Not eat the cake? I gotta just go for it."

Zeke put his hands up.

Swallowing her bite of cake, Domi rinsed her hands in the sink, then checked the fridge. Pulling out a half-gallon of milk, she took a swig. "Nothing like some milk with cake!"

"Seriously, Domi, this is depraved behavior," Zeke commented.

She shrugged at him unapologetically. "It's the end of the world, dude. What am I supposed to do, act all prim and proper, mind my p's and q's? Lift my pinky when I drink tea from a cutesy little teacup? World's over. I'm gonna enjoy what I can."

Zeke snorted but couldn't come up with a comeback. He shrugged instead. "Yeah, I guess so, right? Might as well enjoy it."

"So? You gonna have some cake or not?" Domi asked.

Zeke hesitated, then walked over. *It might not be worth much food to me, but I can still taste. After all the metal I've been eating, the pure sugar would be a good palate cleanser.*

"After all that, you're going to eat the cake?" Mia asked, crossing her arms.

"I mean...Domi's right, right? End of the world, might as well enjoy it." Zeke smashed a handful of cake into his mouth and chewed it down, enjoying every moment of the sweet, soft cake.

A robot burst into the break room. "Now I've got you!"

Mia's sword lashed out, glowing brighter than the overhead fluorescents. The robot crashed to the ground in two pieces, the edge glowing where Mia's sword had cut.

Slashing down, Mia dismissed her sword. She looked at them. "So, shall we move on before they all catch up with us?"

Zeke licked his hand clean. "Yeah. Let's go."

Domi gave the cake a last, longing stare, then followed the other two out of the break room.

54
TO THE CENTER

Putting the breakroom behind them, they wandered through a big, empty maze of white hallways. There were no more wires to string after them, so Zeke simply dragged his finger along the wall, carving a dent in the relatively soft sheetrock to mark their path. Every now and again, a robot lunged toward them from around one of the corners, but Mia, Domi, or Zeke easily dispatched them.

"You know, this lady's supposed to be a Mad Scientist, so how come we're still fighting the same kind of robots?" Domi asked.

"What do you mean?" Zeke asked distractedly. He peered around the next corner and found another open office space. As opposed to the gray cubicles and boring default desk furniture of the first one, this one had bright white furniture and no cubicles at all. Instead, desks scattered at random around a large, warehouse-like space. Office chairs mingled with bean bags. Brightly colored diagrams sprawled across whiteboards. A ping-pong table sat unattended in the corner.

"Ohh, neat. Offices like these are meant to have free food and shit," Domi said, peering out with him.

"What is with you and snacks right now?" Zeke asked.

Domi waved him down. "I haven't had anything since breakfast, lay off. I'm eating a lunch on the go right now."

"Oh, yeah. Yeah," Zeke muttered, half to himself. *My eating pattern is so weird right now that I totally forgot that most people eat three meals a day. Whoops.*

"Mister Eats-Anything getting on me for a little snack attack, can you believe it?" Domi asked Mia.

"Sounds like Zeke," Mia said.

They walked out into the open office space. Zeke plopped down on one of the bean bag chairs. He rolled around on the chair, enjoying the squish and fall. "Wheee."

"Anyone wanna play a round of ping pong?" Domi offered jokingly. She glanced around. Her eyes lit up, and she beelined for a mini fridge in the corner. A moment later, she retreated in regret. "Beer. Yuck. I hate beer."

"It just doesn't taste good," Mia agreed.

Zeke rolled around on his chair a little more, no opinions to share. *So what if I was a good kid who didn't do any underage drinking? My parents would have killed me!*

Man. My parents.

Nothing welled up. So little emotion came to him that it scared him a little. He heaved himself upright and walked on, putting it to the back of his mind. *The Apocalypse is eating at all of us. In visible and less visible ways. And there's nothing we can do about it.*

Nothing...until we destroy the System. And the System Apocalypse.

Another roar rattled out, closer than before. All three heads snapped up.

"We're almost to the center of this office lollipop," Domi commented.

"Let's keep moving. Don't want the robots to catch up," Zeke said.

Mia nodded.

They fell into line again, walking on through the office. There was nothing to visually block their path forward, with no cubicle walls or narrow hallways, but the room flowed on anyway. It gently shifted and flowed in a subtle way. They never reached the wall ahead of them, while behind them, the wall slowly encroached from behind. New wacky desks and strange appliances appeared, then vanished behind them.

A chuffing sound came from before them, like a very large animal sniffing at the air. Something creaked and cracked, and heavy steps made the office furniture jump. A shadow passed along the outer wall, thrown by something around the next corner.

Zeke glanced around at Mia and Domi. They nodded back. Drawing closer together, they approached the sound with caution.

"Ahaha! I've got you!" a robot shouted. Its voice echoed from around the corner behind them, and it burst toward them with a blast of fire, heat, and smoke.

The bestial grunts from around the corner fell silent, then erupted into a roar.

Domi grimaced and reached for her phone, but Zeke grabbed her by the shoulders and dove behind a table before she could explode the robot. Mia glanced after them. She froze for a moment, then leaped behind the table with them.

"Futile! You can't hide from my genius—"

Heavy, sharp steps echoed off the wall, like a giant pair of heels clicking on the tile floor. The robot stopped where it stood. Its eyes traveled up, up, up, all the way to the top of the unfinished ceiling. "Oh, fuck..."

SMASH!

Metal parts flew everywhere. Jetpack fuel lit on fire and smeared across the floor, burning in strange shades of orange and blue. A black hoof kicked the robot's remains away, and a loud *huff* rolled through the room. Crinkling and crunching, something stood over the robot.

Zeke peered up, trying to get a better look. *A Minotaur?*

An enormous body loomed over him, heavier around the shoulders and chest, leaning out around the midriff. Powerful legs recurved down to thick black rooves. Instead of skin or fur, though, its body was covered in plastic and wallpaper, its legs covered in the same bland carpet as the floor. Its hooves were asphalt. A pair of computer monitors glowed in the place of its pectorals. Two red LEDs glowed where its eyes should be, and office char arms arced from its skull as faux horns.

An office Minotaur...wait, an office monitor? Someone didn't like a little friendly surveillance from their fellow employees. Zeke snorted to himself. *If an office monitor is anything like what a hall monitor is, anyway.*

The Office Minotaur lowered its head. It stared directly at the three of them.

Zeke chuckled. He waved.

"What are you waving for, you idiot?" Domi rolled out from the other side of the table and tossed a ball of orange fire at the Minotaur. The fire slammed into its chest and sent it stumbling back. Its feet sizzled in the burning jetpack fuel.

Zeke rolled out the other side. Immediately, he activated **Manipulate Wires,** but severing all the wires in the Minotaur's body did nothing. He grimaced. *Guess that was too much to hope for. This thing is more magical than 'scientific,' I see.*

"Zeke!" Mia slammed into him from the side and threw him away, seconds before the Minotaur's massive hand smashed the floor where he'd been standing.

Tossed into the air, Zeke flared his wings and flapped up,

perching atop the free-swinging fluorescents overhead. The Minotaur roared and swept after him. Zeke released the light and flapped to the next one. The Minotaur's sweep brought down the light he'd been sitting on, but only snagged the edge of the one he flapped to. Sent swinging, Zeke gripped the top of the light with his arms and legs.

"Back off, asshole!" Domi loosed a barrage of orange orbs at the Minotaur, knocking it back. It stumbled. The monitors on its chest flickered. It turned toward Domi and snorted in rage. Whisps of dark smoke escaped its deep nostrils.

Before it could close in on Domi, Mia charged in from behind. She leaped, landed on a platform, and propelled herself higher so she could drop down on its ankle. The gold blade sliced through the carpet skin with a horrible burning smell. The Minotaur screamed and launched a back kick at her, but its heavy asphalt hoof dangled off its half-slit ankle. It flopped uselessly instead of landing a punishing blow on Mia.

The Minotaur stumbled, unable to find its footing with its injured foot. Zeke's eyes glittered. *Now!*

He dropped down from the ceiling onto the Minotaur's back like an avenging angel, his wings arced over his shoulders, hands slammed down. He caught hold of the severed wires at the back of the Minotaur's back and yanked its head back, leaning around its shoulders to bite at its throat.

"Get up on the Minotaur's back!" Domi shouted.

"He already is," Mia pointed out.

"It's..." Domi coughed. "Anyway."

Plastic cracked. Putrid cold coffee poured out, mixed with something acrid and sharp. Zeke gulped it down despite himself, unable to resist the urge to satiate some of that unbearable hunger.

The Minotaur screamed. It reached up, big ham hands gripping toward Zeke.

Mia's eyes widened. She sprinted forward. Her gold sword leapt out, severing its hand at the wrist.

From the other side, a blast of orange flame shoved its big, fat palm away. Domi laughed. "Try again, asshole!"

Zeke bit again and again, barely aware of anything else. It tasted horrible, absolutely disgusting, but with every bite, his stomach filled, even if just a little. Again and again. The putrid coffee flavor was replaced with the hiss of out-of-fashion air fresheners, and then the Minotaur's eyes darkened and winked out. It staggered, then dropped to a knee, finally falling out prone on the ground. Zeke yanked back at the last moment before it struck the ground. He crouched over it, dark fluid dripping down his chin, and viciousness burned in his eyes.

"Zeke...?" Mia asked, afraid.

He snapped to face her. For a moment, he stared blankly through her. His tongue snapped out, and he licked his lips.

Instinctively, Mia backed away. "Zeke, c'mon."

Zeke cracked a grin. He wiped his mouth and jumped off the Minotaur, nodding at the other two. "Scared you, huh?"

"Scared? More like, that's a typical day for Zeke," Domi grumbled. Still, she eyed him from a distance, a hint of wariness in her gaze.

"Aww, I thought I got you," Zeke said, rubbing the back of his neck.

Internally, he tensed. *What was that? I was gone. Completely gone for a moment. Not here at all. What was that? Who was in my body if it wasn't me?*

He shook his head and looked around them. The office space had snapped back to normal. In the distance, the robots bustled around, shouting at one another.

"In any case, we should get out of here before those dang robots catch up," Zeke said, thumbing toward the back exit.

"Agreed," Domi said, hurrying for it.

"Don't have to tell me twice." Mia ran after Domi.

Zeke paused one last second. He looked down at the Minotaur, at its ravaged body, and ran a hand over the back of his neck again.

I told you.

"Shut up. Just give me the levels," Zeke grumbled.

Defeated Office Labyrinth Apocalypse!

55
BACK ON THE STREETS

Defeated the Office Labyrinth Apocalypse!

Level + 3.01
Level: 115.34 > 118.35

Please assign your stat points.

Please choose your skills.
Morph Space

The list ended there. No more skills appeared, no matter how long Zeke waited. As he walked out of the building, following Domi and Mia on autopilot, he furrowed his brows. *That's it?*

The rest of its skills require a static Domain.

Zeke sighed. He ran his hair back, then glanced at the skill. *What does Morph Space do?*

Within the confines of your Domain, weakly twist or warp space to disorient the opponent captured within.

Can I use it outside of my Domain?

No. Domain must be active.

He paused, then shrugged. *It's not completely useless. I'll take it.*

[Morph Space]

Zeke dismissed the screens and jogged a little to catch up to Domi and Mia. Together, the three of them hurried down the twisting city streets, leaving the office building and the robots far behind. Before long, the building vanished behind them.

Pausing, Zeke wiped his brow. "Whew. It's been nonstop since we got here."

"Almost like someone tried to set up some kind of death-match," Domi commented dryly.

"I mean, yes, but..." Zeke spread his hands. "Even so, I feel like it's been nonstop battles. No chance to catch our breath. I wonder if she's just using us to wear one another out?"

"It is the simplest answer," Mia replied with a shrug.

A shadow passed overhead. Zeke craned his neck, staring up at the sky. A winged outline arced overhead, circling in the sky. Brown and crème wings caught the sun.

"Ah!" Zeke flared his own wings and beat down, shooting up into the sky. *Why wonder about the Apocalypse's plan for us when I can ask one of her minions?*

The Scouting Apocalypse looked down. Startled to see Zeke flying at him, he sped off. Before, he'd been able to outspeed Zeke, but now, Zeke had the Rollerblading Apocalypse's skills. Plying them to their full strength, he shot after the Scouting Apocalypse and quickly caught up. The Scouting Apocalypse stared over his shoulder, startled. Zeke beat one more time, catching up to him. He reached out.

The Scouting Apocalypse flicked his wings and rolled to the side, avoiding Zeke's grab.

[High Speed Maneuvering]

Zeke followed the Scouting Apocalypse's maneuver with ease. He crashed into the other boy, grabbing him around the body and closing his wings. The two of them tangled up and spiraled toward the ground. With all his strength, the Scouting Apocalypse flapped his wings, but his and Zeke's weight combined proved too much for him. He plunged toward the ground.

Seconds before they struck the road, Zeke stretched his wings out and helped to slow their descent. "Mia!"

"Got it!" Mia threw her hands out. Gold platforms boxed the Scouting Apocalypse in on all sides, closing him into a small space.

Still holding him tight, Zeke narrowed his eyes. "So? Why has the Apocalypse Alliance brought us all here?"

"Like I'd—tell you!" the Scouting Apocalypse grumbled. He slapped a hand on Zeke, and a fire burned to life in Zeke's wings.

[Fire Manipulation]

The fire instantly went dead. Zeke didn't so much as flinch. "I'd tell, yeah, if I were you."

The Scouting Apocalypse's nose wrinkled. He spun around. A bow and arrow materialized in his hands.

Without hesitating, Zeke went for the throat and bit down. **Devour** finished the job. He dug into the Scouting Apocalypse, biting over and over, not giving him a chance to fight back. *I brought him to us. I'm not going to let him hurt anyone.*

"Zeke...Zeke!"

Zeke startled. He looked up. "What?"

"He's already dead," Mia said, something between shock, despair, and fear on her face.

Zeke looked down. A bloodied, torn lump of flesh lay beneath him. He blinked. *When did...why...I...* Lifting his hand, he touched his chin. Warm blood, soaking down his neck, all the way to his shirt collar. *What happened? I blacked out. I wasn't even thinking. I just...*

Domi tossed him a scrap of cloth. "You got a little bit..." She gestured to her mouth.

"Yeah. Thanks. I know." Zeke took the cloth and wiped his face. He stepped away from the body, unable to look at it any longer. *I didn't do that. It wasn't me. The Apocalypse did that. It took over and...*

I warned you.

Yeah, well, what am I supposed to do about it? Zeke bit back. He couldn't stop now. If he gave up on earning stats and skills, he'd never beat the Apocalypse Coalition. Even if it killed him, he didn't have an option because the other option was to roll over and let the rest of the Apocalypses destroy him. *Do you not understand that?*

I understand that, but—

Then, stop being so damn smug and give me my rewards! If you have helpful comments, share them, but if you're just going to gloat every time I beat someone or mess up, shut the fuck up!

That's not—

It's what you're doing, whether you mean to be doing it or not. I don't care what you think you're doing. Listen to what I tell you you're doing because it's what you're actually doing.

...

Defeated the Scouting Apocalypse!

Level + 2.22

Level: 120.57

Please choose your skills

Skills
Flight
Eagle Wings
Firemaking Merit
Bow and Arrow Merit
Farsight
Map Merit
Binoculars Merit
Statistics Merit

Zeke squinted. "Why are they all Merits?"

He was the Scouting Apocalypse.

"Scouting...*oh*. Oh! I get it. Not just 'to scout,' but 'kiddie scout,' got it," Zeke said, nodding. He tapped his lips, thinking.

"Is Zeke talking to himself...?" Mia asked.

"Yeah. Uh, you know. Of everything you should worry about when it comes to him, that's probably the least?" Domi said, not quite certain.

Zeke pursed his lips, cutting his gaze at Domi and Mia. He shut up. *I can still use it like a normal skill? Even if it says Merit?*

Yes.

Okay. Then... Flight, will that improve my ability to fly?

Yes.

Good. I want Flight, uh... He looked over the skills again. *Eagle Wings would look cooler than my pigeon wings, and they might even be an improvement on my flight skills as well, but I don't desperately need more—or better, for that matter—wings. I'll shelf that one. Come back to it if I can't find something else. Firemaking... he used that to set me on fire. I already have Flame Manipulation. I can use it to level up Flame Manipulation, which is nice, but that's the end of it. Bow and Arrow... Eh. I don't know if I'd use that or not. It feels like an early game skill, and this is the late game. On the other hand, it does improve my long-range attack abilities. Farsight sounds nice. I could always use better vision. Binoculars...how does that differ from Farsight?*

Binoculars is related to your use of vision improvements. Farsight gives you better base vision.

Huh. Okay, garbage. And we're not in math class, so I don't need Statistics. He nodded to himself. *Flight, Firemaking, Bow and Arrow. Let's go with those three.*

Gained skills: Flight, Firemaking Merit > Fire Manipulation +5, Bow and Arrow Merit.

Zeke looked up. "Well, I went after him to get an answer to why the Apocalypse Coalition brought us all here, but uh, he didn't feel like talking."

"Especially not after you started savaging his throat," Domi commented.

Zeke nodded, allowing her comment. "Most people don't feel like talking once I do that."

Mia threw her hands up. "You guys are joking about that? *Joking?* You're not terrified? That wasn't horrifying to you?"

"It was."

She frowned at Zeke. "Then why—"

"What do you want me to do? Break down and cry?" Zeke asked. He rolled his eyes, exasperated. "My life has been fucked up since this started. It's just been getting more and more fucked up with every passing moment. What am I supposed to do? Scream? Cry? Break down every time it gets a little more fucked up? I'd rather laugh. Even if it's fucked. Even if I shouldn't. Better to laugh than cry. Better to laugh than give up and go home."

"Still, there's a limit," Mia said.

"Is there? Can there be? If there's a limit to our actions, we lose this battle. If we hold ourselves back, someone else will go that little bit further and edge us out. We can't—I can't. I can't be 'normal.' I can't even be *good*. I'm just...I'm trying, but..."

Domi put a hand on Zeke's shoulder. "Deep breaths. Like you said. Now isn't the time. It isn't the time to break down. We get through this. We come out the other side. Then we can cry."

Zeke nodded. He swallowed, turning away. *It's so hard. No matter what I do, it gets worse. On all sides, there's people harassing me. Mia, the System. The other Apocalypses. No one gives me a break. No one—* He took a deep breath and forced it down. Shaking his head, he rubbed his brows, resetting himself mentally. *Like Domi said. Now isn't the time. I need to stay strong. After all of this, once we destroy all the Apocalypses—then I can break down. But not now. Not yet.*

Mia lowered her eyes. "I'm sorry."

"No. You were in the right. If the world was normal, you'd be right. It's just...the world isn't normal right now. We can't afford to be in the right. We can't afford to be normal." Zeke gave her a forced smile. "We have to keep moving."

"Yeah. Keep moving."

They walked on, leaving the Scouting Apocalypse behind.

56
THE NEXT BATTLE

They walked on, down the streets and farther into the city. Apocalypses clashed all around them, some of them heard but not seen, fighting on nearby streets, others fighting in the sky overhead. The three of them just walked, taking a bit of a break. After their argument, *or whatever you'd call that mess,* no one was looking at each other. They walked in silence, without saying anything or even pointing things out to one another.

"So, uh..." Mia licked her lips. "Should we go...find another fight?"

"Please," Zeke grumbled under his breath.

"Yeah. I think we're all ready for a battle," Domi said, laughing to herself.

Overhead, another flash of gold light demanded their attention. The same female voice cleared her throat. "Ahem. Can everyone hear me?"

"Yes," Zeke said, mostly to himself.

"Zeke's really going nuts. He thinks the big voice in the sky can hear him," Domi mocked him.

Zeke gave her a look, narrowing his eyes.

Domi grinned, waggling her brows at him. "Huh? What's that look for?"

The voice continued. "A few of you have hit Level 120. Congratulations! Those of you who have hit this amazing benchmark, I welcome you to the next realm!"

"The...what?" Zeke asked.

"The next realm...?" Mia asked, confused.

"Kaaaay," Domi said.

A set of gold stairs traveled down from the sky. Forming one step at a time from molten gold, they dripped down the drops and flats, slowly descending to the roof of the tallest building.

"Come on up! Those of you who are this strong, have qualified to face my Subordinates. If you think you're strong enough to take them on, step forward!"

"Is she saying, if you aren't at least this level, you aren't even strong enough to level by Subordinates?" Domi complained.

"It might be true," Zeke said, cutting a look at Domi. He'd been getting less EXP from lower level Apocalypses and Subordinates. Almost none, nowadays, especially from Subordinates. It was possible that the main Apocalypse and her Subordinates were too high level to gain any EXP from anyone lower than Level 120. *But how high level do you have to be that you need someone to be Level 120 to gain EXP from them? How did she get that strong?*

"I know. And it's kind of terrifying."

Mia looked at the others. "I'm close to 120. What about you guys?"

"Just hit it," Zeke admitted.

"Yep, just scraped over the edge, but I'm there," Domi said. "No Level 120 bonus, though. Hey, System! What's up with that?"

"The System's in a mood. It's being rude right now. Don't think you'll be able to get through to it," Zeke said.

Domi wrinkled her nose. "Pity. I could use a new type of bomb."

"How many types of bomb do you need?" Zeke asked.

She gave him a look like he'd asked a stupid question. "All of them."

Zeke laughed. "Yeah, makes sense. I kinda feel that, actually."

"Uh, so, are we, uh." Mia shifted in place awkwardly. "Are you guys gonna head up, or..."

"Huh? Nah. You're close, right? Let's get you leveled first, and then we can all head up together," Zeke said.

"Really?" Mia asked.

"I mean, it's obvious, right? It's a tactical advantage to have more people on your team. If we head up alone and abandon you down here, not only will we be disadvantaging ourselves, but we'd also be abandoning you to die. I'm not going to do that to a friend," Zeke said firmly.

Mia nodded. She smiled and skipped a little, looking at the ground.

"I'm not gonna abandon you because we argued a little," he muttered, half to himself. *What kind of monster would do that?*

"Soooo, now that we're all made up...who do we want to take on? We've got fights going on left, right, and center. Can't turn around without smacking into another Apocalypse. Where do we wanna start?" Domi asked.

"I know I *don't* want to face that stupid robot Mad Scientist Apocalypse. Anything but that," Zeke said.

"Maybe we should just wander around until we run into one naturally? We could take a little break here until we encounter something. Or we can hang out and watch, wait until a pair of combatants get weak..."

Domi chuckled, nudging Mia. "Look at you! Now you're on team 'attack 'em while they're down.' Learning fast!"

"Well, I—either they get tired, or we do," Mia defended herself, embarrassed.

"That's exactly what I've been saying this whole time," Domi said firmly, very pleased. She glanced around, then pointed up. "Not to attract that Mad Scientist again, but we can watch things better from the rooftop. Plus, there's lots of aerial battles in this part of the city. We're only missing out by keeping our feet on the ground."

"Agreed." Zeke grabbed them.

"Are you gonna do that freaky gravity thing again?" Domi asked, giving him a dubious look.

"N-no," Zeke said, looking aside.

Mia cleared her throat. "I can just...you know. Make a platform elevator."

Domi stared at her. "Why didn't you say so from the start?"

"Er, well, Zeke seemed to be enjoying himself so much, I couldn't just kill his fun," Mia said, embarrassed.

Domi laughed. She thumped Zeke on the shoulder. "You do seem to enjoy yourself."

"I mean, flying is fun," Zeke said, nodding. "I'll take the break, though, if you want to do the heavy lifting this time."

Mia nodded. "I'm good to go."

A gold platform appeared under their feet. Zeke released the girls, and the three of them flew up to the edge of the nearest building. From the top of the building, they gazed down and around at the other Apocalypses around them.

"How many levels do you have left?" Zeke asked.

"Five," Mia said. "One Apocalypse should do the trick."

Zeke blinked. *Huh? I only get two levels per—wait. What was that the System always said? Half the EXP in return for getting skills? Okay, yeah. Actually? That tracks.*

Two Apocalypses crashed to the ground near them, both covered in wounds. They struck at one another with their hands and feet, kicking and punching, screaming, absolutely lost to the fight.

"Well, well, well," Domi said.

Zeke nudged Mia. "You ready?"

"Yep." Mia walked up to the building's edge and hopped off, plummeting down toward the ground.

"Uh," Zeke said, looking after her. He looked at Domi. "She can't fly, can she?"

Domi pursed her lips. She shrugged.

A gold platform appeared under Mia's feet. Rather than immediately catching her, it dropped at nearly the same rate as her, slowly slowing until it stopped a step above the ground.

"Damn. That was actually cool as hell," Zeke muttered.

"Right? Looked better than getting flown around by Mr. Pigeon Wings," Domi complained.

Zeke looked at her, betrayed. "What's wrong with my wings?"

"They're pigeon wings! What do you mean, 'what's wrong?' Do *you* wanna be toted around by a dude with pigeon wings?"

Zeke shook his head. "You know, if you'd mentioned it a minute ago, I could've fixed that."

"Fixed it how? Grown another pair of wings?"

He opened his mouth, then shut it. His brows furrowed. *If I'd taken Eagle Wings, that would've replaced my current wings, right? I wouldn't end up flying on four wings?*

You would have had four wings.

Zeke raised his brows. "You know what? I'll stick with pigeon wings."

"Yeah? Okay." Domi lifted her arms out and cocked her head at him. "C'mon. Let's get down to the party. Make sure Mia has all the support she needs."

Slotting his arms under hers, Zeke enlarged his wings. He flapped, speeding into the sky, then soared down, circling down toward the ground. *One more kill. And then...*

He looked up, gazing at those golden stairs. Already, Apocalypses flurried at the bottom of the stairs, sparring over the right to climb them. He looked back down, where Mia deftly battled the other two Apocalypses.

And then, we charge into the final battle.

57
TO THE STAIRS

Down below, Mia battled the other two Apocalypses. Despite their preoccupation with one another, they hadn't hesitated to separate and attack Mia the second she interjected. One of them drew back his head and screamed, blasting her with sound waves. The other jumped at Mia, slicing at her with vicious bone claws that jutted out of their every limb.

Mia ducked the sound waves. She parried the claws. She and the clawed Apocalypse struggled for a moment, and then she slashed out. The gold blade sliced smoothly through the claws as if they were made of snow, not bone. The clawed Apocalypse fell back, retracting their injured claw with a hiss.

Chasing after them, Mia immediately slashed again. The sound-based Apocalypse screamed at her. Her body shook from the force of the waves, but her blade found the clawed Apocalypse's throat. It fell, dropping heavily to the ground.

She darted to the side to dodge the scream and jumped back. Her blade transformed into a bow, and she fired gold arrow after gold arrow at the Sound Apocalypse. They darted away, jumping back, away from her arrows.

"I don't think so." Domi lobbed a ball of fire at the Sound Apocalypse. They looked up seconds before the ball struck, but it was far too late. An explosion blasted them, the sound and force washing over their body.

The Sound Apocalypse screamed and covered its ears.

Domi laughed. "Ha, I thought so."

Down below, Mia fired another arrow. This one slammed home. The sound-based Apocalypse wobbled in place, then fell backward.

Mia waved. She gave them the thumbs up. A gold platform under her feet buffeted her up.

"Need both of them?" Domi guessed.

Mia nodded. "They were really weak. Only got two levels per each of them. The decimals closed the gap."

"So...we're all Level 120? Ready to breach the stairs?" Zeke asked.

Domi nodded.

Mia gave a thumbs-up, then paused. "I haven't got a bonus yet. Did you guys get your bonuses?"

Domi laughed. She shook her head.

Zeke grimaced. "Er, Domi and I might be bad people to ask. We had to beg the System for all of our bonuses, pretty much. And it's in a bad mood right now."

Mia frowned at him. "The System has moods?"

"Yeah. You remember my theory, right?" Zeke said.

"Your theory..." Her brows furrowed.

Does she not? Zeke waved his hand. "Don't worry about it."

Domi gave him a look. She frowned at him and mouthed, *She doesn't remember?*

Zeke shrugged. *Compared to Domi and I, who've bargained with the System the whole way here, Mia leveled up smoothly as a Hero. She hasn't even had to grapple with being labeled an Apocalypse. It...might not be a bad thing to allow her to continue to be deceived by the System. There's no harm in her forgetting that the System might be an Apocalypse, and it might be harmful to remember or think about it. I won't remind her. Not for now.*

Mia nodded at them, dismissing their conversation. "Step on my platform. I'll fly us directly up to the top of the stairs."

"Smart. I was going to suggest we fly to the stairs, but good point. Why not fly to the top, part two?" Zeke agreed, nodding.

"We still got teleported last time. Without us noticing it, might I add," Domi said. She pressed her lips together. With trepidation, she gazed at the stairs. "It's not that I think we don't need to go up there, but we need to be on guard. No, on *maximum guard.*"

"Right. We didn't even notice it happening, like you said. We can't even flinch," Zeke agreed.

"If we didn't notice, is there a point to being on guard? We probably won't notice it again," Mia pointed out.

Zeke grimaced. "I'd rather be on guard and fail to notice the attack, than not be on guard and miss it anyway. I mean...if that Apocalypse up on top of the stairs can teleport us freely without us knowing, then the battle's already over. Honestly—she probably can't do that because otherwise she'd already have killed all of us, and I know we already had this conversation, but seriously. Let's be careful. Even if it's pointless."

"Yeah," Domi agreed.

Mia nodded, though her expression told Zeke she hadn't been convinced.

They floated up to the bottom level of the stairs. The other Apocalypses still fought, but a few of them climbed up the stairs while they fought, struggling their way up them. The three of them glided past, ascending easily toward the clouds above.

Domi waved as they passed. "Byeee, get a fly skill, byeeeee!"

Mia nudged her. "Don't taunt them."

"If they could get us, they would've flown to the top already. I can taunt them a little," Domi reasoned.

A dagger hurtled up at them from the scrum. Zeke pushed the girls to the side and snatched it out of the air with his teeth, using **Ranged Devour** to catch it. He swallowed it down, then turned to Domi. Without a word, he cocked a brow at her.

Domi put her hands up. "Okay, okay. Maybe I shouldn't taunt them. I'm sorry."

They continued upward. The very first Apocalypses to climb the stairs looked at them, frowning. One of them gestured, pointing at the stairs. She lifted her hands to her mouth. "You can't fly up. You have to walk!"

"We seem to be flying up just fine," Domi said.

Zeke shrugged back at her. Craning his neck, he looked up at the sky. "If there's a wall or something, we can go back down, but I don't see any reason to not try flying, first."

Domi followed his gaze. "Yeah, I don't see a wall...doesn't mean there isn't one, but yeah. Let's give it a try!"

"If you guys are sure. As long as you don't mind potentially getting set back, I'll give it a try."

"Yeah, I don't mind showing up a little later to the fight, when everyone else is already tired," Domi said with a nod.

Up, up, up. The second set of stairs stretched as long as the first had. The other Apocalypses fell away, and they soared up alone, nothing but them, the stairs, and the clouds. Zeke looked down. The city seemed tiny below them, a little blot of gray in the middle of the ocean. The other Apocalypses faded into the gold staircase.

Zeke frowned. He touched his neck. At this height, he expected his breath to come short, the air to be thin and cold, but instead, he breathed easily. Nor was the air unusually cold. Pleasantly cool, maybe, but not icy cold. *Why's it so...normal, up here? It shouldn't be, right?* He looked at the clouds overhead.

Something glittered atop them. A palace, maybe? Something beautiful, that absolutely should not be able to be supported on water vapor.

Yeah, okay. I guess I can't expect too much logic from an Apocalypse. Especially not one that's this high level. Are we still inside her Domain? Is this entire space her Domain? He lifted his head, gazing out to the horizon. To the edge of the world, where the curvature of the earth swallowed up the visible lands, all he could see was water. *Surely this ocean isn't her Domain too, right? But...then, it would explain why we entered the city and found ourselves teleported here, if this entire space is shaped by her powers.*

After a second, he shook his head. *Doesn't explain how everyone else ended up here, so eh. Can't win 'em all. Might be totally off-the-mark with this guess. Yeah, it's more likely to just be an ordinary old teleport to her Domain, in the middle of whichever ocean this is.*

This whole thing is kinda bullshit, to be honest. What's her Apocalypse? The Weird-Ass Teleportation and Illusions Apocalypse? What on earth encompasses everything we've seen so far?

They approached the clouds at last. Zeke turned his eyes upward. *I guess I'm about to find out.*

58
ABOVE THE CLOUDS

Abruptly, Zeke slammed into a wall. He dropped back against the gold platform. Beside him, Domi, too, fell flat, trapped between the invisible wall and Mia's platform.

Mia jolted to a halt. Her brows furrowed. Casually, she gestured upward.

Pressure slammed into Zeke. He lifted his hands and pushed against the invisible wall, fighting to gain a little breathing room. Gasping, he looked at her. "Mia—please!"

Confused, she looked around at the flattened Domi and Zeke. She sat upright, not at all bothered by the wall that crushed the other two. Staring in concern, she patted Zeke's face, a little lost. "What's happening? Guys? Are you okay?"

"We're—being crushed!" Domi hissed.

Mia looked around. She backed off a little. "What? By what?"

Zeke heaved a breath. He went to sit up, only to bang his head on the invisible wall. "Ow," he muttered, putting a hand to his aching forehead.

Domi sat at a lean, patting the invisible wall. Her palm flattened up where the wall stretched. "You don't feel that? It doesn't hit you at all?" she asked.

Mia shook her head. "I don't feel anything a all. It's just normal air. Just like usual."

Zeke snorted. He glanced at Domi, lying flat like him, then Mia, sitting upright. "Wonder if it's because you're a Hero, not an Apocalypse."

"Is that what the other Apocalypses meant, then? They already knew about the invisible wall. The only way up is for us to climb the stairs," Domi guessed. She looked at the stairs, climbing up just beside them, then at Mia. "I mean, we could still cheat?"

"Let me try. I can catch myself if it rejects me," Zeke offered. He rolled off the platform and spread his wings, catching himself out of the barrel roll. Flapping over to the stairs, he swung his body down and aimed his feet at the stairs.

An invisible wall slammed into his soles. He skidded down it. Remembering his childhood days climbing slides, Zeke spread his feet and leaned his weight forward. Even with his best slide-climbing techniques, he still slid down. An invisible surface slipped by under his hands, as slick as ice. His feet slipped, rubber tennis shoes providing no help. There was no traction to be found.

Clumsily, Zeke kicked away from the slick surface and flapped his wings, catching the air again. He circled away from the stairs and climbed back up into the air. As he drew close, he asked, "Mia, can you lower the platform?"

Mia gestured. The platform lowered a bit, enough for Domi to sit upright. Zeke slid into place, folding his wings as he landed.

"No luck?" Domi asked.

"Stairs have an invisible wall, too. They really want us to climb," Zeke informed her, shaking his head.

Domi snorted. "What a game-like anti-cheat technique, huh?"

"Matches the game-like system," Zeke pointed out.

"Wonder if we could clip in? Like, lean against the wall and jiggle a lot until we sliiiiide through," Domi suggested.

"I don't know. Let's start with reality as far as we can see it." Zeke nodded at Mia. "Mia can pass through the invisible wall, and so can the platforms Mia makes...right?"

Mia gestured. She summoned a little platform beside Zeke, then pressed it upward well over her head. "Looks like it."

"What if you wrap me and Domi in the gold platforms? That way, the wall only sees your platforms, and lets them through. We sneak through without the wall ever realizing we're there, and when we're on the other side, it's already too late," Zeke said.

"Oooh, like a Trojan Horse," Domi said, nodding.

"Exactly," Zeke replied.

Mia frowned. "What if the entire area up there rejects you? If it's something like Domain Rejection, instead of Invisible Wall?"

"Can you keep us wrapped in your platforms?" Zeke asked.

She shook her head. "Not long term. That's why I'm bringing it up. It's easy for me to create one, simple platform for a long time, and I can easily create weapons, shields, or other pre-defined items. If I branch out, though, and create a custom item like a whole-body wrap, it takes all my concentration. One would be pushing it. Two? I'd pretty much be completely immobilized. I don't know that I'd have enough brainpower left to walk, let alone fight. And if you two started moving..." Mia made a face. She shook her head.

"All right. Well." Zeke looked above them, then shrugged. "Let's hope it's just a wall. If it isn't..."

"If it isn't, Zeke and I go back and climb the stairs. You go up alone," Domi said, nodding.

"No," Zeke said sharply.

"No?" Domi asked.

"What, think I can't take it?" Mia asked, crossing her arms.

He grimaced. "It's not that I think you can't take it, it's just... we all only have so much energy. I don't want you to face all the other Apocalypses alone, and waste all your energy and strength staving them off, before Domi and I get there. Not to mention that the main Apocalypse might be waiting up there to pick us off."

He met Mia's eyes, then Domi's. "It's not that it's you, Mia. I just don't like the idea of *any* of us passing through alone. Me, you, Domi. None of us should fight alone."

"So, what would you want me to do, then?" Mia asked.

"I think it's better to hover up here until you see me and Domi, and then we can all pass through at once and fight our way through together."

"Assuming we can't pass through right here, right now," Domi said.

"Right," Zeke said, pointing at Domi.

Mia nodded. "Okay. I get it. I'm okay with that." She lifted her hand. A gold gauntlet appeared around Zeke's hand. "See if it works, before I waste energy wrapping your whole body."

Zeke looked at his hand. He opened and closed it, feeling the *nothing* on his skin. Slight warmth, mild tingling, and nothing. No weight. No resistance. The armor easily flowed, no matter what gesture he did, or how he flicked his fingers. *Wow. That's actually really impressive.*

Mia cleared her throat. "Zeke...?"

"Oh— Right." Jolted back to reality, Zeke quickly lifted his hand. He pushed it up, up, all the way up into the sky. His brows furrowed. *Where* was *the wall?* Picking up his other hand, he reached up, and immediately touched the sky...or at least the invisible wall.

He turned, pursing his lips and nodding at Mia. "I think it works."

"Then let's get this show on the road." Mia furrowed her brows and held her arms out, pointing her palms toward Zeke and Domi. That slight warmth surrounded all of Zeke and Domi, wrapping them in a golden glow. His vision became suffused with it. The whole world glowed in a golden tint.

Mia trembled. She bit her lip, her brows furrowed in intense focus. She lifted her hand up, carrying them into the sky. They passed the invisible wall with absolutely no sensation whatsoever. Nothing. With the gold surrounding him, what had been a solid wall became no more than air.

"Are...are we past it?" Mia panted.

"Yeah. Go ahead, let go," Domi said gently.

Mia relaxed. The gold glow vanished.

Zeke and Domi both tensed. Nothing happened. No great power descended on them. They simply sat there, and a great nothing happened.

"Is everything okay? Do I need to put the coatings back on?" Mia asked, concerned by their silence.

Catching sight of Domi wincing, Zeke laughed, and a moment later, Domi did the same. Both of them relaxed. Shaking his head, Zeke climbed to his feet. "We're fine, Mia. You got us through. Thanks!"

"Oh. Phew!" Mia wiped her brow. She laughed, too. "Thank goodness. I was worried you two would get squashed, or something."

"If the wall would do that much damage, she wouldn't refuse to let us in," Domi pointed out.

Zeke nodded. "Yeah, that'd be a pretty overpowered skill, if she could just instagib anyone who walked into her Domain."

"This girl has *got* to be dangerous as hell, though. We keep brushing up against tiny little fragments of her power, and pretty much every time we do, we have a discussion about how it could kill us if it was a little stronger than it is," Domi pointed out.

"Yeah, well, when she has things like invisible walls and teleportation..." Zeke pointed out, finishing the statement with a shrug.

"She's kind of like a combination of me and Ryan," Mia pointed out. "Teleportation, that's Ryan, and force walls, that's me."

Zeke's eyes widened. "Holy shit, could it be?"

"What?" Domi asked.

"This girl...what if she isn't an Apocalypse? What if she's a Hero?"

59
FACING A HERO

"What if she isn't an Apocalypse? What if she's a Hero?"

Domi raised her brows.

Mia startled, then squinted. "Wait, but...does that change anything?"

"I don't know. It...could mean she's way higher level than us," Zeke mused. He spread his hands. "I always get a little scrap of a Level for beating a cockroach, no matter how small because they're classed as 'Survivors.' If her Levels behave the same way, but for Apocalypses..." He let his words trail off.

Mia squinted. "Can Heroes have Domains, though? I never got an option for a Domain."

"For that matter, can Heroes recruit Apocalypses as Subordinates?" Domi asked.

Zeke spread his hands. "We can ask the System for any moves we want. Domi and I begged our way out of a proper Domain, why couldn't a Hero ask for one? As for recruiting, I was able to recruit Mia, right? And when it comes to Heroes and Apocalypses...well, we all remember what happened to Ryan, right?"

"Uh...what happened to Ryan?" Mia asked.

"He was a Hero. He turned into an Apocalypse for destroying the world," Zeke filled her in.

"He...what?" Mia asked, more confused.

"It's a long story. Don't worry about it. The point is, Hero and Apocalypse...as far as I can tell, they're just labels the System hands out at random. There's no real difference between a Hero and an Apocalypse except that one's meant to fight the other."

"Why introduce Heroes at all?" Mia asked.

Zeke shrugged. "I don't know. Maybe it was a way for the System to allow more than one person to survive the domes? Or maybe all the Apocalypses got chosen at the start, and adding Heroes let the System Apocalypse add more players to the field. We can't know for certain unless we face the System down and shake some answers out of it."

"Yeah, good luck getting a straight answer out of the System on anything," Domi complained.

"But it does mean that she's potentially way higher level than us and might be better at killing Apocalypses than the average Apocalypse. After all, if she's a Hero, she's built to kill us, unlike Apocalypses, who are built to kill...well..." Zeke grimaced.

"People. The world," Domi offered.

"Yeah. One of those," Zeke said, nodding.

Mia put a finger on her chin, thinking, then looked up sharply. "Oh, I get it! Usually, the two of you have the upper hand because you chose to invest your power into yourself instead of establishing a Domain. But if you face a Hero, who usually doesn't have a Domain..." Her brows furrowed. She looked at the clouds around them. "But...she has a Domain...?"

"Right. I think the potential Level disparity is the biggest difference," Zeke said.

"If she gets bonus levels for killing Apocalypses? Yeah. That'll be a problem," Domi agreed. "And it's only going to get worse, the more Apocalypses climb up here to face her."

"At least I only got, like, 0.01 Levels for killing cockroaches," Zeke muttered to himself. *Hopefully it's the same for her.*

"Guess that's why she was fattening us up by having us fight each other down below," Domi muttered back.

Zeke twisted his lips. He nodded. *Yeah. I thought up a lot of theories for that, but in the end, it comes back to the simplest one. She wanted Levels, and we were too low level for her. Yikes. That's scary as hell.*

Upside, though: You only get full Levels for fighting people who are close to, or on, your level. Means she fattened us up to be strong enough to fight her seriously. He took a deep breath. *Yeah. That's what I'm going to tell myself.*

The platform flew to the height of the clouds. Zeke and Domi hopped off, and Mia stepped after them, dematerializing the platform behind her. All three of them stared, drinking in the beauty of the city in the clouds.

Fluffy, idealized buildings stood all around them, stolen from all over the globe. From European castles, with tall towers and peaked roofs, to minarets and rounded, plump buildings, to pagodas and intricate shrines, every beautiful type of building stood around them. All of the buildings were formed from clouds, sculpted into their unique shapes. The way the light hit the clouds, or maybe the composition of the clouds themselves, gave the buildings different pastel colors. They were no match for many of the buildings' original brilliant hues, but they gave the entire area a kind of gentle, pale, even color palette that pleased the eyes.

"It's not a palace in the skies, it's a whole city of palaces," Mia murmured.

Zeke walked over and knocked on one of the walls.

Although it looked like an immaterial cloud, the surface was solid under his fingers. It gave a little as he knocked, but ultimately held his fist. "Kind of reminds me of a non-Newtonian fluid."

"Neeeeeerd," Domi commented. She walked over and pushed at the wall, then raised her brows. With open hands, she kneaded the wall, playing with the weird texture. "Heehee..."

"Calls me a nerd, then immediately gives in to the charm of a non-Newtonian fluid," Zeke commented dryly.

"Only nerds call it 'non-Newtonian fluid,'" Domi replied.

"Okay, cool kid, what do you call it, then?" Zeke shot back.

Domi grinned. "Cool kids call it the squishy-squishy-stiff-stuff."

"Uh huh." Zeke gave her a flat look, unamused.

Mia giggled. "It is fun to play with, though."

Zeke shook his head and forcibly removed his hands from the wall. "Okay. Focus. We're the first ones up here. She doesn't necessarily know that we're here yet, since we didn't take the stairs. While we have the stealth advantage, let's poke around and get the lay of the land."

Mia nodded. Domi saluted. Zeke took the lead, and the three of them wound through the streets, passing by replicas of famous buildings shaped out of clouds. Underfoot, the cloud had the same feeling as the cloud walls did, giving way at first, then holding strong. Zeke stomped on it and heard no noise. *It masks footfalls. Good for us, but also good for our enemies. Likewise, it absorbs some of the force of your step. It'll be hard to kick off and do quick jumps. Like fighting in sand, or stiff mud.*

"Keep your heads on a swivel. We won't necessarily hear the opponents coming," Zeke said quietly.

Domi nodded. Mia gave a thumbs-up.

Those normal people who teleported the bodies away...what

happened to them? Are they up here, now? Or still down below, picking up bodies? Zeke frowned, putting a hand on his chin. *But even if they're down there, the bodies should be up here. I wonder what they're doing with them.*

Argh. Could actually use Olivia right now. Bet she'd be able to sniff out the fresh blood. Or Sparkles. He's a dog, after all. Ought to be able to find a dead body or two.

He peered in the next building they passed, sneaking a glimpse around the door. The inside was hollow, the building nothing but a hollow shell. Zeke raised his brows. *Are there not many people living up here? How many people are in her Apocalypse Coalition, then? Or are all the Apocalypses fighting down below, rather than hiding up here?*

Zeke walked on. He peeked into the next building, and the next. One after another, all of them hollow, all of them vacant.

"Wait, stop," Mia said.

The other two paused. Zeke looked back. "You okay?"

"I'm fine, but..." She turned, looking down the street beside them at a giant cathedral with grand flying buttresses. "I don't know. Something feels off about that building."

"Apocalypse Locator pinging you?" Domi asked.

"I don't have a skill that convenient. It's just Hero's Intuition, and half the time, it goes off when there's a kitten stuck in a tree," Mia explained.

Domi startled. "You actually have a Hero Sense skill?"

"Yeah? It's kind of useless, like I said, though," Mia said. She shrugged. "I usually ignore it, but up here...probably not a kitten, right?"

"I'm down to test it out," Zeke said with a shrug. He turned down the street Mia had indicated, and the three of them crept up to the cathedral.

A massive cloud-stone façade gazed down at them. Carvings of saints held various strange objects in their hands. Angels flitted around. Shaped from cloud rather than stone, the intricacy of the work and the lightness imbued by the techniques was somewhat lessened, the details softened away, the imbued lightness less impressive in a material already lighter than air.

As they grew closer, Zeke squinted. *That angel, is that...*

"The Scouting Apocalypse," Mia said, startled.

Zeke looked over his shoulder at her. "You thought so, too, huh?"

"Yeah. That angel, right?" Mia pointed.

Zeke nodded. "Yeah, that one. The one holding the bow and arrow."

"They made the Scouting Apocalypse Cupid?" Domi asked.

"Wrong religion," Zeke said, shaking his head at her.

She threw her hands up. "Have you never visited cathedrals? They throw Cupid in there sometimes, just for fun! Don't blame me because medieval Europeans liked to toss Greco-Roman symbolism into their churches."

Zeke chuckled. He reached for the massive double doors.

Domi stepped up behind him, massing an orange ball between her palms. Mia pressed her back up against the wall, ready to dart in.

The doors swung wide. A massive, sunlit space opened before them. The bodies of dead Apocalypses laid in neat lines down the center of the space, heads facing the sun, feet facing the shadow. No matter how destroyed or tattered, they were all collected here. Zeke recognized the rollerblader and the construction worker, among others.

He frowned. *Why are they collecting the bodies, though?*

"Oh! Oh, I'm not ready yet. I'm not ready!"

A frumpy-looking girl came rushing out of the back. She waved her hands at them, pushing up her glasses with a nose-wiggle as she ran. "Please. I need more time!"

"Uh...what are you doing?" Zeke asked.

"Huh? I'm the Zombie Apocalypse Apocalypse. I'm doing what Madame Pearl told me to do: collect their bodies." She glanced at the floor and poked her pointer fingers together. "I'm sorry. It's a weird power. I probably...shouldn't have asked for my Apocalypse to be the Zombie Apocalypse. But it worked out for me, so..."

"Zombie Apocalypse...Apocalypse?" Zeke repeated. He eyed the Apocalypses' bodies, and suddenly it all came together. *Ooooh, I get it. She's not the Zombie Apocalypse—she doesn't make ordinary zombies. She only makes Apocalypses into zombies. So that's why there's no clash with Osiris, the Undead Apocalypse!*

Holy shit, she turns Apocalypses into zombies? Does that mean she gets to control all their original skills, too? Zeke's eyes widened. He glanced at Domi and Mia, obscured behind the door.

Domi nodded. Mia gestured with her head.

Right. Sounds like we all agree. Zeke lunged in, racing at the girl. He fired off a **Ranged Devour** as he closed in.

She screeched in shock and threw herself back. The bite snapped up the air inches in front of her throat, cutting a line across her skin. Startled, she stammered, "E-enemies?"

Domi jumped in. Mia charged, closing in a few steps.

Even as they ran at the girl, the gurl whirled and ran past the bodies on the floor. As she passed the bodies, they twitched, then rose. One by one, the zombie Apocalypses stood off the ground and faced them, raising their arms.

Zeke licked his lips as he chased the girl. *Welp. I think we might've kicked off the next wave of battle a little early...*

60

ZOMBIE APOCALYPSE...
APOCALYPSE

Zeke closed in on the girl. He opened his mouth.

Before he could bite in, a zombie Apocalypse lunged in front of him. His bite sunk into rotting flesh instead. Zeke tore the bite away, needing his jaws free for another attack. Unfeeling, the zombie closed the gap to grab him. An expressionless face bit at Zeke, strange, scarred arms wrapping around him. The arms extended, swirling around him like taffy.

Confirmed, the Apocalypses keep their skills. This girl is a problem.

As the arms closed in around his, Zeke snapped one hand up and shoved the zombie's head back. He chewed his way through the zombie's neck, and its head struck the floor. For a second, its body still bound him before it finally went slack. Its skill ended, and the arms wound back to their normal length.

The rollerblader closed in on Zeke nearly as soon as the other Apocalypse dropped him. Zeke jumped back, using its own **High-Speed Maneuvering** skill against it. He swept a low kick at the zombie's skates, and the zombie tripped and fell on its face. Numb, it shoved back up, but Zeke stomped it to the ground instead, firing a dozen **Ranged Devour**s at its back to finish it off.

"They have their skills, but they're stupid! They can use their powers, but they don't know how to use them well. They aren't as strong as they were the first time!" Zeke shouted.

"Yeah, except for the part where they don't feel pain and you need to behead them to kill them. Except for the part where they're almost unkillable, they're easier," Domi mocked him.

"Okay, yeah, but...you know what I mean," Zeke said. The construction worker charged at Zeke, and he flapped his wings and took to the air. The construction worker ran past under him and slammed into the intricately carved cloud wall behind him.

"Yeah, yeah." Domi backed toward the doors, throwing explosion after explosion behind her. The zombies fell back, battered by the explosions, but unlike actual Apocalypses, the burns and pain didn't stop them.

"Domi, pause for a second!" Mia called.

Domi lifted her hands. "Move fast!"

Mia darted in. Running close, she swept at the zombie Apocalypses with her sword. Her strikes severed tendons and hacked limbs rather than taking heads, but it left the Apocalypses helpless on the floor, unable to close in on Domi. With the Apocalypses downed, Domi easily finished them off with a few precision blasts.

"Good teamwork! Hell yeah, girl team!" Domi said, pumping her fist.

"I'm here, too," Zeke said.

"Yeah, but you're not on the girl team," Mia said. She glanced at Domi, and Domi glanced back. They high-fived.

Zeke shook his head. "And let me guess, I'll never be on the girl team?"

"Not without *significant* effort," Domi said, flicking her eyes up and down his body.

Zeke rolled his eyes.

The other zombies closed in on them. The four of them turned away again, facing the enemies.

Footfalls shook the ground all around them. The zombies closing in on Zeke stumbled, then fell to the side. A huge, lumbering hulk closed in on him—the remains of the construction worker. Zeke wrinkled his nose. He darted to the side as the construction worker swung at him. Despite the deathly pallor on the worker's face and the blood staining his body, he still struck at Zeke with all the same force he'd possessed in life. Zeke backed away one step at a time, wary of those swinging fists.

Something struck him in the back. Zeke whirled. A ball of long black spines loomed behind him. *Where the hell did that come from?*

A heavy strike slammed into Zeke's chest. He fell toward the spike ball. Immediately, Zeke threw himself to the side, twisting away from the spike ball.

The spike ball scurried after him, persistently remaining beneath him. It twisted to look up at him, tiny black eyes watching in eager anticipation.

I can't hold back any longer. I use it, or I die! Zeke activated **Transform.** Black armor twisted over his body, and long tendrils swirled behind his head. Mouths opened on all his limbs.

He struck the spikes. With all the upgrades to his armor and his transformed mode active, the spikes broke rather than piercing him. He pointed one of his hand-mouths toward the core of the spike ball.

[Ranged Devour]

A delicious, somewhat chewy bite of meat transferred to his

hand-tongue. Zeke raised his brows. *Guess that was a sea urchin. Seems like it wasn't too dead if it still tasted that good.*

It took time to describe, but in real life, the zombie sea urchin went still in the blink of an eye. The construction worker charged Zeke in the next instant. Both arms raised for a hammer blow, it swung them down toward him.

Zeke threw himself out of the way at the last second. The construction worker's hands slammed into the sea urchin's spikes.

"Ha, take that," Zeke said, pleased with himself.

Numb, the construction worker lifted his hands. The urchin's spiny body stuck to its fists. From blunt objects of utter destruction, the construction worker's hands transformed into bladed fists of utter destruction.

Zeke took a deep breath. He clicked his tongue at himself. "Did I just upgrade my enemy? I think I just upgraded my enemy."

The hammer fists slammed at Zeke again. He dodged backward, rolling away from the blow. The spines scraped by his nose, nicking his armor.

Carried by the force of its blow, the construction worker overswung. Zeke spied an opening. He drew back his leg and slammed it up between the construction worker's.

The construction worker lifted into the air a little, but that was it.

"Right. He's dead. Doesn't feel pain." Zeke pressed his lips together, displeased. *Not the greatest scenario, no.*

Without hesitation, the construction worker swung at Zeke's head.

Zeke ducked again, backstepping into a blade. He rolled away, only for the bladed Apocalypse to chase after him. A person in full fencing gear, their white chest guard stained with blood, lifted a rapier at him.

"Oh, come on," Zeke complained.

The fencer flicked their thin blade and jabbed it at him. Zeke swayed back, only to get hammered by the construction worker's meaty fists. A third Apocalypse kicked him in the shins. Zeke staggered, all but falling with the shin strike. The third Apocalypse, dressed in soccer gear, hauled back her leg to kick again.

Zeke threw himself to the floor and rolled head-over-heels, using his whole height to move horizontally. Behind him, the three Apocalypses clashed. Sparks flew as the fencer parried the construction worker's spiked hand. The soccer girl bounced back, startled but unharmed. The three of them whirled, chasing after Zeke again.

Turning, Zeke ran a few steps, just to put a little distance between him and the construction worker. Both the fencer and the soccer player kept up, but the construction worker lumbered in the back. Zeke whipped around. "Allen!"

Subordinate Allen has shared his STR.

Zeke grabbed the fencer by the shoulders and reeled them in. His mouth gaped wide. Sharp teeth slammed down on the fencer's helmet.

Crunch.

Gripping his mouth, he retreated in pain. *My teeth...that definitely broke some of them! Did that fencer reinforce their helmet with skills? No—I bet that's exactly what they did! Foolish me, trying to bite through a helmet that didn't get damaged, even after the fencer died!*

Before he could even mourn the loss of his teeth, his gums itched. He lifted his hands feeling the edges of his gums. His old teeth fell out, but new teeth quickly replaced them.

Wha...? Oh, right! The tooth replacement skill from the Shark

Apocalypse. What was it, the Zombie (modifier) Shark Apocalypse or something like that?

Man. Didn't expect that one to come in handy.

The fencer twisted. Drawing back their arm, they jutted their foil out, stabbing toward Zeke's heart. Zeke jumped back, but too slow. The foil struck his armor.

It's just a foil, though, so I should be—

The slender blade pierced his armor like butter and sank deeper into his chest.

Zeke batted the sword away. It sliced through his armor on the way out, but at least it no longer pierced him. He darted his head in. Getting his teeth on the fencer's arm, he took a big, vicious bite, tearing out a chunk of meat and bone.

The fencer's arm drooped. They still tried to stab him, but their arm refused to obey their commands. Confused, they looked down.

Pushing past them, the soccer player lobbed a vicious kick at Zeke.

It's been a while, but I think it's time to revive this move! Lifting his fingers to his mouth, Zeke whistled.

[Whistle Blast]

A wave burst from his mouth and struck the soccer player in the face mid-kick. She jolted, stunned by the blast's secondary effect, and stumbled back. Zeke closed in on her. His mouth closed around her neck, and he bit down fiercely. Putrid blood gushed into his mouth. The soccer player struggled one last time, then stilled.

The moment he stood still, the fencer closed in. That thin blade arced toward his head. Zeke snapped his head back and snapped the blade out of the air with his teeth. Twisting his head, he clung on with all of Allen and **Devour**'s strength.

The fencer held on tight. The two of them battled, while between them, the metal strained, twisted and twisted until—

Snap! The blade broke.

Zeke spat out the blade and closed the gap. Just as he opened his mouth to bite the fencer, the construction worker loomed up. His eyes widened. Rather than bite, he kicked the fencer away, toward the construction worker. The construction worker slammed his spiked fist down. Black spikes shattered on the fencer's helmet but pierced through their thin cloth armor. The fencer crumbled, done in by the spikes and the construction worker's strength together.

The construction worker lifted his hand. The fencer went with him, stuck to the urchin's spikes that were, in turn, stuck to the construction worker.

"Ha, I've re-un-empowered you," Zeke said, smirking. A moment later, he paused. "W-weakened you. I've weakened you. Yeah."

Still as numb as ever, the construction worker lifted his fist again.

Zeke stood his ground. He stared up at the construction worker. *I can't be afraid of him forever. He's already dead. I already helped destroy him. I can kill him again now.*

The construction worker dropped its fist on Zeke.

Zeke opened his mouth.

[Devour] [Devour] [Devour]

As the fist dropped, he tore the fencer off the construction worker's hand. The next **Devour** took the sea urchin. The third one took the construction worker's fist.

How much farther can I go? Zeke pointed his jaws at the remnants of the man's arm and kept going. One chunk of arm after another, tearing the man's arm off at the elbow, then shoulder. He kept going. Chewing through his shoulder, past his shoulder blades, and into his chest. The first **Devour** only left marks on the man's chest. The second left shallow holes. On the third, those holes deepened, and on the fourth, he chewed away a hunk of chest. One after another, rattling off **Devour**s as the construction worker wobbled in place, off-balance and half-stunned. His body toppled backward, and he hit the ground.

Zeke blinked, snapped out of the moment. He wiped his face and looked down at the construction worker. *Guess you, uh, sometimes have to chew your food before you eat it. I can't always hork off giant bites and swallow them whole.*

He lifted his head, checking on the girls' battles from where he stood.

Domi fired off explosions, back against the wall. She hadn't Transformed, and she handily kept the zombie Apocalypses at bay with her nonstop carpet bombing.

Makes sense. She was always a good match for low intelligence, mob enemies like these. Zeke glanced over at Mia.

Mia's sword darted out. Gold light traced after it as it slashed one line after another in a massive enemy. Bright gold light burst from its body, and it quivered once, then fell apart, falling into sharp-edged pieces.

Man, that was cool. Looks like a video game kill animation. Zeke looked around. *But where did the boss Apocalypse go? The Zombie Apocalypse Apocalypse, or whatever? The Apocalypse so nice we Apocalypse'd it twice.*

His ordinary vision showed him nothing, not even with the Scouting Apocalypse's upgrade. Zeke activated **Heat Vision** and scanned the room again.

In the back of the room, a single bright spot hunkered behind a pew, far away from the fighting Apocalypses.

I bet that's our girl. Zeke jumped into the air, snapping his wings out. He flapped once, twice, getting just enough air, then swooped across the room toward the heat spot.

The bookish girl sat there, her hands over her head, holding her breath and staying completely still. Her eyes flew open as Zeke's shadow fell over her. She staggered back, terrified. "Please don't hurt me! I'm just doing this to survive, I—"

"I don't care." Zeke opened his mouth.

[Devour]

The girl screamed once, then went still. All around them in the church, the zombie Apocalypses fell to the ground.

Congratulations! You defeated the Zombie Apocalypse Apocalypse.

Level + 2.12
Level: 122.69

Please choose a skill
NONE

Zeke squinted. "Okay...I guess I'll take the NONE skill."

Nothing happened. No more messages popped up.

He frowned. "System? Hey? Are you okay?"

No response.

Zeke pursed his lips and squinted at the air. *Now it's just ignoring me entirely? Where's the professionalism I've come to expect? Where's the serious and hardworking System?*

Ha, who am I kidding? The System hasn't been professional for a long time now. It's out here doing whatever, and it's getting away with it.

I mean. Who's going to stop it? It's not like it has a manager or anything. It can just slack off.

"Earth to Zeke?"

"Huh?" Zeke whipped around, startled.

Domi waved her hand in front of his face. "We beat the Apocalypse, yay!"

"Yay!" Zeke repeated half-heartedly. He looked down at the Zombie Apocalypse Apocalypse's body. "She wasn't that hard. Just...kind of an ordinary person."

"Put all her points into SPR, I bet. Probably invested a single stat harder than any of us," Domi offered.

"Yeah..." Transforming back to human form, Zeke ran his hand through his hair, still looking at her. "Imagine, though. If she'd loosed those things on the city below, where no one could reach her..."

"Oh, I'm imagining it," Domi muttered.

The door to the cathedral opened. "Rebecca, we have some more—"

The trio they'd seen earlier collecting bodies stared at the three of them. They stared back.

"Hi?" Mia tried, with a friendly smile.

61

WHAT ARE YOU DOING HERE?

Mia tried a smile. "Hi?"

The three newcomers frowned. They exchanged looks, then turned to Mia, Zeke, and Domi. One of the girls stepped forward. "Who are you?"

"We're, uh...new here?" Zeke tried. *They haven't attacked yet. I'm not Transformed, and neither is Domi. Maybe they didn't recognize us as enemy Apocalypses at first glance.* He glanced down at the mutilated Zombie Apocalypse Apocalypse at his feet. Gently, he nudged her a little farther under the pew. *If they see that, the game's up.*

"You've become enlightened?" the boy asked.

The other girl frowned. "Why are all the bodies so... jumbled?"

"I don't know. She called us here to help out. Something about the zombies getting out of hand," Mia said.

"No idea where she went, though. You guys see her?" Domi asked.

"She isn't enlightened," the boy said, as if it explained everything.

"Ah, yeah. Not enlightened. Real, uh, real disappointment there," Zeke said, nodding.

Mia shot him a look. Zeke gave her a tiny shrug back. *The hell am I supposed to say? I don't know what he means, and neither do you!*

To his surprise, the boy nodded in agreement, a sage expression on his face. "If she were enlightened, she wouldn't have lost control of her underlings in such a crude manner. It's truly disappointing to all of us."

"Yeah. To all of us," Domi agreed.

One of the girls squinted at them. "When did you three join? I don't recognize you."

"Oh, recently, just recently. I'm sorry, I think we haven't met yet. I'm Mia," Mia said, offering her hand to shake.

The boy approached. The girl put her hand on his arm, holding him back. "If you're one of us, prove it. Show us the basic technique to reach enlightenment."

Mia, Zeke, and Domi exchanged a look.

Domi took a deep breath. She stepped forward.

Zeke raised his eyebrows. *Does she know what to do? I guess I'll watch and see what happens. I mean...maybe she saw something I didn't? Picked up on some hint I didn't? If she knows what this Apocalypse...or maybe Hero, is, she might actually know what to do here.*

"The hell, guys? Why do we need to prove ourselves to you? Are you bullying us because we're new? Yikes, man. I thought this was a cool place, but here you are hazing us." Domi shook her head at them in disappointment.

Ah, fuck. Throwing the Hail Mary, huh? Well...here goes nothing. Zeke grinned embarrassedly from behind Domi. Casually, he tensed his core and adjusted his stance, ready to attack.

On the other side of Domi, Mia took the same stance. She put her hands behind her back. A gold sword materialized in her hand.

The boy frowned at the girl. "She's right, Amy. Why are you being so rude?"

"Sean, are you serious? They're crazy suspicious. Vicki, back me up," Amy returned.

Vicki glanced at the three of them. Zeke smiled and waved. She looked at her two friends. "I don't know. They were helping out. You're being kinda harsh, Amy."

"Were they? Where is Gina?" Amy demanded, glaring at the three of them.

Zeke spread his hands. "We already told you. She wasn't here when we got here. Just walked in and found everything messed up like this. I don't know why you guys are wasting time here yelling at us while whoever did this is getting away."

Domi cast him a look. She shook her head a little bit.

"Why aren't you chasing them? You got here first," Amy said, narrowing her eyes.

"We barely got here before you!" Zeke returned.

"Let's go after them now. It's not too late," Mia said, smiling.

"It's not too late to stop you!" Amy shouted. She charged at them.

Mia jerked forward, but Zeke grabbed her arm. He jumped back instead, shocked.

"Amy!" Sean grabbed Amy and tackled her to the ground. Vicki piled on, holding her back.

"Let me go! They're the ones who attacked Gina! They're the ones who killed her zombies! Why are you guys blind?"

Sean looked up at them. "Get out of here, quickly! We'll talk Amy down."

"Thanks!" Zeke called. Drawing Mia with him, he ran away. Domi followed, close on his heels. They all ran out the door and onto the street.

As the door fell shut, Domi turned back. She spread her

hands and ran them along the edge of the door. Little orange blips appeared behind her palms, flickering on the door.

"What are you doing?" Zeke asked, pausing and looking over his shoulder.

"Leaving presents. What does it look like I'm doing?" Domi asked.

"They weren't going to attack us," Mia said, aghast.

Domi stepped back to admire her handiwork but didn't let it stop her from giving Mia a look. "Uh huh. And when they find the Zombie Apocalypse times two's body? What about then?"

Mia licked her lips. She nodded, slowly. "Right..."

"Right. So, I left them some gifts," Domi said. She dusted off her hands.

"How long will they stay there?" Zeke asked.

Domi pursed her lips. She pulled out her phone and checked something on its screen. "An hour. Should be long enough."

"Yeah, I'd say." Zeke nodded. "Let's get out of here before they find her body...and Domi's presents."

Mia nodded back. The three of them sprinted away, deeper into the strange cloud city.

62

CITY IN THE CLOUDS

"Well, so far, we've killed one Apocalypse, trapped three Subordinates, and wandered around half the city. What else do we want to do before everyone else gets here?" Domi asked.

"Right, I almost forgot," Zeke muttered. He looked down, but all he could see was the pillowy soft floor. *The other Apocalypses are on the way up. They're already climbing the stairs. Some of them were pretty close.*

I'm not too worried, since they'll be tired when they get here, but...

Wait, hold on. They'll be tired when they get here. Zeke put a hand on his chin, thinking.

"What're you cooking?" Domi asked.

"I was just thinking," Zeke started.

"Congratulations," Mia replied.

Zeke glared at her. Mia giggled.

"Anyway. If they climb the stairs, they're going to be tired. That's by the design of the person who runs this place, Hero or Apocalypse. They want to take advantage of it. But what if we get there first?" Zeke lowered his hand and turned, meeting Domi and Mia's eyes.

"They'll still be tired, but we'll be the ones to capitalize on it," Mia murmured. She pursed her lips. "It's not...*good,* but..."

"Yeah, well, we're Apocalypses, so. I think it's a great idea. Work smarter, not harder. They worked harder, so let's punish them for it!" Domi said. She pumped her arm and slapped her bicep. "I'm ready to go. Let's do this."

Mia hesitated, then nodded. "Okay. It is the fastest way to handle it. And it's not like they aren't going to attack us."

"Exactly. Attack so we aren't attacked. Easy," Domi said, nodding.

Zeke cleared his throat. "We probably still have a few minutes before the first ones get to the top, soooo...anything else we wanna do?"

Mia thought for a moment, then pointed. Zeke followed her finger.

The road sloped upward. The buildings stood here and there, graduated along the path up into the sky. From the top of the hill, a massive Greco-Roman temple dominated the landscape. The cloud suited the usually pale-marble temple well. White columns marched off under a heavy roof, and from where they stood, statues could faintly be seen within.

"Up there. I want to check there first. Carefully, since the boss might be there, but..."

Zeke nodded. "Makes sense. Check out the final boss's lair...or the big temple that should give us hints as to the final boss's lair."

"But quickly. They're gonna get here any minute," Domi said, looking over her shoulder.

"Right." Zeke paused. "Domi, do you want to go guard the path up? I can fly up really quickly, and Mia can use her platforms. I know you can kinda fly, but..."

"Yeah, I get it. I'm the slow one, and you're tired of carrying my heavy ass," Domi said.

"I didn't say that—"

"I know, I know. I'm just joking." Domi tossed him a wink and ran off, down toward the stairs.

"If we find anything else like the Zombie Apocalypse squared, we'll call you!" Zeke called after her. *I have Hands-Free Calling, after all. It's not hard for us to keep in contact at a distance, even without phones.*

Domi gave him a thumbs up over her shoulder. Her form grew smaller and smaller, until she was nothing but a small, colorful blot amidst the sea of white.

Zeke spread his wings. Beside him, Mia hopped on a platform. They flew up toward the temple together.

The closer they grew, the larger it became. When they stood at the bottom of the hill, it loomed hugely over them, but as they climbed up to the top and grew closer, the true scale of the temple was revealed. The massive white columns went from distant and large to twice as wide around at the base than Zeke stood tall, and dozens of times his height. The temple itself could easily fit multiple stadiums. Just on the front of the temple, intricately carved statues depicted a girl about their age in multiple poses. She tended to the sick and cared for the weak, offered a scroll to a lowly peasant, stood tall holding the scales of justice, wielded a sword, and offered bread from a basket.

"Damn. Get you a girl who can do it all," Zeke muttered to himself.

"I know, right?" Mia muttered back.

The two of them dropped to the ground and walked inside. Zeke walked slowly, taking it all in. Various statues stood down the ends of corridors. Unlike the statues on the front of the temple, these freestanding statues depicted other people than just the one woman. A man, a woman, a pair of children, holding hands. All of them frozen in cloud-stone, at the peak of their beauty. The statues on the front of the temple wore long, flowing robes in the ancient style, but these people wore modern clothes.

Zeke licked his lips. "Greco-Roman...people frozen as statues... Hey, Mia, don't look any snake-haired women we meet in the eyes, okay?"

"It wasn't just me, huh? You were getting Medusa vibes, too?" Mia whispered as if afraid to speak too loudly.

He cast a look her way. "You know, the Scouting Apocalypse always called it the Apocalypse Coalition, but we haven't seen very many Apocalypses, have we? Only these people, frozen as statues."

"Well, there were the ones that fought us over the Ice Cream Apocalypse," Mia pointed out.

As they walked, the statues' eyes seemed to follow them. Zeke froze, watching them for a moment, but not a one moved. They all remained completely still. He ran a hand over the back of his neck, uncomfortable. *They're too real, that's the problem. Even the statues on the front of the temple were posed, but these... they're just people. People, holding completely still. If I take my eyes off them for a moment, they'll come to life.*

He snapped around, looking at the statues behind them. They remained exactly as they had, unmoving. He wrinkled his nose. *It's all in my head. I know that. But it's so damn uncomfortable to turn my back to them.*

Mia's words filtered through at last. He glanced at her. "What if they could be un-frozen at will? If they're fully Dominated, she might even be able to overwrite their memory of being frozen or brainwash them to be okay with it, so they wouldn't even complain. Plus, she doesn't have to worry about feeding them or making sure they don't get sick, or any of that."

"It does sound kind of convenient, when you put it like that."

"Yeah. I, uh...I don't know. I don't think we should stay up here without Domi. I'm getting serious final-boss vibes," Zeke whispered.

"Yeah. And we definitely aren't high enough level to face the boss yet. Let's go finish levelling. Then, we can destroy this Apocalypse, once and for all," Mia said firmly.

"Could be a Hero," Zeke reminded her.

She gestured at the statues around them. "After this? No way."

"You ain't wrong," Zeke said.

The two of them reversed, heading out the front of the temple. As they went to exit the temple, a man walked out from between the pillars. He wore a long, skinny white jacket over black wide-leg trousers and a black turtleneck. Half-moon glasses glinted on his nose. A thin ponytail hung over one shoulder, black as night.

"I don't think you're from around here," he murmured, lowering his glasses to peer over them.

"Er...just got recruited, actually!" Zeke said, smiling. He went to push past.

In the distance, a series of hearty explosions rattled off.

The man lifted his hand to block Zeke's way. His other hand pushed up his glasses. "Mmm. And I suppose you'd have no idea what that was?"

"N-no idea at all," Zeke said.

The man laughed, just once. And then he vanished.

Zeke looked around, startled. He jumped back, raising his hands defensively.

Beside him, Mia let out an *unf* and flew backward. A second later, something whipped toward Zeke, and he, too, went flying.

His shoulders struck a pillar. Marble dust flew, his head hitting the stone with a *crack!*

Zeke dropped to the ground. He slumped, stunned. *What... where...*

"Little rats, scuttling around. Let me put you where you belong."

A shadow loomed over him. Zeke looked up, bleary-eyed.

Fangs. A wide-open mouth. A slender tongue.

A giant snake's mouth gaped wide, the vicious beast one second away from eating him whole.

As its mouth darted forth to swallow him up, Zeke thought only one thing:

Hey, that's my job!

63
THE TRUSTED ADVISOR

The snake struck, its wide-open mouth lunging down at Zeke. Zeke stared up at it, his vision blurry, still dazed from hitting his head against the pillar.

What a way to go.

As the snake struck, clarity suddenly burst in Zeke's mind. Time slowed. His skills flashed before his eyes. *What do I do? What can I use? I can't let it strike me. Those fangs are venomous.*

Two skills leaped out in his vision. Zeke's eyes widened. *Like that! I see it. I can survive!*

Activating **Create Coffee**, Zeke squeezed it through his teeth, creating a thin spray of droplets. With **Manipulate Aerosols** and **High-Speed Navigation,** he directed the spray at top speed around the snake's mouth and into its eyes.

Hot coffee mist struck the snake's eyes. It jerked its head back reflexively. Its jaws snapped shut a hair before its fangs sunk into Zeke's flesh.

Gold light flashed. Mia dashed into the snake's neck, slamming a hammer into the monstrous beast's jaw. Its head snapped back, away from Zeke. "Zeke! Are you okay?"

"I'm fine. I'm..." Zeke shook his head. He hauled himself

upright. Regeneration worked on his body, slowly clearing his disoriented vision. "Phew. That was a big hit."

"No kidding." Mia peered at him, then nodded. "You look good."

"Aww, thanks." Zeke grinned at her.

A faint pink crawled over her cheeks, and she glanced away.

Zeke raised his brows. *Huh? What was that?*

"Don't ignore me, you flirting bastards!" the snake howled. It lunged at them, slinging the coils of its long body at the two of them.

Mia hopped into the air and let a gold platform carry her away. Zeke leaped up and caught the air with his wings, yanking his legs up after him. The coil slung by inches below his toes, so close he felt the air of it passing against his legs. He jabbed them down and kicked off the snake's body, using that to propel himself into the air.

Immediately, Zeke almost ran into the pillars that filled the temple. They were spaced at close intervals just like in an actual ancient building, and that left little room for Zeke to maneuver in the air. He flared his wings and barely caught himself before he ran into one of the pillars, then used that shift in direction to slam his feet into the pillar. He leaped down at the snake, his hand pressed into a blade. The faint glow of **Pierce Through** glimmered on his fingertips.

Below him, the snake whipped around. Glowing yellow eyes pierced through him, and Zeke felt his body grow cold.

Wait—it's not a snake, is it? His mind flashed to the statues, and he averted his gaze. *It's a basilisk! Basilisk Apocalypse, what the hell? Why are you so specific?*

Snake Apocalypse has entered the battle.

Eh? It's just a Snake Apocalypse?

Wait, no. It makes sense. It's a snake, so it managed to beg basilisk-like abilities from the System. Sure! Makes as much sense as anything we've encountered, anyway.

Then, if we defeat him, do all the statues return to life?

Zeke eyed the dozens of statues lining the temple. *Do we want that?*

The snake lunged, baring its fangs again.

No time to worry about that! Zeke let his hand fly, into the snake's mouth. Borrowing Allen's STR, he pierced it into the roof of its mouth. Blood burst out, warm against his fingertips. The snake reared back again, retreating from Zeke's strike. It coiled around itself, hissing in displeasure.

"Don't meet its eyes!" he warned Mia. Flapping his wings, he circled around the snake, darting glanced at it to avoid its eyes.

"Got it!" Mia replied. She darted in from behind, raising a spear high.

The snake whipped around to face Mia. It lunged at her, striking as fast as lightning. Mia whirled her spear around, and its fangs clashed off the gold spear.

Zeke jumped at it from the other side, drawing his hand back to strike again.

Abruptly, the snake retreated. Zeke's hand glanced off its snout and flew at Mia instead.

Zeke canceled his skill and closed his hand into a fist, unable to pull back the blow. His fist smacked against the spear's shaft.

"Good block. Sorry about that," Zeke said.

"No worries." Mia leaped away.

The snake slithered farther into the temple, openly fleeing battle. Turning, they both chased after the snake, but only a few steps before Zeke grabbed Mia's arm.

"What?" she asked.

"Wait! What if he's going to the boss?"

"Then we should definitely kill him before he gets her!" Mia urged him.

"No, we should run back to Domi. We don't want to face her without Domi...and plus, we haven't leveled up yet. It's fine if the boss knows we're here. She's the one who set up the golden stairs and teleported us all to the city. We don't want to fight her until we're absolutely ready," Zeke argued.

Mia hesitated. She looked into the depths of the temple.

"Come on. Besides, what if killing him unlocks all the people frozen in stone?" Zeke asked, gesturing.

"Wouldn't that be good...?"

"Not if they're enemies," Zeke pointed out.

Mia pursed her lips. "They might just be nice statues."

"Oh, come on. He's a basilisk. It's a matter of putting two and two together." Zeke showed her his hands, with the very tips of his fingers already dusted with grayish stone. His Regeneration rate ate slowly away at the stone, but if he'd kept the snake's gaze, it would have turned him into a statue.

She hesitated one more moment, then looked up. "And it was a tough fight..."

"Right. A tough fight, that we should level up and come back to," Zeke argued.

"Let's go meet with Domi, then."

In the distance, a blast of red fireworks flew into the air. Zeke grinned. "Perfect timing. Looks like Domi just asked for us."

"It wouldn't do to keep a lady waiting," Mia replied.

Together, the two of them left the temple behind and swooped down toward the fireworks.

64

CLIMB THE STAIRS TO ME, THANKS

Domi waved as Zeke and Mia approached. She stood alone at the top of the golden stairs, looking down. "Apocalypses are almost here. You guys find anything fun?"

"Yeah. Got stoned by a basilisk up in the temple. Not the fun kind of stoned, either." Zeke showed her his fingertips.

Domi raised her brows. "Holy shit. Yeah, that doesn't look good."

He thumbed over his shoulder. "There's a ton of statues in there. We were worried that if we killed the basilisk—"

"*You* were worried," Mia clarified.

"Yeah, yeah. I was worried that if we killed the basilisk, it'd loose all those Apocalypses upon us. I mean, granted, probably what the boss is planning to do anyway, but you know. Figured we should farm easy levels first, then go run the gauntlet," Zeke reasoned.

"Gotta say, agree that we should level up before we go face the final boss," Domi said, nodding.

"We let him go, though. That means the boss knows we're here," Mia warned her.

"Boss is gonna know we're here when we start farming the Apocalypses she sent up here to farm herself," Domi pointed out. She gave Zeke and Mia a meaningful look. "We should be prepared to get attacked on both sides while we're camping the Apocalypses. We're pretty much in agreement that she's probably funneling us Apocalypses up here to level her men, right? So...I'd expect her to send people to go get that bread, if you know what I mean."

"Right. That bread, meaning us."

"If we're bread, who's the fillings?" Mia asked.

Zeke and Domi both stared at her.

"If we're making sandwiches," Mia said.

Domi frowned at Zeke. "Did Mia hit her head in there?"

"No, actually...I did, though," Zeke said, delicately patting the back of his skull. With Regeneration working hard, the lump was mostly gone, and the soreness had faded to a dull ache.

Domi snorted. "Figures. So long as you can see straight and throw punches, it's all good."

"Yep, I'm good to go on that front," Zeke agreed.

The first Apocalypses reached the final few stairs. They were the same ones who had told the three of them that they'd have to walk up the stairs to enter the city. At the sight of Zeke, Mia, and Domi waiting for them atop the stairs, the lead Apocalypse's eyes narrowed. She hefted her hand and pointed at them, panting from exertion. "You...cheaters!"

"Don't be jelly," Domi said, looking down on them.

"Yeah. Work smarter, not harder," Zeke said, shaking his head.

Mia shrugged and gave her an apologetic smile. "Sorry!"

Growling under her breath, the Apocalypse charged up the last few steps toward them. As she closed in, the air grew thicker around them. Zeke suddenly found himself underwater.

The light wavered, flickering over the ground. He couldn't breathe, trapped in an orb of liquid.

"Ha! You mocked me, but now you die!" the Apocalypse crowed.

Zeke kicked off the ground and swam toward her at full speed. *Underwater, the quickest way to close in on an opponent is— to kick off the wall and butterfly kick! Don't underestimate a competitive swimmer!*

The Apocalypse startled. She jerked back, swaying her hands at the water. Compared to Zeke's combination floor-and-butterfly-kick, she might as well have stood still. Zeke's jaws closed around her throat, and blood stained the water.

With a splash, the water around them struck the ground. Zeke chewed and swallowed, wiping his mouth.

"The hell was that?" Domi asked, shocked.

"Zeke was our high school's top swimmer," Mia explained.

"Huh. Guess it doesn't come up often in the end of the world," Domi muttered to herself.

"Yeah, doesn't really, I have to admit," Zeke said, grimacing. He shrugged. "But every now and again, it's nice."

"I bet," Domi muttered, grinning.

Mia nodded at them. "Look alive. There's more where she came from."

"Right." Zeke turned to face the stairs.

Beside him, Domi gazed down them with a thoughtful look on her face. She pressed her hands together and formed a spark bomb, then dropped it down the stairs.

It bounced down toward the tired, climbing Apocalypses. The first one startled and ran up the stairs, but the next one behind him looked up just as the spark bomb lit up. The explosion blew them directly off the stairs, and they plunged down toward the city below. The bomb kept on bouncing down the stairs, splitting off smaller sparks as it went. The Apocalypses ran, fleeing to the edges of the stairs, but the explosions just kept going. And going. And going.

Zeke frowned. *That's a lot of explosions for one bomb.* He looked at Domi. *Did she get an upgrade?*

Domi pressed her hands together, then released another bomb down the stairs. The second that one bounced away, she started forming another one. A steady barrage of bombs tumbled down the stairs, blowing the Apocalypses below them away.

"Oh," Zeke said. *Yep. That explains it.*

"What?" Domi asked.

"Doesn't it seem a little unfair—"

Subordinate Domi has defeated an Apocalypse. Distributing EXP.

Subordinate Domi has defeated an Apocalypse. Distributing EXP.

Subordinate Domi has defeated an Apocalypse. Distributing EXP.

Subordinate Domi has defeated an Apocalypse. Distributing EXP.

Subordinate Domi has defeated an Apocalypse. Distributing EXP.

A cheeky grin appeared on Domi's face. She waggled her brows at him. "Yeah?"

"You know what? Nothing. Never mind. You're doing great, keep up the good work," Zeke said, giving her a thumbs up.

"Aye-aye, Boss!" Domi turned, enthusiastically continuing to rain fiery death on the slowly climbing Apocalypses.

"It is unfair, though," Mia mused, watching the other Apocalypses run, hunker, or simply topple off the stairs altogether.

"Yeah? But if they got up here, they'd try to kill us. We're just saving ourselves some time and effort," Zeke pointed out.

"No, not that. I mean, yes, that, but all's fair in love and war, after all. I mean...us. You, me, Domi." She looked up, meeting his eyes. "We—none of us have a Domain. All those Apocalypses have been stripped out of their seat of power. A good third, no, probably more like half of their strength has been stolen away. We're able to trample them because we have our full strength, and they're fighting at a massive disadvantage."

"Kind of the goddess to hand them to us on a silver platter like that," Domi muttered.

Goddess? Zeke looked over his shoulder at the giant marble temple atop the hill, and shrugged, tilting his head back and forth. *Yeah, I guess it does make sense for her. She's got a temple, her followers are talking about enlightenment...sure, she's a goddess.* "It's really just a smart move on the goddess' part for herself, but we're taking advantage of it. It's like...uh...you know, in a MMORPG, where you come across a party who's killing a boss, then slide in at the last second and swoop the kill. It's like that. But the party in this context is a world-destroying Apocalypse. So, we're totally justified."

"Uh huh. Are you trying to convince yourself, or something?" Domi asked, snorting at him.

Zeke shrugged. "I don't think any of us are 'good,' not anymore. But we're at least not actively trying to destroy the world, so that's a plus, right?"

Domi nodded, dropping another few spark bombs on the ground. "Right. Speaking of, what happened to our little world destroyers? Zel and Ryan and Erica and Sparkles? Well, okay. Erica's hanging out with the world-destroyers. She's innocent. And Sparkles is a dog. And come to think of it, we don't know where the hell Zel is, so..." Domi shrugged.

"I don't know. Let me call them while we're waiting." Zeke lifted his hand to his ear and activated **Hands-Free Calling.**

Hey, Ryan. Can you hear me?

Yeah.

Zeke waited a few seconds, but that was all. Ryan didn't continue.

He licked his lips. *Right. That is how Ryan is, sometimes.* Clearing his throat mentally, he spoke again in his mind. *You guys still down below in the city?*

You're up above the golden staircase?

Yeah. I'll take that as a yes. Hey, let us know before you come up, okay? We're kind of, er, blocking up the stairs.

I'll just teleport up.

You can't— Wait, do you still have Hero status? Because Mia—

"Yeah, why?" Ryan asked in his ear.

Zeke jolted. He jerked away, putting a hand over his ear. "God, Ryan, why?"

Ryan grinned. "Because it's funny."

"It was pretty funny," Erica agreed primly, resting both hands on the top of her staff.

Beside her, Sparkles barked and wagged his tail.

Zeke glared at all of them. "I didn't ask you."

"You asked me, though."

"Yeah, well, fuck you," Zeke grumbled.

The two of them looked at one another, then broke out into laughter.

Mia and Domi met gazes. Domi shrugged. "Boys."

"Yeah, damn," Mia muttered back.

Erica walked over beside Domi, then raised her staff. With pinpoint sniper precision, she trained her pink heart-shaped beam on one Apocalypse after another, picking off the few Apocalypses who managed to dodge Domi's explosions. Mia joined them, arching the more distant Apocalypses.

Ryan, Zeke, and Sparkles looked at one another. Sparkles wagged his tail and tilted his head.

"We're useless," Zeke mourned.

"We're resting. It's excellent," Ryan informed him.

"I feel useless," Zeke amended.

Ryan snorted. "Well, *you* might be useless, if you insist."

Zeke glared at him.

Lifting his head, Ryan looked around them. "Where's the other you? What are you calling him, Zel? Where'd he go?"

"I kind of thought you were keeping an eye on him," Zeke admitted, raising his brows.

"Nah. I got better things to do with my life," Ryan said.

"Huh," Zeke muttered.

"You think he's here?" Ryan asked.

"I hope he's here. Don't want to know what he'd be doing otherwise," Zeke grumbled.

"Can't call him?"

"No."

The two of them gazed down the stairs for a minute, silent. Abruptly, Ryan pulled out a knife and threw it into the head of a particularly vicious-looking Apocalypse. The Apocalypse fell backward, sliding down the stairs. Ryan raised his hand, and the knife appeared back in it.

He cut his eyes at Zeke and grinned. "Useless."

"Oh, come on," Zeke muttered, rolling his eyes.

65
PLAYER FARMING

This is almost too easy. It feels cheap, Zeke thought, looking down the stairs at the Apocalypses.

As if responding to his thoughts, a steel-coated Apocalypse suddenly burst up the stairs. Domi's explosions bounced off his silvery surface. Erica's beam reflected. Mia's arrows only cut shallow wounds. Ryan narrowed his eyes and threw the knife, but the man batted it out of the air. He charged the top of the stairs, howling out a war cry.

Zeke stepped forward. "I've got him."

"Are you sure?" Domi asked.

Zeke narrowed his eyes silently in response. He focused on the man, drawing back his head, then thrust it forward.

[Ranged Devour][Bite]

With all Allen's STR, he chomped down on the man's skin. His teeth barely scraped the surface, but nonetheless, he cut open a small hole.

The man laughed. He locked eyes with Zeke and charged even faster.

Zeke narrowed his eyes. He opened his mouth again, biting down two, three more times. The taste of metal filled his mouth, but he ignored it. *One more—*

The man reached him. Ignoring Zeke, he drew back his fist to punch Domi in the gut.

Erica hauled back her staff and smacked him in the skull. A bell-like tone emanated from his head. "Don't you *dare*."

The man staggered to the side, reeling a little. He shook his head.

Before the man could recover, Zeke planted a foot on the man's chest and kicked him backward. He fell head-over-heels down the stairs, rolling back into the blasting zone. Once again, he pushed to his feet and climbed resolutely upward, eyes still locked onto the prize.

"Erica, can you use any of your big attacks?" Zeke asked.

She harrumphed. "Against a small fry like him?"

"Do you...not want to, or can you mechanically not?"

She looked down at him in silence.

I'm just going to go ahead and take that as a no. Zeke glanced through his skill list again, considering his options. He pointed at the man.

[Negate Gravity]

The man stepped forward and simply glided upward. He waved his arms around, startled, then looked up. When he found himself soaring directly toward Zeke, he grinned.

Maybe not. Zeke cancelled the skill, and the man thumped back down to earth. *That skill is super situational. I'm not even sure if I can use it properly. Still, I've got plenty of time, so let's try another new one.* He pointed his finger again.

[Morph Space]

Something strange happened right in front of the man. The man paused, looking at it. A tiny window opened in front of Zeke, and through it, he could see the man's neck.

Oh. Well. That's convenient. Zeke jerked forward, opening his mouth, and dug his teeth in deep. Metal shavings fluttered over his tongue. The man backed away, but Zeke came with him, popping his head through the hole. Doggedly, he chewed away at the man's metal throat.

"Zeke, watch out!" Domi called from far away.

Zeke didn't hesitate. He yanked his head back through the hole and closed it. A second later, the man's hand whistled through the space where he'd been.

What else, what else.

At the very bottom of his list, a skill leaped out at him. **Bow and Arrow Merit.** Zeke stared at it. *All this time, I had a ranged skill?* Shaking his head at himself, he activated the skill.

His body assumed an archery pose all on its own, and a bow and arrow appeared in his hand. He fired the bow, and the arrow shot forth. Just like all the other projectiles, it bounced off the man's steely skin.

Laughing, the man shook his head at him.

Zeke pursed his lips. *Right. I don't know what I expected.* He released the skill and turned back to his skill list. *I've been making progress by chewing on his throat, but I don't know if that's the way to devour him. Surely I have some skill that will speed this up. Something...*

His eyes landed on a skill, and he laughed. *I totally forgot about this one. Yeah, that'll work!*

Quickly, Zeke activated **Morph Space.** Rather than reach his head through, though, this time, he hauled his head back and horked a lob of acid through the hole, thanks to **Acid Spit.** The acid sizzled where it landed, eating into the hole he'd already bit in the man's neck. The man wiped it away immediately, but he quickly spat again. The man's face distorted in anger. He punched the hole in space.

The second his fist emerged out the other side, Zeke immediately closed the hole. The man's metal hand clanged to the floor, neatly sliced where the spatial hole had been.

Zeke raised his brows. *Isn't that a little OP? Why didn't the Labyrinth use that on us?*

Well, then again, maybe it couldn't. Zeke lifted his hands and tried to form a spatial rift around the man's neck, but the skill refused to activate. It fizzled out until the man walked through the space, and then activated, opening behind him.

He closed his hands and opened them again, aiming in front of the man. He turned the edge of the hole toward the man's neck. Again, the hole fizzled when it touched the man.

Huh? Zeke frowned. *What's going on?*

Restriction: the victim has to willingly enter the hole in order for Morph Space to be used offensively.

What? Boo, Zeke complained.

The System didn't respond.

He shrugged. *Oh, well. It doesn't stop me from horking acid on him.* He opened another hole and spat acid, steadily eating into the man's neck. The man ran faster, hurrying up the stairs. Rather than let him charge up easily, Domi launched big explosives at him. They couldn't hurt him, but they slowed him and knocked him back down the stairs a few at a time. With Zeke spitting acid, it was only a matter of time before they won.

At last, the man dropped to one knee. He touched his neck, then fell, going limp on the stairs.

"Thank goodness," Zeke said, wiping his brow.

"Thanks, Zeke," Mia said, beaming.

"No problem." Zeke turned away to hide his blush.

Domi looked at them and clicked her tongue. "The two of you need to admit you care. It's the end of the world, man. If not now, when?"

Zeke glanced at Mia, but she turned resolutely away, pretending not to have heard. He turned to Domi and shrugged.

"Just do it! Just..." Domi growled in frustration and spread her hands to the sky. She shook her head. "Honestly..."

66

FINISHING THE STAIRS

The stairs slowly emptied, as either the last of the Apocalypses climbed them, or Apocalypses stopped attempting to climb them, knowing that Zeke's party and their barrage of ranged attacks awaited them at the top. Zeke wiped his brow and nodded at Mia and Domi. "Think that's all of them?"

"I hope it is," Mia murmured, exhausted.

"Better be," Domi agreed.

Zeke pulled open his status menu, checking his level.

Level: 150.83
STR: 10
CON: 20
DEX: 20
SPR: 66

He grinned. *Those kills were worth a lot of levels, even if Domi, Mia, Ryan, Erica, Sparkles, and I were splitting the EXP. Feels good to see that sixty-six SPR, too. I'd like to see another Apocalypse with a SPR stat that high. Good luck hitting me with your status effects!*

I should bring back Whistle Blast. It'll do good work again, now that I've got so much SPR. Stunning people mid-battle is OP no matter what level you are.

Zeke scanned over his team. He nodded at all the others. "You guys ready to go take on the boss?"

"Could use a bit of a breather, honestly," Domi admitted.

Mia sighed. She sat down on the clouds and nodded, taking a minute to catch her breath.

Ryan, Erica, and Sparkles exchanged a glance. Ryan stepped forward. "We're still good to go."

"Mind if the three of us take a break?" Zeke asked, sitting beside the girls.

Ryan shrugged. He crossed his arms. "I guess."

Zeke shook his head. *It's not like we're asking you to do something. We're just asking you to chill out and rest. Don't have to make it a big deal or anything.*

"Have you heard from other you? Zel, or whatever you decided to call him?"

Zeke glanced up. "Not since you asked five minutes ago."

"Hmph. I don't like that neither of us are keeping an eye on him," Ryan muttered.

"So...this is your first time through this loop?" Zeke asked.

Ryan frowned at him. "You told me not to use Regression. I haven't."

"Oh, I meant, like, the little ones. The ones that didn't destroy the world, or whatever you said."

"Oh. Yeah, first time."

They stood there in silence for a while. At last, Zeke rubbed the back of his head. He glanced up at Ryan. "You still, uh, hung up on...you know."

"I lived *lifetimes* in the loop. I spent longer inside than I've lived, total, outside. Counting before *and* after."

Zeke coughed. "So, uh...that's a yes?"

"Yes."

He sighed. "Can't forgive me? I wasn't even the one who—"

"You were. Not you, but *you*. Someone with your face and your voice, who acted like you. Imagine watching me corrupt, until you couldn't recognize me anymore, and then the next day, there I was, exactly the way I started, with no memory of any of the horrible things I'd done to you."

"I mean, I'm not saying it wasn't awful, but like, dude. Come on. End of the world. You still can't forgive me? Even now, here at the end of the line, fighting to save the world?" Zeke asked, putting a hand on his chin.

Ryan took a deep breath. He looked at Zeke. Zeke looked up at him, giving him his purest, sparkliest eyes. "C'monnnn. Do you really wanna die hating me?"

"No," Ryan admitted.

"Let's be friends again. Let's go back. I mean, I never left those days. You've been one-sidedly an asshole to me this whole time. You don't have to be an asshole until the end." Zeke offered Ryan his hand.

"Hell of a speech," Ryan commented.

"Yeah, well, never said I was a motivational speaker. Friendship speecher?"

Erical looked up. "Friendship speeches?"

"Yeah. That. I'm not good at them. So uh, wanna be friends anyway, even though my friendship speeches are shit?" Zeke asked.

Ryan laughed. He shook his head, running a hand down his face. "I..."

"Yeah...?"

"All right, dammit. Fine. Let's not go into the end of the world hating one another. I'll...I'll try to forgive, or at least forget. We'll be friends."

Their hands met. Zeke beamed. Mia clapped. Even Domi gave an approving nod.

"My, my. How beautiful. It's too bad I've come to kill all of you."

Zeke jumped up. Ryan vanished. Mia and Domi leaped to their feet. "Who—?"

The man from earlier stood over them, his hands clasped together, smiling placidly. All at once, his body twisted and deformed, then whipped around. A thick coil lashed out at them, threatening to knock them all down the stairs.

Zeke stood his ground. He opened his mouth wide and took a big bite, tearing the snake's scales open. The snake flinched back, but only for a second. In the next, it regrouped, then smashed out at the party again.

Domi flew into the air. Mia soared on a golden platform. Erica stood her ground alongside Zeke, while Sparkles simply leaped over the snake and darted forth, going for its vitals.

A wall of reddish-brown scales rushed at Zeke. He braced himself, planting his feet, and opened his mouth wide. For a second, he felt scales against his tongue, and then he bit down. His teeth pierced through soft flesh. Hot blood gushed into his mouth. He swallowed, closing his eyes to relish the sensation. *This is what I want to eat. Live, hot, meat. The meat of something powerful. Something strong.*

The snake coils slammed into him, lifting him off his feet and carrying him out over the stairs. Rather than lift his wings or dodge away, Zeke grabbed onto the coils. He dug his hands into the bite wounds he'd torn in the beast's side. His fingers sunk into muscle and sloshed around blood. Bone pressed up against the backs of his hands. He held on tight, gripping deeper, harder, and dug into the snake's flesh. Over and over again, gulping down mouthful after mouthful of muscle.

The snake recoiled, then lashed out again, using its prodigious length to whip Zeke off its body. The coils snapped, and Zeke flew away, soaring toward one of the could monuments. He stretched his wings out and caught himself in midair. Without hesitation, he darted down onto the snake again. His bloodstained mouth opened wide.

If I can't hold on, then I'll just have to make runs.

Zeke swooped again and again, stealing mouthfuls of the snake as he passed. Around him, Mia battled its head beside Erica, Ryan stabbed it repeatedly down the spine, and Domi rained explosions on its tail. Even Sparkles fought, biting it and shaking it as only a dog would.

Mindless of the rest of the battle, Zeke chewed. He flew up high, only gaining height to have more force when he swooped down for another mouthful. Each bite was ecstasy, only to be replaced by the loneliness of an empty mouth when he swallowed. He licked his lips, eyeing the hole he'd dug. Bones shone, slicked with blood from the deep wound. But it wasn't enough. More. Deeper.

He flapped up high into the air, higher and higher, until the battle looked like little more than a blot on the ground. From there, he dropped. Mouth open, screaming down from the sky, his eyes locked on the snake's side.

Without even thinking, he activated all his skills. **Devour, Bite, Pierce Through,** anything and everything that would help him bite harder and deeper.

The snake's flesh flew up. The bones rushed at him. Zeke slammed his mouth shut.

Crack!

Bone shattered. He turned his head, spitting a mouthful of bone fragments, and crawled deeper. Half his teeth were cracked, but it didn't matter. A new row of teeth were already pushing their way through his gums to replace the first set, thanks to **Tooth Regeneration.** The second his new teeth sprouted, he bit deeper. The snake's soft internal organs rushed up at him, spilling out the hole he'd dug.

The snake thrashed, keening in pain. Caught inside its body, Zeke held on. He dug deeper, biting deeper into the snake. It couldn't hurt him when he was inside it. Couldn't throw him out if he was buried in its body, eating it from the inside like a parasite. Dark, hot flesh closed in around him. Blood soaked into his clothes. He slithered through the snake, chewing his way into its guts.

Fangs slammed through the snake's body just ahead of him. Zeke flinched back, startled back awake. He froze. *What the hell am I doing?*

Wait. Where the hell did those fangs come from? Sparkles? But he turns into a robot, not a giant dog.

The fangs retreated. Zeke peered out through the holes punched in the snake's body. The snake's head retreated, blood dripping from its fangs.

Zeke lifted his brows. *It bit itself?*

Well, then, I guess snakes don't have a whole lot of options when it comes to dragging things out from inside its body. Though...why did I go in here? I mean, it's working, so... Zeke looked around him. He shrugged. *Might as well keep going.*

Opening his mouth, he chewed deeper into the snake. One bite at a time, he ate his way through the snake's guts. It thrashed and twisted, trying to throw Zeke out of it.

"You'll need hands if you want me out of here," Zeke said, grinning. A second later, he paused. *Wait. What the hell happens if he turns back to human while I'm still in here? Where do I go? Where does he go, for that matter?*

Maybe I should get out of here.

Just as he thought that, a steady throbbing thud sounded from just ahead. Zeke whipped up. *If the heart's right there...I can't stop now.* He clawed deeper into the snake, toward that steady throb.

His fingers struck a mass of muscle. The snake thrashed again. It struck its own body over and over, searching for Zeke. Zeke grabbed the snake's heart with both hands and took a big bite.

[Devour]

The snake shuddered one last time, then went still. Stuck in its body, Zeke did a little thrashing of his own for a moment, then found the wall of the snake's skin and chewed his way through. Sunlight poured down. He took a deep breath of clean air and staggered out of the snake. His feet caught on the edge of the snake's body, and he dropped to his knees, but quickly climbed back to his feet.

"Hey, you, uh, you...killed it?" Domi asked.

Zeke ran his blood-soaked hair back from his face. He nodded. "Yeah. I killed it."

"Oh. Uh, good." She licked her lips and nodded.

Silence. No one made eye contact with anyone.

Zeke clapped his hands together, inadvertently splattering blood all over the cloud around him. "Uh, so...final boss?"

"Yeah. Final boss," Mia agreed.

"Let's fucking go," Domi muttered under her breath.

Aloof, Ryan watched from a nearby roof. He said nothing, but his eyes narrowed. He vanished.

Zeke tensed, but nothing happened. A few moments later, Ryan reappeared. He nodded over his shoulder. "Boss is right up ahead, at the top of the hill. Let's go."

Zeke and Mia exchanged a glance. *We already knew that...* Zeke shook his head just a little. *Let's let him have his victory.*

Mia nodded back. *Understood.*

"What are you two doing over there?" Ryan asked, suspicious.

"Nothing, nothing. Final boss!" Zeke threw his fist in the air and ran up the hill, charging toward the temple atop it.

67
TEMPLE ON THE HILL

Together, the six of them climbed up the hill toward the distant temple. The imposing structure bore down on them with every step. The perfectly aligned pillars marched into its shadowed depths like teeth into a mouth. The preponderous top stone with its carvings of the woman looked down on them, the pathetic, buglike beings that they were. Still, they climbed, in defiance of everything the temple stood for.

"Everyone good to go?" Zeke asked.

"Yeah?" Mia replied, a little lost.

"Timers off cooldown? All abilities cued up?" he prompted.

Domi gave him a thumbs-up.

"Everyone all healed up?"

"Yes, *dad*," Erica said, shaking her head at him.

Zeke nodded. "Just checking. We wanna be in top shape for this battle."

"Weird hearing that from a guy who's actively dripping with blood," Domi commented, eyeing him.

Zeke looked down at himself. His whole body was stained

red. Blood dripped from every limb. His clothes stuck to his body, soaked with the stuff. "It's not mine."

"As if that makes it better."

"From a fighting standpoint, it does," Zeke argued. "Plus, it was the easiest way to kill the giant snake. It had tough scales and eyebeams that petrify on contact. Get inside it and tear it up from the inside out. It's no problem."

"You still hungry after all that?" Domi asked.

Zeke snorted. "Yeah." *I'm never not hungry. It's just become default for me. I'll always be hungry, no matter what.* Nowadays, satiation only lasted for a few seconds before his hunger kicked back in. His life was sprinkled with brief respites from his hunger, rather than hunger being a temporary condition. It wasn't something he wanted to admit, not with Ryan right there. *Besides, it worries me, too. This all-consuming hunger. Even if we beat the boss...well, I've never been able to come up with an answer for 'what next,' and I still don't have one.*

This is it, though. The final Apocalypse. The final big Apocalypse, anyway. After this, it's just a matter of cleaning up the little ones. And then...uh. And then we rebuild, I guess. Try to get the world back on track. We didn't get destroyed, so we'll carry on, without destroying the world this time.

He took a deep breath, gazing up at the temple above them. *It doesn't feel real. None of this feels real. But it's been insane for so long that I'm not even sure what 'real' feels like anymore.*

One stair after another, they approached the temple. The hubbub of conversation bubbled out from the marble interior, and Zeke frowned. He licked his lips. "Uh, guys. I just thought of something."

"Yeah? Is it the same thing I just thought of?" Mia asked.

"You know that snake we killed? The basilisk, the one with eye beams that turn people to stone."

"Oh, it is. Yep."

Zeke pointed. "When Mia and I came up here earlier, there were statues lining the sides of the temple. Super, hyperrealistic statues of people. All made of stone."

Domi hissed a breath through her teeth. "I see where you're going with this but keep going."

"So, when the basilisk died, um, what do you think happened to those statues?" Zeke asked.

"They all stayed statues because they're just normal statues and that was it," Mia muttered to herself sarcastically.

"Yeah. I wish."

Domi rolled up her sleeves. "One final gauntlet to run, huh?"

"Yep." Beside her, Zeke clapped his hands together.

"Let's hit them fast. Before they even know what's happened, they're dead," Ryan said, his voice low and tight.

"Agreed." Zeke tensed, preparing to run.

Mia frowned in disapproval but said nothing. Beside her, Erica nodded in approval and swirled her staff, warming it up.

"Three. Two." Ryan vanished.

Zeke sprinted in. Domi and Mia charged with them, Sparkles bounding by their side. Erica jogged cutely alongside them, somehow keeping up despite her terribly cutesy running form.

They passed through the first row of pillars uncontested, then the second. At the third, a young man jerked upright, lifting his hands. "Whoa, whoa—"

Domi shoulder-slammed him and fired a dozen explosions at his body. They rattled off behind them, leaving very little behind.

A scream sounded from somewhere deep in the temple. Blood splattered across a white pillar, lurid red.

From the side, a woman ran toward them. "What's going—"

Mia's sword darted out. The woman's head tipped back, then rolled off her neck and hit the ground.

Feathers flew as a ferociously angry bird flew at them. Zeke lifted his head and shot a **Ranged Devour** at it, plucking it out of the sky. He chewed, grimacing at the crunch of bones. "Not a whole lot of meat on that chicken."

"It was a cardinal, not a chicken," Mia shot back.

"Well, that'd explain it," Zeke replied.

Domi rolled orange ball after orange ball into the temple as if they were bowling balls, rolling them down the clear, broad expanses between pillars. "This is a real 'are we the bad guys' situation right here."

"They'd destroy the world if we didn't," Zeke pointed out.

"Yeah, but still." Domi rolled another bowling ball-sized explosive into the temple. Distantly, the first round of explosives blasted off. "I mean, it isn't stopping me, but…"

"Yeah. I get what you're saying," Zeke agreed.

Light glinted off metal. A dozen swords flew at them from the side. Zeke ducked, dragging Domi and Mia down with him. Mia threw up her hand, forming a gold shield between them and the swords. The swords fell back, clattering to the ground.

From the other side, the unmistakable bark of a gun sounded out, over and over. Zeke instantly activated his **Transform.** Pushing Mia and Domi back, he charged toward the gunfire.

An old man unloaded a rifle in his direction, shouting something incoherent. The bullets chipped away at Zeke's body even with the armor. Zeke grimaced and ran faster, charging headlong into the bullets. Pain sparked along his front as the bullets dug in. *I can't get there fast enough. I need more speed.*

Mid-run, he activated **Hands-Free Calling.** *Hey, Domi. Mind lending me your DEX for a minute?*

Uh, sure? I guess?

Subordinate Domi has shared her DEX.
DEX: 20 > 55

Instantly, Zeke sped up. His reactions grew faster, and even his vision improved. The bullets were no longer an unavoidable hail, but instead a speeding group of individual shots. With the help of **High Speed Maneuvering,** Zeke dipped to the side, easily dodging a cluster of bullets.

The man's gun had kicked up a little. He dragged it back down, but too slow for the recently sped-up Zeke. Zeke grabbed the gun and shoved it away. He leaped for the man's throat.

The man shouted something, but his words were lost on Zeke. Zeke bit down. Lifeblood flowed into him as he tore out the man's throat. With a few last kicks, the man went limp.

He stood, running a hand over his head. *I can give Domi back her DEX now.*

Subordinate Link terminated.

Across the way, steel rang out on steel as Mia pinned a sword to the ground with her own sword. Stomping on it, she lifted her sword and dealt the final blow, severing the inferior blade with a blow that cut through the marble below.

She turned, and her eyes met Zeke's. They nodded at one another, then ran deeper into the temple.

"Wait, guys. Wait up! I'm coming!" Domi called, chasing after them.

"You should be fine. You have fifty-five DEX!" Zeke shouted over his shoulder.

"Just because I have it, doesn't mean I like running!" Domi replied.

Robotic barking caught Zeke's attention. He whirled to find Sparkles backing a huge rat into the corner. The rat hissed, its fur all puffed up and its teeth bared. Blood spotted its mottled gray fur. Sparkles barked again, then jumped in to finish the kill.

"I think he's got that one handled," Zeke said to himself.

"Imagine, the Rat Apocalypse winning? How disgusting would that be?" Mia asked.

"Rats are actually pretty clean—"

"Not when they number in the thousands and they're crawling all over you," she countered.

Zeke snorted. "Fair enough. Although..." *I mean, it would solve my food problem. Maybe I'll just capture one of these animal-based Apocalypses and obtain an infinite meat supply.*

But that'll have to happen after we finish off the boss.

The far end of the temple loomed out of the pale mist that obscured the temple's depths. A woman stood in front of an enormous throne, holding a spear. Simple white robes draped her body, not unlike the Ancient Greeks' robes, pinned at the shoulders with large gold brooches. She waited, watching them, her body and eyes both incredibly calm. It was as though she stood in the middle of an empty meadow, rather than a battlefield. Even as one of her Subordinates screamed and blood soaked the floor at her feet, she didn't so much as blink.

In that instant, Zeke was already sure of it. Just looking at her, without any more knowledge, he knew everything he needed to. *She's insane. Fully, truly, and deeply.*

"Welcome to my temple, mortals," the woman bellowed. Her voice came loud, but her posture and mouth moved as though she merely spoke. She lifted the spear and pointed its blade at them. "You are brave to challenge a god, but ultimately foolish. None can best me. Not any of the other Apocalypses, and not you, either. For I am Holy. I am Beyond. I am more than a mortal, ascended from a mere Apocalypse. And I am your death."

"Oooh, a proper boss speech. I like it. It's refreshing," Domi said, blasting a nearby Apocalypse with a half-dozen balls of orange force even as she spoke.

"This lady's crazy," Zeke muttered back.

"Well, obviously. You don't make boss speeches when you're sane," Domi returned.

The woman flourished her spear. She stepped forward. "This temple shall serve as your resting place. I will bury you alongside my loyal Subordinates, as children of the clouds."

"I don't think so," Zeke returned.

Domi clapped. "Someone had to do it, and I'm glad it's you, Zeke."

Zeke nudged her. "Hey, don't snark me. I'm being cool right now."

"Is that what you're doing?" Ryan muttered.

Zeke whirled, but Ryan had left again before he spun. He narrowed his eyes. "Did he really teleport in just to sass off?"

Mia giggled. She nodded. "Yeah."

"You dare laugh? You dare ignore me?" The goddess' eyes flashed. She pushed off the ground and vanished.

Zeke tensed. "Watch out!"

68

GODDESS FIGHT

Mia threw her hand up. Gold shields spawned between them and the goddess, layers and layers of them, one popping up after another.

"I don't think that's—"

The goddess reappeared. Her spear slammed toward them. It pierced through the first shield, the second, the third, shield after shield popping as her spear passed smoothly through, barely impeded by the force of Mia's glowing shields.

"—necessary...it's necessary, it's necessary!" Zeke threw himself to the side as the last shield popped, barely avoiding the thrust.

The goddess stumbled past. Before she could whirl, Zeke opened his mouth and cast **Ranged Devour** on her back.

His head rebounded. Even though he'd used the ranged version, his head was knocked back. His teeth ached. Blood flowed from his gums. He backed away, closing his mouth and eyeing her warily. *Was that her skin I bounced off? Her skin? How tough is this lady? Is she even human anymore?*

He looked around him, at the temple, and sighed. *Right, how could I forget? She's a god. Well. In her mind, anyway. And right now, that's what really matters.*

Allen! Now more than ever, I need your STR!

Subordinate Allen shared his STR.
STR: 10 > 75

Hot damn! Allen isn't playing around, huh? Did he even put points in any other stat?

Not that I'm complaining. It's super useful for me.

The goddess turned. She stared at him with a doleful gaze, her eyes full of vengeance. Rearing back, she lifted her spear high.

Zeke lashed out with the tendrils on the back of his head. The thin golden strands struck the goddess. She looked at him, her brows faintly furrowing.

[Electric Tendrils] [Electrify] [Zap Enhancement]

Golden lightning coursed down his tendrils and lashed over the goddess. She jerked in place, quivering from the force of the electricity.

Oh? That hurt her? Zeke lashed out with his tendrils again, sending more electricity into her.

"Merely...a tingle!" the goddess shouted. She slammed the spear backward. The butt hurtled toward Zeke's gut.

Zeke jumped back, but without Domi's DEX, he was too slow. The spear struck his stomach and sent him flying backward. He smashed into a pillar. Marble dust flew around him. Chunks of marble cascaded down over his body. Stunned, Zeke laid there, mashed into a hole in the pillar.

"And now, foul beast, die." The goddess appeared over him. She lifted her spear high.

A blast of pink energy sent her flying backward. Erica ran up beside Zeke and offered him her hand. Zeke looked at it, his eyes blurry, then groped for it. She hauled him up.

As he climbed to his feet, green energy swirled around him. Warmth flowed through him. His vision cleared, and the headache throbbing around his temples dissipated.

Subordinate Erica has used The Healing Strength of Companionship on you! Condition: Stun removed!

"Thanks," Zeke said, a little surprised.

"A magical girl can't neglect her squad," Erica returned firmly.

Eh? I'm on Erica's squad? No, she's on mine! Zeke opened his mouth, then shut it. He shrugged. *Oh, whatever. It doesn't matter. We can all be on each other's squads.*

Mia dashed across the room, fast as blinking. She lifted her sword, lashing out at the goddess.

The goddess parried her blow. The two of them battled back and forth for a moment, before, with a great sweep of her spear, the goddess sent Mia flying back. She spun her spear and struck a pose, looking down at Mia with disappointed eyes.

"Is this what a Hero amounts t—"

BAM!

A massive blast exploded up from her feet. It shattered the marble floor and sent the goddess tumbling into the air. Dust swallowed her up, a great cloud of it billowing through the semi-enclosed space. Zeke hunkered, lifting his hands to block the cloud and narrowing his eyes against the dust.

From the dust, a clap echoed forth. A great wind blew, separating the dust into two walls, then dissipating it entirely. In the depths of the cloud, the goddess stood there, her hands clasped, the spear momentarily stuck in the marble. "Foolish attempts to desecrate my temple...will all stop here."

"Yeah? Says who?" Domi challenged her. A barrage of orange orbs bounced toward the goddess. They trembled, on the verge of explosion.

The goddess lifted her spear and swung it. The wind from the swipe sent the orbs flying back from whence they'd come. Domi's eyes widened. She snapped her fingers, and the orbs vanished.

In the next instant, she tensed. Her body trembled. She stumbled to the side, then leaned forward and puked.

"Domi?" Zeke asked, leaping up.

The goddess harrumphed, coldly amused. "To not even know oneself. At this level of immersion, you have become your Concept. To cancel your Concept is to deny yourself. Did you think you could so easily prevent that which you are, without harming yourself?"

"Is that why you're roleplaying a goddess?" Ryan asked, appearing behind the goddess. His knife lashed out, slicing into her throat.

It bounced off, unable to harm the goddess' alabaster skin. She reached over her shoulder and grabbed Ryan by the shirt, tossing him to the floor. Without hesitating, she lifted her foot and stomped on his collar.

Crack. Ryan screamed, squirming on the ground.

"And this one, the most deluded of all, who remembers naught. Neither what he is, nor what he should be. You cannot kill me." She lifted her spear and struck down at Ryan.

Mid-scream, Ryan vanished. The spear drove into marble. Dust flew up where it hit home. The goddess clicked her tongue. She gazed into the distance, shaking her head. "It would be better to let me purge the infection. Prolonging it like this will only hurt you worse."

"Infection?" Zeke stepped up, deliberately drawing her attention. *The last thing I want is for her to kill Ryan. I definitely don't trust that he can't use Regression.*

She nodded. "He has a virus. In his System. A ruinous, self-destructive skillset."

"You mean Regression?" Zeke asked. *Or does he actually have a virus in his System? Wait, but...can a System have a virus? I mean, I wouldn't be surprised if his was wonky from so much looping and world-hopping, but still. It would mean my guess was totally wrong if the System turned out to be a computer and could get infected with viruses.*

The goddess ignored his question. "And you. You are a virus upon this Earth. I ought to purge you first."

Ahhh. We're speaking in metaphors. Well, it makes sense. A lot of religion is told in metaphor. "What's your Apocalypse, anyway? God Apocalypse? Goddess Apocalypse?"

God Apocalypse.

"Oh. Got it. I mean, as far as Concepts go, can't go wrong with infinite power," Zeke reasoned. "It's like picking genie for your Concept."

"Except without the convenient storage lamp," Mia said, stepping up beside him.

"Yeah. Except without the glaring, obvious weakness," Zeke agreed. *Gods don't really have weaknesses, the most of them, anyway. We'd have to know her specific mythology to target her weakness even if she has one, since a lot of the time, they're weird and random anyway. A single vulnerable spot on the ankle, or the first strike from the seventh-born son, something like that. I think we can pretty much give up on that, which leaves one option: brute force.*

The goddess lifted her spear and slammed it into the ground. A shockwave flew through the marble floor, sending the marble rolling like a wave. Zeke jumped before the wave hit him and flapped his wings, climbing into the air, but the others weren't so lucky. Mia yelped, scrambling onto her platforms. Domi cursed, firing explosions behind her as the wave knocked her into the air. Erica squealed, unable to do anything against the wave, and simply staggered into a pillar. Sparkles growled, then started barking wildly.

"Enough of this," the goddess declared. She spun the spear, and the ancient temple melted all around them. Marble tumbled down from the sky.

Zeke looked up. The massive headstone that formed the roof plummeted, dropping toward them. His heart dropped into his stomach. *The fuck do I do about that?*

69
SKY DROP

The enormous stone that formed the temple's roof plummeted toward them. Zeke stared at it, swallowing. *The hell do I do about that?*

At top speed, using **High-Speed Maneuvering,** with Domi's DEX, he could escape, but that meant leaving Domi, Mia, and all the others behind. *Ryan will escape. Mia...can probably get out of it. Domi might be able to blast her way through. But Erica and Sparkles? And it's not like it's a sure thing with Domi—*

"Everyone! To me!" Mia shouted. She lifted her sword high. Gold light glimmered on the blade. The faint outline of a dome, lit up in sparkling star-dots of gold, appeared around her.

"Dammit!" Domi staggered toward Mia. She limped heavily, dragging her left leg. Blood stained her pants from the calf down, her leg barely able to hold her weight.

Zeke swirled in the air. He darted down toward Domi, snatching her up, then flapped back toward Mia. Stones crumbled all around them. Chunks of the roof broke off, plummeting down all around them. One crashed past so close it slammed through his right wing's flight feathers. Zeke leaned away from it, flapping harder. He swooped toward Mia's dome, surging down with all his strength.

Domi grabbed onto him hard, her grip almost painful on his shoulder. "Faster...faster!"

Zeke grunted. He locked his eyes onto Mia and her globe. *We're going to make it. We are!*

Rocks plummeted down, blocking his way ahead. Dust clouded the air, so thick he could barely see through.

"Fuck, we're dead, fuck, fuck, fuck," Domi muttered, tightening her hold.

Between two huge falling rocks, a tiny smidge of gold light glimmered through. Zeke beat his wings one more time, then folded them close to his body, flying for the hole like a rocket. Domi screamed. The rock brushed by his wings, disturbing the feathers as he passed, and then he popped out the other side.

Mia's dome stood inches before him. Zeke flared his wings and drew to a halt, dropping down into the thin light. Erica nodded at them, already standing within the safety zone. Sparkles barked at him, running over to sniff him and Domi. At the sight of Domi's injured leg, he opened his mouth. A greenish spray shot out and landed on Domi's leg.

"What the—huh?" Domi pulled her pant leg back to reveal smooth flesh, the last of the injury vanishing as though it never were.

"Saves me having to heal you," Zeke muttered, half to himself.

Domi smacked him, annoyed.

Thump. Rocks slammed into Mia's barrier. She gritted her teeth and held on, pushing her sword up higher. Her brows furrowed with concentration. Her arm trembled from effort. Sparks glittered down on them, raining from the dome.

"Mia, do you need help?" Zeke asked. *Not that I know what I'd do, but I'd do anything she needed.*

"I-I think..." Mia gritted her teeth. The dome flickered. Her expression turned grim, and she fell silent, putting her all into raising her arm again.

"What do you need? Just tell me," Zeke said, concerned.

A soft hand pressed on Zeke's shoulder. Erica pushed him out of the way and strode to Mia's side. "Now isn't the time for boys. Now is the time for Magical Girls."

"Uh...okay?" Zeke said, completely lost.

Erica put her hand on Mia's, resting the other one on Mia's shoulder. Leaning her head against Mia's, she closed her eyes. Pink energy glowed around her. It swirled, then flowed into Mia, supplementing her own golden energy. The dome around them streaked with pink and grew stronger. No longer did sparks rain down, nor did Mia sweat or tremble. She stood strong, her sword raised high. Erica leaned against her, the two of them glowing with a pink-gold light that melded together so perfectly Zeke couldn't tell where one ended and the next began.

"Now *that* is some magical girls shit," Domi commented, crossing her arms.

"Yeah...I guess so," Zeke said.

"Friendship? Love and companionship? Putting absolute trust in one another to strengthen both of you, together? Don't tell me you can't see it," Domi said, glancing at Zeke.

He shrugged. "I was never the biggest magical girls fan."

Domi snorted. "Me either, but man. You know it when you see it."

Zeke looked around. "Where's Ryan?"

"Why are you asking me? I know even less about the guy than you do."

"I dunno. Figured I should ask anyone I could," Zeke reasoned.

The last of the rock tumbled down. It melted into the cloud

beneath them, no longer heavy. Erica stepped back, and Mia lowered her sword.

All around them, the city in the sky crumbled. Monuments shuddered. Blocks tumbled. With a great *crash*, a tower smashed down into the center of a castle. A steeple road its church downward, standing erect until the moment it struck the ground. Statues struck the ground, throwing up great puffs of cloud as they sunk into the ground. Under their feet, the hill shook as it flattened to the earth. Only the throne at the far end of the temple remained, empty, as ever.

"What is she doing?" Zeke wondered.

"Man, you are just full of questions no one knows the answer to right now, huh," Domi commented.

"Flattening the clouds," Mia offered, a little more helpfully.

"But why," Zeke muttered, half to himself.

Across from them, the goddess swirled her spear. The clouds twisted around her, morphing and rising up beneath her feet. They took shape, forming not a building, but a horse.

"A...horse?" Zeke asked, lost.

"Yeah. A horse. You never seen horses before?" Domi asked.

Zeke gave her a look.

"Did she flatten the floor to give herself a better ground for her horse?" Mia asked.

Erica lifted her lip, wincing. "Flat ground, a spear, a horse? If she had a full cavalry line behind her, we'd be in bad shape. Even with one horseman—"

The goddess' horse reared, showing off six legs instead of the ordinary four. Thrusting her spear into the sky, the goddess shouted.

The floor around the goddess churned once more, but more of it, and farther. One after another, horses climbed out of the clouds. On their backs, men and women with spears shouted war cries.

Although they were shaped from clouds, these women and men weren't perfect, idealized humans, nor were they feature-less mannequins. They were ordinary people, some of them overweight, some muscular, some handsome, and some less so. They wore office clothes, street clothes, sweatpants and scrubs, some even dressed in their underwear. The cloud people roared alongside the goddess, all of them raising their spears in concert with hers.

"Never mind," Erica said.

"Ride, my Valkyries!" the goddess cried. The horsemen stampeded toward Zeke.

Zeke pinched his chin. "I get the intent, but like, the Valkyries were the ones who collected the people who fell in battle, not the people who fell in battle themselves."

"Yeah, well, I think our goddess is playing a little fast and loose with myths over there," Domi muttered. She spread her stance and reached out, flexing her fingers. A ball of orange light condensed in each hand.

Zeke nodded at her. "Time for our Domains?"

"I think so."

The two of them charged toward the spearmen. As they ran, domes appeared around them, orange for Domi, black for Zeke. Instantly, Zeke's hunger pinged in his stomach, but he used the hunger to push himself on, toward the charging spearmen.

Seeing the two of them charge, the spearmen split, one contingent breaking off to deal with Domi, another chasing after Zeke.

A thousand horses charged toward him. A thousand people roared, hefting spears. The drum of hooves on the cloud sounded like drumbeats. They pounded in his ears, painfully loud. Zeke roared back, but his voice was nothing compared to a thousand voices working in concert. They grew closer and closer. White cloud horseflesh labored, chests heaving as they closed in on him. The people atop glared down at him, nothing but hatred in their eyes. Not people at all, but merely the pawns of a hateful Apocalypse, moving at its whim.

He opened all his mouths and leaped, jumping toward the first row of spearmen.

The black dome struck them before he did. Being constructs, and not humans, they felt no hunger. They charged onward, closing in on Zeke without stumbling a single step. Even so, their bodies and the horses withered. In equal measure, Zeke's stomach filled, his body growing stronger.

He chuckled under his breath. *It doesn't make any sense to me, but I won't question it. I'll take whatever advantage I can get.*

His eyes swept over the army, and the chuckle turned into a grin. *And did the goddess ever give me a hell of an advantage.*

70

I LOVE MOB BATTLES

The spearmen faltered as they reached Zeke. Their horses' legs gave out, and they tumbled to the ground, sending their riders rolling. Zeke trampled them, letting his foot-mouths do the final blow. Fluffy, ephemeral cloud melted on his tongues. He wrinkled his nose. *It's like eating cotton candy, but none of the sweetness. Just the unsatisfying part where you take a big mouthful and swallow a hard, sad little lump of sugar.*

Even as the first ones fell to his Domain, the next wave charged in, spears held high. Rather than charging into his Domain, they thrust from outside it. Behind them, yet another wave of spearmen threw their spears at Zeke. He looked up and found himself at the center of an inescapable orb of blades. Spears flew at him from all directions, their blades white and fluffy like clouds but no less deadly for it.

Zeke threw his head back and **Roar**ed. A blast of sound burst from his mouth and blew the spears coming down from directly overhead back. The second they parted, he kicked off, simultaneously activating **Gravity Negation**. He floated up, then, cancelling his **Gravity Negation** skill, he flared his wings and flapped up over the spearmen. His domain descended in a dome below him, just as it soared over his head as a dome, the two halves forming an orb around him. The spearmen he flew over crumpled the same as the rest. A rain of spears chased after him. He swooped left and right, dodging the blades.

One caught him on the side, slashing straight through his armor as though it was paper. Zeke glanced down, startled. *I can't get hit by those things. They're way more dangerous than they look!*

Flapping caught his ear. Zeke peered over his shoulder.

Some of the spearmen chased after him, their horses winging it after him, powerful white wings beating them through the air.

"Fucking..." Zeke wrinkled his nose. *Valkyries. Right. Of course, they can fly. Honestly? That's my bad.*

He opened his wings wide, using **High Speed Maneuvering** to jerk himself to a sudden stop. The leftover momentum dragged at his body. Rather than fight it, he threw himself into it and let the momentum flip him around. Facing the Valkyries upside-down, he flapped one wing and spun in a barrel roll to right himself. He winged toward the Valkyries as fast as he could.

The Valkyries lowered their spears, closing in on him. Zeke grinned. *They've only seen my Domain. That's all they think I have.*

Their loss.

He opened his mouths and activated **Ranged Devour.** The Valkyries crumbled, their heads rolling away. Again, the unsatisfying sensation of eating empty cotton candy dissolved in his mouth. The horses flew on, but without their riders, they rushed into Zeke's Domain blindly and dissolved.

Zeke touched his stomach. *Even if they can't really be eaten, I can at least absorb them with Absorb from my Domain. This goddess is doing more to feed me than almost any other Apocalypse so far.*

Well. Maybe except for the Ice Cream Apocalypse. I really appreciated that one. Living ice cream, so I could enjoy delicious ice cream and get full at the same time? Should've captured that Apocalypse and kept it alive forever, honestly.

Too late for regret now.

Another group of Valkyries charged toward him, letting out their hollow war cries as they swooped up at him. Zeke turned to meet them, winging down at the masses.

All around, his allies fought on. Valkyries flew into the air, lofted by big orange explosions. Beams of pink light cut across the battlefield, mowing down swathes of Valkyries all at once. Mia held off the front lines, fending them off with bright slashes of her gold sword and blasts of gold sword energy. At her side, Sparkles, in his robot dog form, used metal teeth to tear apart Valkyries. Blasts of energy from his eyes melted the clouds, while every bark threw dozens of Valkyries ragdoll-style through the air.

Ryan dropped out of the sky, falling toward the goddess. Zeke's eyes widened. He stared for a second, but then a spear sliced past his cheek, drawing his attention. He turned back to the Valkyries, slamming directly into the first one. Chewing on their head, he rode atop the horse, guiding it toward the other Valkyries. The Valkyrie he rode dropped her spear. He grabbed it out of the air and slashed out toward the other Valkyries.

The spear removed the first Valkyrie's head, then melted away. Zeke wrinkled his nose. Leaping off the winged horse, he sent another blast of **Ranged Devour**s at the oncoming spearmen. The spearmen fell. Their horses flew away, wandering randomly through the sky.

Zeke dropped down, using his Domain to absorb spearmen again. He stared after Ryan. *What happened? He didn't die, did he? I'm not going to let him die this late in the game.*

The goddess sat tall on her horse, unbothered. Ryan lay

behind her, crumpled into a little ball. Blood poured out of his eyes, nose, and mouth.

Zeke tensed. *Fuck!* Ignoring the Valkyries, he sped toward Ryan and the goddess. *She doesn't know what she's playing with. And Ryan, what the fuck was he thinking? Attacking the goddess alone, while none of us could support him?*

He needs to learn that he's not a solo hero. He's a member of the squad, the same as all of us. Whether he's on my squad or Erica's, or anyone else's, we're a damn team, and he needs to figure it out already.

The goddess lifted her head and saw him coming. She laughed. "You think you can touch me, in this form? Cloaked in my power?"

"Why can't I?" Zeke challenged her. *Yeah, go on. Tell me your skills, dumbass.*

She laughed. Tossing her head, she looked down at him. "Because I am a god, and you are a mere mortal."

Okay, fair. I don't know what I expected. Girl has a god complex, I get it. She's off in lala land, on cloud nine. Her tether to the real world snapped a long time ago.

He glared back at her. "What's to say I'm not a god, too?"

"Because I took that Apocalypse."

"So? Maybe I took the Goddess Apocalypse. Did you think of that?"

The goddess stared at him. Her jaw gaped, words failing her. At last, she managed, "What?"

"Hahaha!" Zeke drew back his fist and swooped down on her.

She tossed her head again. Her defiant eyes gazed directly into his, daring him to land the blow.

71
DON'T FLINCH

The goddess stared up at him. Zeke dropped at her, fist drawn back.

At the last second, Zeke flinched away. He flew past her, so close their bodies almost collided, and landed beside her. Two steps. Cancelling his Domain, he snatched up Ryan and jumped again, flying away from the goddess with all his might. "Fucking hell, Ryan, do you *think* before you act?"

Ryan laughed but said nothing.

Pressing his lips together, Zeke flapped away. He activated **Ninja Healing** as he went, burning some of the extra fullness he had from Devouring the Valkyries to heal Ryan's injuries. Ryan's face stopped bleeding, and he sat up in Zeke's grasp, wiping his face.

"She's a tough nut to crack," he declared suddenly.

"No fuckin' kidding. She's a goddess," Zeke returned.

"I've tried everything. I can't damage her. I'm hit with backlash, or she takes no damage, or both. There's no in between."

"You hit her once," Zeke said, confused.

Ryan looked at him.

Zeke rolled his eyes at himself. "...and then you replayed that moment in time a hundred times. Got it."

"Right. She can't be hurt. It's not possible. This...might be a loss."

Zeke snorted. "Don't give up yet."

"Why shouldn't I?"

"What do you mean? You're a gamer, dude. Come on. Think. When you can't kill the boss and there's a shit-ton of adds on the field, what do you have to do, nine times outta ten?"

Ryan twisted his lips. "Kill the adds?" he muttered reluctantly.

Zeke nodded approvingly. "Now you're thinking with— well, not time, or portals, but you know. You're thinking."

"Thanks. Appreciate it."

"You're welcome. I knew you could do it."

Ryan stared at Zeke, deadpan. Zeke stared back.

Abruptly, they both broke into laughter. Ryan shook his head. "If we have to kill all the adds, then let me go and get back to it."

"I'm in midair, dude. You sure about that?"

Again, Ryan looked at Zeke. Without another word, he vanished.

"Fair. I earned that one."

Down below, the other Apocalypses on Zeke's team cornered the Valkyries, whittling them down. A few flew at Zeke, but he quickly **Absorb**ed them before they could hurt him. He circled overhead, then hovered over Mia. "Mia! Can you box the remaining Valkyries in with your gold panel things?"

"Huh? Yeah," Mia said. She lifted her hands. For a second, nothing happened. Sweat began to form on her forehead, and her face turned red.

"If you can't do it, don't hurt yourself," Zeke said.

Ignoring him, Mia wrinkled up her face in concentration.

Her hands clawed at the air as her attention densified. Every fiber of her body tensed. Abruptly, she screamed.

"Mia! Don't force yourself—"

Big gold panels formed on the battlefield, vaguely surrounding the Valkyries. They slammed down, setting the clouds below them into a flurry. Scraping over the earth, they closed in, forcing the Valkyries into one clump.

"Domi, Erica, Sparkles! Fire all the beams and AOEs that you have!" Zeke shouted.

"You got it, Boss!"

Erica spun her staff.

Sparkles threw back his head and barked.

Orange explosions crowded the box. A pink beam and Sparkles' green beam swept across the box, obliterating all the Valkyries in their path. The masses crumpled, unable to handle the damage the three of them could manage at once. As they died, some turned and fled, running toward the walls, but the walls held strong, boxing them in.

Zeke swooped overhead, **Absorb**ing the dying Valkyries to strengthen himself. He felt the faintest tingle of guilt at their overkill but repressed it. *They aren't human. They're just constructs. Just sad echoes of what were once human beings, forced to fight at the goddess' command. If anything, we're doing them a favor.*

The last Valkyrie crumpled. Bare seconds later, the gold walls vanished. Mia dropped to her knees, panting, absolutely exhausted. She pushed sweaty hair back from her face and tried to stand, but her legs gave out under her.

Domi walked up beside her and patted her shoulder. "You stay down, girl. Rest. You deserve it."

Panting too hard to reply, Mia nodded and sat back down.

"Ryan!" Zeke shouted.

"Already on it!"

Ryan blinked across the battlefield, only appearing for a moment before he vanished again. With each teleport, he reappeared closer to the goddess.

The goddess shouted. She pointed her spear at him. Lightning lanced across the field at Ryan, but he always vanished in the split second when it should have struck. She roared in frustration and jabbed her spear at the sky.

Overhead, lightning crackled. Thick beams shot down toward all of them. Zeke activated **High Speed Maneuvering.** The lightning slowed. He flapped hard, dodging around the lightning beams and closing in on the goddess.

At the same moment, Ryan reached the goddess. He lashed out, slamming his knife toward her.

She swung her spear, parrying his blow. But even as she did, his knife skittered over her shoulder, drawing a thin red line.

Overhead, Zeke grinned. *Ha, I knew it!*

Ryan laughed. "What was that about being beyond mortals?"

The goddess' face flushed red with fury. Her expression twisted, and she reared on her horse, striking at Ryan with its six hooves.

Ryan vanished. The horse slammed down, and the goddess hefted her spear once more. "This will not stand!"

Clouds flew toward her body, swirling around it. The entire floor swooped toward her. Every single bit of the clouds drew toward her, leaving nothing behind. The edge of the cloud swooped toward the rest of the party. Sky gaped, threatening to swallow them up.

"Mia, Domi, Erica, Sparkles! Guys!" Zeke shouted, startled. *Mia's tired. She can't support them. What are they going to do?*

72

BATTLE OF THE TITANS

As the floor swooped toward the rest of the party, the four of them jumped toward one another. Erica swirled her staff, and a pink bubble formed around them. It lowered slowly toward the ground, drifting as gently as though it were a soap bubble.

Zeke let out his held breath. *Thank goodness. They're safe.* He turned back to the goddess, slowly beating his wings to hold his place.

Clouds swirled around her. She was nothing but a giant lump of cloud, every bit of her obscured. Slowly, the cloud took shape. It formed a giant horse, then the goddess. Their bodies were soft and fluffy, formed of cloud, but incredibly huge. As tall as a cumulonimbus, flickering with lightning, dark and ominous. The goddess turned toward Zeke and lifted a spear as large as a skyscraper.

"Hey, hey, I'm not even the one who hurt you!" Zeke grumbled. He lifted his wings and flew toward the goddess, closing in on her. Eyeing the spear, he prepared to activate **High Speed Maneuvering**.

A small form materialized right in front of the goddess's

eyes. Ryan latched onto her nose and drew back his knife, slashing away at the cloud. The cloud regenerated faster than he could slash it. Even his deepest cuts only managed to shallowly slice the goddess, unable to inflict any serious wounds.

The goddess lifted her fingers and flicked. Ryan vanished a second before the flick hit, reappearing on top of her head. He grimaced at Zeke and spread his hands. "Nothing doing."

The spear shot forth. It moved quickly, but it was so huge she couldn't help but telegraph the blow. Zeke flapped away, not even needing his maneuvering skill. It was a lot like running away from a car. Sure, the car was moving at forty miles per hour, and he could only manage ten at best, but the car had so much momentum that it couldn't turn or chase him easily. It flew forth as if on rails, and he easily dodged. The spear swooshed by. Wind flew around Zeke, sending him spinning in the air. The earth and sky spun around him, mixing into one wild blur.

Zeke jolted to a halt, barely avoiding the urge to vomit. He glanced around him, then blinked. *Hold on, I'm upside down.* With a strong flap, he righted himself.

The goddess swung toward him again, trying to hit him on the backswing. Zeke flapped up, soaring into the sky. She altered her strike upward, but he dodged aside. The cloud-cloaked spear swooped past. The wind howled, loud as a hurricane. Zeke lofted up, thrown higher by the spear.

"You cannot defeat me. You cannot harm me. Be crushed, bugs, and die!" the goddess shouted.

Zeke chuckled. He looked at Ryan. "I think it's time."

"Yeah. Go wild." Ryan vanished.

Zeke rolled his shoulders and activated **Modest Gigantification.** He grew larger and larger, his whole body and wings growing as one. The goddess stared at him, then drew back her spear and stabbed toward him.

Ryan reappeared in her eye socket and stabbed her right in the eye. "Fuck off, douchebag."

The goddess recoiled, screaming. She put a hand over her injured eye. Ryan teleported away seconds before her hand struck.

The spear sagged in its strike, no longer supported by two hands. Already halfway to his giant size, Zeke batted it away. The goddess recoiled, thrown off-balance by his strike. He closed in, reaching out to grab the goddess.

The goddess reared her horse. Its hooves bit at Zeke, slamming down toward him.

Zeke opened his mouth and clenched his jaw.

[Ranged Devour]

The horse's leg vanished. Bones stuck in his throat for a moment before he forcibly swallowed them. An earthy, copper flavor chased after the bony limb.

He frowned. *It tastes like a real horse, not like cloud. What's different about this horse, compared to all the other constructs so far?*

The horse screamed in pain. It jumped under the goddess, bucking and tossing its head. The goddess put a hand to its side, calming it. She murmured sweet words in its ear. The horse stomped on its remaining five legs, trembling in place.

Zeke flapped in close and grabbed the goddess while she was distracted. "Allen!"

Subordinate Allen has shared his STR.

"Domi!"
"Huh? Oh, sure!"

Subordinate Domi has shared her DEX.

With his new higher stats, he wrestled the goddess. "You're going down!"

The goddess thrashed. Her horse kicked and reared, fighting Zeke. Zeke stopped flapping, letting his body sag down toward the ground. The goddess started falling toward him. She grabbed onto the horse's mane, refusing to let Zeke pull her off. "You mere mortal—"

Zeke opened his mouth and **Devour**ed her.

She jerked back. His mouth snapped shut on the air. Only a little bit of hair entered his mouth. It tickled his mouth and tasted like conditioner. He swallowed anyway, but it did nothing for him. Zeke grabbed on tighter and bit again, but she kicked him away. Her spear whirled around and jabbed toward him.

Zeke reached out with both hands and caught the spear as it dropped down toward him. The shaft slipped through his hands. The blade pressed down, scratching against his armor. Like before, the seemingly soft blade easily cut through, as if his armor was paper.

This thing is dangerous. Zeke looked at his hands, then shrugged. Shifting his grip, he set a hand-mouth against the spear's shaft and used **Devour** again.

The shaft snapped off. The blade tumbled down onto his chest. Zeke stretched out his neck and snapped up the blade with a quick bite. It tasted like clouds.

This is back to being cotton-candy-nothing flavor. The horse tasted like horse, but the blade tasted like cloud. Is the horse...a real horse? But where was it? I didn't see a horse in her temple.

This has got to be some kind of weird skill from her Apocalypse. Something I don't understand. No point wasting too much thought on it.

Frustrated, the goddess lifted her severed shaft. She swirled it in the sky. Clouds swirled around it, flying to reform the shape of the spear. The missing inches of shaft returned, and a blade grew at the end of the shaft.

Zeke wrinkled his nose. *Dammit. Wait! Is that it?*

He looked down. The horse's leg remained missing. *That makes sense. It can't regenerate because, due to whatever rule is operating in her mind, the horse is real. The spear isn't real, and so it can regenerate. Got it! If it tastes like what it is, it can't regenerate.*

He licked his lips and eyed the goddess. *Her hair tasted real. She's real.*

Ha. All I need to do is kill her? Easy.

"Ryan. It's time!" Zeke shouted.

The goddess startled. She looked around.

"Time for what?" Ryan asked.

Zeke darted in. Opening his mouth, he surged toward the goddess' neck.

73
EATING GOD

Zeke darted, open-mouthed, for the goddess' neck. She jerked back, and he slammed into her. His weight threw her off her horse, which startled and ran, galloping across the sky. The two of them plummeted. Wind whooshed by. The earth loomed, but so far away it was only a distant thought.

Grappling the goddess, Zeke bit at any part of her he could reach, his hands, feet, and mouth all devouring. His mouths tore off chunks of the cloud, biting deeper and deeper into the goddess.

"Release me! Unhand me, cur!"

Zeke's hands reflexively released her, compelled by one of her skills, but his hand-mouths didn't. They tore into her soft, cloudy flesh, chewing down on flesh-flavored cotton candy.

Honestly, I couldn't recommend flesh flavored cotton candy. It's not a good experience.

The goddess struggled in his grasp. Pain burst out in his gut as the spear sliced through it. Zeke grimaced but pushed the pain back with **Resilient Regeneration.** *It doesn't hurt. Not now. Nothing hurts. Nothing matters, except for finishing this fight.*

He tore the goddess apart. The goddess' body melted around him, falling apart like dissolving clouds after a storm. The goddess stabbed him, but his wounds healed rapidly as he continued to eat her. The two of them tumbled uncontrollably, plunging toward the earth.

At last, he ripped the last layer of cloud open to find the woman in the middle. She glared defiantly at him. "You will never overcome me."

"Wanna bet?" Zeke darted his head down and gulped her up.

[Devour]

The goddess fought inside his throat. The spear poked out from his Adam's apple. Zeke gagged. Blood welled up, and he swallowed it rather than choke on it. His nose wrinkled. He swallowed again and again, trying to clear the goddess into his stomach. *Go down, dammit. Go down!*

Ryan appeared on his shoulder. He dodged as the spear shot out of Zeke's neck, then grabbed it with both hands and wrenched it away. The goddess punched Zeke's neck from the inside, and Ryan punched from the outside. She fell, dropping lower in Zeke's throat.

Zeke swallowed again, more firmly than before. The goddess clung to his throat with all her strength. Ryan twisted his nose, then looked up at Zeke.

"Don't swallow me."

Huh?

Ryan vanished. A second lump appeared in his throat. The two figures punched back and forth, slamming into Zeke's throat walls and scraping him up from the inside. Zeke pressed his lips together, dissatisfied. *Could we not hold the final battle inside my throat?*

Though...I guess this is my fault.

Ryan appeared on his shoulder again, his hair a mess, his clothes torn. "Now!"

Without hesitation, Zeke activated **Devour** once more, swallowing at the same time. The lump finally cleared from his throat and plunged down into his stomach. There were a few pangs from his stomach, and then it went silent.

Defeated God Apocalypse

Zeke released his gigantification and spread his wings, slowing his plummet. "So? What now? Is that all of them? Are there any Apocalypses left?"

The System was silent.

Zeke pressed his lips together, lost. "I guess that's a no?"

"Someone must have hidden away somewhere," Ryan said. He paused, cutting his eyes at Zeke. "Or...the Apocalypses and Heroes have to fight to determine the final victor."

"Yeah? You're on my side anyway, even if that's the case. The only Hero here is Mia," Zeke returned.

Ryan tipped his head back and forth. He shrugged, then vanished again, jumping another ten or so feet down. "Arguably true."

"True according to the System."

"Yeah, but the System is bullshit."

"That...does seem to be true," Zeke said, nodding.

Below them, the city crumbled. The ocean awaited them far below, dark and unforgiving. Erica's bubble drifted downward, destined for the sea.

Zeke pursed his lips. "Anyone have sailing-based skills?"

"No," Ryan said, snorting.

"Yeaaaaah. Not uh, not the greatest prognosis there for our forthcoming sailing adventure," Zeke commented. *I can fly, but for the thousands of miles needed to cross the ocean? Fat chance.*

Abruptly, the world shifted. Everything swirled around them, wavering like a mirage. Something drew Zeke backward, back into the sky. Below him, the bubble floated up. The city reformed.

"What's happening? Ryan?" Zeke asked, looking at Ryan beside him.

Ryan threw his hands up. "I'm not doing this!"

Then who? Some other Apocalypse with time powers? Is there a hidden boss? Zeke glanced at Ryan. "Stay close to me. Whatever happens, if we stick together, we'll have an advantage."

Ryan nodded. He gave Zeke a suspicious gaze. "I'm not taking my eyes off you."

"What? Why?"

Ryan gave him a look.

Zeke blinked at him, then rolled his eyes, understanding at last. "Dude. I only got one skill from eating your arm, and I picked Regression."

"This could be Regression."

"Is this how Regression works?" Zeke asked.

Ryan paused. He shook his head. "No."

"Oh. So you know it's not me."

"Hmm." Ryan shrugged noncommittally.

They were placed back on their feet, back atop the crown of clouds. A throne sat before them, formed from cloud. Empty. Waiting.

"Uh...is someone supposed to be on that?" Zeke asked.

"It does feel like a boss intro scene, but one where the boss clipped through the chair and fell out of the world, so we're just kind of chilling," Ryan agreed.

Mia, Domi, Erica, and Sparkles ran up behind them. "What's going on?" Mia asked.

"Wish I knew," Zeke told her, shaking his head. He gestured. "I'd guess that throne has something to do with it."

Mia squinted. "Should we sit on it?"

"You wanna try it?" Zeke asked.

Mia pursed her lips. She shrugged, then stepped forward.

Before she got more than five paces away from them, a figure stepped out from behind the throne. Moving casually, he sat down in the throne and lounged, looking down on them with a smile on his face.

"Hello, Zeke," the figure said.

"Hello, Zeke. Or did we agree on Zel?" Zeke returned, looking at his alternate-universe self. "Is this your endgame? Turning on us, after we kill all the other Apocalypses? One last duel to the death?"

"No. *This* is." Zel snapped his fingers.

74
ME VS ME

Zel snapped his fingers. The world went dark. Only he and Zeke remained, staring one another down. He still lounged on his cloud throne, but it stood alone in the black now.

"What do you want?" Zeke asked.

"You know what I want. The same thing you do. To destroy the world."

Zeke crossed his arms. He looked at Zel. "I already told you. I'm not going to destroy the world. I'm going to save it."

Zel spread his hands. "And? You've killed all the Apocalypses but me. Go on. Save the world."

Zeke opened his mouth, then closed it. *He's got a point. How am I going to save the world from here? I killed all the Apocalypses, but that doesn't undo what's happened. It doesn't un-kill all the people the Apocalypses killed or undo all the destruction they caused. I have to rebuild the world, but how? Where do I even start?*

Zel snorted. He rose to his feet. "Right. You don't know. I know because I also don't know. None of us do. Not one of us."

"None of us?" Zeke asked.

Ryan appeared beside Zeke. Panting, he looked around. "You're here? How'd you get here?"

"Huh? What do you mean?" Zeke asked.

"This is the space between. This is...you shouldn't be here," Ryan said.

"I didn't allow you in," Zel said. He lifted his hand and waved dismissively. Ryan vanished.

Zeke startled. He looked around. "Where'd you send Ryan?"

"Away. We don't need him here."

"I'm suddenly feeling like we need him here," Zeke muttered, only half to himself.

Zel sighed. He stepped toward Zeke. "The thing is, Zeke, there can only be one of us. One Zeke."

"Why? I'm cool with you chilling out over there. It's not hurting either of us for two of us to exist."

Zel shook his head. "You're not getting it, Zeke. We are the basis of the time loop. Because of us, Ryan keeps going back. It's made us more than human."

"What?" Zeke asked, squinting.

Ryan appeared again in the air over Zel. He dropped down toward him, lashing out with his knife.

Zel snapped his fingers. Ryan vanished once more. "We're a nexus, Zeke. We're the center of the time loop. Unknowingly, Ryan has elevated us to something far greater than we once were.

"I've tried killing him. I've tried killing Ryan. Countless times, I've succeeded. But it doesn't matter. He always comes back. And that's when I realized: I was going about this all wrong."

"What do you mean?" Zeke asked.

"I've been going about this all wrong. I don't need to kill Ryan." Zel lifted his hand and pointed at Zeke. "I need to kill you."

"Why?"

"If there's only one of us, the timeline will collapse. There will only be one timeline left, and it'll be shaped by the last Zeke standing. And when I eat you, that'll be me."

"You've eaten all the other Zekes?" Zeke asked.

Zel laughed. "That doesn't matter. The point is, I'm much closer to success than you will ever be."

Ryan appeared behind Zel. He charged in, striking toward Zel's heart.

Zel waved his hand. Ryan vanished again.

Zeke narrowed his eyes. "If that's what you wanted, why didn't you attack me off the kick? Why wait this long?"

"Those who are about to die don't need to worry about such details," Zel declared.

"Unless...it's because you want my timeline, too. Yours is fucked beyond all belief, so you want a timeline that isn't trash. You let me play out all my battles until I almost won, then swooped in to steal the victory." Zeke shook his head at Zel. "Cheap. How cheap of you. Didn't even bother to help me out, just sat back and waited to see if I could win."

"Yeah? Come at me, bro. Who cares how I get to victory, so long as I win."

Zeke pressed his lips together. "That does sound like something I'd say."

"It is. Because I'm you. So hey, don't worry about it. When I eat you, it'll be just the same as if you ate me. We're the same person. I'll take care of Mia and everyone for you. I've even got a plan for fixing the planet. So just sit back, relax, and let the better Zeke win, huh?" Zel advanced slowly, his hands out peacefully.

"Yeah, the thing is, I'm not really that excited about being eaten," Zeke said, backing away. He eyed Zel. *Do I have to eat him? Is that what it's going to come down to? Eat or be eaten?*

Ha. What a fitting way to end this. Eat or be eaten. Live by the eat, die by the eat. He chuckled at himself despite everything. *God. What a stupid way to die.*

"You know you're going to lose. Give up. Come to me," Zel urged him.

Ryan appeared inches from him, stabbing at his gut. In between appearing and striking, Zel waved his hand, and Ryan vanished again.

"Well, you know what? I've thought about it. And you know, you're me, I'm you. I feel like I have a pretty good idea of what goes on in your head," Zeke said.

"Yeah?" Zel strode forward.

Zeke continued to back away, keeping his distance. "You're talking to me. You're trying to convince me. Stalling for time. Because you're pretty sure you can't beat me. You're scared. More scared of me than I am of you."

"One of us is backing away," Zel pointed out.

"Well, yeah. That's because I'm not stupid. I know how dangerous I am. I'm not going to stand here and let you eat me. But I don't think you've got a guaranteed win, either. I think you're talking me down because you know...I'm stronger than you. Way fucking stronger. Actually...I might be the strongest Zeke you've ever encountered," Zeke said suddenly, everything connecting at once. *He said he didn't leave the dome. No—Ryan said it, too. He always left before the dome opened. That means I'm the only Zeke to leave the dome. The only Zeke to power up outside of the initial scenario. I'm stronger than him. I'm stronger than all the Zekes out there.*

This one knows it. He's talking me down. Trying to get me to give up before I even try. Because he knows that I'm stronger than him. He knows I can wipe the floor with him. And not just that—that's why he didn't attack me until now. Why he didn't contribute to the fight. I'm sure he hunted some Apocalypses in the city below the clouds, but aside from that, he's been hiding his strength. Not because he's strong, but because he's weak.

If all the other Zekes are coming here to devour me, they're in for a bad time.

Zeke stopped backing away. He held his ground. Lifting his head, he looked down on the other him. "So, why don't you come here, and we'll see who eats who?"

75
EAT OR BE EATEN

Zeke stopped dead. He spread his arms and grinned at Zel. "So? Come over here, and we'll see who eats who."

Zel snorted under his breath. "Cocky."

"Aren't we both."

Zel stepped forward. He cracked his knuckles. "I take it you're not going to go quietly."

"Are you?" Zeke returned. He walked toward Zel, lifting his arms. *Not yet. Not yet.*

"Of course no—"

Ryan appeared behind Zel, knife already striking. Zel's shirt darted backward and twisted around Ryan's hand, binding it in place. Zel glanced over his shoulder. "Are you done?"

The second he looked away, Zeke darted in. His fist flew toward Zel's chin.

Zel's shirt twisted up again. In one direction, it held Ryan, and in the other, it caught Zeke's hand. Zel clicked his tongue. "What a cheap trick. You aren't smart. I can see right through you."

Rather than answer, Zeke bit toward Zel's neck. He yanked

toward himself with his caught hand, using the shirt that grabbed his hand as a way to draw Zel toward his mouth.

Zel's shirt released Zeke's hand. Zel jumped back before it could retract to Zel's body, Zeke turned his mouth down and snatched a bite of shirt out of the air.

In the next moment, Zel reappeared behind the throne, out of Ryan or Zeke's reach. He grimaced. "You're underestimating me. I'll destroy you both."

"All right, then prove it," Zeke challenged him.

Zel glared at him. Black, stringy strips of armor wrapped around his body. Sharp teeth pressed out of his gums. Long, slender tendrils thrashed around his face. He glared at Zeke for a moment, then vanished and reappeared in Zeke's face, his fist already halfway to Zeke.

Zeke darted back, but something caught his arm. Zel's punch sent him reeling but didn't let him fall back. He glanced down. The shirt snagged his arm, fine cotton wrapping him in place.

Zel lifted his fist and punched again. One, two, punches rained down on Zeke. He snarled and opened his mouth, biting at Zel's hand. Zel snatched it out of his reach before he could bite down, far too fast for Zeke. Zeke grimaced. *I don't know where the hell he got his super speed from, but it's a pain in my ass!*

A knife flashed. It slammed into Zel's neck, and dark blood spurted out. Zel stumbled, slowing his assault for just a moment.

Zeke threw himself at Zel's shoulder.

Cursing, Zel kicked backward, sending Ryan flying. Ryan vanished, teleporting away before Zel threw him too far. He jumped away from Zeke.

Rather than let Zel go, Zeke spun his wrist and caught the shirt, jerking Zel back to earth. He pulled it toward him with all his might, then used his other hand's mouth to gnaw through it.

As Zeke's hand-mouth swallowed the shirt, Zel jerked away at last. Only rags remained of his Oxford, most of the shirt torn away. He shook his head at Zeke. "Ruining a man's look?"

"Ruining your annoying-ass defenses, more like," Zeke shot back.

"You're just jealous that you don't have them," Zel returned, sticking his long, weird tongue out.

"Sure. Nothing like a super-cool office shirt to defend me," Zeke said, rolling his eyes.

Zel blurred toward him. Before he struck, Zeke activated **High Speed Maneuvering.** For a moment, the world slowed. He saw Zel hurtling at him, and the fist flying for his face.

Zeke swayed to the side, narrowly avoiding the punch. Zel's eyes widened. He yanked his hand back.

Zeke grinned. He jerked his head forward, opening his mouth.

[Devour]

Swallowing, Zeke nodded at Zel. "Too slow."

Zel made a face as if he'd eaten a bitter lemon and backed away, holding his wrist. A single, small bite wound opened in his flesh. "You got lucky."

"Sure. When I get a hit, it's luck. When you get a hit, it's skill. Uh huh," Zeke snarked.

Zel's face twisted even further. He charged at Zeke again.

This time, Zeke expected it. The world slowed again, and Zeke bit at Zel's arm once more. Zel yanked his arm back, too fast for Zeke to sink his teeth in.

Zeke grabbed onto Zel's midriff. He stepped on Zel's foot. With all his mouths, he dug into Zel's flesh.

Zel shouted, startled, and retreated. This time, Zeke chased after him. He couldn't keep up, even with **High Speed Maneuvering,** but he didn't have to. A shadowy figure appeared behind Zel and stabbed down into his chest.

Zel stumbled. He slowed to a halt. Kicking blindly behind him, he sent Ryan teleporting away. Once again, only Zeke and Zel stood in the darkness.

Lifting his hand, Zel jabbed his finger at Zeke. "I could kill you. If you were alone...you wouldn't even know what happened. You, and Ryan, and this whole world. I could destroy it all."

"Yeah, sure." Zeke paused. "This whole time, was it all fake? Did you never consider yourself part of the team?"

Zel laughed. "Don't be ridiculous. You have everything. Mia. Friends. A home base, and people to protect. Warriors who fight alongside you. Even...fucking...Ryan. You're throwing it in my face. Every day, you throw it in my face. How much you have. How little I have. It's not fair. What did you do, that I didn't?"

"Win," Zeke said. "Got good."

"Sure. Sure. Because I didn't try. Because I didn't..." Zel shook his head. He backed away, then pointed at Zeke. "I'll kill you and take your place."

"Oh. That's what this is about, huh?" Zeke crossed his arms. He snorted. "What a stupid reason. You know, you can have it all, too. You can be part of the team, just like anyone else. Make friends with Domi. Cozy up with Mia."

"But only one person can be *with* Mia. Only one person gets to lord it over everyone else."

Zeke glanced around. "I don't think I'm really lording it over anyone."

Zel's lips twisted. He shook his head. "Even if I ignore all that, it doesn't matter."

"Oh, really?" Zeke asked.

"There's more. More than just me. All the worlds that Ryan destroyed...there's Zekes from all of them. Zekes that are far more hungry for your blood than I am. Zekes who would do anything to tear down everything you've built." He looked up at Zeke. "I...could have lived like that. Maybe. If I'd let myself. If I had the option. But that's not true for all of them. And if I didn't attack...one of them would have. One of them would've taken your whole world from you, before you even knew what was happening."

"What? What are you talking about, dude?" Zeke asked, suddenly lost. *He was going on about how he wanted my life, but now he's...I don't know, he doesn't care? He was doing this to train me, or something? Is this bullshit, or was the earlier part bullshit?*

Or is there some truth to everything he's saying? Do both halves reflect some part of the whole truth?

"So, I figured I'd take it first. Take your world and become you. Devour all the other Zekes and win. But you're a pain in the ass to—" Ryan appeared behind him, and he cursed and darted away, frustrated.

Zeke nodded. *Oh. Now it all comes together. He wants to win. Win, and live. Well, I understand. I, too, want to win and live.*

It's just that he attacked me first. A strange choice, since I'm stronger than him.

"I think it's time we end this," Zeke commented.

"Yeah. It's time for you to die," Zel agreed.

Zeke snorted. He lunged for Zel.

Faster than his eyes could track, Zel darted in.

"Now!" Zeke shouted.

Zel stuttered. He dug in his heels, surprised.

Zeke jumped at Zel. He latched onto him with his hand-mouths and opened his mouth wide. He slammed it shut on Zel's shoulder, tearing out a lump of flesh.

"You—fucking—tricked me?" Zel snarled.

"Oldest trick in the book," Ryan answered for Zeke. He tapped Zel on the back of the head. "Go still."

Zel froze. He completely stopped moving, paused in time.

Zeke nodded his thanks. He tore into Zel, using **Devour** over and over again. Blood flew. Bone shattered. He swallowed, gulping down Zel one bite at a time until nothing remained.

And then it was over. He and Ryan stood in the darkness, all alone. Zeke wiped his mouth and looked around. "What now?"

Ryan shrugged. "I don't know. No one else has ever dragged me into the space between."

Congratulations! You defeated the

The message stopped dead. Zeke looked up, confused. "What's going on with the System?"

"Doesn't know how to handle you devouring yourself, I bet," Ryan guessed.

"Huh. Yeah. Is that also why we're stuck here?" Zeke asked.

Ryan shrugged again. "I don't know anything about what's going on. Where are we? Why can't we go back? Why did other-Zeke…Zel, why did he know Regression?"

"Did he eat you, in his universe?" Zeke asked.

"Not all of me."

"Some of you?"

Ryan hesitated, then shook his head. "No."

Zeke twisted his lips. "I wonder if he got Regression, or a similar ability, from one of the other Zekes. He seemed pretty convinced they were real, and that they were going to kill me and maybe also him. Maybe he encountered other Zekes already."

"You think he was being honest? That he wasn't deluded?" Ryan asked.

"I mean, he seemed pretty convinced of it," Zeke said.

"I've never encountered any Zekes in the space between until this fight, right here. If there were other Zekes, I feel like I would've seen them," Ryan said.

Zeke shrugged at him. "Space between's a big place, right? They could be somewhere else."

"Yeah...I guess." Ryan looked around them again. "But more importantly, how do we get out of here?"

Zeke hesitated. He looked around him and pursed his lips. Black stretched in all directions. Pure, featureless black. The cloud throne slowly melted away with no one to maintain it. Once it was gone, there was nothing but the void. They could have been standing at any angle, or falling into oblivion, and Zeke would have had no way to tell. The darkness was complete and pure, and yet, he could easily see Ryan standing across from him.

"I don't know," Zeke said, shrugging.

Ryan shrugged back. "Well then. I guess we just die here?"

76

SPACE BETWEEN

"Guess we just die."

Zeke chuckled. "Yep. Nothing we can do, might as well give up." He turned and walked off, heading deeper into the darkness.

"Where are you going?" Ryan asked.

"I'm finding a good place to give up," Zeke called over his shoulder.

Ryan stared after him, then shook his head and jogged to follow Zeke. "You know, I wasn't actually going to die."

"Yeah? I know." Zeke walked on.

Ryan drew up with him. For a while, they walked silently into the darkness. Nothing changed. As far as Zeke could tell, they might as well have been walking in place.

"Can you use Regression to get out of here?" Zeke asked, glancing at Ryan.

"Huh? No. Already tried. This is where Regression takes me. So...it can't activate because I'm already here. And if the skill can't activate, its back-half effect where it takes me out of here also can't activate...or something." Ryan shrugged. "It's the System. Sometimes things get weird."

"Yeah...huh," Zeke muttered. *I could use skills in here. Actually...* He spread his hands. The hand mouths opened hungrily, and armor twisted around his palm. *I'm still Transformed. I wonder if I can transform back to human?*

Not that I want to, right now. If there's more Zekes to fight, as Zel suggested, then I can't let down my guard yet.

Just to test it, Zeke activated **Regression.** Just as Ryan had said, though, nothing happened. The skill activated, but nothing changed. He stood in the dark world, unable to escape.

He pressed his lips together and shrugged. Casually, he deactivated the skill. *Guess that's it. Ryan was telling the truth. We can't escape here through Regression. There might not be a way to escape at all.*

After a moment, he turned to Ryan, his brows furrowed. "Wait, huh? Can't you leave?"

"No...?"

"But when you were fighting Zel, you kept popping in and out."

Ryan stared at him, then laughed. "Oh. Yeah. I mean, I did, yeah."

"So...you can't leave now? Why not?"

"Well, I wasn't popping in and out of the space between. I was just travelling within it. I usually teleport somewhere out of sight, reposition, then teleport back in. It keeps my opponent on their toes. I was doing the same for Zel."

"What about when he waved you away?"

"Yeah, that part was confusing. He must have had some kind of skill to manipulate the space between because he was..." Ryan paused for a second, then gestured. "Sending me places. Reverse-teleporting me, almost. I don't know how. I mean, maybe that's all it was. Maybe he had a reverse-teleportation skill." He turned to Zeke expectantly.

Zeke put his hands up. "I don't have anything like that. Don't look at me."

"Guess you two don't share that one. But yeah. That was something else, but he wasn't expelling me from the space between."

"Now that I'm thinking about it, how did you follow us in?" Zeke asked. "Zel only grabbed me, right? He didn't seem to want to bring you."

Ryan nodded. "I'm pretty familiar with the space between. When I recognized what was happening, I latched on. Used a partial activation of Regression to follow you two here. But..." Ryan spread his hands. "In the end, it locked me here."

"Didn't know that would happen?"

"Nah. I've never partially activated Regression before. It seemed like a bad idea, and surprise! It was," Ryan said, chuckling under his breath at himself.

"I mean, yeah, fair," Zeke said, nodding.

They walked on. Darkness continued to provide a monotonous setting. Zeke looked at his feet, watching them impact nothing. Non-ground. Darkness. There was nothing to indicate where the walls, floor, or ceiling were. *I could be walking through a tiny, narrow corridor, or a huge ballroom. I wouldn't know the difference.*

Ryan glanced at Zeke. "You...okay?"

"Huh? Yeah."

"I mean, you just ate yourself. Just committed auto-cannibalism. That's not, you know, messing you up in the head or anything?" Ryan asked.

Zeke shrugged. "Zel wasn't me. It didn't bother me any more than eating anyone else. I mean, it bothered me a little bit, but...not like, a lot. You know?"

"I don't, no. I don't eat people, so I wouldn't know," Ryan said, looking Zeke in the eye.

Zeke looked back at him. They both started to laugh.

"Yeah, I guess you wouldn't know," Zeke said at last, wiping a tear from his eyes. He shook his head.

"We just walking for fun, or?" Ryan asked.

"Kinda hoping something would change if we kept walking. You know. Something would happen. We'd run into the System Apocalypse, or another me, or something."

They kept walking. The darkness stretched on, silent as ever. Even their footsteps made no sound. No light, no change in scenery, no depth or distance. Zeke glanced up. *It's like floating at the bottom of a deep pool. There's no sensations. We're moving, but there's no feedback. No up and down, no right and wrong. There's gravity here, I guess, but...in general, the sensation is pretty similar. That weightlessness. The sensation of lack.*

It's almost...peaceful.

Zeke glanced at Ryan. "You come here often?" he joked.

Ryan snorted. "More often than I'd like."

"I missed on one. Zel decided he wasn't part of the team. What about you, Ryan? Are you in it to win it? Is my reality your reality?"

Ryan spread his hands. "It always was. I've always seen the world I'm in as the real world. Maybe it's wrong, but...I was never really confronted with the idea that I've been swapping worlds. I knew it was happening. Actually, sometimes Zekes would cross over, chasing me. But it still felt like the real world all along. There was never anything to confront my sense that this was the real world."

"Unlike Zel, who immediately met me," Zeke said.

"Right," Ryan said, nodding.

Zeke sighed. He shook his head. "I really wish Zel could've adapted. Become one of us. There's no reason we couldn't have both lived on the earth together. I mean, there's a lot of world.

We don't both need to be next to each other, or even acknowledge that we both exist."

"Is there not?" Ryan asked.

"What do you mean?"

Ryan pointed at Zeke. "You need to eat constantly to survive. And not just eat but eat living things. It escalates over time. By now, you need to eat what, people?"

Zeke hesitated, then wiggled his hand. "Er, kind of. More or less?"

"Is it all the way to Apocalypses by now?" Ryan asked warily.

Zeke pressed his lips together. "Maybe...?"

Ryan looked at him. He shook his head. "And you say you and Zel can exist on the same planet. I'm not sure Earth can support one of you, let alone both of you."

Zeke spread his hands. "Look, man. I mean, hypothetically, it's not a problem."

"Hypothetically, a lot of things work that don't work out practically. Practically, you and Zel are *both* problems, and when you're together, you combine into one big problem."

Zeke went to argue, then shrugged. "Fair. I can't really disagree with that."

"Maybe it's better for you to stay here. Never leave. We won't have the eating things escalation problem here," Ryan mused.

Zeke narrowed his eyes. "Hey..."

Ryan shrugged. "Doesn't matter. I can't leave, and neither can you. Don't have a method of escape, either. I'm just pointing out the upsides of our shitty situation, you know?"

"Oh, yeah, yeah, I get it. The upside of being eternally trapped is that we're eternally trapped. Makes sense," Zeke agreed, nodding.

Ryan snorted. "Oh, come on. I didn't say that."

"You did kind of say that."

"Okay. Maybe a little," Ryan allowed. "But hey! I mean, it solves one problem, right?"

"Yeah, yeah. It also causes a problem," Zeke pointed out. He lifted his finger at Ryan. "Namely, I'm still gonna get hungry. And there's only one thing in here to eat."

"Hey."

"What? As long as we're making the best of a bad situation, I oughta point out my emergency food is you," Zeke said, shrugging.

"I'm not emergency food."

"Not to you," Zeke muttered darkly.

They made eye contact. For a few moments, they stared at one another, tense. Abruptly, Zeke waggled his brows and grinned. "I'm kidding, just kidding."

"Kind of kidding," Ryan said.

"Well, sure. But I'm not going to eat you until I have no other option," Zeke promised him.

"Wow, thanks. You know, it really makes me feel secure when my cannibal friend says he'll eat me last, and I'm the literal only other person around."

"Hey now. I didn't say that," Zeke complained.

Ryan grinned back. "Now you know how I feel."

"Yeah, yeah." Zeke pushed Ryan.

Again, they walked. Darkness and silence. Shapeless space. Time passed. It could have been a long time, or no time at all. Zeke couldn't tell. There was no indication as to the passage of time. No sun to cross the sky, or light to grow and fade. Just pure black in all directions, dark as the void of space.

Zeke glanced at Ryan. *If he wasn't here, I might go crazy. But because he's here, I'm able to anchor myself. Up and down, left and right; I have a frame of reference for all of that, thanks to Ryan. And I'm not stuck in here alone, wondering if anyone even remembers me.*

I'm here, and Ryan's here. If nothing else, we can always work together to escape...though I don't think either of us have a good idea on how to accomplish that.

Ryan caught his gaze. "What?"

"Um...are we good now?"

"What do you mean?"

"Do you still want me dead, basically?" Zeke asked.

Ryan let out a breath. He ran his hair back. "I... Jeez. What a question."

"It's a pretty important question to me."

"I..." Ryan shrugged. "I'm not sure?"

Zeke snorted. "'Do you want to kill me?' 'I'm not sure.' The hell kind of conversation are we having?"

"An important one."

"Yeah, I agree. Still."

Ryan put his hands up. "I don't know. Am I good with you? I don't know. I mean, we just killed a version of you that was— well, he was everything I was afraid of. Every part of you I hate. And you helped me. You fought alongside me. So, I-I don't know. But I feel like I'm moving in your direction?"

"You're in your Zeke-killing refractory period," Zeke said, pinching his chin and nodding sagely.

Ryan made a face. "Don't put it like that."

"Am I wrong?"

"I mean...yes, very, but also...not really." Ryan shrugged. "I'm not sure. And I won't be, for a little while, I don't think. But gun to my head, yes or no, I'd say...yes. We're good."

"I like that answer," Zeke said, nodding.

"Also, please never call it a refractory period again."

"What? Oh, come on. You're killing me, and *I'm* not allowed to be crude? Shakin' my head, dude. Shaking my head."

Ryan snorted.

They walked and walked. On and on, through the void. Zeke

lifted his hands again. Still Transformed. *Time is weird in here, but I feel like enough time has passed that my Transform should be over. Maybe my counter doesn't count down in here. Maybe time is so strange that it's not passing, even though it's passing for me.* He considered asking the System, then shook his head. *One, I don't really want to draw its attention right now. Two, if this is a glitch, I don't want it to realize that I'm out of time and penalize me for it now, when another Zeke could show up at any moment.*

Zeke paused. He looked at the world around them.

"What?" Ryan asked.

"I wonder if..." Zeke hesitated. He shook his head. "No. It was a stupid idea. I'm embarrassed to say it."

"Oh, come on. Like any idea is stupid right now. I'd do anything, if it could get us out of here," Ryan said.

"Okay. But you're not allowed to laugh," Zeke said firmly.

Ryan crossed his arms. He leaned back. "Sure. Go on. What is it?"

Zeke took a deep breath. "What if—" He leaned in and whispered.

Ryan stared at him, then broke out laughing.

77
OM NOM NOM

Zeke leaned in. He whispered, "What if I eat...this? The space between, I mean."

Ryan stared at him, then busted out laughing. A second later, he sobered up. "Oh wait, you're serious?" He laughed again, harder than before.

Zeke scowled at him. "You said you wouldn't laugh."

"Well, yeah. But some things need to be laughed at, promises aside."

"Is it really that ridiculous?"

Ryan shook his head, suddenly turning serious. "No. It's actually a really good idea." A grin crept in. "But the funny part is you suggesting eating things as the first idea every time. Problem? Eat it."

"Well, I mean. It's worked out for me," Zeke said, gesturing helplessly.

"Yeah, yeah. It is your concept. It makes a lot of sense."

"Right."

"So, uh. How are you planning to eat...this?"

Zeke licked his lips. "That's the part I hadn't quite worked out yet. But I haven't tried yet, either. So, you know what? Let's give it a shot and see what happens."

Ryan gestured for him to go ahead.

Taking a deep breath, Zeke took a step forward. There, he paused. "The fuck did I do that for? It's not like there's a wall here."

"I dunno. Vibes?" Ryan asked.

Zeke snorted. He looked at the darkness. Nothing stood out to him as bitable, but then, nothing stood out to him as impossible to bite, either. He opened his mouth.

[Devour]

His jaws clamped down on something. It slipped out of his mouth, but he felt it. For an instant, it was there. *Something.*

"Welp. Didn't expect that to work," Ryan sighed.

"No, hold up. It worked. Or...something happened," Zeke said, distracted. He reached out and grabbed Ryan's hand.

Ryan tensed. "Huh?"

"In case I succeed. I don't know if I can pause and grab you or not. I don't want to leave you behind."

There was a pause. Ryan relaxed. He looked at Zeke in surprise. "Oh."

Zeke opened his mouth again. He activated **Devour**. Again, the sensation of biting down on something slippery passed through his mouth. Frustrated, Zeke stepped forward as it slipped, but that didn't help. The thing he bit wasn't physical and couldn't be physically approached.

Zeke wrinkled his nose. "Dammit. I'm not letting this get away so easily."

Rapid-fire, he activated **Devour** after **Devour,** almost chewing at the air. Every time, the *thing* slipped away. Zeke wrinkled his nose. "I can't catch it!"

"What if I use Regression? Regression pulls me into the space between, so maybe it'll...I don't know, activate it," Ryan suggested.

Zeke shrugged. *I can use two skills concurrently, but I'm not sure if I can activate two skills at the same exact instant. It's easier if Ryan does it, anyway.* "Let's go for it. On three." He opened his mouth.

Ryan looked at him. Zeke stared back, mouth open.

"Oh, you want me to count down. Right. Three. Two. One!"

Zeke bit. The thing tried to slip away again, but then he felt something else twist it, holding it for just another moment. He slammed his mouth shut, tearing into it.

The darkness ripped. A hole opened in the void, and light streamed through. Zeke grabbed at it, but his hand slipped through. He frowned.

Oh. Duh. I have to keep using Devour. "Grab my wrist," he told Ryan.

"What?" Ryan shifted his grip up, freeing Zeke's hand.

He set his hand-mouths into the tear and pulled, activating **Devour** on both of them.

The darkness tore. His hands chewed up whatever came away in the tears. It slipped down his throat like Jell-O, sliding easily into his stomach. Zeke shuddered. *So weird. But so good.*

He lifted his hands again, tearing off strips of the darkness until a human-shaped hole formed. On the other side, pale, blurry light glowed. Indistinct shapes moved, like a television seen through blurry lenses.

Distracted, Zeke eyed the edges of the hole instead of the blurry light. *I could eat more...*

"It's closing!" Ryan shouted. He ran through the hole, dragging Zeke after him.

Aww...I could've eaten more of that. It was tasty. And filling!

They staggered through the hole in the darkness and into

the light. They stepped out into a well-lit area. After all the time in the darkness, the bright light blinded Zeke. He squinted and lifted a hand, trying to see.

"Whoa..." Ryan breathed.

"What is it?" Zeke asked. He blinked his eyes, trying to hurry up and unblind himself so he could see.

"What *isn't* it," Ryan said quietly.

Zeke's vision faded in. He blinked a few more times and could finally see clearly.

Sheafs of colorful light hung all around them. Different colors spotted the sheafs, the light stacked up like coats hanging in a closet. The lights stretched before them, behind them, in all directions, thousands upon thousands of them. An uncountable number. There was something ephemerally beautiful to them, like light shining through stained glass. It made him feel as though he were somewhere sacred, somewhere holy. A place where he shouldn't be loud, or even move too quickly.

They floated in the midst of this bright realm, their feet touching nothing, and yet on flat ground. The lights hung overhead and above them as well, shining in all brilliant colors. It almost reminded Zeke of being in a clothing store as a little kid and hiding under a rack of colorful T-shirts or dresses, but on all sides instead of just overhead. Surrounded by the sheaves. Hidden by the lustrous, shimmering, smooth lights.

Zeke caught his breath, his eyes wide. *Wow. Beautiful.*

"What is this? Where are we?" Zeke asked.

Ryan shook his head. "I don't know."

Zeke turned, slowly, taking it all in. "Is this, like...the center of all the worlds? A nexus?"

"Might as well call it *the* nexus," Ryan said, but he didn't disagree.

"Damn," Zeke whispered. He paused, then, thinking, then bit his lip. "Er...but how do we figure out which one's ours?"

Ryan shrugged. "How do we enter the worlds? I don't know."

"Huh," Zeke muttered.

A claw closed on his shoulder. "Doesn't matter. You die here, fucker."

78
DIE HERE

A claw closed around his shoulder. It yanked Zeke back, toward an unseen opponent. Zeke whirled, jerking away. Beside him, Ryan vanished, doubtlessly teleporting to a superior vantage point.

Black armor. A vicious mouth. Tongues lashed from hands. Zeke stared at himself.

"Oh," he said.

The other Zeke drew back his fist.

Rather than let him land the blow, Zeke activated **High Speed Navigation** and thrust his head toward the other him's neck. The other Zeke jerked back, but Ryan appeared behind him and shoved the other Zeke forward. A throat entered Zeke's mouth, and Zeke bit down.

The other Zeke choked. He stumbled backward, grabbing his neck. As Zeke watched, the wound began to regenerate.

"Yeah, nah." Zeke chased down the other him. The other him turned and fled but couldn't move fast with a torn neck. In a few moments, Zeke reached him and **Devour**ed him, leaving nothing behind.

For a moment, he stood there all alone, half-floating in the strange space. Zeke looked around. "Ryan...? Where'd you go, man?"

Ryan reappeared beside him. "Bad news."

"What?"

"There's more of you."

"I guess that's not a surprise," Zeke said. He dusted off his hands and nodded at Ryan. "Where are they?"

"Moving in. Your arrival seems to have started a kind of feeding frenzy," Ryan said.

"What, like they have a hive mind or something?" Zeke asked.

"Huh?"

"Like sharks..." Zeke went silent.

Ryan stared at him. "Sharks don't have a hive mind."

"I—sorry. I don't know what I was thinking," Zeke said.

"Of bees, maybe? Ants? Ants will all go on the attack if you injure one ant," Ryan said.

"I guess? Let's go with yes."

"Sharks do the blood-in-the-water thing, but it's not because they have a hive mind or anything."

"Yeah, I know. I said the wrong word, okay?" Zeke grumbled.

"If that's what you meant, then you're right. They're like sharks. Jumping on the fresh meat," Ryan said, his voice turning dark at the end.

"And I'm a big bloody T-bone steak, fresh off the cow," Zeke replied.

Ryan chuckled. "Fresh off the cow. You would bring it back to food."

"Hey, man, what can I say? I'm a growing boy. Need my nutrients."

Ryan opened his mouth to answer, then shut it. Abruptly, he straightened up and drew his knife, spinning it between his fingers. He nodded at Zeke. "They're closing in. Be on guard."

Zeke nodded back. He looked around, but only shimmering lights surrounded them. Still, he tensed, ready to fight. *Maybe Ryan saw the future, or some shit. The one thing I can trust Ryan to be, is a decent scout.*

Some of the lights began to shudder. A dark claw jutted out from one of them. From another, a head burst through, looking left and right from the torn fabric of the light. On and on, Zekes began to crawl through the lights, a *hunger* to their motions. An edge. An urge. One tilted its head to the side, watching Zeke, a bestial quality to its gaze.

"Uh, Ryan? Weird question, but...how many times did you turn back time, again? Asking for a friend."

"I've already told you. Lifetimes' worth—" Ryan cut off. He looked around them, then swallowed. "Oh."

"No kidding, 'oh.' I think each of these lights equates to a reality you created. Which means we have to fight as many Zekes as numbers of times you activated Regression," Zeke complained, glaring at Ryan.

"How was I supposed to know?" Ryan muttered.

"I mean, you probably could've guessed."

"Sure, but. At the time...have you ever done something that you could immediately go back and start over? Something where you don't have to invest too much, and you can just quickly go back and start again when you make a mistake?"

"Dude. Is that seriously how you saw the loops?"

Ryan shrugged, grimacing a little. "I had no idea how it worked at first. I thought there was no cost. By the time I realized what was happening, I'd already spawned so many worlds that I thought a few more wouldn't hurt."

"Fuckin'...damn. Well. I guess we've got a lot of Zekes to contend with, huh?" Zeke muttered under his breath.

Ryan clicked his tongue. "Hey, look on the bright side. I'm trapped in this hell with you."

"Oh, great. Two against a billion, instead of one against a billion. Huge improvement."

"It's not a billion. Just a couple thousand."

"*Just* a couple thousand."

Ryan looked at Zeke. Zeke gave Ryan a look back.

The first of the dark-armored figures crawled out of the lights and raced at them. Turning to face them, Zeke and Ryan lifted their blades and claws, ready to fight.

The lights the armored figures had left behind darkened, then faded away. Zeke's eyes widened. *Each light represents a Zeke? Then I only have to fight...*

He looked around him, taking in all the multitude of lights that shone in all directions. He pressed his lips together. *Right. I only have to fight that many.*

One of the dark-armored Zekes rushed at him, and Zeke snapped his eyes back to the fight. He charged to meet them, opening his mouth. The other Zeke also opened his mouth, and the two of them ran toward one another, jaws open.

Zeke noticed the trajectory of his strike, noticed the trajectory of the other one's strike, and internally sighed. *You know, I never considered the downslides of fighting mouth-first until now. I wonder how many people bite their clone in the mouth when they're fighting? I've got to be the first in that particular weird-ass situation, right?*

Their jaws clashed. Resisting the urge to flinch, Zeke bit down instead, relying on his skills and Allen's STR to overpower the other Zeke. With a horrible crunching sound, he smashed through bone and bit the other Zeke's face open. Blood gushed out. The other Zeke tried to retreat, but Zeke caught him by the shoulder and bit deeper, chewing into his skull. After another few **Devour**s, the Zeke went limp.

There was no time to finish eating him. The next Zeke closed in on him, striking toward his spine. Zeke tossed him aside just in time to bat the new Zeke aside. They exchanged hand blows. The new Zeke's hands were sharp as blades, and sliced ruts in Zeke's arm armor, but unlike Zeke, he didn't have hand mouths.

Zeke grimaced as pain burst from his arms. He spun his wrists around and slammed his hand-mouths into the other Zeke's wrists. Activating **Devour,** he bit through the other Zeke's wrists. The other Zeke screamed, staring at his severed hands, and Zeke quickly finished him off.

Another Zeke darted in to fill the gap before that Zeke hit the ground. This one shone, his body covered in a metallic luster. He punched Zeke in the gut before he could react, and Zeke stumbled back, all the air rushing out of him. The metallic Zeke lifted his fist to continue the pounding, but Zeke threw his hands up and caught it with all his strength. He gasped a breath, unable to do anything but stave off the Zeke's punch for a moment.

Bam! With his other fist, the metallic Zeke struck a blow to his solar plexus. Zeke wheezed. He held onto the metallic Zeke's fist with all his strength, but his whole body trembled, losing power. *Dammit! I can't—I can't stop both fists. I need more stats, dammit!*

Another Zeke darted in. This one hadn't transformed, but he did carry a fearsome blade. He drew back, readying a slash with both hands.

Oh, fuck. I don't know if I can take that hit.

Subordinate Mia has shared her DEF.
Subordinate Domi has shared her DEX.
Subordinate Erica has shared her SPR.
Subordinate Sparkles has shared his STR.

Subordinate Allen has shared his STR.
Subordinate Link level up! You can now stack Subordinate
stats on top of your base stats!

Strength flowed into Zeke. His armor thickened, and the metallic Zeke's punches no longer took all the wind out of him. He shoved the metallic Zeke back easily. Startled, the metallic Zeke stumbled toward the blade-wielding Zeke. The blade-wielding Zeke struggled to stop his sword, but it was too late. It smashed into the metallic Zeke, scoring a deep mark in his side.

Before either of them could recover, Zeke used his newfound speed and strength to close in on them. He snatched the blade-wielding Zeke's throat in his hand-mouth and tore out his larynx. At the same time, he lunged with his head and, using all his STR and SPR, **Devour**ed the metallic Zeke's neck straight out of existence. A metallic head clonked to the ground beside him.

The kills bought Zeke a moment's respite. He caught his breath and scanned the battlefield. More Zekes closed in. Most of them were monstrous humanoids, with some variant on his armor—it had no tendrils, or more tendrils, or spikes, or a metal coating, but the theme remained the same. A few remained completely human, either un-Transformed or Trans-form-less. One or two had completely lost their human semblance. One in particular oozed along the ground, vital organs floating deep in a semitransparent goop.

Zeke grimaced. "That one took the liquefy ability I had the option to take way back, didn't it? Glad he survived…I guess. I'm not sure if he is."

He backed away. His shoulders struck Ryan's, and the two of them exchanged a glance.

"I've got two, you?" Ryan asked.

"I thought you couldn't kill me," Zeke returned.

Ryan scoffed. "Sure. Plenty of these I couldn't kill run one, or two, or twenty. I got better, believe it or not."

"Right. I think...uh, three, four for me? Somewhere in that range," Zeke said.

Ryan smirked. "I've killed five."

"Blah, blah, blah," Zeke muttered, rolling his eyes at Ryan. Running forward, he gave the metallic head a swift kick and sent it flying into the gut of the nearest Zeke. He flew backward, colliding into the Zekes behind him, and for a moment, they all piled up together. "Why are they all coming to kill me, anyway?"

"Fucked if I know. Because you're standing by me, maybe?"

Zeke gave him a look. "Good luck, I'm out."

"Oh, hey."

He grinned. "A joke, it's a joke." Turning back to the crowd, he lifted his fists as they closed in. "Let's get back to it."

They parted once more, rushing toward the mob of Zekes.

79
ZEKE CENTRAL

Zeke tore throats. He punched guts. He kicked balls. There was nothing fair or particularly coordinated about his fighting style, but then again, neither were his opponents particularly coordinated. None of them had ever learned to fight properly, so they fought like animals, vicious, no holds barred, to the death. Blood slicked the immaterial floor around them, finally giving shape to the invisible thing. One after another, the light sheafs dimmed, and one after another, Zeke bodies piled up at Zeke's feet. He began to feel full, his stomach barely able to take it, but he pressed on anyway. Every now and again, one of the other Zekes would activate Absorb, and relieve the pressure a bit.

There was no level up chime. No message. And yet, his level climbed. He felt it in his **Devour**s, in his armor, in the weight of his punch and the speed of his kick. There was no time to allocate stats, but neither did the System bother him with a menu. He **Devour**ed. Zekes fell. His body grew stronger, on and on.

A pile of bodies grew at his feet. He'd always wondered about that when he'd read accounts of ancient battles. Where would the warrior stand? Why would people keep rushing him? And here he was, in the midst of it, blood and gore all around him. He stood on the bodies because there was nowhere else to stand. The Zekes kept rushing him because leaving him alive was not an acceptable option. They climbed the bodies of those who fell before them, slipping on the gore, **Devour**ing what they could, neither honor nor humanity in their battle.

Zeke's awareness slipped as the hours ground on. Sometimes he fought, fully aware of his actions, battling with all his strength. Sometimes, he moved on autopilot, his limbs acting on their own. Sometimes, he lost himself to his Concept, nothing but a ball of Hunger, **Devour**ing every scrap of flesh he could reach. And his opponents were the same; half mad, going mad, or gone, they clawed and bit, slashed and bashed, smashed into him and launched projectiles at his head. There was nothing in those moments. Nothing left of Zeke at all. Just the battle, and the Hunger, and his horrible, horrible new instincts.

Ryan flitted about the battlefield like a wraith. He appeared for a fleeting second to deliver a knife strike, then vanished again, only to reappear somewhere else. He no longer fought his own battles but fought around Zeke. Weakening the ones who drew too close. Darting in when one was about to land a vital blow to block, attack, or hinder. He stayed out of Zeke's reach. In his fleeting moments of clarity, Zeke felt immense gratitude toward Ryan for that. If Ryan had drawn too close, he would have doubtlessly met the same fate as all the others. In the state Zeke was in, he rarely maintained the ability to tell friend from foe.

Nor did he try to. The battle was too long, the toll to high, the fight too hard. He had to attack everything that entered his reach because if he waited the split second to tell the difference between another Zeke and Ryan, it would be his end. If not for the stats his friends had shared, he would have been dead long ago.

Subordinate Timmy has shared his DEX.
Subordinate Sara has shared her SPR.
Subordinate Heather has shared her DEF.
Subordinate Olivia has shared her STR.

One after another, all of them reached out to him. Giving him extra strength. More power than his own stats alone. Zeke blocked another Zeke's blow easily. The other Zeke glared at him, huge muscles bulging. Without a word, Zeke tore those muscles apart with his teeth. Relying on his own stats wasn't enough. All these Zekes had done that—rely on their own power. They'd raised their stats as high as they could, in whatever time Ryan had given them. But they hadn't had Subordinates willing to trust them with their stats. They didn't have the supplemental STR, and DEX, and everything else that Zeke had, thanks to his Subordinates. Over and over again, they confronted Zeke with that reality: he couldn't win this battle alone. They had all tried to, and they had all failed. Only he had come this far with a team. Only he had brought everyone along to the end of the game. Not physically, no. But in spirit.

He tore another Zeke's neck out and chewed it down. His body was drenched in his opponents' blood. The cracks in his armor were gummy with viscera. He swallowed with effort, his seemingly bottomless stomach full for the first time in forever. From the peak of the dead Zekes' bodies, he gazed down, exhausted.

He stood alone. Alone, save Ryan. All the light sheaves had extinguished, except for one.

Zeke took a deep breath. He wavered where he stood. His whole body trembled with adrenaline. His muscles ached from exertion, his jaw weary. He stumbled down to the floor and slipped, almost back into the bodies. The ground was a macabre ice skating rink, slicked with fresh blood and riddled with limbs. He gazed at it, barely able to process what had happened.

I did that. I did.

I Devoured all the other Zekes. I ate them all. I'm the only one to remain. The only—

"Hello, Zeke."

Zeke whirled. Ryan materialized a distance behind him, watching the newly approaching figure warily.

A final Zeke walked toward them. He smiled, spreading his hands. Not transformed. Not armed. Dressed in ordinary clothes, without a scrap of armor in sight.

Zeke backed away instinctively. The tendrils at the back of his neck stood on end. "Who are you?"

"I'm the first," the Zeke said. "I'm the only real Zeke. You're all fragments of me. Even you."

Behind Zeke, Ryan startled. "That's not...Zel was..."

"Zel thought he was. Many of these Zekes thought they were the first. I watched them all be born. Here, in this darkness, I waited, watching as every world came to life. Helpless to stop it. To stop...*them.*"

"How? You— How did you get here?"

The final Zeke nodded at Ryan, a beneficent smile on his face. He waved ever so slightly toward Zeke. "I'm not the only one to have attempted to take your skills, no? I've seen other Zekes intersect before. Land in one another's world and wreak havoc. When you left my world behind, I took your Regression. I activated it in a misguided attempt to follow you, but I landed here instead. Maybe my concept wasn't fully developed yet. Maybe the System still wasn't at its full power. Whatever happened, I was marooned here. And I've lived here, watching all of you, through all those lifetimes of yours in the loop."

"But that's not..." Ryan's voice faded.

"The System's been getting stronger?" Zeke asked. *If it's an Apocalypse, that makes a lot of sense.*

"Slowly but steadily. It's hard to fulfil a concept like System. They use their skill once, and from there on out, how are they supposed to gain points? On my loop, all the skills were much weaker. Ryan, you must have noticed it—how skills were growing stronger with time."

Ryan grimaced. "I regressed in power every time I leveled down. After the first run, I-I had to start from zero, so it was hard to tell. I thought it was on me. That I was having bad runs. That my first run was lucky."

"That it was a skill issue?" Zeke asked.

Ryan gave him an eye roll.

Zeke turned to the other Zeke. "What do you want? You didn't have to reveal yourself. I would've assumed that the final light was our world, not...the last world that belongs to someone else."

"Ah, right. These lights...they have an end, no? They're all failed worlds. Or in the eyes of the true apocalypse...successes." His expression darkened. He gazed intently at Zeke.

"W-what?" Zeke asked, a little disconcerted.

"The other Zekes knew it was suicide. That this was their final stand. Oh, they all fought, don't get me wrong, but no one expected to win. Maybe some convinced themselves they'd get lucky. I suspect most didn't. After all, you're the first one to ever reach Level 150. Hell, thanks to Ryan, we were lucky to leave the dome. Our deaths were a necessary sacrifice, and our last gift to you."

"Gift?" Zeke asked.

The first Zeke nodded. "A gift. Our levels, our power. Take them. Grow stronger. And overthrow the true root cause."

"The real apocalypse. The one that speaks in all caps and

handed out Concepts. Not the System, but the thing that gave the System life," Zeke said.

The other Zeke nodded. He smiled at Zeke. "I wanted you to know. So, you wouldn't be burdened by guilt. We wanted someone to win, and that someone was you. So please. Feel no regret and take our strength to the final battle."

"Then...what about you?" Zeke asked.

The first Zeke gave him an enigmatic smile. There was some pain in it, some regret, but no fear. He stepped forward. "I'm the first Zeke. I'm the weakest version of all of us. It was never in the cards for me to lead this fight. Devour me. Become the true Zeke. The only Zeke. And go forth."

"I..." Zeke hesitated. He backed away. *I don't understand. Why? Why did this have to happen? Why was everyone willing to sacrifice their lives? For me? They're putting all their hopes on me? But I'm just blundering through the same as anyone. I don't have any particular skill, or ability, just a good Concept and a few nice skills. That's all. Anyone could have—*

"I know what you're thinking. Anyone could have become the main Zeke, right? But you did. So stop worrying about it, and come over here and finish the job already. Kill the last side world. Merge the worlds back together, and make them yours," Zeke declared.

"Is that how this works?" Ryan questioned.

The other Zeke just smiled.

Zeke looked around him. At the dark hanging lights, and the single one remaining. The one that also came to an end. It stretched into the distance, but just like all the other lights, it had an edge. A border. It wasn't infinite, but merely a little more finite. He frowned.

Something feels off about this. About all of it. I don't—or rather, I didn't feel any desperation or giving up in the Zekes I fought. Sure, maybe they all fully committed to trying to be Zeke prime, or whatever this guy is trying to sell, but I doubt it.

They were vicious. Hungry. They wanted to win as much as I did and didn't hold anything back. They fought like the idiots we are, putting their whole heart into it. And if any of them had won, they wouldn't have hesitated to Devour me. Just as I didn't hesitate to Devour them.

He eyed the final Zeke. His eyes flitted up and down the boy's body. He wore the same clothes Zeke had on the first day of the Apocalypse, the same worn old jeans and T-shirt. He wore his hair the same way. Even his shoes, the shoes Zeke had abandoned in the Coffee Apocalypse right out the gate, were exactly as they had been on that first day.

Exactly. That's it. That's what's wrong. Zeke backed away. He put his hand up, protecting Ryan. He activated **Hands-Free Calling.** *That isn't me, Ryan. That isn't a me. That's something else.*

Something else? What makes you say that?

He's me from day one. Exactly the way I was on day one. I lost my sneakers that same day. My shirt got drenched in blood and torn. Hell, didn't you say it yourself? I usually pick up some kind of Shirt Apocalypse and wear a dumb Oxford for half the dome. Half the other Zekes were wearing the dumb thing.

Ryan cut a look at Zeke. He raised his brows. *Holy shit, you're right. I didn't even notice.*

Besides, he talks like a preacher, not like me.

I mean, he has had a long time in here to, you know, mature.

Yeah, mature. Like you did. Maturing like milk left in the sun.

Harsh, and yet, fair.

Zeke nodded. Returning to the subject of the conversation, he added, *Whatever this thing is, it wants us to have our guards down, and it wants me to Devour it—or so it says.* Even as he spoke to Ryan, his thoughts straightened out, connecting the dots. Zeke's eyes widened as it came to him. *But if it really wanted to be*

Devoured, it would've rushed into the mob. I wouldn't even have noticed. I would have Devoured anything. This thing...it doesn't want to Devour me. It wants me alone. Me, and not any other Zeke.

To teleport you somewhere? Regress you? What does it want? Maybe it wants to Devour you, Ryan murmured, half to himself.

Zeke shook his head. *I don't know. But we shouldn't get close.* Quietly, he slipped one hand behind his back and activated his bow and arrow skill.

A suspicion glimmered in the depths of his mind. A possibility he didn't want to admit to himself, much less give voice to. He held it in, quietly, eyeing the man. *He could be—*

"What's the wait? Hurry up. You can't end this as you are," the thing pretending to be the other Zeke said, spreading his arms wide.

Ready? Zeke asked.

On three, Ryan agreed.

Three. Two. One.

Ryan hurled his knife at the figure at the same time Zeke launched an arrow. They hurtled toward the smiling man.

His smile never once shifted. His hands didn't lower from where they were, spread out to either side of him. The weapons struck an invisible shield in front of him and fell to the earth. Zeke's gold arrow fizzled out. Ryan's knife vanished, returning to Ryan's hand a moment later.

The Zeke lowered his hands. His smile turned vicious, his eyes malignant slits. He shook his head. "You couldn't make it easy, could you?"

80

NOT ZEKE

"You couldn't make it easy, could you?"

As the man spoke, his voice changed from Zeke's lighthearted tone to a dark, vicious tone. His form shifted. The façade of Zeke melted away, revealing the man beneath. He wore white, all white. Simple clothes made from fine cloth, the kind of simple that only the wealthy could afford. His skin turned pale, almost paper pale, deathly pale. And his eyes went cold.

"What are you?" Ryan asked.

The man chuckled. He waved his hand, and the scenery changed. Whiteness replaced the color, a calm, white box forming around them. "Guess."

"The Apocalypse?" Ryan tried.

A mean grin spread across his face. "Perhaps."

"No. He's not," Zeke said abruptly. He narrowed his eyes. "The System?"

The man laughed. "Perhaps."

No. Not that, either. He doesn't strike me as someone who's had a whole lot of control. Nor does he have the System's lazy can't-do-it-I'm-busy attitude. But he knows too much. He knows about the

System. He knows too much about how it levels. He's something...
adjacent to it. Something... "Maybe...more like an Administrator?"

The man's eyes widened, just a hair. Zeke startled. "Really?
Huh. Guess you expected to have...like, leadership powers, and
not to be treated like a web admin for a lazy System?"

"I didn't know how the System was going to interpret it
when I picked. I didn't even know what I was picking," the man
defended himself.

"Picked a shit Concept and got dumped in the space
between? Sucks to suck, man," Ryan said, chuckling.

The man's face twisted, contorting with rage. A moment
later, he repressed it. "And yet, I have still existed here for all
that time. Here, alone, growing stronger. There is nothing I
cannot do. Give up."

Zeke frowned. A trickle of anxiety wandered into his gut,
but at the same time, he scoffed at himself. *Yeah, sure. If he really*
could do anything, we'd be dead right now. He wanted me close to
him for a reason.

The arrow...the knife. Zeke's eyes widened. "Ryan, watch out.
He—I'm guessing here, but I think he has administrative
control over the area immediately around him."

"You don't know anything," the man said, his eyes
narrowing to slits.

"Wait, hold up. I want to probe the whole web-admin-for-
the-System thing. Did you have to moderate its requests?
Handle the traffic when users asked for new skills? How did
that work?"

The man's nose crinkled. He spat. "It was thankless and
purposeless work. I hated it. That fucking lazy ass System
didn't want to do anything, so I was stuck pulling all the
weight—"

Abruptly, he regained his composure. "Perhaps. Something
like that."

Zeke and Ryan exchanged a glance. *I wonder if he's the final barrier between us and the System. But...if he has absolute control of the space around him, how do we attack? If we get close, he'll have absolute control over us. Any projectiles will bounce off. Our ranged abilities will get blocked, and...*

Our ranged abilities...

Huh.

Zeke stepped forward. This time, it was his turn to offer his open hands to the man. "Why not let us through? You don't like the System. Let us go have a nice little talk with it. We'll even see if we can negotiate overtime pay for you, or something."

"If I would, I could. My Concept is—" The man's face glitched. His demeanor changed abruptly. "—I would never dare. I am the Administrator. If you want to access the System directly, you have to go through me."

Zeke's brows raised. *I'm not the only one who's getting eaten by his Concept, huh?* "Jeez. Sucks, man. I know how that feels."

"Know how what feels? You couldn't fathom my emotions, you petty user."

Ryan grimaced. "Man. I feel like I'm in a 1980s, 90s era movie set inside a computer."

"Yeah, like the air should be kind of milky and everything should be blue, and like, maybe we get to ride really cool neon bikes?" Zeke suggested.

"Yeah. That one."

"Are you mocking me?" the man asked, suspicious.

"Yeah, but we're also pitying you. We feel bad for you, man. It sucks to suck. Dunno what to say," Zeke said, shaking his head.

"You understand *nothing*." The man strode forward evenly. Behind him, the wall closed in.

Zeke glanced over his shoulder. The wall of the white room the man had created drew close behind them as well, boxing them in toward the man's absolute control. He bit his lip. *This is going to come down to the wire. If I'm wrong, we're fucked.*

Beside him, Ryan vanished, only to appear pressed against the ceiling a moment later. He dropped to the floor, landing beside Zeke with a thump. His expression remained cool, but a hint of tension shone in his voice. "I can't teleport out."

"I've **Isolated** you. There's no escape. You will approach me, and you will die," the man said simply.

"Yeah, about that." Zeke glanced over his shoulder, then took one final step forward. He reached toward the man.

[Ranged Devour]

The man laughed. "You fool. That will never wo..." His words caught. Blood ran down his chin. He staggered, his brows furrowing. "Hurt. That hurts." He touched his chin and looked at his bloody fingers. "I-I'm hurt?"

Zeke shrugged. "It was a bit of a long shot, but it was this or try to Devour my way out of your Isolation. I figured you controlled everything around you, but what about inside you? I mean, conceptually, right? An Administrator doesn't have absolute control over themselves. No one does."

The man blinked at Zeke disbelievingly. He fell to his knees. His eyes flickered.

For a moment, clarity shone through. He met Zeke's eyes. "Thank you."

And then he went limp. The white room faded. They were back in the room with the extinguished lights, but now, even the last one was dark.

Zeke ran a hand over the back of his head. He pursed his lips. "That one...that one didn't feel good."

"Yeah. Well. We're all victims of the System, man," Ryan drawled like an old-fashioned rocker.

Zeke glanced at him. With some effort, he managed a grin. "Let's go stick it to the System, huh?"

Ryan nodded back. "Let's."

Zeke lifted his hand. His hand-mouth gripped the fabric of reality again, this time more easily with his boosted stats. He tore, opening a hole in this strange layer, and peeling back the final one. *Or at least, what I hope is the final layer.*

He stepped through the gap, Ryan close by his side, and found himself in a familiar space. Too familiar, almost. He blinked, lost. *What? How? Huh?*

"Whoa, hey! You can't come in here!"

81

CAN'T COME IN

"Whoa, hey! You can't come in here!"

Stepping out from behind Zeke, Ryan clicked his tongue. "Too late, here we are. Whoops."

Zeke stared, struck dumb. At last, he managed, "The hell...?"

They stood in a cozy bedroom. Plush, dirty carpet stretched underfoot, with crumbs, broken toys, crushed-in crayons, and wrappers scattered all around, plus more stains, marks, and globs that Zeke didn't care to identify. Four walls were painted a pleasant pastel lavender. A window overlooked a quiet street lined with trees and the house on the other side of it, a mini fridge sitting just under the window. To Zeke's left, an unmade, messy bed lay, and to his right, a desk long due a cleaning huddled against the wall, complete with the requisite desk lamp and out-of-date laptop. There, a teenaged girl sat, her hair a mess, dressed in comfortable, loose, soft clothes. She lowered her headphones, startled, and stared at them from the other side of thick glasses. "What—what are you doing here? You can't come here. You can't! No one can."

Oh. Not like, "I don't want you in here," but "I've never seen someone enter." Zeke looked around him. Aside from the quickly healing gap in reality, the room had no doors. Only the window, gazing out at the daylight outside.

The girl scrambled upright, pulling her shirt back up over her shoulder to hide her bra strap. "Uh, uh, what the hell? What do you want?"

"Calm down. We're not looking for you. We're looking for the System," Ryan said.

Zeke looked at Ryan. "Ryan, I think, uh...I think we found it."

The girl raised her hand. "That's right. Present."

"What the fuck?" Ryan asked, startled. "This...*this* is the System?"

The girl coughed. "I prefer she/her, thanks."

Well. It certainly explains the lazy vibes the System gave off. This place is a mess. Zeke looked around him, eyeing the overflowing trash bin and the filthy carpet, the rumpled sheets and the messy desk. He hesitated, then nodded at the girl. "Um. Can you, like. Turn it off?"

"The System?" she asked.

"Yeah."

"Can you turn off your Concept?"

"Er, no."

She nodded. "Yep. Same. Besides, I'm not sure you want me to turn it off. I'm the only thing standing between us, and..." She cast a quick glance at the window but quickly looked away as though she were afraid to see what awaited outside.

Zeke walked to the window and peered out, gazing up at the sky and down at the ground. Ryan raised a questioning brow. He shrugged. *I don't see anything weird.*

"A-anyway. Don't kill me, please. I didn't do anything wrong. I'm just trying to make the best of a bad situation, okay? Just like all of us."

"You run the System," Zeke pointed out.

She rolled her eyes. "Yeah, 'cause I read too many K-novels

and made a bad pick, okay? Not because I'm evil, or something. Just like you. I got handed my Concept, and I did my best to handle it."

"Did you make that guy outside your Admin?" Ryan asked, a bit of an edge to his voice.

"No. He picked a shitty Concept and got shit handed to him. I didn't even know he was out there until recently. Thought he was, like, an automatic task function in the System. I apologized to him, but of course that wasn't enough. And by then, he was pretty far gone..." She shrugged helplessly. "There's nothing I can really do. Weird shit is happening left, right, and center, and I'm the one scrambling to put it all together at the last second, before it all collapses. I mean, this whole thing is hanging on by threads. I'm tippity-tappin' my little fingers to death trying to make it keep working, and it still crashes sometimes. Sometimes, I have to do it all manually. Talk about hell on earth. I have to *talk* to *people,* can you imagine?"

Zeke raised his brows. "You seem pretty okay talking to us."

"Easy when you're right there. You misunderstand something, we can have a little chat and clear things up. Waaaay different when you're on the other side of reality and have a character-limit on your responses. That's so hella stressful, you know? I've gotta sound polite and reasonable to people in life and death situations while handing out bonuses, coming up with skills, and giving out stats to a thousand people at the same time. I only recently unlocked free-text messages."

"Wait...you have to unlock things? But you *are* the System," Ryan said, lost.

She shrugged at him. Her shirt slipped off her shoulder again, and she pulled it back up. "I don't know what to tell you. It's just my Concept, bro. I'm the System, sure, but that just means I'm the one translating the bullshit your Concept puts out into neat and tidy skills you can understand. Isn't that nice of me? But yeah, I do still have a system, and levels, and shit. That's me making sense of the bullshit my own Concept is giving me. I don't know. It's complicated, man. I'm just out here doing my best, and everyone's screaming a thousand different criticisms at me all at once. More skills, less skills, more bonuses, just give it to me now, I don't want any of this, like it's my fault, when I'm just the same as all the rest of you."

"Your Administrator said that, too. That he was a victim like us. Before he tried to kill us, that is," Zeke pointed out.

She put her hands up and rolled her eyes. "Brooooo, calm down. I'm like, a hundred pounds of skin and bones, and you're a fuckin' chow monster of ultimate destruction. I don't have offensive skills. Even if I turned off your System, you'd still benefit from your Concept and its progression. I'm like, the opposite of a threat."

"Fucking chow monster of ultimate destruction," Ryan repeated. He chuckled and shook his head.

Zeke narrowed his eyes. "It wasn't *that* funny."

"It's what he is, isn't it? It's what he is," the girl said, looking over her shoulder at Ryan. "Mister Loopy-doopy-can't-get-it-right-poopy."

"Mister—? Could you repeat that? Like, a few times. Really loud," Zeke requested. He grinned deviously at Ryan.

Ryan cleared his throat, suddenly all business. "So, you've been watching us, this whole time?"

The girl shrugged. "Can't stop won't stop. But like, literally." She spread her hands, and from her shitty old laptop, a thousand screens filled the walls of the room around them. Each one showed a perspective of Zeke, of Ryan, of one of Zeke's subordinates or the other survivors. "It's my job, you know?"

Zeke pursed his lips. *I'm starting to feel like this girl isn't the final boss I thought the System would be.* "Speaking of, what's your name? I feel bad calling you 'the girl' in my head all the time."

The girl looked at him. Her eyes went empty, and she tilted her head a little. In a drone, she said, "The System doesn't need a name."

Zeke backed away a step instinctively. Ryan jolted, calling his knife to his hands.

She snapped back to life. Seeing the two of them standing over her threateningly, she jolted and threw her hands up. "Whoa, whoa, guys, chill. What happened? Did I say something? I swear I'm not a threat, I'm really not," the girl insisted.

"No. I think you're right. You aren't a threat," Zeke said. *Even if I Devour her, that won't stop this. It'll only stop the System, not the Apocalypse. There's more. Something else. Another layer.* He nodded at her. "But if you aren't a threat, then what is? Is there anything we can help with?"

Fear flashed across her face. She glanced at the window again. "N-no. Nothing." She swallowed visibly and forced her usual cheerful expression back on. "Nothing you can do anything about, anyway! So just, y'know, chill here and enjoy the end of the world with air conditioning and a mini fridge. It's got snacks in it." She paused. Turning, she eyed it warily. "It always does."

Zeke watched her gaze, and suddenly, he realized the horror of the situation she'd found herself in. Locked in a room. No doors, no exits. Something outside the window that terrified her. And yet, provided for. Given a bed, a desk, a laptop. Space to complete her task, but no more. No escape. No outlet. No alternatives. She was kept.

Like a pet.

Outside, lightning flashed. Zeke startled, turning. It had been clear moments ago, but now the sky brimmed with dark clouds. Lightning flashed between them, and thunder rolled out, sharp and clear, closing in on them with every passing second.

The girl jolted. She shivered where she sat. "Oh no. Uh oh. It's noticed you. It's noticed you. I didn't do it! I didn't let them in! They came in on their own!" She dove into the bed and pulled the covers over her head, shivering like a small child hiding from a storm.

Zeke and Ryan exchanged a glance. Zeke stepped toward the window. He undid the latch and pushed at it, trying to lift the lower pane, then shifting and trying to lower the upper pane.

Stuck. Completely motionless. As if it were one pane, and not a two pane window at all.

He swallowed. *Somehow, I'm not surprised.*

"So?"

"Won't open," Zeke said, glancing at Ryan.

Ryan shrugged. "Then make it."

Zeke glanced at the window, then shrugged. He pulled back his fist. "Here goes nothing."

The girl peeked out from under the comforter. "No, no, don't do it, don't do it—" Her voice pitched up, escalating to a whine, nothing but fear and horror.

Crash! Zeke punched through the window.

82

THROUGH THE WINDOW GLASS

rash! Zeke's fist shot through the window. Glass shattered, flying toward him rather than away, in defiance of all physics. Zeke lifted his arms to protect himself against the sharp edges.

The girl ducked low, her head pressed against the bed. "It wasn't me. I didn't do it. I said nothing. It wasn't me. I was safe, I was safe, dammit! I was safe!"

The glass fell. Zeke lowered his arms and stared.

Everything up until now had been unbelievable. The pure darkness. The sheaves of light. The Administrator and the System. But this, somehow, this took it a step further. Not because he couldn't recognize what awaited outside the window, but because he did.

A blue orb, floating in a diamond-studded void. In the distance, a tiny but intense ball of fire burned. Closer, orbiting around the orb, a godforsaken pale rock circled.

The Earth. The Sun. The Moon.

"What the hell," Zeke muttered.

"No kidding," Ryan agreed.

The girl grimaced. "I told you not to. I *told* you. I even erased your memories, but no..."

Zeke glanced back. "So, uh, what was so scary about this? I mean, it's scary shit, but the oxygen doesn't seem to be escaping and we're not decompressing, so I'm guessing there's some kind of invisible airlock-pressure lock skill going on here? Or something? In which case...are you afraid of space, or something? Claustrophobic? Or no, that's tight spaces. What's that other one called. The opposite of claustrophobic. Agoraphobic! Are you agoraphobic?"

The girl hunkered in her bed, muttering repeatedly to herself.

Ryan cleared his throat. "I don't think she's gonna help us out much here."

Zeke waggled his brows. "Did she ever?"

"Oooh, zinger," Ryan said, shooting finger guns back at Zeke.

They fell silent. Sobering, they gazed out the window again.

"How do we get back?" Zeke wondered.

"Fucked if I know."

He frowned. "I really thought there'd be...you know, something. Something to be scared of. I mean, space *is* scary, but it's not, like, hide-under-the-bedsheets-screaming scary."

"Is there something we're not seeing? Or something we can't see?" Ryan peered up and down, searching all around them, but shook his head. "I'm not seeing anything."

"Me either, but...it feels off. There's something wrong about this whole thing," Zeke commented. He put a hand on his chin thoughtfully, squinting into the void.

"What do you mean?" Ryan asked.

"It's...I don't know. Space is big, you know? But it's super empty out there. Isn't there supposed to be a shit-ton of space junk up here? Old dead satellites, and stuff like that. Even the live satellites were supposed to be getting pretty numerous. But there's nothing. Or, well, I can't see anything. It just...it feels off. Like there's something just a little bit weird about it."

Ryan squinted. "I mean, we are pretty far away. Maybe we just can't see the satellites. I'm gonna go see if I can break the walls down and get out somewhere else."

"Maybe," Zeke said, and then the darkness shifted.

He jolted. "Did you see that?"

Ryan turned back. "See what?"

"See—" Zeke gestured. *How do I describe what I saw?* "See space moving. It kind of..." he wiggled in place. "Shivered. Like jiggled around."

"Uh, sure. Did you eat too much? Are you seeing things?" Ryan asked.

"I'm not...come on, Ryan. Look. It did it once, it'll do it again," Zeke said adamantly.

Ryan rolled his eyes. "And this is better than trying to break down the walls?"

"What do you think that'll even do? We're floating in space."

"I dunno. The window seems like a portal to me. Why wouldn't the walls be portals, too? Or not-portals, in which case we can walk away and forget about our space adventure."

"Ryan, come on. Look, at least. It's weird. It really is weird."

"Yeah, yeah." Ryan walked over to the window and looked out.

The space around the Earth moved again. It drew back, as if a curtain, or perhaps a sleeve. A pale hand appeared in the dark. The hand reached for the Earth, as if plucking an apple from a tree.

Ryan jumped back. "Holy fuck."

Zeke's jaw dropped. "How are we supposed to fight that?"

Abruptly, the girl sat up. She looked at them. "I know a way."

"What?"

"Eat me."

83
EAT ME

Zeke spread his hands to the sky. "How many people are going to tell me to eat them today?"

"At least two, but it's weird it happened twice."

"Thank you, Ryan." Zeke looked at the girl. "How does that help? If I eat you, what does that change?"

"I'm the System," she said, as though it was obvious.

Zeke squinted at her.

She spread her hands, simultaneously rolling her eyes. "I'm *the System*. I'm the means through which its power flows to Earth. It wasn't supposed to happen this way, but it left the whole Apocalypse thing too vague, and so, anyway..." She took a deep breath, visibly composing herself. "The point is, due to my weird-ass choice of Concept, and thanks to Ryan repeatedly reversing the timeline, I am the most powerful Apocalypse of all. I've become the nexus through which all that monster's power flows. The, uh..." she waved her hand, struggling for the word, "you can think of me as the international internet cable of Apocalypse power. Big, thick, the chokepoint through which everything passes."

"And if we sever that point, then..."

"Then, then, well, I'm dead, and I'm not too happy about that, but I'm barely alive anyway. When it realized what had happened, it boxed me away here. To keep me safe. I'm a prisoner. Or...whatever's worse than a prisoner."

"A pet," Zeke offered.

"Pets get walkies and playtime."

"Fair," Zeke allowed.

Ryan lifted a hand. "Wait, hold up. You, uh, you said something about me turning back time allowing you to spread your power?"

"Yeah. Well, you know. In the first loop, my domain was only one dome. But then you turned back time, after my dome had already opened. I had infiltrated the world. And when you turned back time, that thing—the thing that gives us all Apocalypse power—didn't want to weaken its hold. It made an exception—allowed me to keep my expanded Domain. As the loops ground on, I expanded it farther and farther, until it covered the whole Earth," she explained.

"But...I would remember. I can still remember the first loop. Very clearly, even. I—"

She waved her hand. "I can delete memories. And are you so sure you can remember the first loop, Ryan? You've guessed that you've looped anywhere between ten and a hundred, but are you even secure in those numbers? All the Zekes who fought you today came from worlds you created, and not every world spawned a Zeke powerful enough to break through reality. Your mind started slipping a long time ago. You're like me. Already part of the machine, before you even realize what you're doing."

"I'm not—"

"You are. You're weakening the reality of the world by splitting it into so many alternate realities. Or something. I don't get it, but it's part of the *thing*'s plan."

"The Apocalypse's," Zeke offered.

They both looked at him.

"She's the System, so that thing is the Apocalypse. It makes sense, right? System Apocalypse?"

Ryan rolled his eyes. The girl shook her head at him in disappointment. "Try harder, man."

"All right, fine. You come up with a better name."

"Can't. We'll call it the Apocalypse," the girl said easily.

Zeke took a deep breath. He shook his head at her.

The girl gestured, as if to move a heavy object aside. "In any case, back to my original point. You, Zeke, are somehow the Apocalypse present here right now who is least corrupted by the Apocalypse. You at least can still recognize the difference between you and your Concept, whereas Ryan and I have *become* our Concept, at least in part. I want that horrifying thing dead no matter what. If you have to eat me, so be it. I'll sacrifice myself to save the world. It's a boring-ass role and I get no enjoyment from it, but what needs doing, needs doing.

"You'll never find another conduit like me, Zeke. If you don't act now, I'm sure the Apocalypse will act to keep me from doing this, giving myself up to you. It makes new rules whenever it remembers I exist, in fact. So. Go ahead." She cocked her head and pointed at her neck. "Go to town."

"I... Look, this doesn't feel right. I've been angry at you for a while, but still, I don't really...I don't want to kill you," Zeke explained.

"What happens to our skills when you die?" Ryan asked, more practically.

"I'm barely me anymore. I don't have a name. I'm a puppet. End my suffering, while I'm still sane enough to realize I'm suffering," she said, staring up at Zeke.

After a moment, she turned to Ryan. "It doesn't matter. My rigid corpse will be forced to complete the same role, I'm sure. Life and death are nothing to that thing. It can bring someone back to life as easily as it can end their life—without a thought. All it needs to do is wipe my mind and resurrect my corpse just neatly enough that I don't go completely 'brains, braaaains,' and it's just as happy as it is right now."

"That seems...that can't be right," Zeke muttered. But even as he said it, his brows furrowed. *But isn't it? How many inanimate objects has the System brought to life? How many dead legends did it revive? I mean, we even had a literal Undead Apocalypse. It clearly does not pause for something as petty as mere death.*

She pointed at him. "You get it. You understand. It's something so far beyond our understanding that it might as well be a god. As far as I'm concerned, that thing can do whatever it wants. Literally anything. At any time."

"Then why hasn't it already corpsified you?" Ryan asked.

The girl shrugged. "Do you deliberately zombifiy an ant? Do you pick a particular bacterium and kill it, then resurrect it because it *might* obey you better? I'm a little bit vital right now, but it still barely knows I exist. It paid attention for long enough to ensure I didn't starve in this shitty little room, and that was it. Period. End of sentence. Unless I do something drastic that actually disrupts its plans, it isn't going to care."

"Like feed all your Apocalypse energy to me," Zeke muttered.

"Like that, yeah. But at that point, we're all hoping it makes you a big enough deal for that thing to care. Because...if it doesn't, if even using its power against it is hopeless...we're fucked. For real."

"There has to be another way," Zeke muttered.

"Does there? Does this really end any other way than with you eating me? Eating the System? You need to become Hunger incarnate if you're going to face that thing. Something beyond human. You've already killed all—almost all the Apocalypses.

You've already consolidated all the versions of yourself. You even ate my Admin."

"Well, yes. I do eat a lot," Zeke allowed.

The girl gestured at him. "In what world did you, the Hunger Apocalypse, storm into my room and not end up eating me? Like, seriously. What was your plan? If you weren't planning to eat me, why did you even come here?"

Zeke licked his lips. "To demand answers."

"And you thought I had them? I know you already suspected there was something beyond me."

"You seemed to know about that 'something beyond.' And, I mean, what can I say? You *did* answer my question." He gestured at the window. "There it is. That thing I was looking for. Right there in front of me."

"Well, okay. You win that one. But my point stands. Any time you run into someone else, the only way that battle ends is with you eating them. I was being completely reasonable to assume you'd eat me, just like you ate all the rest."

Zeke grimaced. "When you put it that way..."

"How else am I supposed to put it?" she asked, exasperated.

Ryan leaned in. "Zeke doesn't like it when you point out that he's crazy."

"Oh. Well, no one does," the girl allowed, nodding.

"I don't—that's not..." Zeke sighed. He shook his head. "Honestly."

"But we're all crazy here. It's fine. You're among friends," the girl reassured him, patting him on the shoulder. The motion jostled her rolly chair, and she spun a full circle, quietly murmuring, "Wheeee."

Zeke gave her a look. *I'm not sure that came off the way you wanted it to.* He sighed. "So you really want me to eat you. You think it's the one way to save the Earth?"

"Well, yeah. Duh. I mean, ideally, you eat me *and* that guy," she said, pointing at Ryan.

Ryan backed away. "I didn't agree to that."

"He's got Dead Man's Switch, anyway," Zeke pointed out.

"I can turn that off," the girl offered.

Ryan's eyes widened. He looked at Zeke. "Don't even think about it."

"I'm not, I'm not. I'm not even sure about eating her," Zeke said, putting his hands up.

"But he has to, Ryan." The girl looked him in the eyes. "You are the looper. You have the power of thousands of loops imbued in your body. You're the second most powerful being in this mess, after me. I'm the System. All the Systems. Every System. I power the whole Apocalypse, basically. If you combine the power both of us have, Zeke might have a chance."

"*Might* have a chance," Ryan grumbled.

"What if we all work together?" Zeke offered. *Seems reasonable to me.*

The girl shook her head. "Individually, none of us pose the slightest threat to that thing. I mean. Look at it." She gestured behind her, to the giant pale hand the size of the Earth.

Zeke grimaced. "I'm not sure that all our powers combined kill that thing."

"Not if we work together, no. But if you get the firehose of that thing's power—me, and the multiverse power multiplier—Ryan, then you might be able to chug enough power to kill it outright."

"Might?" Zeke asked.

The girl shrugged. "No guarantees. I mean. Look at it."

Zeke looked at it. He nodded. "Yeah."

"Does he *have* to eat both of us?" Ryan asked.

The girl nodded emphatically. "I was giving myself up first because it seemed like the easier sell, but yes. He does have to eat you as well. If he doesn't get your power multiplier, and he just gets one universe's System's worth of power..." The girl made a face. She shook her head.

"No good?" Zeke asked, grimacing.

She shook her head again, emphatically this time. "I'm a straw, and that thing is a swimming pool. I'm a dialup internet connection, and that thing's a world-scale server. No good. If you eat us both, then I can tap into Ryan's multiversal connections to draw all the power from all the Systems, and nuke that thing with way more power than it expects, through you, Zeke. We're the chargers, and you're the conduit. Think of it that way."

Zeke gritted his teeth. He glanced at Ryan.

"No." Ryan backed away, shaking his head.

"What if it *is* the only way?" Zeke asked.

"Why are we even listening to her? She's a weirdo who's locked in a room by the System...by the Apocalypse. She can't do anything. How does she know how to kill that thing?"

The girl made a face. "I've run a bunch of numbers, okay? I'm not just talking out my ass. There's math involved here. Math!"

"Yeah? What math? How do you assign values to any of this shit?" Ryan asked.

"Easy. You and I, we're both small infinities, like...like the full list of every whole number. Whole number, right, not fractions. But between one and zero, there's a whole other infinity that's just as large as the list of all whole numbers, more or less. The infinity of fractions. And that exists between every whole number that we list. If you're the infinity of whole numbers, and I'm the infinity between one and zero, then Zeke is the infinity of all numbers, real and imaginary."

"I have no idea what you just said," Zeke muttered.

Ryan shook his head, his brows furrowed.

The girl sighed. She reached under her desk and pulled out a candy jar full of small colored chocolate pieces. "How many chocolates are in that?"

"I don't know," Zeke said.

"Right. It might as well be infinity."

"Well, there's a finite number of—"

"This is an explanation, dimwit. Let me finish."

Zeke shut his mouth and mimed throwing away the key.

"It might as well be infinity," she repeated. Reaching under her desk again, she pulled out a bottle full of sand, about the same size of the candy jar. "How about that? How many grains of sand are in there?"

"Uh...a lot?" Zeke said.

"Right. We aren't going to count them, so it might as well be infinity. But look. Even without counting them, we can say for sure that there's more sand than candies."

Zeke nodded slowly. *I think I'm getting it.*

The girl reached under her desk again and pulled out a fish tank about as wide as the space under her desk and equally as deep. Grunting, she slopped it onto the table. Some of the water sloshed out, spilling toward the candies and the sand. "Now this...this has a certain number of water molecules in it. But we all agree we aren't going to count them, so it might as well be infinity, yes?"

Zeke nodded. "Yep."

"And we all agree, that with a tank this big, and how small water molecules are, that the water tank probably has the largest infinity here, yes?"

"Can't deny that," Zeke said.

The girl wiped her brow and nodded. "So there. That's what I'm suggesting."

"If we mix candies and sand together, we get fish water?" Zeke asked.

The girl threw the sand jar at him. Zeke dodged, chuckling.

"Where'd all that stuff come from?" Ryan muttered, intrigued.

"The thing lets me materialize pretty much anything I want to keep myself sane. I made a gaming computer the first week I was here, then realized I'd have to materialize all the games. I materialized an internet setup, but by then, the web was down...or maybe I just can't reach it from here." She shrugged helplessly. "Threw it under the bed, the piece of garbage. Waste of my time and energy right there."

"That does sound unfortunate," Zeke agreed.

She nodded. "Yeah. *Yeah.*" Staring at the bed for a second, she sighed. Abruptly, she turned back to Zeke. "So? You gonna eat me or what?"

84

THE INFINITY BETWEEN 1 AND 0

Zeke took a deep breath. He threw his hands up. "I don't know! I don't know. It's— Before today, no one ever asked me to eat them, and now everyone's doing it one after the other. I don't even know what to think. I don't know what to do. I don't know."

Ryan crossed his arms. He looked at the girl. "If we, all three of us together, make a fish tank, then how big is that monster compared to that power level?"

The girl grimaced. "I hoped you wouldn't ask that."

"I asked it."

She gestured. "I'm hoping...only as big as this room."

"Only—" Zeke looked at the room, then at the fish tank. It was a large tank, but compared to the room, it was nothing.

"But..." The girl reached out and pushed the tank over. Ryan lunged, but too slow. It smashed to the ground. Water flooded over the carpet. Glass shards flew. Zeke flinched back, startled more than anything.

She looked at the mess, then grinned at them. "But a fish tank can *fuck up* a whole room. A candy jar or some sand in a bottle will make a mess, but it won't fuck the whole room. That takes a fish tank."

"You're pretty decided about this," Zeke commented, eyeing the wet floor.

"Yeah. I've been thinking about it a long time. I think it's the only way we can save reality—" She followed her gaze, and her mouth made an O shape. "You mean the wet carpet."

"Yeah."

The girl waved her hand. The carpet dried. The glass shards vanished. "There you go. Good as new."

"I'm not doing it," Ryan declared abruptly.

"Why not? Don't want to save the world? Oh, right. You did promote from Hero to Apocalypse," the girl said, nodding as if it all made sense.

Ryan shook his head. He backed away, lifting the knife and pointing it at both of them. "I'm not. I want to save the world because I want to live in it. I want to have a good life. There's no point to the world existing if I'm not in it."

"You can't really think that," Zeke said, startled.

"I do. How can you *not* think that? Isn't it weird to think otherwise?" Ryan asked.

Zeke glanced at the planet, then shrugged. "I don't know. I mean, that's everyone. *Everyone*. All the people we know and love, who are all going to die. I think that's worth it."

"Says the guy who's surviving this," Ryan muttered.

Zeke looked him in the eye. "You think I'm surviving this?"

Taken aback, Ryan frowned at him. "Yeah? No one's eating you."

Zeke laughed. He gestured at the window, at the *thing* outside. "Do you really think that if I become something that can battle that monster, that I'll still be able to live a normal life afterwards? Still be able to be human? Still walk around on the planet Earth and talk to people, fall in love, whatever? I mean, come on. You can't really think I'm getting out of this unscathed."

"You won't be dead," Ryan countered.

The girl cleared her throat. "He might be."

They looked at her.

She nodded. "That thing's power...it's fine in small quantities, but in large quantities...I don't know. No one's ever tried what I want to try before. But you have to think—that thing's a huge, reality-defying monster. I'm bootleg siphoning its power away and shoving it all into Zeke. That's not the way people get out of things alive—that is, getting bootleg power shoved into them. It sounds like a great way to die, to me."

"Yeah. So there. We'll all be dead," Zeke said, crossing his arms. He paused a few seconds, then glanced at the girl. "Will I survive long enough to fight that thing?"

She shrugged. "*I* think so. All my calculations indicate that you last long enough to give it a run for its money. You'll have hours, no question about that. It's really at the days-scale where it starts getting a little iffy."

"Oh," Zeke said, sobered a bit. Knowing it in the abstract wasn't so bad, but somehow, hearing it in the concrete made it all hit home. *Days. Once I do this, I'll have days left to live. Not years. Not months. Not even weeks. Days.*

He took a deep breath. *I'm asking Ryan to die right here. I can't balk because I'll die afterwards. That's still hours more than Ryan gets to live.* "Yeah. I-I think it's worth it. Saving the world? Let's do it."

"Why don't we think up another option? One that doesn't leave us all dead," Ryan said, crossing his arms.

Zeke looked at Ryan. "We don't have another option."

"You haven't tried to look for another option," Ryan argued.

Zeke gestured out the window. "Do we have time to wait?"

The girl shook her head. "No. Now that you've won...well,

let's just say it wasn't moving much until you finished off all the others."

Zeke clicked his tongue. "Damn. What does it even want? What does it get out of all this?"

"The same near-infinite energy I'm about to hijack for us?" the girl asked.

"What? I thought we were stealing its energy."

She shook her head, hesitated, then shrugged. "Yes and no? When I say that you, and Ryan, and I all have infinite energy inside us, I do mean that. Something about what we've been doing...maybe consolidating the energy of humanity, or something? But anyway, it's going to take the energy out of us, if we don't use it first. Of course, if it goes according to my plan and hard work, I'll be able to use that link to siphon some of its energy back to us, too. It's complicated. I was really hoping you wouldn't ask questions and would just be gung-ho about this, but here we are."

"You are asking us to put our lives on the line," Zeke pointed out.

"Yeah, should've seen it coming. That was my bad."

Zeke took a deep breath and clapped his hands. "All right. Let's do this."

"No."

They both looked at Ryan.

Ryan brandished his knife. "No. I'll regress again. Reset this whole timeline. We have infinite time to solve this problem. All I need to do is turn back time."

"That's not...did you miss the part where I said that thing is beyond reality? Even if you turn back time, it can turn it forward again. Hell, it might not even bother. Might just cancel your skill," the girl said lazily. She turned around in her chair and cast a bored gaze his direction.

"I don't care." Ryan made an intent expression.

Zeke lunged, calling up his own copy of Regression. "Don't–"

Ryan stood there. Nothing happened. Zeke crashed into him, and they staggered back a few steps.

Ryan blinked. Disbelievingly, he muttered, "It didn't work?"

"Toldja." The girl made intense eye contact with Zeke. She gestured with her head. Opening her mouth, she made biting gestures at Ryan.

Zeke grimaced. *I'd rather talk it out, but...Ryan won't be convinced. There's nothing I can do.* He grabbed Ryan by the shoulders and opened his mouth.

85
TO EAT A FRIEND

Ryan jerked back. Zeke gave him no room to run. He activated **Ranged Devour** and took a deep bite out of Ryan. Ryan shuddered. His eyes locked onto Zeke's, and his lip lifted in disgust. Silently, he mouthed, *I'll never forgive–*

Zeke didn't hesitate. He bit again, and again, until nothing remained. Ryan fell to the ground, what little of him was left. Zeke turned to the girl.

She opened her arms wide, welcoming him. "Come here. Make it quick."

Zeke charged, not thinking about it, not thinking about what he'd done. His heart twisted, aching. He'd killed Ryan. He, himself, had killed his best friend. Even if it was to save the world, Ryan was right. He was unforgivable.

His jaws latched on to soft flesh. The girl didn't struggle or fight. He ate her easily, her flesh sliding down his throat. As she died, she sighed with relief.

He stood there, covered in blood, in that empty room. Zeke looked down at his hands, his whole body trembling. Excitement? Fear? Horror? Relief? He had no idea. Only that he shook, and that he was all alone. So, so alone.

Did it work? Oh, God, please let it work.

Power slammed into him like a sledgehammer. He stumbled forward a step, thrown by it. More power, more than he'd wielded to fight the T-rex with the power grid, more than he'd had charging alongside Erica, more than he'd had with everyone's stats in the battle against the Zekes. He almost puked, burning, over-full, choking on power. *I can't, I have to–burn this off–*

Another blast of power struck him, even stronger than the first. His body shook from the forces surging inside it. His heart raced. Unable to think of anything, anything at all, Zeke went to his go-to to burn power: **Modest Gigantification**.

Instantly, his body surged upward. Taller. Wider. Muscles strengthening as they grew. Bones firming. His head pressed the top of the small room and burst out of it, his shoulders following seconds later. Up and up, surging out of the room and into the void of space.

With his armor on, space barely smarted. He held his breath, then gasped, once, only to find that **Manipulate Aerosols** had gotten there ahead of him. Zeke breathed deep and grew.

On and on, up and up. He kicked his way out of the small room as it passed his waist, still growing. Compared to the monster, he was nothing, but with every passing moment, he drew closer. Larger and larger and larger. He knew his body should be struggling, collapsing, but it kept growing, kept strengthening. Between **Grid**, **Electrify**, **Biogenerator**, and all his other power skills, his body handled the skills automatically, applying them to optimize his growth.

Is that because I won the Apocalypse? Or...I did just eat the System, didn't I.

Yeah, you did.

Zeke startled at the foreign voice in his head. *What the—*

Oh, sorry. You aren't going crazy-not crazier than you already are, anyway. I've got a few last tricks of my sleeve. Last-ditch techniques to cobble together a last few moments of life. For as long as I can, I'll keep helping you. Do everything I can to make your skills flow together. All you have to worry about is the fight.

Thank you.

Thank me after you save the Earth.

Zeke faced the giant figure. It ignored him, continuing its slow reach toward the Earth. Compared to it, he was still a speck, barely the size of an asteroid. He grew on. Moon-sized, then planet-sized. Still small enough to fit int that immense being's palm, but larger than he could imagine. Gazing down at his hand, he struggled to wrap his head around his size. He lifted his hand, and it moved slowly. Not because it moved any slower than it usually did, but because he was so large that even the smallest motion crossed a vastness of space.

The figure turned, taking him in at last. They locked eyes, or rather, Zeke stared at the void where the thing's face should be. Emptiness stared back at him. Aside from the pale hand, all he could make out of the figure was...*nothing.* But it was that nothing that became the figure's defining shape. Wherever the stars failed to shine, wherever the sunlight failed to land—that was where the figure stood.

He flipped it off. "I've fought things with a bigger size-gap before. Come at me, ugly!"

His voice barely escaped the shallow mass of atmosphere around him, but the figure reacted, nonetheless. It turned away from the earth and reached its hand toward him. Two fingers closed in on him, seeking to pinch him away.

"I won't die so easily!" Zeke turned his head up. As the finger closed in on him, he used **Ranged Devour**. The surface of the finger grew slightly pink, as he managed to strip the first layer of skin off, but no more.

Zeke gritted his teeth. He activated **Ranged Devour** again, then again, and then—

Skill Unlocked: [Multi-Devour]

He blinked. *You can do that?*

I'm the System. I can do whatever the fuck I want.

Without hesitation, as the finger continued to close in, Zeke activated **Multi-Devour**. His jaws lurched out of his control, moving at double speed. Devour after Devour sliced into the monster's finger, until, for the first time, he drew blood. A big red drop of it, dangling from the end of the finger.

The figure withdrew their hand. They looked at their finger, something like surprise in their nothingness of a shape.

"That's right. I'm not going to let you get away with this," Zeke challenged it. At the same time, his heart chilled. There was something wrong. Something wrong about that blood.

Nothing was wrong. It's red. Red, like normal blood.

And yet, in the back of his mind, he kept churning, unable to escape the sensation creeping down his spine.

The figure withdrew their hand. This time, they slapped at Zeke. A wall of flesh as large as him rushed toward him, ready to splatter him into interstellar space.

Even as it closed in, Zeke continued to grow. Taller than the hand, first by inches, then head and shoulders. The tiny tidbits he'd sliced from the figure's finger warmed his stomach. They supplemented the power from Ryan and the girl, all mixing to fuel his growth.

I like that. Keep eating whatever that was, the girl said.

Message received. Zeke turned toward the incoming hand. As it struck him, he latched on with hands, feet, and mouth, and dug as deep as his jaws would let him. His main mouth wrapped around the figure's forefinger, and he worked at it with all his strength, struggling to close it. *Bite! Devour! Tear flesh and snap bone!*

With a horrible snap, the bone broke. The soundwave from the snap sent nearby space dust flying, so strong it even buffeted Zeke's atmosphere around him. He slipped backward a little, thrown. *Jeez. Even biting this thing open is no joke.*

Eat that finger! Eat the finger! the girl shouted, almost ravenous.

On it, Boss, Zeke said, mimicking Domi. A pang shot across his chest. *Domi. I'll never get to see her again. Or Mia. Or Erica. Or anyone. None of them. Not one.*

He pushed his sadness away. *But if I win here, they'll all get to live. They, and the whole planet, survives. For that—for that, I'd give anything.*

The figure jerked their hand back, wrenching it away from Zeke. Zeke let it go. He grabbed the severed finger and started eating it from both ends, using his hands and mouth at the same time. Flesh, blood, skin and bone, all vanished into his stomach. With each bite, he grew stronger, larger. Now, he stood about as large as the thing's forearm. The size of a newborn baby.

This is all the further the power I stole can get you. From here on out, it's all up to how much you can eat.

It is my concept, after all, Zeke returned.

Go, go! Eat, eat, eat!

86
BOSS BATTLE

The figure drew their hand back again. This time, they formed a fist, ignoring their bleeding, missing forefinger. Zeke stared it down. He braced himself, spreading his stance and widening his arms, although he knew it was all but meaningless in space. The fist drew back, then shot forth, closing in on Zeke. As it flew, a red glow formed around it.

The hairs on the back of Zeke's neck stood up. *That's bad.* He pointed toward the Earth and cast **Electrify** on a random piece of space junk, then activated **Electric Leap**. The world became tunnels around him but, this time, the tunnels were wider and fewer. He flew toward the wire he'd just electrified, leaving the space he had occupied behind.

The figure's fist slammed through the place he'd been. Withdrawing their fist, the figure looked at it, then turned their head, searching for Zeke.

Oh, shit. I don't want to be seen here. Zeke stared around him, lost, then looked up at the moon. *Right! There's rovers and probes up there. I bet one of them is electric.*

[Electric Leap]

Zeke rematerialized on the surface of the moon. With his new size, he barely fit on the moon. He straddled its horizon with either leg and pierced through its atmosphere from his height alone. His feet struck down with a *thump*, sending the regolith into the thin atmosphere in a visible shockwave. Before the weak gravity drew the dust back to settle, he turned, searching for the figure.

This close to the earth, the figure loomed over everything, so large he could barely see anything else. Zeke gaped, stunned by the sheer size of it yet again. Huge. Beyond huge. Unfathomable.

Incoming!

Another fist flew at him. Zeke braced against the moon and lifted his hands, preparing to take it. As it closed in, he opened his mouth.

[Ranged Devour] [Multi-Devour]

He bit holes in its fingers, swallowing a knuckle with one lucky bite. Still the hand closed in, seemingly heedless of its pain. Blood globbed after it, half-clinging to the hand in that strange way liquid floated in clumps in zero-gravity. Closer and closer, with no real reduction in mass.

Zeke gritted his teeth. *This is going to hurt.*

The fist slammed into him. It drove him into the moon like a hammer drove a nail into soft wood. Huge chunks of the moon broke off, shattering into space. A crack ran down the center of the moon. Dust clouded around Zeke.

He hung there, in the no-gravity, barely holding himself together. The bites he'd stolen powered his **Resilient Regeneration**, but even that struggled to heal his wounds at a meaningful pace. He was shattered, more broken than whole. Thick cracks ran through his armor. Blood welled up around him, mixing with moon dust and bits of its mantle. Vaguely, he heard a voice. *Get up, Zeke! Get up! He's throwing another punch! You have to move!*

Zeke shook his head. He knew he had to move, but he couldn't. There was nothing left. Nothing to move. His limbs were all broken. His body was a mess. Hunger assaulted his body, and it began to shrink. He couldn't fight any more. They'd tried but failed. And now, and now...tears welled up, despite himself. *I'm so sorry. Mia. Domi. Everyone. I failed you. I'm so sorry.*

...Fine. I'll share my power.

A torrent of power shot into Zeke's body. His wounds healed almost instantly, and he continued to grow, matching his old height in the blinking of an eye and shooting right past it. From out of the moon dust stood a man as tall as the figure's knee, and steadily growing taller, until he stood almost halfway up its thigh. Already throwing a punch, the figure balked in surprise, but it was too late. Zeke grabbed their fist out of the sky and bit into it with all three mouths he could bring to bear on it. His main mouth gulped down bites of its fingers and palm, while his hand mouths worked at its wrist, sawing at the joint. The figure pulled their hand back, trying to free it from Zeke's grasp. Zeke flipped around and firmly planted his feet on the figure's waist, pushing back with all his might. *This hand is mine. Mine!*

With one last screeching tooth-on-bone bite, he severed the figure's hand. He gulped it down, barely chewing. Zeke loosed an almighty burp and faced the creature. "So? What next? I'll eat it, too!"

As if in response, the figure reached out. Zeke braced himself, expecting another punch, but the hand swooped by. Bypassing Zeke, the figure reached toward the Earth with its remaining hand.

"No, you don't!" Zeke snapped. Kicking off the remains of the moon, he charged toward its other hand.

87
FINAL BATTLE

He charged toward the figure's other hand. The figure smirked and lifted their hand, going for Zeke. Attacking the Earth had only been a feint. Its fingers smashed toward Zeke.

Zeke laughed, himself. He turned around in the air, biting down at the hand. The hand flinched, surprised.

"Why are you surprised? I already ate your other hand." Zeke activated **Ranged Devour**. He stole a bite off the flesh of the palm before the hand jerked out of his range.

The hand changed directions instead. Once again, it closed in on the Earth.

"Hey!" Zeke stepped in front of the earth.

Force slammed into him. The hand sent him reeling, flying head over heels through space. The figure moved toward the Earth once more.

Zeke turned around. Using **Manipulate Flame**, he blasted in front of the hand. Again, it struck him. **Resilient Regeneration** struggled to keep up. His whole body trembled with pain. He snatched a bite from the hand as it retreated. The bite did little to replenish him. Zeke fell back, staggering.

Once more, the figure reached for the Earth. The figure's arm passed by Zeke, the fabric rustling by.

I'm not going to let you take the Earth! Zeke whipped around. He latched onto the arm with all his strength. The billowy, void-black fabric of the sleeve wrapped around him, bearing him down.

No! Zeke tore into the fabric. He swallowed down great chunks of it, tearing streaks off the cloth. The arm's pale flesh appeared before him. Zeke's weight bore down the sleeve, pulling him toward the elbow. He reached out and grabbed onto the crook of its arm. Without hesitation, he bit into the bicep. A big, meaty chunk of flesh broke off. Zeke bit and bit, eating its arm down to the bone.

The figure closed its arm, trying to squeeze him between its forearm and bicep. Zeke laughed internally. *Ha! My plan worked. You can't go after the Earth if you're too busy dealing with me!*

He jumped, pushing off the figure's bicep, and latched onto its shoulder. Zeke ran for the neck. The figure shrugged, trying to squeeze him against its neck. *Nice! Push me in!*

Zeke opened his mouths wide. He grabbed onto its neck and tore.

Bright red blood. He chewed and chewed, burrowing into the figure's neck. Blood gushed all around him. The figure batted at him with its missing hand but couldn't dig him out. It lifted its good hand and grabbed Zeke around the waist, pulling him away.

Zeke kicked it away. He used his foot-mouth to bite into the hand. The hand ignored his bite, pushing harder, but Zeke let it push him. He **Devour**ed his way into the neck, letting the hand push him as deep as it wanted. Blood rushed down all over him, drenching him in heavy, hot liquid. He grew as he burrowed, tearing the neck apart.

The hand yanked again, this time harder than ever. Zeke tumbled through space, trailing blood after him. Fire blasted behind him, pushing him upright. He faced down the figure. His body grew again, this time to almost half the figure's height.

The figure glared at him. It slapped toward him. Zeke reached out to grab it, stealing a few bites as it passed. The blow sent him flying, but he quickly used **Manipulate Flame** to catch himself. He turned in time for the figure's other arm to club toward him. Zeke braced his forearm and took the blow, then immediately snapped his hands down to take bites.

Blood pooled in space, blobbing around the figure's neck and its stubbed arm. Blood leaked out of every bit of him, everywhere Zeke had bitten. The figure sunk in the void, ragged.

"Stand still and let me eat you!" Zeke said.

The figure turned away. It faced the Earth once more. Reaching out, it clawed toward it, no feint this time, a hunger in the gesture.

Zeke's eyes widened. He glanced around him. He was far from the Earth, beyond the moon. The figure's final trick had worked.

No. It hasn't worked yet. He blasted off with **Manipulate Flame** and **Manipulate Aerosols**, activating **High Speed Maneuvering** at the same time. He chased after the figure, but the figure was far ahead of him.

Electric Leap... Zeke tried to activate it, but it refused to start. He gritted his teeth. *I'm too big. All the electric objects are too small relative to me!*

Okay, Zeke. My last gift to you.

The world went still, but Zeke, and Zeke alone, still moved. He rushed toward the still figure, speeding in.

This...is this what Ryan's Teleportation feels like? Zeke wondered.

The figure jolted back into motion abruptly. Nothing else began moving again, only the figure.

Good thought, but I told you he's beyond things like time and reality, the girl commented.

Thanks, Ryan. Every second counts, Zeke said. He closed in on the figure, but the figure closed in on the Earth. He gritted his teeth. *Faster. Faster!*

I'm diverting all your power into speed! the girl shouted.

Zeke sped up. He charged in. The figure's hand slowly clenched around the earth. The pale fingers pressed into the atmosphere. Fire shot up from its fingertips. The palm pressed the air and magnetism away, reaching for the ground.

Zeke slammed into the figure. He knocked it backward. Its hand knocked away from the Earth. This time, Zeke didn't hesitate, didn't think. He gave himself purely into his instincts. Chewing. Biting. Tearing into the figure's body. Clumps of black flesh, globs of blood, and bits of muscle clouded the space around them. The figure pressed at him, but there was no stopping him now. He tore it apart completely.

And then there was nothing. Nothing but Zeke. Zeke and the void, all alone.

...We did it, Zeke said, barely able to believe it.

We did it.

We did it!

The girl's voice faded out at the end. Zeke startled. *What—Where are you going?*

I could only hang on for so long.

Goodbye, Zeke. Fuck yo—

Wait, hold on. I think I can manage one...last...

Congratulations! You Devoured the Apocalypse!

Silence. He felt the lack, the absence. Both the girl and Ryan were gone.

All alone, he floated in space. The debris of the moon floated around him, mixing with the figure's remains. Zeke looked at the Earth. That beautiful blue marble, rolling off after the Sun.

I did it. It's over.

Now what?

AFTERWORD

Mia gazed up at the night sky. Silently, she watched the stars. There was no moon, not anymore. Just the darkness of the night.

"Looking for him?"

Mia turned. Domi walked up behind her, holding Olivia's hand. Olivia gave a little wave, and Mia nodded back. "Yeah. I always...wonder. If he's going to come back."

"I'm sure he will. Someday," Domi said.

Beside her, Sparkles barked.

Olivia petted the dog. "It's been so long. Is it still possible? Is he still alive?"

Mia grimaced. She turned up to the stars again.

Domi nudged Olivia. Olivia made a face. "My bad. Sorry."

"Is everyone up here?" Erica asked. She wore her hair long, not like the magical girl version of her ponytail. A skirt swished around her legs.

Mia nodded. "Yeah."

"It's been...what, five years?" Erica wondered.

"Yeah. Five long, long years, figuring out how to keep fires running overnight and fire up the steam generators," Domi complained.

"It's not like all the original infrastructure was destroyed. We just need to get to it, and fix it," Mia said.

"Well, yeah, but still. How many people are left? More than just the few of us, but not enough."

Mia shrugged. "Maybe that's for the best. We can start over. Do it better this time."

"Yeah, but do you think we will?" Domi asked.

Mia snorted. "No."

Domi pointed at her.

Mia looked up at the sky again. "Where do you think they are? Ryan and Zeke."

"Ryan's probably in Zeke's belly by now," Domi joked.

This time, it was Olivia's turn to nudge her.

"What? It's just reality," Domi muttered.

Mia sighed. "I really wish we still had our powers, at least."

"Yeah. That'd be awesome. I miss Heather. I miss warm showers," Domi said.

Erica shook her head. "I had no idea she was the Apartment. Or...something like the embodiment of the Apartment? Its avatar? But I was sad to see her go."

"We all were," Domi said regretfully. "Press F and all that."

There was silence for a long, long moment.

Abruptly, Mia spoke, "He's still out there, somewhere. He has to be."

"Yeah. Yeah. Watching over us, or something," Domi said quietly.

They all gazed up at the sky. Watching. Waiting. For something that would never come.

Far, far away.

Zeke wandered the void of space. He drifted aimlessly, supplying his own atmosphere, using **Manipulate Flame** to fly. Nothing happened. For a long, long time, nothing happened.

Zeke's stomach grumbled. He looked around. A stone drifted past. He took a bite and felt full, just for a few moments. Afraid to leave the rock behind, Zeke quickly **Devour**ed the whole thing.

There were no skills, not anymore. But he used the names anyway. It was a crutch. A comfort.

The rocks were few and far between. He'd drift months between one rock and the next. He **Devour**ed dust, stones, the big rocks when he could find them.

And then he came across a *big* rock. A planetoid.

Zeke latched onto it. He drifted with it, chewing it as he went. They flew on, him and the planetoid, drifting on. Away.

Years passed. He ate the planetoid and drifted alone again. His stomach grew weaker and weaker, until he was nothing but a withered husk, full of hunger. Anything that came close, he chomped on without thought or hesitation.

A moon drifted by. Zeke latched on again, chewing into it. It tasted horrible, but it was food. At last, food. Another moon, not so far away. He finished the first one and chased the second, only to find a third drifting on his horizon. That, too, vanished into his maw. One moon after another, until he reached the planet.

What a planet it was. Absolutely massive, soft and gaseous. Somewhere in the dusty depths of his memory, it occurred to him that the planet had a name. Jupiter? Saturn? He couldn't remember the difference. It pulled him toward it, and he let it take him. Welcoming him. *Inviting* him.

Zeke slurped up the atmosphere, swallowing it away. That took him a few years, but he got through it to the core, the small, rocky core. So small. Like an apple. He swallowed it up and turned away, looking for more.

Another big, gassy planet. That one vanished like the first. Then a smaller gassy planet, and beyond that, a few tiny, hard rocks. So much time passed between each one that he barely knew how to quantify it. Decades. Centuries. Millenia. He couldn't tell any longer.

When he ate those final hard rocks, he gazed out at the edge of the solar system and found nothing. Turning, he faced inward. Nothing for a long, long ways...and then *something*. Delicious, glistening *somethings*. A belt of rocks. A red, rocky planet, then a blue one.

At the sight of that one, something tickled in the back of his mind. Something important. Something...

He squinted, then licked his lips. It must be delicious. Why else would he think of something as important?

Turning around, a fell, slender figure flew back into the solar system, mouth watering, on his way to one last meal.

THANK YOU FOR READING APOCALYPSE WORLD

We hope you enjoyed it as much as we enjoyed bringing it to you. We just wanted to take a moment to encourage you to review the book. Follow this link: Apocalypse World to be directed to the book's Amazon product page to leave your review.

Every review helps further the author's reach and, ultimately, helps them continue writing fantastic books for us all to enjoy.

Also in series:
Apocalypse Me
Apocalypse City
Apocalypse World

Check out the entire series here! (Tap or scan)

Want to discuss our books with other readers and even the authors? Join our Discord server today and be a part of the Aethon community.

Facebook | Instagram | Twitter | Website

You can also join our non-spam mailing list by visiting www.subscribepage.com/AethonReadersGroup and never miss out on future releases. You'll also receive three full books completely Free as our thanks to you.

Looking for more great LitRPG?

Check out our new releases!

Order Now!

(Tap or Scan)

A wizard's first quest. An unlikely companion. Grand adventure awaits! Wanda and Wumble are a small pair with vast ambitions. One an aspiring alchemist, and the other her faithful hound, the pair bond as wizard and familiar to begin their pursuit of magic. As a newly made wizard without any training, resources, or even a home to return to, Wanda will have to forge her own way on a path where constant dangers lurk. Even the simple act of furthering her alchemy education swiftly becomes a harrowing ordeal. Luckily for Wanda, Wumble is no ordinary hound. Contained within her one-eyed companion is a power many factions of the world are actively hunting for. A seed with unfathomable potential waiting to sprout. And anyone who trifles with Wumble's wizard is in for a ruff time. **Experience a brand new universe from Drew Hayes, the bestselling author of Super Powereds and NPCs. Featuring a lovable pair of heroes out on their first adventure, learning about both magic and life in a progression fantasy suitable for all ages!**

Get Roverpowered Now!

Order Now!

(Tap or Scan)

he Gods are dead. The Seven Evils reign. Only Hope stands between humanity and extinction... *When Sorin's parent's mysteriously die, he is starved for truth and thirsty for revenge. He begs the Eighth Evil, Hope, for assistance, and his prayers are answered... ...Though not in the way he ever expected. He is made a Poison Cultivator, a rare class who are shunned by high society. Unable to continue his medical practice, Sorin turns to adventuring to make ends meet. Though he's only able to afford to team with a ragtag crew of outcasts as companions—An armored polar bear, a stern archer, a sleep-deprived pyromancer, and a peeping-tom rogue. Oh, and a rebellious rat familiar who won't stop eating the party's loot when no one is watching. Things are looking up, until Sorin discovers his ancestor's hidden research notes about forbidden medical research. What dark deeds was his family up to? Only he can find out... if he and his party can survive the coming Demon Tide.* **Don't miss this new Cultivation Progression Fantasy series from Patrick Laplante, bestselling author of** Painting the Mists. *Featuring loads of power progression, demon slaying, dungeons, loot, crafting, and even a rebellious pet rat, it's got something for everyone!*

Get Pandora Unchained Now!

Order Now!

(Tap or Scan)

A magical new world. An ancient power. A chance to be a Hero. Danny Kendrick was a down-on-his luck performer who always struggled to find his place. He certainly never wanted to be a hero. He just hoped to earn a living doing what he loved. That all changes when he pisses off the wrong guy and gets transported to another world. Stuck in a fantasy realm straight out of a Renaissance Fair, Danny quickly discovers that there's more to life. Like magic, axe-wielding brutes, super hot elf assassins, and a talking screen that won't leave him alone. He'll need to adapt fast, turn on the charm, and get stronger if he hopes to survive this dangerous new world. But he has a knack for trouble. Gifted what seems like an innocent ancient lute after making a questionable deal with a Hag, Danny becomes the target of mysterious factions who seek to claim its power. It's up to him, Screenie, and his new barbaric friend, Curr, to uncover the truth and become the heroes nobody knew they needed. And maybe, just maybe, Danny will finally find a place where he belongs. **Don't miss the start of this isekai LitRPG Adventure filled with epic fantasy action, unforgettable characters, loveable companions, unlikely heroes, a detailed System, power progression, and plenty of laughs.** From the minds of USA Today bestselling and Award-winning duo Rhett C Bruno & Jaime Castle, An Expected Hero is perfect for fans of Dungeon Crawler Carl, Kings of the Wyld, and This Trilogy is Broken!

Get An Unexpected Hero now!

For all our LitRPG books, visit our website.